COLD KILL

When Jane Roberts is found dead in a woodland area, Detective Sergeant Laura McGanity is first on the scene. The body bears a chilling similarity to a woman – Deborah Corley – murdered three weeks earlier. Both have been stripped, strangled and defiled. When reporter Jack Garrett starts digging for dirt on the notorious Whitcroft estate, he finds himself face-to-face with Jane's father and local gangland boss Don, who won't stop until justice is done. As the killer circles once more, Jack and Laura must stop him before he strikes again. But his sights are set on his next victim and he's watching Laura's every move...

COLD KILL

COLD KILL

by

Neil White

Magna Large Print Books
Long Preston, North Yorkshire,
BD23 4ND, England.

British Library Cataloguing in Publication Data.

White, Neil
    Cold kill.

A catalogue record of this book is
available from the British Library

ISBN   978-0-7505-3639-4

First published in Great Britain in 2011 by Avon
a division of HarperCollins*Publishers*

Copyright © Neil White 2011

Cover illustration © Dave Wall by arrangement with
Arcangel Images

Neil White asserts the moral right to be identified as the author of this
work

Published in Large Print 2012 by arrangement with
HarperCollins Publishers

Magna Large Print is an imprint of Library Magna Books Ltd.

Printed and bound in Great Britain by
T.J. (International) Ltd., Cornwall, PL28 8RW

Acknowledgments

I write in a very solitary way. I don't often seek advice during the writing process, and instead just lock myself away until I'm done. Once I re-emerge, squinting in the daylight, I am so grateful that there are people who can make some sense out of what I've put on the page. My editors, Claire Bord and Helen Bolton, have been fantastic, as I knew they would be, and they and the rest of the Avon team work very hard on my behalf.

My wonderful agent, Sonia Land of Sheil Land Associates, has been a source of sound advice and support, as always, and long may that continue.

As much as I enjoy the professional help, I am lucky to enjoy the support of a small band of people who do what they can to help me. In particular, I would like to say thank you to Angela Melhuish for setting up and monitoring my Facebook fan page, and to Liz Wilkins and Belinda Cohen for telling people about me on the internet forums.

For everyone else, I know who you are and I won't forget.

Chapter One

The evening was bright and warm, the sun dipping behind the trees that lined the small copse between the houses, so that the light was filtered, the strips of brightness catching the loop and dance of midges that flitted between the leaves.

He looked at his watch. Nearly time. He knew her routine. Saturday night. A walk to the bus stop on the main road and then into town. She always passed the copse on her route, her head down, rushing to start her evening.

He paced, just out of view, his breaths fast, his chest tight with excitement. Thoughts of her came to him like whispers, so quiet that he could hardly hear them, but with each night they got stronger, so that the whispers became louder, like white noise, a rush, pressing him on.

He fought the urges sometimes, when his drive was low, but those moments were rare, and it was the images of her that drove him. Her hair, blonde and over her shoulders, gleaming against her pale skin. Her small upturned nose. Teeth bright and straight. He smiled to himself when he thought of her skin. Soft skin. Taut. Now that it was time, the noises pulled back, as if they were watching from the wings, breaths held in anticipation.

He knew this one would be different. It would be the strongest buzz of all. No buried body. No burnt out car. No trips to the lake, bound up in chains. This was going to be the best, because he knew it had always been leading to this.

He could almost hear her. The flick of her hair in the breeze, the rustle of her clothes as she walked. Then he realised that the tap-taps he could hear were not the fast drums of his heart-beat or the hum of his pulse. They were the click of her heels, fast steps that seemed to echo along the quiet suburban street. His breaths became deeper through his nose, his chest rising and fall-ing, and he felt himself grow hard. He checked his gloves. No rips. No tears. Nowhere for any trace evidence to escape. He thought about his movements one last time. He had thought of little else all week.

It was time.

He started walking as the clicks got louder, so that he would be on the same side of the street as her when she appeared. As she came into view, she gave him a nervous look, but then she noticed the polo shirt, the police crest on his breast, and the black-and-white ribbon around his cap, a black soft-top.

He smiled, a quick flash of his teeth, and stepped on to the road, so that she stayed on the pavement, the copse to her side. 'Evening,' he said, as she got closer. His words almost caught in his throat as her perfume drifted towards him. The scent of flowers, light on the breeze. He had to stop himself from reaching out to run a finger along her neck. Don't go too soon.

She flickered a smile at him but then looked down again. He followed her gaze. Short black skirt. Legs shaved smooth, tapered into silver heels. He had to swallow, his heartbeat fast, his mouth dry.

His hands were on his belt, fingering for the release of his cuffs. He had practised the move until it was perfect. Speed was key. He had to cut down on the noise.

She was alongside him now. He looked quickly along the street. There was no one around. There were houses, but why would anyone be looking out? If he was quick, they wouldn't suspect anything.

He ran at her, his shoulder ramming into hers, knocking her off balance. His hand clamped around her mouth and he kept his legs moving, pushing her along the path that ran between the trees, her feet pedalling in the air. He pulled his cuffs free and clicked one loop onto her left wrist, loving the click as it went tight around the bone. She was starting to fight now, her head thrashing against his glove. He couldn't release his hand, she would scream, and so all he could do was keep his legs pumping, lifting her along, waiting until the path disappeared into the shadows, where the trees grew thicker.

One of her shoes came off. He would have to get it afterwards.

He was in the trees now. There was a small stream that ran at the bottom of a slope, and he knew that he was well hidden down here. He was close to the path, but he would be quick, he knew that.

The thump of his boots on the path changed into the soft sweep of his feet as he made his way further through the undergrowth. When he got

13

far enough away from the path, he threw her onto the floor, his gloved hand still over her mouth.

She started to fight, flailing with the cuff, the loose metal nearly catching him in the face. He pushed her face down and gripped the cuff, yanking both her arms behind her back. A quick throw of the metal and he heard the clicks again as it locked.

He pushed her onto her back, her arms cuffed beneath her, and his free hand began to scrabble around for dirt and leaves. She had her teeth clenched, but he pulled down on her jaw and pushed some in, before reaching down for more, jamming it in as far as it would go, her eyes getting wider, her chest bucking as she coughed and choked.

His hand did the same between her legs, pushing in dirt, stones, pieces of shrubbery.

Then he started to pull at his belt, his other hand still over her mouth. He groaned as he gripped himself.

He moved his other hand from her mouth to her neck and began to press. As tears rolled down her cheeks, as her legs kicked, as he pressed down harder, his moans became louder.

Chapter Two

It was a few days later when Jack Garrett got the call.

He was on the Whitcroft estate, for an assignment for the local paper's newest editor, Dolby Wilkins, who had been brought in to cut costs and increase circulation. Dolby was all shiny good looks and old money confidence, always in jeans and a casual linen jacket, and his mantra was that two types of stories sold newspapers: sex and prejudice. The local paper left the sex to the red top nationals, so all Dolby had left was prejudice. So he went for the social divide, the quick fix, shock stories over good copy. Immigrants breaking laws, or people on benefits making a decent life for themselves. The first thing he did was to have his business cards printed. That told Jack all he needed to know.

Jack had been staring through his windscreen, uncomfortable with the assignment. He knew that repackaging poverty as idleness got the tills ticking, but Dolby was new to Blackley and he didn't understand the place. He hadn't seen how a tough old cotton town had been stripped of its industry, with nothing to replace it, just traces of its past lying around the town, dismembered, like body parts; huge brick mill buildings, some converted into retail units that held craft fairs on summer weekends, while others had been left to

15

crumble, stripped of their lead, the wire and cables ripped out of the walls, cashed in for cigarette money, the light spilling in through partial roof collapses. The stories were more about no prospects in hard times, but sympathy for the unlucky didn't sell as many papers.

Jack understood that the *Blackley Telegraph* was a business, but he was a freelance journalist, not a businessman, the court stories his thing, with the occasional crime angle as a feature. But the paper bought his stories, shedding staff writers and using freelancers to take up the slack, some of them just kids fresh out of college or unpublished writers looking to build a CV. So Jack had agreed to write the story of the estate, bashed out on an old laptop in his cottage in Turners Fold, a small forgotten place nestled in the Lancashire hills, a few miles from Blackley.

The Whitcroft estate was on the edge of Blackley, the first blight on the drive in. Built on seven hills that were once green and rolling, Blackley seemed like the ugly big brother to Turners Fold. Traces of former wealth could still be seen in the Victorian town centre though, where three-storey fume-blackened shop buildings were filled by small town jewellers and century-old outfitters that competed with the glass and steel frames of the high street. The wide stone steps and Roman portico of the town hall overlooked the main shopping street and boasted of grander times, when men in long waistcoats and extravagant sideburns twirled gold watches from their pockets.

The Whitcroft estate had been built in the good times, an escape from the grid-like strips of terraced housing that existed elsewhere in the town. Here, it was all cul-de-sacs and crescents, sweeps of privet, indoor toilets, but it had divided the town, had become the escape route for the whites after the Asian influx in the sixties. Mosques and minarets were sprinkled amongst the warehouses and wharf buildings now, the call to prayer the new church bells, and so the Whitcroft estate had become white-flight for those who couldn't afford the countryside.

Jack pondered all of this as he sat in his car, a 1973 Triumph Stag in Calypso Red. Young mothers walked their prams on a road that circled the estate. The morning sun gave the place a glow and highlighted the deep green of the hedges, the gleam of the brickwork, and brought out the vivid violets and pinks and reds of the flower baskets. He could hear laughs and screams from the local school, which he could see through some blue railings on the curve of the road.

But that was just gloss.

The entrance to the estate was marked by two rows of shops that faced each other across gum-peppered paving stones, making a funnel for the cold winds that blew in from the moors that the estate overlooked. A Chinese takeaway and a grocer occupied three units, along with a bookmaker's and a post office. On the other side, a launderette and a chemist. There were grilles on the windows and the doors looked old and dirty.

Behind the shops were blocks of housing, four houses to each small row, with pebble-dashed first floors and England stickers in the windows. Some had paint on the walls or wooden boards over the windows. They formed cul-de-sacs that were connected by privet-lined ginnels, so that the quick routes were the most dangerous. Crisp packets and old beer cans lodged themselves in the hedges.

There were small signs of affluence though. The streets were busy with workmen in overalls and young office girls heading out to work, calling in for newspapers or cigarettes at the grocer's. There were porch extensions, gleaming double-glazing, new garden walls. The estate wasn't just for lost causes. A private security van patrolled every thirty minutes, with bald men in black jackets who stared at Jack as they went past. Maybe Dolby wasn't going to get the article he wanted.

Jack climbed out of his car and wandered towards the shop, looking for some local views. Outside the shop, a young mother stood over her pram with a cigarette in her hand, cheap gold flashing on each finger, her hair pulled back tightly.

Jack gave the door of the shop a push. It let out a tinkle as he went in, and he pretended to browse through the magazines until the shop became empty. He went to the counter.

The man behind it barely looked up. Middle-aged and with a cigarette-stained moustache, he was flicking through a newspaper and only stopped reading when Jack coughed.

'Jack Garrett,' he said, and tried a smile. 'I'm a reporter, writing about the estate.' He pointed towards the windows. 'What's it like for you, with the grilles and the bars?'

He stared at Jack, weighing up whether to answer or not. 'The council ruined this place,' he

18

said, eventually.

'How so?'

'Because they turned it into a dumping ground,' he said. 'Have everyone in one place, so they said.'

'Have you been here long?'

'More than twenty years,' he said. 'I inherited it from my father, back when this was a decent place to live.'

'What went wrong?'

He shrugged. 'I don't know, but it doesn't seem like people want to work anymore. The young girls get a house when they get pregnant, but the father never moves in. Or, at least, that's what they tell everyone, but I see them leaving in the morning.'

'I see people heading out to work,' Jack said. 'It doesn't seem that destitute.'

'There are still some people left that make me proud to live here, but it's getting harder every day.'

'Why is that?'

'The kids,' he said. 'They hang around here all evening, circling customers on their bikes, asking people to buy their booze and fags for them, because I know most are too young. If I try and get rid of them, I get abuse. All my customers want is to come in and buy some milk or something, maybe some cans for later, but the kids put them off.'

'Have you spoken to their parents?' Jack said.

The shopkeeper gave a wry smile. 'Drunk most of the time.'

Jack returned the smile and guessed his predicament. 'You sell them the booze,' he said.

'They'd only go somewhere else for it. And they

19

do mostly, stocking up on the three-for-two offers. They come here when they run out, or when they want to start early and don't want to drive to the supermarket.'

'Do the police come round much?' Jack said.

The shopkeeper scoffed. 'Hardly ever, and when they do, the kids treat it like a game, looking for a chase. They shout abuse and then starburst whenever the van doors open. Sometimes one of them trips and the police catch them, but nothing ever happens.'

'Is that why the estate has private security?' Jack said.

'It makes people feel safer.'

'Who pays for it?'

'Whoever wants it.'

'What about drugs?' Jack said. 'Could the police be doing more about that around here?'

'No, not drugs around here,' he said. 'Maybe some weed, but it's booze mainly. Always has been. I'm not saying that no one round here does drugs, but the kids that cycle around causing trouble aren't on drugs. They're pissed.'

'You don't paint a glowing picture,' Jack said.

He nodded to the voice recorder in Jack's hand. 'And I bet you won't either, by the time it makes the paper.'

When Jack started to protest, the shopkeeper jabbed his finger at the paper. 'I read them as well as sell them, and I've seen the way the *Telegraph* has gone.' Then he returned to whatever had occupied his attention before.

Jack turned away, frustrated, and left the shop. He watched the cars heading in and out of the estate. They were mainly old Vauxhalls and Fords, most driven by young men who didn't look like they could afford the insurance. His phone buzzed in his pocket. When he checked the screen and saw that it was Dolby, he thought about not answering, but he knew he needed to keep on Dolby's good side.

He pressed the button. 'Dolby, what can I do for you?'

'There's been another murder,' he said, his voice a little breathless. 'A young woman.'

Jack paused as he tried to work out what he meant, but then his mind flashed back to the young woman found in a pipe by the reservoir on the edge of town a few weeks earlier, a gruesome find for a father and son on an angling trip.

'Whereabouts?'

Dolby told him, and Jack realised that he was only half a mile away.

'Do you want me to cover it?' Jack said.

'I'm not calling to spread the gossip,' Dolby said, some irritation in his voice.

'On my way,' Jack said, and jabbed at the off button.

He gave the shopkeeper a smile, but there was no response.

Chapter Three

It was just after nine-thirty as Laura McGanity looked around at the scene in front of her and tried to shake away the nerves. Someone had died, and now it was for her to show that she deserved her sergeant stripes. Nine months in uniform, working in the community, but now she was back where she wanted to be, on the murder squad. And even though this was a tragedy, she felt a familiar excitement as she took in the blue-and-white police tape stretched tight around the trees and the huddle of police in boiler suits holding sticks, ready for the slow crawl through the undergrowth, looking for scraps of evidence – a footprint, a dropped piece of paper, maybe a snag of cloth on the thorns and branches. This was it, the start of the investigation, the human drama yet to unfold.

She had pulled on her paper coveralls, put paper bootees over her shoes, and now her breaths were hot against her cheeks behind the face mask. But Laura knew the excitement wouldn't last long, because in a moment she would face the lifeless body lying in a small copse of trees behind the new brick of a housing development, just visible as a flash of pink in the green. Then the tragedy would hit her, but for now it was all about concentration, so that she didn't miss something crucial.

22

Joe Kinsella came up behind her, poised and still, his face hidden, the hood pulled over his hair. His eyes, soft brown, showed a smile, and then he said in a muffled voice, 'C'mon, detective sergeant. Let's see what there is.'

Laura smiled back, invisible behind the mask. The title still felt new, but as Joe set off she realised that the back-patting would have to be put on hold for the moment.

The ground sloped down to a small ribbon of dirty brown water that ran into underground pipes that carried it under the houses. Sycamore and horse chestnut trees filled the scene with shadows. Ivy trailed across the floor like tripwire, but Joe strode quickly through it, crunching it underfoot, in contrast to the soft rustles of Laura's suit as she trotted to catch up. Laura was grateful that it was dry, or else she imagined she would have found herself skidding towards the small patch of pink by the edge of the stream.

The body had been found by teenagers, looking for somewhere to do whatever they did in the woods, and since then the area had swarmed with police and crime scene investigators, the ghoulish and idly curious hovering on the street. There was a detective posing as a journalist, mingling with those craning their necks to get a view, snapping pictures of the onlookers, in the hope that the killer might be among them, having come back to marvel at his work. That had been Joe's idea.

As Laura reached the body, she saw that her inspector, Karl Carson, was there. Karl was large and bombastic, shiny bald, no eyebrows, his blue eyes glaring from the forensic hood.

'Looks like we've got another one, McGanity,' he said, his eyes watching her, waiting for her response.

Laura sighed. That word, *another*. It made everything harder, because it meant that the murder wasn't just a family falling out, or maybe a violent boyfriend faking it as a stranger attack.

Laura watched as Joe got closer to the body and kneeled down. She knew that he wasn't looking for forensic evidence, but for those little signs, hidden clues that reveal motivation. That was Joe's expertise: not the *what*, but the *why*. Laura was still new to the team, but she had worked with him before, and so he had eased her into the murder squad. It was good to be back doing the serious stuff. She had moved north a few years earlier, away from her detective role in the London Met, and had done the rounds of routine case mop-ups and a short spell in uniform to help grease the push for promotion, but this was where she felt most at home.

Laura kneeled down alongside Joe, and as she looked at the body, she saw that Karl Carson was right, that it confirmed everyone's worst fear, that the murder three weeks earlier wasn't a one-off. There were two now.

The victim was a young woman, Laura guessed, in her early twenties, more there than the skinny hips and ribs of a teenager but with none of the sag of the later years. There was a tattoo on her left wrist. A pink butterfly. The body had been hidden under bark ripped from a nearby tree, and when it had been disturbed, the kids who found her had been swamped by blue-bottles. Laura gritted her teeth at the smell – a mix of vomit and off-meat, and even outdoors, with her nose shielded by a mask, the stench still made it through. As she looked at the floor, she could see the shifting blanket of woodlice and maggots spilling onto the ivy leaves, their work of turning the corpse into just mush and bones interrupted. The body's stomach was distended by the gases brewing inside, and Laura knew that she didn't want to be around when it was rolled onto plastic sheeting to be taken from the scene, because whatever was inside the stomach was going to come tumbling out of the mouth.

Laura peered closer to try and see the face, so that she could see more of the person and less of the corpse, but it was dirty and disfigured, and so they wouldn't get a better idea until the post-mortem clean-up later. Laura tried to be scientific and dispassionate, but she knew that the sight of a healthy young woman who had been mutilated was something that would come back to her in quieter moments.

Laura took a deep breath, more heat through the mask, and tried to take in what she could.

The woman was naked, the clothes taken away, no sign of them torn up and thrown to one side. Just like with the other one. There were bruises on her body, grazes and scrapes that might have come from a struggle, along with small cuts on her stomach and legs, but it wasn't those that drew her eye. It was her mouth. It was stretched, with soil and leaves jammed in so that it looked like the dead woman had choked on the ground, her cheeks puffed out. There were bruises around the neck, so Laura guessed that it was another strangulation case. Laura looked down at the woman's hips, and she didn't need to look too closely in order to see the dirt trails and scratches where soil and leaves had been jammed between her thighs.

It was the tears that made her angry though. The woman's face was dirty, but there were streaks where her tears had run through the dirt as she choked on the leaves and looked up at the man who ended her life.

'Is it another one of our own?' Laura said.

Carson just shrugged that he didn't know.

The first victim had been the daughter of a Blackley police officer. Gangland revenge had been ruled out, because her father was just uniform, seeing out his career patrolling in a van and doling out advice to young officers who would soon overtake him. Tales of the woman's private life had made everyone think that it was a jealous ex-lover, or a frightened husband worried about his affair leaking out.

'What do you think?' Carson said.

Laura saw that his eyes were fixed on her, and she knew that it was a test. Carson was checking whether Joe had been right to ask for her to be on the team.

She took a deep breath and had another look along the body.

'She was alive when all of that was jammed in there,' Laura said, and pointed to the woman's genitals.

'Why do you say that?'

'Those scratches and scrapes along the woman's legs have drawn blood,' she said, and pointed towards trails of ragged skin that had since dried brown. 'They will have been caused when he jammed the leaves and dirt up there, inside her, and so it must have happened when she was still alive. The dead don't bleed.'

Carson gave a nod. 'Why is that important?'

'It makes it more likely that she was killed here rather than just dumped,' she said. 'And we might get some of his DNA from her thighs or face.'

'Provided he wasn't wearing gloves.'

Laura raised her eyebrows. 'That goes without saying.'

Carson nodded. 'What about the clothes?' he said. 'She didn't walk down here naked.'

'He's got some forensic awareness because he realised that his DNA would be all over her,' Laura said. 'He took the clothes away to stop him from being identified, which makes it more likely that he wore gloves, as a precaution. And he's cool.'

'What do you mean?' Carson asked.

'Look around,' Laura said, and she pointed towards the houses that overlooked the scene. 'All it would take is for someone to look out of their bedroom window, or even hear the struggle, and we would be down here. An eye-witness is the best we can hope for right now, unless he's slipped up.'

'Anything else?'

Laura looked at the body, and as she felt Carson's stare bore into her, she tried to think of something she might have missed. Or maybe he was just trying to make her spout wild theories to use against her later. She wasn't the only woman on the team, but she still felt like she had to prove herself for spoiling the macho party, and she'd heard the little digs that she was Joe's new favourite.

Then it struck her.

'If she was alive when he was filling her with soil, it meant that she wasn't being raped when she died,' Laura said. 'If all of that was in there, he couldn't have been, and so whatever he did afterwards was just to degrade her.'

Carson tilted his head and Laura saw the skin around his eyes crinkle. It looked like there was a smile there. Test passed.

Laura looked at Joe and saw that he was still staring intently at the corpse.

'What is it, Joe?' Carson asked.

Joe didn't respond at first. That was just his way, quiet, contemplative, but then he rose to his feet, his knees cracking, and looked down.

'This isn't going to end,' he said, his voice quiet.

'Why do you say that?' Laura said.

'Because he has attacked before, and once you start, you don't stop,' he said.

'We know he's done this before,' Carson said, his brow furrowed. 'Three weeks ago.'

'No, even before then,' Joe said, and gestured towards the body with a nod of his head. 'The signature is so fixed. The debris and soil in the vagina, the mouth, the anus. Too much like the last one. But why does he do it? No one just chances on that, the perfect method. Signatures grow and develop. This one? It's a replica of the first.'

Carson sighed behind his mask. 'This is sounding like a long haul,' he said, almost to himself.

Joe shot worried glances at Laura and Carson. 'We haven't got the time for that,' he said. 'We need to catch him quickly, because the gap will shorten.'

'Are you sure about that?'

Joe nodded. 'These murders are three weeks apart, but identical methods were used. He's found his style and likes it.'

'Why is all that dirt in there?' Laura asked.

Joe looked down at the body, then he looked at Carson, and then at Laura.

'I don't know,' he said slowly. 'And we will need to work that out if we are going to catch whoever did this, but I do know one thing: he's going to want to do it again.'

Chapter Four

Jack put his camera away as he watched the activity at the crime scene.

He had managed some shots of the white suits as they were bent over the body, knowing that Dolby would like those. And as he'd zoomed in, he'd recognised one of the white suits as Laura McGanity, his partner.

He smiled to himself. No, not partner. Fiancée.

They had been engaged for a few months now, but things had changed since he'd proposed. Laura had thrown herself back into her career, and it seemed they saw each other only briefly in the house, pit-stops between her shifts. She complained that he was showing no commitment, that he was stalling about the wedding, but it was more that they didn't have the time to talk about it. Laura wanted it low-key, because she had been married before, a marriage that produced a son, Bobby, the main brightness in their lives, eight years old now. Both of Jack's parents were dead and so he had no one to offend by keeping it small, but it felt like it wasn't the same big deal for her, because Laura had already had the big white wedding with all the trimmings.

As he watched her, Jack knew that Laura was the reason why Dolby had asked him to cover the story, hoping for an inside line, maybe a loose word over supper. But Jack knew better: Laura wouldn't give anything crucial away. Having a reporter as her squeeze had caused her enough trouble before, hints and jibes that she was whispering secrets along the pillow. It would only take one lazy article, where he forgot what was official and what was secret, and Laura could lose her job.

The crowd around the police tape had grown, from the simply curious passing through, some with dogs straining on leads, the police blocking access to the usual dog-walking path, to the unemployed looking for a way to fill the day. Teenagers hung around on bikes, some just watching, others riding in tight circles, all in black, hoods drawn over their faces in spite of the warmth, laughing and talking too loudly. Young mothers smoked and gossiped, and two men at the end were drinking from a can of Tennent's, which was passed between them as they watched the police at work. A police van drifted across the junction at the top of the street.

All the activity was taking place in a small patch of trees between some houses, the police in the shadows, talking in small clusters. Some flowers had already arrived and been placed by a lamppost, although the identity of the body hadn't been released yet.

Jack approached the crime scene tape, hoping to overhear the police talking, but as he got near, a female officer put her hand up.

'You need to move away,' she said, the light tremble in her voice telling him that she was new to the force.

'I'm a reporter,' he said, and then he pointed to where the body had been found. 'Do we have a name?'

She shook her head and repeated, 'You need to move away.'

'I don't want to get closer. I just want to find out who she is. Do you know yet?'

She was about to shake her head, but she stopped herself and put up her hand. 'Please, move away.'

'Can you tell me anything?' Jack persisted. 'How did she die? When did she die?'

'No, I'm sorry, I can't tell you anything,' she said, her voice firmer now. Jack could tell that he had annoyed her.

He smiled an apology and then turned away as

he realised that he wasn't going to get anything else from the scene. He checked his watch. No information would be released for a few hours, and so it was time to go to court, the crime reporter's fallback, low-life tales of shame from the grim streets of Blackley. That was how Jack made his living, writing up court stories. He would have to speak to Dolby about the Whitcroft article later, because he got the sense that it wasn't going to amount to much, despite the shopkeeper's views. Perhaps he would go back later, when the sun had gone down.

Jack watched the crowd for a few seconds more, as they waited for a glimpse of something they didn't really want to see, like knitters at the guillotine, but it felt grubby, like he wasn't really that different to them. He had just found a way to make money from the excitement, that's all.

He turned to walk towards his car. No one really noticed him going, and so he turned his thoughts to what might be ahead at the courthouse.

The police van drove slowly past the crime scene. He couldn't help but look, but as he glanced over, he could hear a ticking sound. Not loud. Just like a scratching noise on the inside of his skull. It wasn't enough to distract him or make him close his eyes.

He allowed himself a smile. Now was the time. It had taken longer than he'd expected for her body to be found, considering that the path nearby was used by joggers and dog-walkers. He must have concealed it well.

He turned away when he saw people look over. The gaggle of the crowd. Someone taking photographs. Like fucking sheep heading for the pen. The first stretch of the crime scene tape and they all shuffle forward. All of that thrill could have been theirs, but they're spineless, like leeches, second-hand thrill-seekers.

And then the images came back to him in flashes, bright snapshots of her clothes, of her walking, the cloth moving against her soft skin, young and unblemished. Not knowing. Just another night. Then that look in her eyes. The flash of fear replaced by anger, and then back to fear when she knew that her time had come.

Then it came, like always, the sharp focus, where he could see everything more clearly than ever before, in more detail than is possible with the naked eye. Her pupils, black saucers, but he could see the other colours in them too, swirls of dark green and deep blue, the clear view broken only by the flecks of spittle that bubbled up when she first went to the floor. And the coughs of mud. He could see the soil turning in the air in front of him as she spluttered, tumbling in the fading sunlight. Just tiny specks, but he could see their form, uneven and dirty. He remembered the whites of her eyes. He had seen the veins in them and how they were broken by the small explosions of red, just pinpricks, like splashes as the blood came to the surface.

He grinned as he felt the familiar tremble in his groin as he thought of her struggling, the fight under his hand. He knew it would come. He was waiting for it. He liked to feel it, to control it. He could do that, control it, so that it was a present for later, something he had to touch, to feel in his hand as he thought of her struggling and then slowly giving up the fight, her body limp.

He gave the crowd a salute but no one was watching as he slipped away.

Chapter Five

Laura leaned against her car and peeled off her forensic suit. The hood had made a mess of her hair, dark and long, and so she used the wing mirror to tease it back to life. The body had been taken away, rolled onto plastic sheeting and then wrapped up in a bag, and was on its way to the mortuary. Now it was time for the fingertip search of the undergrowth, and she could see the line of police in blue boiler suits waiting to crawl their way through the small patch of woodland. Joe was looking back towards where the body had been found, his hood pulled from his head. Carson was in his car, talking into his phone.

'What is it, Joe?' Laura said, reaching into her car for her suit jacket.

He didn't answer at first, his gaze trained on where the stream headed under the estate. Then he turned round, chewing his lip.

'Something about this isn't right,' he said.

'What do you mean?'

'The location. It doesn't make any sense. Why here?'

34

'That occurred to me too,' she said, and looked again at the houses that backed onto the crime scene, a line of wooden fence panels forming the boundary on both sides.

'It isn't secluded at all,' Joe continued. 'One scream from her and all of those lights are going to flicker on, and what escape route is there? There is only one way to the street, because the other way is down that path, into the woods, but he couldn't get a car down there. So if he drove to the location, he would have had to leave his car on the street, and so he would be blocked in and easy to catch.'

'Perhaps she was just walking past?' Laura said. 'You know, the wrong place at the wrong time, and he was hiding in there, waiting to pull someone in.'

'Same thing applies,' Joe said. 'Too many houses. What if she fought back? If she ran or screamed? There is a whole community to wake. And you saw how the body was concealed, just left on the ground and covered in leaves and bark. She was always going to be discovered.' He sighed. 'It just doesn't feel right.'

'You're giving the killer too much credit,' Laura said. 'How many people do we catch because they do dumb things?' She checked her hair in the mirror again, and then pulled away when the sun glinted off some grey strands. 'So what do *you* think?'

Joe looked around again. 'It must have been the victim he was after, not someone random. He wouldn't have chosen this location unless it was the only place he could get to her, and this is all about the victims, not the killer. We need to know about her.'

They both turned as they heard a noise behind them, and they saw it was Carson, grunting as he climbed out of his car.

'We've got a possible name for her,' Carson said. 'Jane Roberts.'

'Don't know it,' Laura said.

'No, me neither,' Carson responded. 'But I know her father. Don Roberts.'

Laura shrugged, the name didn't mean anything to her, but she saw the look of surprise on Joe's face.

'*The* Don Roberts?' Joe said.

Carson nodded. 'It was called in yesterday, when she didn't return home at the weekend.'

'How sure can we be?' Joe said.

'The description matches, and she doesn't live too far away.'

'It's Wednesday today. Why would Don leave it so long?' Laura asked.

Joe turned to her. 'Because it involves calling us,' he said. 'Don Roberts will not want us digging into his life. He's a long-time thug, Blackley's most violent doorman before he started to run his own gang of bouncers, leasing them out to the clubs. He's turned to clamping as well, and trust me, you were wise to pay rather than contest it.'

'But why would that make him want to keep away from us?'

'Because he makes a lot of money, and that cannot all come from fixing metal clamps to car wheels. However he makes his cash, he won't be happy to see us looking into his life, and I can tell you one thing: we've got trouble now.'

'What do you mean?'

'Because this is one of two things: targeted or bad luck. We need to look into the last murder again, see if there is any link with Don Roberts, and if there is, we can expect the revenge killings to start.'

'And if it is just coincidence?' Laura asked.

Carson almost smiled at that. 'The killer just has to hope that we catch him first, because if Roberts gets to him, he will die, but it won't be quick and it won't be pleasant.'

Chapter Six

Jack was smiling by the time he reached the court, even though the shadow of the court building took away the warmth of the sun.

The drive into Blackley had done its job, with the wind in his hair and the roof down on his Stag, and so the ghoulishness of the murder scene began to seem a little more distant. He had driven as quick as he dared through the terraced back streets, avoiding the traffic lights and relishing the echo of the engine as he shot between the rows of parked cars, hemmed in between the solid line of brickwork dotted by windows and door frames. The car was his father's legacy when he died, and so Jack liked to give it a good run out when he could, the feel of the wheel his link to those childhood Saturday mornings spent with his father.

He looked up to the four storeys of millstone with tall windows and deep sills, decorative pillars built into the walls on the upper floors. The police station had once been next door, the prisoners' journey into court through a heavy metal door at the end of the cell corridor and then up some stone steps, the light of the court-room making them blink as they arrived in the dock. The police station had moved out to an office complex by the motorway, but the court had survived redevelopment, if survival was measured by draughty courtrooms and bad acoustics. The prisoners arrived at court in a van now, the subterranean journey through the tiled cell complex replaced by a short walk across the town centre pavement in handcuffs.

Jack had no expectations as he approached the entrance. He always kept an eye out for the un-usual cases, and so he listened in to the chatter of the lawyers, especially the prosecutors, because they always relished the chance to tell a good story. Something amusing or with low-shock value usually worked nicely, but the best cases rarely ended on the first hearing, so he kept a diary, just to make sure that he didn't miss the hearings. The best cases attracted the internet spies though – those who looked at his reports and then turned up for the sentencing hearings – and so he preferred the unexpected.

He strode up the court steps and noticed how quiet it was. He was used to striding through the haze of old tobacco mingled with nervous sweat and last night's booze, but there was none of that today. His feet echoed against the long tiled corridor cast in yellow lighting with interview rooms to one side. It was almost deserted, apart from three people waiting, staring into space. He glanced at the clock. It was just after eleven. It seemed too early to have cleared the morning list.

It should have been busier. He'd been attracted to crime reporting by the mayhem, the excitement he'd felt for the stories of bad men doing wicked things. It had always been crime that had interested him, from the television thrillers of his childhood to the Johnny Cash prison concerts that his father played constantly. His father had been a policeman, and Jack remembered the pride he'd felt when his father left each morning, his trousers dark and pressed, his boots shined, ready to take on the bad guys. Jack grew more distant from his father as he grew older, when they both retreated into themselves after the death of Jack's mother, but when he was smaller, his father felt like his own private superhero.

He looked back at the security guards by the entrance, old men in crisp white shirts, security wands in their hands. They were already counting the minutes until lunch. So this was it? Jack Garrett, hotshot reporter. He sighed. A quiet court meant nothing to report.

The duty solicitor room – a small square room designed for client interviews usually filled with bored lawyers moaning about how they couldn't make a fortune anymore – was slightly busier.

He put his head in to ask if anyone had a case worth writing up. There was a general shake of the head and then it went quiet. They spoke to him when they wanted publicity or an audience for their wit, but Jack would never be part of the lawyer-clique, he knew that. His old denims and long blue shirt didn't fit in with the dark pin-stripes. Some were doing crosswords, photo-copies from the national papers that got passed around at court. Sam Nixon was there, one of the main players, who practised from a small office over a copy shop, where tattered sofas and plastic plants served as a reception waiting area.

'Nothing at all for you, Sam?'

He shook his head. 'Times are lean, Jack.'

'I've just been up to a murder scene,' Jack said. 'They've found another girl.' Everyone looked up at that. 'Maybe you'll get a slice of that when they catch the killer.'

'You see, us lawyers are not that bad,' Sam said, waving his hand at the others in the room. 'We want the killer to be caught, not stay free.'

'That bad?'

Sam smiled. 'It might keep me in business for another few months.'

'You're all heart,' Jack said, and then nodded at the prosecutor, who was playing with a touch-screen phone. 'And it might generate some excitement from him.'

'I doubt it. I had to blow the dust from him before,' Sam said.

The prosecutor looked up and raised his eyebrows, just greying on the fringes, to match the silver streaks along his temples. 'My activity is all deep,' he said, grinning. 'That's the trouble with defence lawyers: they're all show and no substance.' Then he pointed towards the door as the

40

sound of bold footsteps clicking rhythmically on the tiles got louder and louder. 'Just to prove my point.'

Jack put his head back out of the door and knew who it was before he even saw him: David Hoyle.

He was different from the rest of the defence lawyers. Most of the lawyers in Blackley were sons of old names, the firms passed through the generations, sometimes split up and married off to other firms. Hoyle was an outsider. He had been sent to Blackley to head up the new branch of Freshwaters, a Manchester firm trying to establish a foothold away from the big city. No one had expected it, and Hoyle had just arrived at court one day, in a suit with broad pinstripes and a swagger that no one seemed to think he had earned.

The other lawyers didn't like him, because he made bold promises that made clients shift loyalties. Low-level crooks usually wanted nothing more than someone to shout on their behalf, and David Hoyle did that. And he didn't work out of an office. Freshwaters had premises, but it was really just somewhere for Hoyle to park his Mercedes. He ran his files from home, did his own typing, and visited his clients on their own turf.

His client trotted behind him, a red-faced man in a grey suit, his stomach pushing out the buttons, his shoes shiny underneath the pressed hems of his trousers. He wasn't the usual court customer. Suddenly, Hoyle turned to smile and shake hands with his client, but from the look of regret Hoyle gave, Jack guessed that things hadn't

41

gone his way.

There was the scent of a story, a disgraced professional always gets a column, and so he checked his pocket for his camera; get the picture first, the story later, because the shame sold better if there was a face a neighbour might recognise. It was the part of the job that used to make Jack most uncomfortable, but he'd learned a long time ago that he had to write stories that people wanted to read, and having a troubled conscience didn't help sell a newspaper.

Jack watched them walk past and then headed after them as they made their way to the steps and then outside.

Hoyle had stopped at the bottom to straighten his tie and fix his hair, using the glass panel in a door as a mirror, before lighting a cigarette.

'I'm too good for this place,' he said to his reflection, and then turned round and blew smoke towards Jack, who had appeared over his shoulder. 'Mr Journo, you're looking twitchy.'

'Where's your client?' Jack said.

Hoyle took another long pull on his cigarette. 'Now, what do you want with that poor man?' he said, wagging a finger.

'When there isn't much going on, I have to chase what I can.'

'Didn't you have bigger ambition than that when you first started out?' Hoyle said. 'Dreams of travel, interviewing presidents, uncovering conspiracies?'

'What do you mean?'

He grinned, smoke seeping out between his teeth. 'This?' he said, and he pointed up the stairs. 'Was this your plan when you left reporting school, or wherever you people graduate from, trying to shame people for stepping on the wrong side of the line sometimes?'

'It's not like that,' Jack said, bristling.

'So what is it like?'

'It's the freedom of the press,' Jack said. 'It's about letting the wider community know what is going on around them, where the threats lie. Over the years, it paints the town's history.'

Hoyle raised his eyebrows. 'If that makes you feel better.'

'What do you mean?'

'You flatter yourself, cover yourself in glory talk,' Hoyle said. 'It's all bullshit, this freedom of the press stuff.'

'And this was your life plan?' Jack retorted. 'Did you always dream of giving speeches to a bench of bored greengrocers in a backwater Lancashire town? Why are you here? Did it not work out in the big city?'

'We're both parasites,' Hoyle said, his voice low, stepping closer to Jack. 'Necessary evils, that's all. A fair justice system is essential to our freedoms. That's right, isn't it, Mr Journo? Like a free press.' He scoffed. 'But that isn't why I do it. I like the game, and if that means I help guilty people get away with bad things, so be it, because it is *all* a game, you know that. And if the odds are stacked against me, I've got to make sure that they don't get the punishment they deserve, so they can skip out of court, laughing at the system. You like it that way too, because it means that you can write it up as an outrage. But I like what I do, because

43

I get off on the fight, the challenge. What about you, Mr Journo?'

Jack rolled his eyes. 'Do all defence lawyers think like you?'

Hoyle laughed. 'Deep down, yes, but some are like you and cloak it in bullshit. All the stuff about protecting our freedoms? That is just crap, because it's a dirty game, and you don't pick your fight, your client picks it for you. It's time for you to be honest with yourself now, and stop disguising your courtroom tales as freedom. It's just gossip, tales over the garden fence, revelling in someone else's downfall. God help us if the world is ever as bad as the papers make out.'

'I can't believe I'm having a debate about morals with a lawyer,' Jack said.

Hoyle checked his watch and then winked, before flicking his cigarette stub onto the pavement outside. 'You're not,' he said, with a grin. 'You've been delayed. My client should be in his car by now, and well away from your camera lens.'

Jack sighed. Didn't Hoyle ever stop playing the game?

'You need to stop wasting your time in there,' Hoyle said, pointing back up the court steps. 'Go after a proper story.'

'Give me one to think about.'

Hoyle smiled. 'A good story always involves me,' he said, and then patted Jack on the shoulder. 'Next time, ask my client the questions, not me, because I'll just protect my client every time,' and then he set off, walking away from the court, a brown leather bag thrown over his shoulder.

Jack leaned against the door frame and watched him go. It was characters like Hoyle who made the courtroom a livelier place, made the day less tedious. And despite Hoyle's brashness he knew Hoyle was right, he *did* need to kick-start his life again, instead of trying to get by on inquests and court stories.

Dolby had used the recession as an excuse to cut costs and streamline the paper, except that Jack knew it wasn't just that. Newspapers were changing, with people going to the internet for the news, and so there was no longer the luxury of a cadre of staff reporters, with Jack providing the freelance stories. Dolby had just two full-time reporters left. He used freelance for the rest, and because there was always some eager new hack ready to provide the stories, Jack wrote whatever Dolby wanted. He hadn't written anything of his own choosing for nearly a year now. It wasn't why he went freelance, but he knew that his career was gone once Dolby looked elsewhere for material. He had thought about writing a book, but on the days he'd set aside for it, his fingers had just hovered over the keys and he'd written nothing.

Jack knew that the problem was deeper than just Dolby though. The court routine had become too comfortable, because going for the big stories had become too dangerous. Criminals were bad people, it came with the job description, but reporters didn't come with the protection that police or lawyers enjoyed, because they weren't players in the game. They were on the sidelines – observing, annoying, interfering. He was sick of the risk and had been hurt – badly – a couple of times.

Jack smiled ruefully as Hoyle disappeared from view, and then his mind drifted back to the murder scene. He thought about the victim from a few weeks earlier. The two deaths hadn't been officially linked yet, but he ought to make the connection in his story, so that once it was confirmed, the story would be ready to run. An update from the first victim's family would be a good way to start.

He glanced back up the court steps. There was nothing going on there, and so he walked back to the Stag, parked further along the road. It was time to concentrate on the murder story.

Chapter Seven

Laura chewed her lip as Carson approached the home of Don Roberts, a shiny redbrick detached house, with bright double-glazing and pillars under a small porch. A bay window jutted out towards the lawn. It wasn't how she thought it would be. Joe had made Don Roberts out to be the local thug, and so she was expecting something a bit less suburban, although she did spot stone lions on either side of the front door, *de rigueur* for the criminal set. There was an Audi parked at the front, an RS8, black and sleek. Although Don's house looked like the flashiest on the street, Laura guessed that he was still looked

46

down on by the rest of the neighbourhood.

They'd come straight from the crime scene, and so they hadn't had much time to plan what to say. When Carson looked at her, Laura nodded. She was ready.

A metal gate blocked the driveway, and it clinked loudly as she opened it. This was the part of the job she hated most, delivering bad news, knowing that whatever shade of normality was behind the door, it would soon be gone forever.

Carson took the lead, rapping loudly on the door. Laura noticed the lens of the CCTV camera in the shadow of the porch, and when the door opened, a woman appeared, her hair streaked blonde and pulled tight into a ponytail. The darker roots were showing through and there was a line of foundation around her face. She had a stud in her top lip and the pucker of lines around her mouth showed her as a heavy smoker.

'Helen Roberts?' Carson asked.

She nodded in response, her hand gripping the doorjamb. Her stare was hard, as if she was used to dealing with the police at her doorstep, and Laura knew that they had been clocked straight away as that. But Laura sensed her uncertainty. Bad news or another pointless warrant?

Carson gave her a regret-filled smile. 'Can we come in?'

'Why?' she said, the colour draining from her cheeks.

'It really would be better if we came inside.'

'Is it about Jane?'

Carson paused just long enough to give away

the truth, and the woman's eyes widened in shock.

She seemed to recover quickly, her default reaction to the police coming back, but still she couldn't help swallowing hard when she asked, 'Have you found her?'

Carson stepped towards her and let out a long, heavy sigh. 'Did Jane have a butterfly tattoo on her wrist?'

At that, Mrs Roberts' grip on the door slackened, and her eyes glazed over before she slumped to the floor.

Carson looked at Laura and then stepped forward to help her into the house.

Jack rooted through the newspapers he kept in his car to find the name of the first victim – Deborah Corley. He remembered her house, he had driven past it on the day she'd been found but had been beaten to the scoop by one of the employed writers. The newspapers were now strewn across the passenger seat, with pictures of Deborah and posed photographs of Deborah's parents, looking tearful, a framed photograph of their daughter held on the mother's knee.

The house was a large Victorian semi on the edge of Blackley, with a small square patch of flowers behind a low stone wall, the red brick of the house dark and covered in moss in places. A flower basket hung by the front door and the curtains in the white-framed sash windows were tied back neatly.

Jack stepped up to the front door. A woman watched from the house next door, and her look

48

of disapproval said that she knew what he was doing: intruding. He steeled himself and turned away. He knew that her parents didn't deserve the attention. He had the jump on the other media though, because he was on the spot. Blackley wasn't a large town, and young women didn't get murdered too often here. When the out-of-town press made the connection, this quiet crescent of driveways and two-car households would become busy with cameras.

He rang the doorbell.

There was a pause as the soft chimes echoed around the house, but then there was a twitch of a curtain, and when the door opened a few seconds later, a woman with a pale face and bags under her eyes looked out. Jack recognised her from the newspaper, although he could already see the weight dropping from her.

'I'm sorry for the intrusion, Mrs Corley,' he said. 'My name's Jack Garrett and I'm a reporter. I've come to see how you are doing, whether you've got any more news.'

She looked at him for a moment, as if she was going to slam the door in his face.

'If Deborah's killer is going to be caught, we need to keep her story in the news,' he said.

She faltered at that, and then just turned and went inside. Jack followed.

It looked like she had spent the past three weeks cleaning the house, perhaps just to keep herself occupied. There was a strong smell of air freshener and the stair rails that climbed out of the hallway looked polished.

Jack followed her along a tiled hallway, stepping

past a fishing rod and bait box, and into the room at the front. There was a dining table in the room behind, and the brief glimpse out of the rear window gave a view of a neat lawn surrounded by a splash of flowers. The room looked spotless. There were the tracks of a vacuum cleaner in the carpet, and the fireplace gleamed, the flowered tiles reflecting the light streaming in through the window. Photograph frames sat in a neat row on the mantelpiece. This had been a happy home.

As Jack looked out of the window, he was surprised to see the reservoir in the distance, where Deborah had been found. What must it feel like to see that all day, knowing what it meant?

'I know this is not a good time,' Jack said, as he settled into a chair, to make sure he stayed, 'but I meant what I said, that we need to keep Deborah's story in the news.'

She looked at the television for a moment. It was playing but the sound was turned down, as if it was there for the sake of distraction, not entertainment.

'The police told me that, but it doesn't make it any easier,' she said. 'Reliving it.'

'And how are you?'

Tears welled up in her eyes and she took a deep breath. 'Just getting by.'

'What about your husband? How is he doing?'

She looked down. 'Not good,' she said. 'He wants to go back to work, but he can't face being there, because he knows everyone will be talking about Deborah.'

Jack shuffled in his chair, knowing that he was getting to the difficult part. 'You know there's been another?' he said.

She stared into space for a few seconds before looking down at her lap. 'Yes,' she said. 'The police called earlier and told me to expect press visits. I'm expecting Mike back soon.'

'Where did he go?'

'For a walk,' she said. 'He does that a lot now.'

Jack couldn't respond to that. 'Can you think of any reason why your daughter should be a target?' he said instead.

Her chin puckered and her hand shot to her eyes, to wipe away the tears.

'None at all,' she said, her voice breaking. 'It's a bloody cliché, I know, but she was a lovely girl, would do anything for anybody, and then some bastard comes along and just takes her away.' She wiped her eyes. 'I'm sorry for swearing,' she said, her voice softer now, 'but that's what he is. Can you imagine what it is like to watch your daughter leave the house and never return? It had seemed like just another day. If I'd known...' and she shrugged. 'Well, things would have been different.'

'You would have kept her safe at home, if you'd known,' Jack said gently. 'But you couldn't know, and that's why it is so cruel.'

She nodded, a smile breaking through the tears. Then there was the slam of the front door, followed by footsteps.

'It must be Mike,' she said, her eyes suddenly wary.

A small black-and-white mongrel bustled into the room and sniffed at Jack's hands, checking out the stranger in the house.

'He's harmless,' she said, her voice husky, and then looked up when Mike Corley walked in. He was dressed in jeans and a jumper, holding a dog lead. Jack guessed his age as early fifties. The faint boozer's flush to his cheeks and the sag of his belly told him that he was dealing with his loss quite differently to his wife.

When he saw Jack, he scowled.

'Hello, I'm a reporter,' Jack said.

'I guessed that much,' he said sharply. 'You didn't waste much time.'

'I know the police have told you about another girl being killed.'

'So you want one more quote?' he said. 'Well, I'll give you one: get out of my fucking house and leave us alone.'

'Michael!' Mrs Corley said.

'I'm sorry, Mr Corley,' Jack said, 'but the more press exposure you get, the more chance the police will have of finding whoever killed Deborah.'

'I'm a fucking police officer. Do you think I don't know how the police work?' Mike said, tears brimming onto his lashes 'You see, it's not really about Deborah, is it, because when it was hinted that she'd had affairs with married men, it was like some kind of sick fatal attraction story, an excuse for you people to pick apart her life just to sell your papers? You don't care who you hurt, provided that you put a few words on the page. So no more. Not from me.'

'I'm not saying the press are perfect, but this is your chance to tell Deborah's story.'

Mike pondered that for a moment, and then

shook his head. 'And I don't want anything to do with it.'

Jack stood to go, and then pulled out one of his business cards and handed it to Mrs Corley. 'Call me if you change your mind,' he said.

Deborah's father didn't move as Jack left the house.

Chapter Eight

Laura tapped her pen against her hand as she sat opposite Don Roberts.

He was a thickset man in tracksuit bottoms and a black T-shirt, two gold chains around his neck His grey hair was cropped close to his head and large tattoos dominated his forearms: a bulldog in boxing gloves and a black panther, the claws scraping along the veins that bulged under his skin. Middle age was making its mark, and although Don was well-built and muscular, the curve of his paunch was visible under his T-shirt.

Don hadn't said anything since their arrival. He had stared at Carson, and then at her, and then at Carson again. But Laura could see the hurt in his eyes, the desperate need for someone to tell him that it was all a mistake, that his daughter would walk into the house and they would all go back to normal. His hands were trembling, but he continued to stare fixedly at Carson, ignoring his wife's wails from the kitchen.

'Mr Roberts,' Carson began, but then fell silent

as Don raised his hand.

'Why didn't you find her?' Don Roberts asked, his voice quivering and loaded with emotion.

'We don't know how long she was there,' Carson said. 'Once we've done a full examination...'

'Bullshit,' he snapped. 'Jane was missing and you didn't find her because you weren't looking hard enough, because of what you think of me.'

Laura saw Carson take a deep breath to calm himself, because what he really wanted to say was that if the call had come in earlier, then perhaps they would have had a better chance of finding her. Instead, Carson shook his head. 'We treated her like we treat everyone,' he said. 'Just tell us what you can about the last time you saw her.'

Roberts clenched his jaw. 'That won't bring her back,' he said, his teeth gritted.

'It will help us catch her killer, stop him from doing it again.'

'Where are you looking?'

'We haven't started yet,' Carson said. 'We're hoping you might help us, give us some pointers. Who were Jane's friends? What about a boyfriend?'

Roberts stiffened at that, and then took a deep breath and sat forward, slowly and deliberately, the leather chair creaking softly underneath him. 'I am not having you dig into Jane's life. It will become about me, not her, because I'm hated in this town.'

'Who hates you?'

Roberts shook his head. 'I know who hates me, so I'll do the searching. And since you couldn't find Jane alive, I'll be the one to find out who

54

killed her.'

'Mr Roberts, please, let us do our job.'

Don slammed his hands on the arm of his chair and rose quickly to his feet. 'Why should I?' he bellowed, his face contorted by rage, tears in his eyes. 'Would you, if you were where I am, because even if you do find the killer, which I fucking doubt, it will all be for nothing, because how long will he go away for? Ten years? Fifteen? And then he's out. That's if you even put him in jail. And you want me to spend those years waiting for him to come back onto the streets, back into my community?' He stood over Carson, his hands balled tightly into fists. 'I'll find the murdering bastard, and I'll make sure it won't happen again, you can trust me on that.' He jabbed his fist towards the door. 'You need to go, now.'

'Mr Roberts,' Laura said, to deflect Don's attention away from Carson. 'We need to find out what we can about Jane.'

'So do I,' Don said, and then he stood up to leave the room.

Laura exchanged quick glances with Carson, but then she was taken by surprise when Roberts gripped her arm and hauled her to her feet.

'I said out!' Don said, and pushed Laura towards the door.

Laura looked at Carson, unsure what to do, but Carson pushed past her, pausing only to put his business card on the mantelpiece.

'If you want to tell us anything, Mr Roberts, give me a call,' Carson said, his voice measured. 'I investigate murders, nothing else. This will be about Jane, not about how you make your money.'

Don Roberts didn't say anything as they left the house, and when they were back on the path outside the front door, the door slammed behind them. There was silence for a few seconds, but then it was broken by the sound of sobbing from Mrs Roberts, audible even outside.

Laura blew out. Murder was just as much about the living as it was about the dead. She looked at Carson, who shook his head and then walked towards his car. He didn't need to say anything, Laura knew that. Don Roberts was blinded by his dislike of the police, and if he found the killer before they did, there would be another death to deal with.

Chapter Nine

Laura was in Carson's slipstream as he rushed into the police station, past a television crew that was still unpacking its gear and through the large wooden entrance door, banging it hard against the wall behind. One more hole for the maintenance team to fill.

The station was busy, just as Laura had expected. The day was rushing on, nearly one o'clock already, and it seemed like all rest days had been cancelled. There was going to be a high police presence in Blackley today, to provide reassurance to the community. Everyone was hanging around and waiting to be despatched, talking in small groups in the canteen, which was situated in the centre of the station in a bright and airy atrium, lit by the sun streaming through the high glass roof. Two police drivers pushed their way through, pulling trolleys behind them, one containing bags of files to be taken to the prosecution office, and the other filled with large brown exhibit bags, heading towards the forensic laboratory a few miles away.

Carson had commandeered a room on the ground floor, a large glass-fronted space with views over one of the car parks. The squad was based at the constabulary headquarters on the other side of the county, and so they had to set up base camps in other stations whenever a murder took them further afield. Desks lined the room. It was used mostly for training, the new boom industry, with computer terminals around the edges, the white board at the front filled with the enquiry routes from Deborah Corley's murder. Laura saw Joe at a computer screen, and as she walked in, he looked up and waved tiredly.

'What are you looking for?' Laura asked.

He sat back and ran his hands through his hair. Laura noticed a few grey streaks.

'I'm trying to find similarities,' he said. 'He must have done something like this before.'

Laura heard Carson grunt behind her. 'He did,' he growled, and he pointed at the photographs on the wall. 'Three weeks ago.'

Joe didn't answer, just flashed Laura a half-smile, and she guessed that he had learned to let Carson's moods blow themselves out. Carson was bad-tempered and aggressive, and he didn't have the bedside manner of some, but if Laura ever wanted a copper on her side, it would be him.

Carson sat down and sighed. 'Go on then, hotshot,' he said to Joe. 'What have you got?'

Joe twirled his pen in his fingers. 'So far, nothing. At least not in Lancashire.'

'What, you think he might be from out of the county?' Carson said.

'Maybe,' Joe said, nodding, 'but not too far. He had to have known the locations well enough. And I just don't believe that a fantasy is this well-developed without there being something else before it.'

'Fantasy?' Carson said.

'The strangulation. The leaves. The dirt,' Joe said, before standing up and going to the wall at the front, which was covered in photographs and maps. He tapped at the first picture: naked legs, flaccid and pale, sticking out of a large overflow pipe that took water from a reservoir into a nearby river. 'Deborah Corley,' Joe said. 'Just the same. Leaves and dirt and grit jammed into her mouth, her vagina, her anus, dumped so that she could be found easily. I thought at first that the dirt might have been for some forensic reason, to make it harder to pick up DNA, but now I'm not so sure.'

'Just because it is repeated doesn't mean that it wasn't done for the same reason,' Carson said.

Joe shook his head. 'When it's repeated, it's more than that. It's the fantasy, part of the act. Remember what we said from the scene, that she was alive when he jammed the stuff in there. They both died from strangulation, so if we go with the forensic clean-up, then he must have attacked her and then jammed her full of debris, but that doesn't fit in with a violent sexual offender. Sex attackers get off on the violence, so it doesn't seem right that the violence would come after the sex. That's when they are normally trying to get away. Some even stay to apologise, to try and comfort the victim.'

'Maybe he couldn't finish the job and acted out of frustration?' Laura said.

'What, twice?' Joe said, his eyebrows raised. 'Frustration suggests lack of control, because it wasn't planned, but if you are out of control, you don't act identically twice.'

'So what do you think?' Carson said.

Joe chewed on his lip for a few seconds, and then said, 'The best I can come up with is that the removal of the clothes from the scene is part of the forensic clean-up. I think the debris and the strangulation is part of the act, and the motivation will have been sexual. If he didn't have sex with her, he must have got his kicks in some other way. My guess is that he masturbated at the scene, maybe even onto her when she was still wearing clothes. That might be why she was naked and there were no clothes at the scene, because when her clothes went, his DNA went with them.'

'Perhaps they were trophies?' Carson said.

'Possibly,' Joe said. 'Do you remember the small cuts on her body and legs?'

Laura and Carson exchanged glances and then nodded that they remembered.

'I think that happened when he cut off her clothes,' Joe said.

'So what scenario do we have?' Carson asked.

Joe looked at the photographs again, and then he went back to his chair. 'He attacks the victim and fills her mouth with dirt and debris, perhaps to keep her quiet. He jams her with dirt wherever he can, for some sexual motive, and then strangles her. As she dies, he masturbates over her, and then cleans up.'

'So it's a pure sex attacker?' Carson said.

'That would be my guess,' Joe replied.

'What about a diversion?' Laura said.

'What do you mean?' Joe said.

It was Laura's turn to walk towards the photographs, but this time she went to a glamour shot of Deborah Corley, a soft-focus picture from one of the high street makeover studios, her hair over her face, her top pulled down from her shoulder.

'From what you've said, Jane Roberts is from a bad family, the sort that makes enemies,' Laura said. 'Nothing like Deborah. Her father's a copper, for Christ's sake, a different world to Don Roberts. She was rebelling a bit, maybe, sleeping around, but no different to a lot of young women.'

'So what are you suggesting?' Carson said.

'Do you remember the whispers we heard about Deborah's father?' Laura said. 'Good cop on the street, bad man at home; that he was a bully, spent too much of his off-duty time with a bottle in his hand. His wife has called in twice when he's come home drunk and got too heavy-handed. Maybe he got the same with Deborah, argued about her private life, and ended up killing her? Was Jane Roberts just a cover-up, to distract us from the first family, to make it look like a serial killing rather than someone closer to home?'

'Why expose himself a second time, just to rig up a smokescreen?' Carson said. 'It's too much of a gamble. If he wasn't seen the first time, and there is nothing forensically to link him, he is taking a big risk in doing it again. No, if Deborah's father was behind it, he would sit tight and wait for it to blow over.'

'And it wouldn't be so sexualised,' Joe added. 'But it could be a distraction for a different reason.'

'What do you mean?' Carson said, sitting forward now.

'Some kind of turf war,' Joe said. 'Perhaps someone found out how Deborah died and replicated it, so that it hurt Don Roberts and distracted us.'

Carson shook his head, unconvinced. 'Don Roberts is an old-school crook,' he said. 'So are his enemies. Just small town big fishes. They would tear each other's fingernails out, but they still play by certain rules. You don't go into each other's houses. You keep family out of it. The rules are the only things that keep things stable, because they don't want to attract attention. That's why all the new drug dealers get spotted, because they think the game is all about power and Bentleys, about baseball bats and guns. It's not. It's about secrecy.'

'But was the dirt in the vagina meant as an insult, not a sex act?' Joe said. 'We're only guessing that he masturbated.'

Carson groaned and put his head back. 'How many bloody angles do we need?'

'But she was the target, we know that,' Joe said.

'What do you mean?' Carson said.

'The location. There was too much risk of being seen, because it's overlooked by houses. And nice houses, where they would perhaps be more likely to investigate a scream or a fight. If it was random, I would expect the killer to be somewhere more secluded, or driving around, looking for the right victim.'

'Maybe he was driving around?'

'But if you had transport, would you choose that location for a dumping ground?' Joe shook his head. 'I wouldn't expect so, and so it makes me think that Jane Roberts was meant to be the victim. But why?'

'We do know one thing, though,' Laura said. 'We have only ever told the press that the first victim was strangled, and so the girl we found today was either killed by the same person, or by someone who knew all about the first.'

'Do we keep it secret from the press again?' Carson said.

Joe sighed. 'It will stop anyone copying if we do,' he said, 'but it will also stop anyone from recognising the method. There is no easy answer.'

Carson nodded and pulled at his lip, before he said, 'Keep it quiet for now. We could let it out later, if we get nothing from the phones or the scene in the next couple of days.' He checked his watch, and then looked at Laura. 'The press will be here soon. Will Jack be?'

Laura felt her cheeks flush. 'Probably. He was at the scene earlier.'

'I know, I saw him,' Carson said.

Laura was rescued by the opening of the door and a detective appearing, holding a camera in the air.

'Who wants to look at the gawkers?' he said. He was dressed in his scruffs to blend in, jeans and a T-shirt, but the short hair and muscles gave him away as police. The detective went to a computer terminal and hooked up the camera. He clicked the first photograph to make it fill the screen, and then stepped back as Carson stepped forward.

'McGanity, you need to look at these,' he said. 'You've been based in Blackley.'

'Look for people who are standing apart from the crowd,' Joe said. 'The person who is alone, not talking to anyone.'

Laura nodded as Carson began to flick through the pictures. It seemed to be people from the near-by estate, teenagers on bikes and young mothers. Nothing of interest there. Then Laura saw something.

'Stop!' she said. 'Go back.'

Carson looked round. 'Which one?'

'The picture before.'

Carson clicked the back button and scoured the screen for someone of interest. And then he saw him, loitering at the back of the scene, his hands in his pocket, distant from everyone else.

'Do you recognise him?' Laura asked, and she could tell from the frown on Carson's face that he did.

'Deborah Corley's father,' he said quietly, before he looked at Joe. 'It looks like we are going to have to look into more than just sex fiends.'

Chapter Ten

Jack strode into the offices of the *Blackley Tele-graph,* a seventies relic of glass and concrete next to the bus station, made dusty by the passing fumes. The reception area was typical of a newspaper office, with a high counter and low chairs, the latest edition spread out over tables, the walls lined by recent photographs and framed past editions. There was no one at reception though, so he just strode through into the offices behind.

He missed the buzz of the newsroom. The shouts, the banter, the rush to make deadlines. Things were different now though. Most stories were done on the telephone, and the noise was just the sales staff trying to drum up advertising space. It was past two o'clock in the afternoon and people were busy trying to finish work on the next day's paper. Dolby Wilkins worked from a glass-fronted office at the end of the room. He was leaning back in his chair, talking into a telephone.

Jack walked between the desks, smiling the occasional hello, pausing to knock on Dolby's door, who waved him in impatiently. Jack settled into a leather chair opposite and read the newspaper cuttings pinned to the wall as Dolby finished his call. They were all headlines from after Dolby had arrived, part of the new style that he wanted the paper to adopt: unsubtle and edgy.

Dolby liked to attack the police whenever he could, and once that became stale, he turned to the other easy targets, *asylum seeker* appearing often.

The phone went down and Dolby grinned, showing off bright white teeth, and swept his hair back, a habit of his, although it only ever flopped forward again. He was younger than Jack, only just past thirty, but he had the confidence that a good education brought.

'How was it at the murder scene?' Dolby asked.

'Pretty much the same as always. Police en masse and everyone kept back.'

'Do we have a name yet for the woman?'

Jack shook his head. 'Not mentioned to me.'

'There's a press conference in thirty minutes,' Dolby said. 'There should be enough padding in that to make up the front page.'

Dolby could get one of his staffers to do it, Jack knew that, but this was about the power balance. Dolby gave out an assignment as an order, not a request, and being freelance was just like being a staff reporter, but without the paid holidays.

'It will delay your Whitcroft feature,' Jack said. 'You wanted it today, but I can't do it if I'm running around doing this.'

'How is that story?' Dolby said.

Jack frowned. 'It's not the hell-hole you want it to be,' he said. 'Just people like all of us, trying to make their way in life. It's just that some do it better than others.'

'Knock on some doors. We could run a *good life on benefits* story instead,' Dolby said.

Jack sighed. He knew how they worked. You talk

to people about their struggles, and then make sure you get a picture of them in front of the big television, grinning.

'What do you want, someone with plenty of kids, or a brown face and a foreign accent?' Jack said.

'Don't be like that, Jack,' Dolby said. 'It sells papers, you know that. It gets people talking in the pubs.'

'And it gets innocent people beaten up.'

'Okay, okay, you've tweaked my liberal conscience,' Dolby said, sarcastically. 'What about delinquent kids, causing mayhem as their parents sit in drinking?'

Jack smiled. 'Lucked out again, Dolby. They have private security on there now, and so even those kids are probably better than they used to be.'

'Private security?' he said.

'There's a van that patrols the estate. Just a couple of bald men in black satin jackets, you know the type. It sounds like the residents pay for them.'

Dolby thought about that and then said, 'Find out what you can about that. Why are people on the lowest rung paying someone to do the work the police should be doing?' He leaned forward. 'You never know, this could turn out to be a story to fill your pinko heart, the noble working class looking after itself.'

'You really are an arsehole, Dolby,' Jack said, shaking his head.

'I know, but I write your cheques, so be nice to me.' He tapped at his watch. 'Press conference soon. I don't want you to miss the show.'

Jack got to his feet and managed a small smile as he headed back towards the sunshine.

He was a spot of calm surrounded by noise. The jumpsuits and boots. Detectives deep in consultation. The air around him felt still. No one saw him. No one spoke to him. He could see them though. He watched them, saw how they gathered in small groups. Talking, laughing, always moving around him as if he wasn't there.

He could tolerate the uniforms, because they knew their place, that it was all about eight-hour shifts and then home, nothing more. It was the detectives that he fucking hated. Glory hunters, just egos in pastel shirts.

He smiled, and then lifted the cup to his mouth to hide it. Beware the quiet man.

Chapter Eleven

Jack had to park some distance from the police station because the spaces were taken up by the out-of-town television crews sorting out their equipment, and the growing huddle of newspaper journalists who sucked on cigarettes as they waited for the show to start.

The police station was shiny and new, on the edge of town and visible from the motorway, its red brick and high windows towering above the low-rise office complexes that surrounded it, high steel fences guarding the car park. Jack saw Karl Carson ahead, Laura's boss, a bald-headed bully of a man, making chit-chat with some of the reporters. They'd come across each other before, had fallen out and then made up again, and so when Jack got up close, Carson just smiled and made sure he used plenty of force when he slapped the *visitor* sticker onto Jack's shirt.

Carson turned and walked back into the police station, holding the door as the journalists trooped past. When Jack got close, Carson muttered, 'No trouble, Mr Garrett.'

'Not if you behave yourself, Inspector,' Jack said, and winked.

They were ushered to a room on the ground floor that looked out onto the police canteen. Jack went to the back as everyone else fixed their microphones to the tables at the front, the television people jostling for a prominent spot, so that their question could form a part of their edited highlights, ego over news. Cameras lined the back of the room. Deborah Corley's murder three weeks earlier had provided fodder for columns filled with tales of her social life – how she was a pub regular and liked the company of married men. The television people just wanted to fill the late afternoon news slots, but the newspapers were wondering what the new murder might give them, needing to write it up for a deadline, and so the air crackled with tension. It went quiet though as Carson entered, with Joe Kinsella and Laura right behind him. As everyone settled into place, Jack ended up behind a television camera, his view restricted to what he

68

could see over the cameraman's arm.

Carson and Joe sat down behind a long white table and glanced at the cluster of microphones in front of them. On a board behind them was the logo of Lancashire Constabulary, a police crest over a blue ribbon. Carson reached for a jug of water and poured a drink. Jack watched Laura as she moved to the back of the room, tall and dark, in a grey trouser suit, her dimples flashing as she smiled her thanks at those reporters who moved aside for her. Jack made a space for her and she joined him against the wall. He straightened himself. Although just under six feet tall, his slouch made Laura look taller than him.

He leaned towards her. 'I suppose there is nothing you can tell me that Carson won't say?' he whispered.

She raised her eyebrows. 'No special favours, you know that.'

He smiled. 'I missed you this morning. It was an early start.'

Laura blushed, and then her eyes went to the front as Carson cleared his throat into the microphones. He heard her sigh. 'I'm sorry,' she whispered, 'I'll make it up to you later.' And when Jack looked, he thought he saw some mischief in her eyes.

One of the cameramen looked at Laura, the trace of a smile on his lips, and then Jack noticed the boom microphone and the headphones clamped to his head. He must have heard their exchange, but he just shrugged an apology to Jack and then shifted his focus back to Carson, who was getting ready to speak.

69

'Thank you, ladies and gentlemen,' Carson said, his voice coming out with a slight tremble. 'I will make a short statement and then answer a few questions.' He looked at the press corps, and then read from a sheet of paper. 'This morning, the body of a young woman was discovered in woods in Blackley. She died a few days ago. We believe that this may be connected to the death of a woman in Blackley three weeks ago, Deborah Corley, the daughter of a Blackley police officer. We are trying to confirm the identity of the dead woman, but when this has been done, we would ask that you respect the privacy of the victim's family.' Carson took a breath and looked around the room again, his bald head reflecting the gleam of the camera lights as he tried to catch the eye of each journalist in turn. Then he looked directly towards the cameras at the back of the room, keen to make the most of his chance to address the public. 'We are not ready to reveal details of her murder, but I would like to say this: whoever carried out this barbaric act must be caught. If you know something, don't keep it back. Don't shelter this man. If you have any information that might help to catch this person, come forward.' Carson paused to let his words sink in, and then said, 'I will be limited in what I can say, but if you have any questions, please ask them now.'

Someone stood up at the front.

'Martin Ashton, Sky News,' the man said. 'Do you think this is the work of a serial killer?'

Carson pursed his lips for a moment, and then said, 'That term tends to overexcite. The post-mortem examination has not yet taken place,

70

but, yes, we are looking at the possibility that the same person killed both women, if that is how you define a serial killer.'

Someone else rose to his feet.

'Ian Bramley, BBC,' he said. 'Both the victims are young women. Is there any other connection between them?'

'That is something we will try to establish, but until we know the answer we must assume that all women will be in danger.'

Jack scribbled some notes, and then watched as the questions petered out, each television network satisfied that they'd asked a question. Carson stood to go, and so everyone began to collect their microphones and laptops, all keen to edit the piece for the afternoon news.

'I've got to go,' Laura said.

Jack grabbed her hand and pulled her close. 'Can't you give me a name for the dead woman?' he said, his voice low.

She squeezed his hand and smiled. 'Nice try,' she said, and then rushed to go after Carson, threading her way through the crowd.

Jack tried to follow her, still hoping for an insider quote, or even just for a longer talk, but an officer stepped in front of him and made it clear that journalists were to be escorted out. Instead, he watched her walk away, deep in conversation with Joe and Carson, just three suits making their way through the tables of the police canteen.

Jack sighed. One of the drawbacks of being involved with a police officer, he supposed, was that her job could sometimes be so damn important. He thought of how Laura could be when

71

she was away from the station, fun and light-hearted, but also how absorbed she became when a big case came along. But as he watched her go, and thought of the two dead young women, their murderer still not caught, he knew that he wouldn't have it any other way.

Chapter Twelve

Carson waited until they were clear of the journalists before he asked, 'How do you think it went?'

Laura was surprised. Carson was a brute, direct and strong, but there was a hint of self-doubt in his voice. 'It said enough,' she said. 'Maybe the serial killer question will help, because it scares, and it puts the word into people's heads without our having to use it.'

'But should we have said more?' Carson persisted.

'No,' Joe said. 'Say too much and you risk getting things wrong. Let's see what comes in today, and if there is anything forensic to work from.'

Carson nodded his agreement as they headed away from the atrium and towards the Incident Room. Everyone was already lined up and waiting for them, and so Carson went straight to the front as Laura made her way to the back. The front two rows of desks were occupied by those keen to be spotted, the shirts pristine, pastel colours and bold ties, one uniform replaced by another. Joe sat behind Carson, in a corner, to observe, as always. The room was full, all the door-to-door detectives coming back for the press conference debrief, and everyone was attentive and quiet. The discovery of the body was still too new, and so no one wanted to break rank and crack a gag, although she guessed that the respectful silence wouldn't last to the end of the next day.

'Two murders in less than a month,' Carson said, and he banged the whiteboard behind him with the flat of his hand. 'We'll get the blame for the second one after not catching him first time round. Remember that,' and he pointed around the room, his finger going to each face. 'If you miss something, you might be explaining it to the High Court, because Kinsella,' and he jerked his thumb in Joe's direction, 'he reckons that this isn't going to end here.'

Carson looked around the room slowly. The detectives had settled into clusters, with those who had been knocking on doors separate from those who had been with the extended family and friends, and they shuffled nervously as Carson met their gaze, one by one.

'So has anyone got anything?' Carson shouted at the room, prowling along the front, his paces making the photographs taped to the whiteboard flutter as he went past.

No one spoke at first, just exchanged glances, but then someone just in front of Laura, a small man with a crew cut and moustache, coughed and strained his neck so that he could be seen.

'We did the houses that back onto the scene,' he said. 'It's busy down there. The local kids use the path as a mini-moto run, buzzing round most nights. And if it isn't them, it's kids boozing in groups. Some of the residents have had abuse when they've looked out of their windows, been called paedos and things like that, and so they might not have noticed any noise.'

'But if it's busy, maybe the body hasn't been there as long as it looks,' Carson said. 'We can check that in the post-mortem.'

'Oh yeah, we got a call on that,' said another voice, and a post-it note was passed forward. 'Tomorrow morning. The doc didn't want to rush it, so he'll do it first thing and take as long as we need.'

'Who have we got?' Carson asked.

'Doctor Pratt,' the same voice said.

Carson nodded approvingly, and then he pointed to the detective who'd spoken first and asked him, 'Did anyone make you suspicious?'

'From the houses?' the detective said, and then shook his head as he answered his own question. 'No. Just normal young families.'

'Do you know how abnormal the killer looks, or who he lives with?' Carson said, his eyes wide.

Laura saw the embarrassment creep up the back of the detective's neck, a blush to match his lilac shirt.

'No, I don't,' the detective replied.

'So run everyone's name through the computer, and see if anything pops up,' Carson said. When the detective looked to his colleague, who had suddenly developed an interest in the floor, Carson added, 'You did get everyone's name, didn't you?'

The detective looked down.

'Fucking hell,' Carson said, and slammed his hand on the whiteboard. One of the photographs slid off. 'That's your next job,' he barked. 'Go back and get everyone's details, and then run them, see what you get. Convictions, intelligence, incident logs. And look for any link to either of the dead women or their families!'

Carson pointed to two young detectives standing next to Laura. 'I want you two to go through the Sex Offenders Register,' he said. 'Visit everyone on it who targets women. Forget about the child porn and kiddie fiddlers. I want the flashers, the gropers, the closet cameramen. If they haven't got an alibi for either death, then they're suspects.'

'And look for violence,' Joe said. 'The flashers should be the first stop on the list. Ask around, speak to the beat cops and PCSO's, see if they can think of anyone who is dangerous but hasn't been caught yet. And concentrate on white offenders.'

'Why is that?' someone asked.

'Common sense,' Joe said. 'The victims were white. The girl this morning was found in a white area. An Asian man would stand out, be remembered, wouldn't venture onto that estate. So a white man is most likely.'

A female detective put up her hand. Laura recognised the glossy blonde hair and the frosty body language. It was Rachel Mason, sitting in the middle of the room. Laura had crossed her before, except that now Laura was a sergeant and Rachel was still a constable.

'I spoke to the extended family,' Rachel said. 'They know what Jane's parents do, but they say that Jane was different, not part of that set-up. She worked for a travel agent in town and was just trying to make her own way.'

'Boyfriend?'

Rachel shook her head. 'They split up a couple of months ago, but nothing in it. Childhood sweethearts who grew out of each other.'

'If the wider family don't know of a link between the two women, we can leave them alone for a while,' Carson said. 'The Jane Roberts murder is linked to the murder of Deborah Corley. We need to find out what it is that links the two women.'

'We got a nod from an informant that Don Roberts has already put out a reward,' said a voice at the side of the room. 'Fifty grand, so I was told.'

'Great,' Carson said, rolling his eyes. 'The security racket must be doing well. How do these people grow fortunes?' He shook his head. 'The back streets of Blackley will be crawling with amateur sleuths right now, none of them fit for fucking purpose. Can you imagine what it will be like when all the local smackheads think they've got a path to easy money. Don will get more names than fucking Lloyds.'

'Maybe we can persuade the drug squad to muscle a bit of info out of someone,' the same voice said. 'You know how it is, they'll do anything to stay out of a cell.'

'Try everything,' Carson said, and then turned his attention to two detectives sitting at a table near the front. 'Anything from the phones?' he asked.

The detectives shook their heads in sync with each other. 'Nothing yet, except people telling us that it might be gangland, because Jane's father is a crook,' one said.

'Has anyone else got anything that can take this investigation forward?' Carson asked, his eyes scanning the room. No one answered.

Carson sighed. 'So it looks like it's forensic results or nothing for the moment. Anyone got an idea?' The room stayed silent, and so Carson clapped his hands. 'Come on, back to it. Phone your families and apologise that you'll be out for most of the night. If they moan, just be glad that they're alive.'

Carson grabbed his jacket and nodded at Joe. He raised his hand to the back of the room, towards Laura, gesturing at her to follow. As she excused herself past small muttering cliques, Rachel Mason flashed her a glance, but Laura turned away. She didn't have time for squabbles about Rachel being left out.

As Laura got close, Carson said, 'We'll check whether anything was found at the scene, and then you go to Mike Corley's house. We need to find out more about Deborah. People might remember more now, because the news is less fresh for her. Go over again where she went, who she slept with, who she knew. We might just find a link between the two women.' He turned to Laura. 'Try and speak to Corley's wife alone, if you can. Talk to her as a mother, not as a copper. You might just get something from her that way.'

Carson walked out of the Incident Room, Laura and Joe following behind, and turned into a room that sometimes got commandeered for meetings with community leaders and criminal justice committees. It was the murder squad's turn now. There were two officers in there, supervised by a young female Crime Scene Investigator, cataloguing everything that had been collected from the scene. The table was filled with exhibit bags, and notes were being made about which officers had yet to provide statements detailing their finds. This was part of the routine, the exhibit trail, some of the grunt work done by those away from the frontline. A CSI used to be called SOCO, Scenes of Crime Officer, but American TV had glammed them up.

'Is there anything that looks promising?' Carson asked.

One of the officers looked up and shrugged. 'You're the detective.' When Carson scowled, he added, 'Just the usual scrap metal collection. Ring pulls, bottle tops. There are some cigarette ends, but they are so mashed up that I can't see them being much use.'

'Get them analysed anyway,' Carson said.

'I'll speak to forensic submissions, but I wouldn't hold out much hope,' the CSI said. 'The budget doesn't stretch to speculative stuff these days.'

Carson looked surprised. 'Doesn't it?' he said, grimly. 'Well, I don't fucking care about pulling back, because when we have another death on our hands, the case will get even more expensive. Tell forensic submissions that if they refuse to

78

send anything off that later proves to be crucial, I'll give their number to the next victim's parents so that they can explain why they couldn't afford to save their daughter.'

The crime scene investigator looked at the floor, clearly not wanting to take Carson on.

'We're not looking at someone who hung around there, waiting for a victim,' Joe said, his voice soft and quiet. 'It's a dumping ground. We're looking for snags of cloth, that kind of thing.'

The two police officers shook their heads. 'Nothing like that, but if the body had been there for a while, he hadn't, and his traces might have gone.'

Carson turned away. 'I guessed as much.'

'So what now?' Laura asked.

Carson sighed in frustration. 'Unless Mike Corley can tell you anything new, we wait for the phone call that gives him up, or for the post-mortem to yield something. Apart from that, we just hope.'

Chapter Thirteen

Jack was sitting in his car, writing the story on his laptop, his phone plugged into the side, acting as a modem. This way he could send the story straight to Dolby when he had finished. He was by the Whitcroft estate again, feeling like he was spinning plates as he moved between court and assignments, looking again for quotes for the feature.

He sat back and stretched his fingers. The murder story was done. It was short, with just a description of the murder scene and the bare details from the press conference, padded with the ongoing grief of the Corley family. It told everyone what they needed to know, that a young woman from Blackley had been murdered. The police hadn't released much else.

He read through it, saved it, attached it to an email, and then sent it to Dolby's inbox, all from the front seat of his tired old Triumph Stag.

He looked at the estate through his windscreen. It was nearly six, and he saw people returning from work, some of the ones he had seen earlier in the day. There were some kids ahead, in their late teens, sitting on bikes and watching young girls walk past with their prams. The soft glow of a cigarette passed between them, although from the way their fingers snapped for their turn it seemed that the paper contained more than just tobacco. People who spotted them in time crossed over when they got near. The tallest of the group leaned to talk into a white van that had pulled up alongside them. It was the same security van Jack had seen earlier. He noticed letters on the side this time: DR Security.

Jack put his laptop away and strapped the bag over his shoulder as he climbed out of his car. There was no point in putting it into his car boot, because the group had seen it. He pulled out his voice recorder and hovered near the shops. Every time someone came near, Jack asked if he could speak to them about the problems on the estate, or whether the police were doing enough, but no one seemed keen. They just rushed into the shop or kept on walking. It looked like he was going to have to do the door-to-door stuff. He glanced over to the group again. They were still watching him.

Jack headed away from the shops and towards the first cul-de-sac. He was about to knock on the first door when he heard the sound of tyres scraping along the kerb behind him. As Jack looked around, he saw that it was the white security van.

'Can we help you?' the driver said through the open window, his hands fat around the steering wheel.

Jack bent down to his level, and said, 'No, I'm fine.'

The driver and his companion were just as Jack expected, bulky and wide-necked and tattooed.

'I'll put it a different way,' the driver said. 'What are you doing?'

'Just doing my thing,' Jack said.

'Which is what?'

'It's my thing, not yours, which sort of ends the conversation,' Jack said, and then he turned to walk away.

Jack didn't expect the conversation to end there, but he had to let them know that he wasn't intimidated.

'No, it doesn't,' said a different voice.

Jack turned around and saw that they were both out of the van now. They were dressed identically: black trousers and black silk jackets, with hair shaved to the scalp. The second man was much shorter than the driver, and one thing Jack had learned from seeing drunken pub fights is that the big man will hurt you the most, but the little man is more likely to start the fight.

'Okay, let's talk,' Jack said. 'Who pays for your services?'

The two men exchanged glances, less confident now. 'What do you mean?' the taller one said.

'Just that,' Jack said, and he gestured around him. 'These people aren't millionaires, but they've got you two looking after them. The police come free. Why you?'

'We're here all the time,' the tall one said again. 'The police only ever come round with search warrants or to arrest people. You never see them just looking after people.'

'Very noble of you,' Jack said. 'Who is *DR?*'

The two men exchanged glances again, until the taller one said, 'Look it up, if you're that interested.'

Jack nodded. 'I think I am. Thank you.'

'Where are you going now?'

'Like I said, I'm just doing my thing,' Jack said. 'If you want to follow me, well, that's your choice. That's what they pay you for, I suppose.'

'You can't go knocking on doors,' the smaller one said.

'If I pull out an axe, you can earn your money, but until then I'll make my own choices.' Jack flashed them a grin. 'You can be in the story if you like.'

The small one scowled and clenched his fists, but the big one just put a hand on his elbow, to keep him in check.

'If we get any complaints, we'll see you again.'

'Understand one thing,' Jack said, stepping closer, stopping only when he could smell the staleness of their breath. 'You have no power to do anything. You can't speak to me, you can't escort me anywhere, and you cannot stop me doing my job.'

Jack turned away and carried on walking. He expected to hear footsteps coming after him, but he didn't, and eventually he heard their van start up and head off.

Jack was starting to think that the estate could be a dangerous place.

Laura and Joe were on their way to the home of the first victim when Laura glanced at her watch and realised how late it was getting.

'Bobby?' Joe asked.

'He's gone to a friend's house, so he'll be all right for now.'

'But you're still worried about him,' Joe said.

Laura gave a weary smile. 'I'm his mother. I'm supposed to be there for him.'

'What about Jack? Can't he do more?'

'He does a lot, but I don't want Bobby to become a chore.'

'Don't worry, you'll get home to him,' Joe said, and then he smiled. 'Maybe not today, though.'

'And what about you, and the rest of the team?' she said. 'What about your home lives?'

Joe raised his eyebrows but didn't answer straight away. Instead, he kept his eyes on the road before eventually saying, 'My home life is best kept there, at home.'

Laura took the hint and didn't probe any further.

'We'll probably go for a drink later on,' he said, and looked over at Laura. 'You could always join us.'

Laura pulled a face. 'I was never any good at the team bonding thing,' she said.

'Too macho?'

'Well, maybe, but it doesn't mean that I don't care about the team.'

'That's not how I meant it.'

'It's how it feels though,' Laura said. 'I wouldn't have thought it would be your scene either.'

'Why's that?'

'It sounds all a bit too *Sweeney* for you,' she said.

He laughed. 'We all need to unwind sometimes, and like it or not, those are my friends. And yours.'

'It was an observation, not a criticism,' Laura said, and then turned to look out of the window. She watched as the main road out of Blackley turned into a stream of warehouses and car showrooms. A large supermarket dominated one side, and then soon after Joe swung his car into a street of tall Victorian houses, with large sash windows and dark millstone fronts. They wound their way around curving streets, along tree-lined avenues, the kerbsides dominated by new cars, all large and polished.

They stopped outside the Corley house, and as they got out, Laura smoothed down her suit jacket and reminded herself of the purpose of the visit. Take it easy. Play it like a sympathy visit.

Don't let on that Mike Corley had been spotted at the murder scene and see if he volunteers it.

They walked up the short path and were about to ring the doorbell when the door opened. They were confronted by a large man with a crew cut whose scalp bore faint scars that looked like the remnants of a knife attack. He was wearing a black T-shirt and black combat pants, almost police-style, except for the thick gold chain around his neck.

He stopped when he saw them, surprised, but then he eyed Laura up and down, before he looked back into the house.

'There's someone to see you,' he shouted, his voice gravelly, broad and local, before he set off down the path. 'Looks like the Mormons,' he added, and then he flashed Laura a sneer. As she turned to watch him go, he gave her a wink.

There was a noise behind, and as she turned back to the door, Mike Corley was there. He nodded at Joe and then turned to go back into the house.

As they followed, Laura asked, 'Is your wife in?'

Mike Corley shook his head. 'Gone to her sister's house. She just can't cope with all the visitors and the intrusion.'

'Looks like she missed a well-wisher,' Laura said. 'She needs to know that people are there for her.' When Corley looked confused, Laura pointed towards the window. 'The man who was just here.'

'Oh him,' Corley said, and then shook his head as if the visit meant nothing. 'Just an old friend.'

He didn't look like the sort of person a policeman had round for afternoon tea, Laura thought, but didn't say anything. Instead, she sat down on the sofa, just to emphasise that it wasn't a quick visit. Corley stayed on his feet, his eyes flicking between her and Joe.

'How much have you been told today?' Laura asked.

'Not much,' he said. 'A reporter came here earlier, but he just told me what I already knew.'

'Can you remember his name?'

'Garrett,' he said. 'Joe or John.'

Laura blushed, before she said, 'Jack?' She coughed. 'Jack Garrett?'

'So you know him?'

Laura nodded, trying not to give anything away. 'Yes, I know him. What did he tell you?'

'Just that you didn't catch my daughter's killer and he has murdered someone else,' he said. 'That just about sum it up?'

Laura looked at Joe, who was pursing his lips.

'You know how it is,' Joe said. 'We don't always catch these people straight away.'

Mike shook his head, his hands on his hips, his tongue flicking across his lips with tension. 'I know that you lot cruise around the station like we are supposed to be in awe of you,' he said. 'But how often do you get it right?'

'The woman's name was Jane Roberts,' Laura said. 'Do you know her, or Jane's father, Don Roberts?'

Corley's anger stalled at that, and he gave a quick shake of his head. Too quick.'

'You seem pretty certain,' Laura said.

'I know who I know.'

'What about your daughter? Did she keep any address book that you haven't already handed over? Jane's name might be in there. If they are connected in any way, it might help to find your daughter's killer.'

Again, Corley shook his head.

'Have you checked?' Laura said.

'I don't need to,' Corley said, angrier now. 'Deborah's life was turned inside out by the press before she was found, and it didn't let up after. All they wrote about was her love life, because she'd had a couple of married boyfriends, just because it made the story a little seedier. How do you think that made us feel, that we had to find out things about our daughter that we didn't need to know, that no one needed to know?'

'That was the press, not us,' Joe said. 'We can't stop them from printing whatever will sell their papers, but you can use them, to keep Deborah in the public eye, make them see the real Deborah, not the one they have shown until now.'

'That's what the reporter said earlier. You must work from scripts.' He snorted a bitter laugh. 'Is that why you've come here, to get me to talk to the press?'

'No,' Joe said. 'I just want to find out whether you can think of anything else. It's been three weeks now.'

Mike Corley gritted his teeth. 'I know exactly how long it is,' he said. 'I have felt every day of it.'

'So have you thought of anything else?' Joe asked.

Mike Corley shook his head. 'No, and now someone else has died.'

Joe nodded, and then looked at Laura to let her know that it was time to go.

'If you come across Jane's name, will you tell us?' she said.

Corley nodded slowly, but then said, 'Could you please leave? All I see right now are detectives who have failed us. Speak to me when you find out who killed my daughter.'

Laura exchanged quick glances with Joe, and then she nodded. 'Sorry, Mike. Thanks for your time.'

As they headed for the door, Laura stopped and looked back. 'Why were you at the scene this morning?' she said.

Corley's eyes widened in surprise, and then he shook his head. 'So that's why you are here, to catch me out.'

'It's not like that,' she said. 'We saw you, that's all, and were curious.'

'So if you think I had something to do with it, I'm not the cleverest, am I?' he said.

Laura realised that she didn't have an answer for that.

The door almost hit Laura as they got to the doorstep and it slammed shut behind them.

'Not my finest hour,' she said.

'It was never going to be,' Joe said. 'He doesn't like us at the moment, and do you know what, I'm not sure I would in his shoes.'

Once they were in Joe's car, Laura glanced towards the Corley house, tranquil from the outside, but raging within.

'So do you fancy that drink now?' Joe asked.

'I should be getting home,' she replied.

'Bobby will still be there later on.'

Laura wavered, and when Joe raised an eyebrow and smiled, she relented. 'Come on then,' she said, sighing. 'I've time for one.'

Chapter Fourteen

Jack checked the clock. Just gone nine. Bobby was playing on the floor with some action figures, talking to himself, playing out a scene. He should be in bed, but Jack wanted him to see Laura before he went to sleep.

The piece on the murder had long been submitted, and so he was idling, lying down on the sofa, just waiting for Laura. Johnny Cash boomed out of the speakers, as usual, the *Orange Blossom Special* album, boxcars and railroad drum rhythms, but it gave the house an energy that he didn't feel.

There were some wedding magazines on the coffee table, with brochures for venues tucked in like bookmarks. Jack reached over for one, knowing that they had to start making some decisions, but as he flicked through the glossy shots, it didn't hold any interest for him.

Bobby looked up and smiled, and Jack saw Laura in him for a moment, with small dimples in his cheeks.

'What time is Mummy coming home?' he said.

'Soon,' Jack said, although he didn't know whether that was true or not. He knew that she would be tied up for most of the night, the first days of a murder are like that, where all the hope is for a quick hit, but the day had long since gone.

He pulled his phone from his pocket to call Laura, just to see if she was going to be much longer, but he paused. She might be in a meeting, or driving. And was he ringing for updates, ever the reporter, or was he just missing her, wanting to hear her voice? Or was it worse than that; was he just bored?

The album played itself out and the house fell silent again, except for the creak of the stylus arm as it moved slowly across to its resting place. Jack listened to Johnny Cash because it reminded him of his father. He had been killed a few years earlier, but he had spent his life collecting and playing Cash records. In the line of duty was the phrase they had used when he died, although Jack didn't think he'd volunteered for that part of the job. And it wasn't just the songs that brought his father close again. It was the album sleeves, the paper inserts, the orange Columbia labels. Jack kept his memory alive by driving his car and blowing the fluff from the stylus.

He turned back to Bobby, who was engrossed in his game once more. Bobby made them a proper family, but Jack knew the truth: if he parted with Laura he would just become a distant memory to Bobby, despite the years he'd put in. It would mean nothing in the end, because they were bound only by Laura.

And there had been some rocky patches. Laura took a long time to settle in the north, and their first couple of years had seemed like a constant battle with Geoff, Bobby's father, who was still in London and wanted Bobby nearer to him. There had been arguments, and when things had got really strained, Jack could see Laura's uncertainty about life in the Lancashire hills.

But they loved each other, and so far that had taken them through the difficult times. Jack hoped that their marriage would settle any doubts she might have left.

His melancholy was interrupted by the rumble of a car engine. He sat up and looked towards the window, expecting it to be Laura. He groaned. It was Dolby, his Jaguar making Jack's Stag look shabby and old. As he climbed out of the car, Jack felt his hackles rise. He tried to stop it, knew that it was an ego thing, because Dolby looked like he could fall into just about anything he wanted. His jeans were designer, and as he walked to the door he threw on a linen jacket. One quick run of his fingers through his long blond locks and then he knocked.

Jack forced a smile as he opened the door. 'It's late, Dolby. What have I done to deserve this visit?'

'Jack, don't be like that,' Dolby said, his hands spread. Wide grin. Perfect white teeth. Only to be expected. 'I was in the area, and so I thought it was a good time to talk.'

Jack stepped to one side and let him go past, until Dolby turned round and said, 'It might be better if we spoke alone.'

Jack bent down to ruffle Bobby's hair and whispered in his ear that it was time to go up-stairs. Once they were alone, Dolby sat down on the arm of the sofa. Jack didn't object. It made Dolby look like he wasn't staying long.

'How's the press conference piece?' Jack said.

'It's good, and it's on the website, but we need more than that now,' Dolby said.

Jack was confused. 'What do you mean?'

Dolby smiled in that condescending way that he had. 'Jack, it's old news now, and you know what sells newspapers? Anger, that's what. People are dying and the police can't catch the killer, but people can get that from the internet. What about a campaign? Make the people scared. We need to make the paper stand for something again.'

'And that something is spreading fear?' Jack said, surprised. 'The police shouldn't have to spend their time combating the press, they should spend it catching the killer.'

'How very fucking noble of you,' Dolby said, flicking at his hair. 'Nobility doesn't keep the paper afloat. The world's changed, Jack. It's a tough economy for local papers. You know how it is. It was hard enough before the banks sent us all down. We're in a different news culture than the one you trained in. It's instant now, and so we have to do something different. I want to run a campaign, getting at the police, asking why this killer is still loose.'

Jack held back his first response, that he didn't need a lesson in newspaper politics. Instead, he said, 'You know it's difficult for me. Laura's on the murder squad, for Christ's sake.'

'So that's a no, is it?' Dolby said, his eyes wide, and Jack guessed the subtext, that there were plenty of eager young hacks getting ready to step in, and that it wasn't just the one story that was up for grabs.

Jack sighed. 'No, it isn't,' he said quietly.

Dolby slapped his legs with his hands and jumped to his feet. 'Good man, I knew you would. Can you get something to go in tomorrow?'

Jack pointed at the clock. 'It's too late.'

Dolby shook his head. 'I've held back the front page. We've got the headline set, with a picture of the crime scene. We need just two hundred words to go underneath.'

'How soon?'

'An hour.'

Jack sighed, and then he shrugged and nodded.

Dolby slapped him on the back and went towards the door. Just as he got there, Jack said, 'Just one condition.'

Dolby turned round. 'Name it.'

'Print it under a different byline. For the sake of my pending marriage, if it ever happens, I could really do with Laura not knowing.'

Dolby flashed that grin again. 'No problem.'

As the door closed, the silence that descended felt heavy, because Jack knew he'd just promised to undermine Laura's investigation.

He went to the computer and navigated to the *Telegraph's* website. The write up from the press conference had attracted some interest. Forty-eight comments. Maybe it was the Simon Cowell effect, but it seemed like a story wasn't really a story until everyone knew what Bert from Burnley thought of it all. He flicked through them anyway.

The first few were expressions of sadness, but

then the identity of the woman must have leaked out. Jane Roberts. It meant nothing to Jack at first, but when the posts turned nasty and he saw the name of Jane's father, Don Roberts, he wondered whether there was more to the story than a random attack. Jack was a crime reporter, and so he had heard the name Don Roberts bandied around. Don never turned up on the court lists, but there were always whispers and hints that he was the big man around town.

Jack stopped reading when his phone buzzed in his pocket. The screen told him that it was Laura.

'How's your day going?' Jack said.

'Are you speaking as Jack the boyfriend or Jack the reporter?'

'Jack the boyfriend,' he said, laughing.

'Long,' she said, 'and about to get a lot longer.'

'What time are you coming home?'

Jack heard the fatigue in her voice as she said, 'I don't know, Jack. I'm sorry. That's why I'm calling. The post-mortem is tomorrow, and so we are going to have a briefing and then see how the night looks.' She paused, and he heard her steel herself before she said, 'Say goodnight to Bobby for me.'

'I will,' he said. 'And I'll wait up for you,' and as they said their goodbyes, he glanced over to the kitchen and remembered the wine that had been in the fridge for a couple of days. It was no way to fill the slow hours, because the hill only ever slopes downwards, but just then, it seemed the right thing to do.

Laura clicked off her phone and looked at Joe,

who noticed the clench of her jaw and raised his eyebrows at her.

'Why didn't you just tell him that we were going for a drink?' he said.

Laura paused as she thought about this. She felt a blush creep into her cheeks. 'It's not that,' she said. 'It's Bobby. I should be there for him.'

'Having a career doesn't make you a bad mother,' Joe said.

Laura looked at Joe. He looked thoughtful, his brown eyes soft. 'I know that,' she said. 'I just feel like I don't do enough for him.'

'That's natural, but he'll grow up proud of you, because of what you do. It all comes good in the end.'

She reached out and touched his hand, gave it a squeeze. 'Thank you,' she said, and let out a long, slow breath. She looked in the car mirror and teased out her hair, before frowning. 'I look tired.'

'You look fine,' he said.

'*Fine* is no good,' she said, smiling now.

'Okay, more than fine,' he said, laughing with her. 'Attractive, sexy.'

Laura's blush took over her face. 'Enough about me. What about you?' she said.

'What do you mean?'

'When are you going to let a lady sweep you off your feet?'

Joe smiled. 'I analyse things too much, so nothing seems to happen naturally.'

'What about Rachel Mason?' she said.

'What about her?' Joe said, his hand paused on the door handle.

'You know she likes you,' Laura said. 'She stares at me whenever I'm with you, as if I've trespassed into her territory or something.'

'Come on,' Joe said. 'The rest of the squad will be waiting.'

'Is that your way of avoiding the subject?' she said.

'Something like that,' he said, and stepped out of the car.

Joe was still smiling as she joined him on the pavement. Laura glanced upwards, at the darkness of the sky, and took a deep breath. Getting on wasn't just about turning up for work. There was this side too, being a squad member.

But why did she feel so reluctant?

She looked at Joe and her smile returned. 'Your round,' she said, and then headed for the pub door, Joe close behind.

Chapter Fifteen

He rewound the footage again, as he had done for the last ten minutes.

It was Inspector Carson on the news. A stern look to the camera. *We are not ready to reveal details of her murder, but I would like to say this: that whoever carried out this barbaric act must be caught.* And then the flashback from the press conference three weeks earlier, images of Corley in distress. Oh, he liked that, but when will they be ready to disclose more?

The image was back in his head. Corley's daughter this time. Less fight than Roberts. A scream and then she was crying. She almost gave up, it had been too easy. Her choice. The wrong choice. She could have walked a different way, or put up more of a struggle, but she chose surrender, as if he was going to maul her and run. He was different. She should have realised.

He was aroused again. His breaths were fast, and he knew he had to look at Jane again, but something wasn't right, wasn't how he expected it.

He went to his study, really just something he had crafted from the space under his stairs, so that the slope of the steps was just in front of his face, smoothed out by plasterboard and wallpaper. It was cramped, and so his knees had worn blue marks into the wall where he turned in a tight circle on his chair. He couldn't move back much, but it was private and felt like somewhere separate from the rest of the house.

He felt the space close in as he shut the door behind him. The light from the screen bathed his face in flickering lights and his head was filled with the soft hum of the computer fan.

Normally he liked the darkness, the confinement, but it wasn't the same today. Jane was supposed to be the finale, the crescendo, but it didn't feel any different from before.

He closed his eyes. He could feel the hiss of the pressure release, like a loose valve. He had tried to smother it, but it was impossible, like a song in your head that never stops going round. You can try to ignore it, but eventually the beat gets in your fucking head and you just go with it. But, oh Christ, the thoughts of her. Her look of fright, short squeals, drowned out by his hand, tight around her neck, squeezing, her skin soft, bruised. His breaths came as short gasps, loud in the confined space.

His hand went to his belt, but he stopped himself. Don't waste it, not here.

He went to the website of the local paper and read the story. He saw the outrage in the comments, but then he read the scorn for Jane. He remembered her differently. The swish of her hair, the soft scent of her perfume as he pressed her down, the roar of his thoughts as he gripped her. The struggle. The fight.

He took a deep breath. He had to calm down. He had projects to complete, he knew that now. Jane was supposed to be the last one, but the need was still there. It didn't feel like he was finished. He needed that final rush, to get somewhere near the intensity of his first time. And he should listen to that need.

But it was hard not to think of Jane. The young woman. Pretty. Scared. The dirt. He had seen the buzz around the station, the big shirts wheeled in, and still they didn't know of the connection. Jane and Deborah. He had to do more.

He saw the reporter's email address at the bottom of the article. It was time to go public. That had always been his plan.

His fingers started to tap on the keys, soft clicks that echoed in his tiny office.

Chapter Sixteen

Jack's movements felt sluggish as he read the words on the screen. He had thrown together Dolby's article, questioning why the killer was still at large, a rehash of facts from the press conference mixed in with the article he had submitted earlier. It would appear in the paper in the morning. He had just opened a second bottle of wine and his vision was starting to swirl, fingers moving clumsily over the keys as he headed to the *Blackley Telegraph* site to check for the latest comments.

He took another drink of wine as the page loaded, his name writ large at the top, and saw that snipes at Jane's father had taken over from sympathy. Some had even found a racial angle, putting forward one ethnic group as potential suspects. Jack knew that the comments were moderated, but Dolby usually took a relaxed view because he knew that bile kept the page counter turning.

He was about to shut down the computer when it flashed up that an email had arrived. He went to the inbox, expecting an offer for bogus medication, but instead there was a message entitled *Blindness*.

He started to read:

You're writing the wrong story, Jack Garrett. So another woman has died in Blackley, just the daughter-whore of the town's biggest thug. My message to him is that you've wrecked lives too, so how does it feel now? Both fathers. Both sinners.

Spot the link, win the prize, because they won't, I can guarantee it, those special boys in blue. Yes, spare a thought for the girl in the woods who gorged on the floor, but don't think too long, think then of Daddy at last feeling the pain.

Jack put down his drink, surprised. That was strong stuff. He checked the email address. It was a Google address, so it would probably be hard to trace the owner.

He sat back and tugged at his lip. Crime reporting certainly attracted its fair share of oddballs, from those who sat at the back of court, just for the public viewing, to those who sent out paranoid emails without a second thought. But why the reference to gorging on the floor? And what was the link between the two victims? The police had hinted that they were random, that *all* women were in danger.

Jack looked around for a notepad, and felt a familiar tremble of excitement in his fingers. If the police were holding facts back, he needed to know.

He pressed the reply button and typed, *Gorged on the floor. What do you mean?*

He clicked send and drank some more wine, wondering what the reply would contain. He didn't have to wait long.

Good to see that you're alert, Jack, but this is just for you and me. If you tell the police, I'll know. I'll hear the whispers. But what about a poem, an ode to Jane:

What is this that I can see,
Cold icy hands taking hold of me,

For Death has come, you all can see,
Hell has opened a gate to welcome thee,
He'll stuff your jaws till you can't talk,
He'll bind your legs till you can't walk,
He'll tie your hands till you can't claw,
And he'll close your eyes so you see no more.

Jack took another drink of wine. It seemed like the story had taken a new twist.

Chapter Seventeen

Light streamed through the open curtain, making Jack groan. He lifted his head off the pillow and the bed seemed to shift. He shouldn't have opened that second bottle of wine, and he could still taste it as he smacked his lips.

He put his hand out, expecting to feel the rise and fall of Laura's body, or the spread of her dark hair across the pillow, but she wasn't there. He squinted at the alarm. Eight o'clock. He flopped back onto the pillow. Everything felt heavy, and quick movements sent flashes of pain through his head. He lay back and listened for the sounds of Laura downstairs, chatter with Bobby or the noise of the hairdryer, but there was only silence.

He tried to think through what had happened the night before. He couldn't remember Laura coming home, but he remembered her weight against him in bed, her naked skin, warm and close. Yesterday's clothes were discarded on the floor and he could smell the flowery haze of her perfume spray.

He clambered out of bed and shuffled to Bobby's room, just to check that he was awake. He wasn't. His dark hair peered out above his England football duvet, a remnant of his World Cup mania from the year before. Jack rubbed his eyes. He would have to rush now, and he didn't feel much in the mood for speed.

Jack nudged Bobby gently until he stirred and then pointed at his school clothes, set out by Laura.

'Time to get moving,' he said, although his voice still had a slur.

It was going to be a slow morning.

Laura threaded her way through the Incident Room, her coffee in her hand, the smell of stale booze hitting her, the remnants of the trip to the pub the night before, everyone more bleary-eyed than the previous day. Mornings were always the toughest part of a murder investigation, because they were no nearer the killer and hours of uncertainty lay ahead.

As she got to Joe, he looked up and smiled. 'Did you get in trouble for being back so late?'

'Jack was all tucked up when I got back,' she said, and returned the smile. 'I enjoyed myself. Thank you for making me go.' She took a sip of coffee and then nodded towards some sheets of paper in front of Joe. 'Is there anything new?'

Joe looked down and then shook his head. 'Not much to get excited about,' he said. 'Just last night's calls, and unless Don Roberts had a change of heart overnight, all we'll have today is tips from friends.'

'So when was Jane last seen?'

'Last Saturday,' Joe said. 'A routine night out, she was supposed to go to a friend's house. There was a group of girls waiting for her, but she never showed up. They called her house but Don said that he didn't know where she was and told them not to worry. They went out and forgot about it. Some of her friends texted her, but didn't think much of it when they didn't get a reply.'

'They don't seem like close friends,' Laura said.

'They were used to the disappearing act,' Joe explained, as he reached for a photograph. 'It seems like the ex-boyfriend wasn't that ex.' He passed her the picture of a young man, good teeth and skin, dark hair teased over his forehead. 'Adam Carter. They were making like single people, but they weren't, because they were still an item. They just had to keep it quiet from Don.'

Laura picked up the photograph. 'Why is that?'

'We'll find out later,' he said. 'But that's why Jane's friends weren't worried, because they thought she was with Adam.'

'So is Adam a witness or suspect?'

'Everyone's a suspect,' Joe said. 'All we know about Adam is that he's just finished university and is trying to find a job. Jane's friends seem to like him, but I suppose that doesn't mean too much.'

'But if he's anything to do with Jane's death,' Laura said, 'he's done it as a copycat, to make us think that Jane was killed by Deborah's killer. How would a young student find out so much about Deborah's murder to pull that off?'

Joe smiled. 'I didn't say he was high up the list.'

'At least we've got a list,' Laura said, looking at the picture and then tapping it against her hand. 'What about her workplace?'

'The same as with her friends,' Joe said. 'She didn't show up, and when they called home, they spoke with her father. The same answer as before, that he didn't know where she was but not to worry.'

'I don't get it,' she said. 'Why would Don shut everyone out when his daughter was missing? Was his hatred for us more important than finding Jane?'

'Maybe it is more complicated than that,' Joe said. 'People who behave in that way often have something to hide.'

'What, you think that Don Roberts might be involved?'

'I don't know, but we have to look,' Joe said, and then pointed to two detectives at the back of the room, scouring through papers and then looking at a computer screen. 'That's their job.'

'What are they looking at?' Laura asked.

'Just old intelligence reports, to check for any allegations of sexual abuse within his family.'

'Do you think she was about to expose him?'

'Maybe there was nothing to expose,' Joe said, 'but I would rather we looked and found nothing than not look and miss it. A lot of men who kill their daughters do it because they are about to be exposed. It's a mixture of betrayal and sexual confusion and downright fear that they are about to be shown up for what they they really are. So they lash out.'

'And stuff their daughter's vagina with leaves and dirt?' Laura said, her eyebrows raised.

'Well, that's pretty extreme,' Joe replied, 'but like with the boyfriend, that would be all part of the cover-up, to deflect attention, to make it look like the murder was done by the same person who killed Deborah Corley.'

'But we didn't disclose the details of that murder,' Laura said.

'So we need to see if there is a leak anywhere,' Joe said. 'Don might have some friends in the police. Yes, he's a crook and a thug, but some officers think that they might pick up some useful information if they keep their enemies close, but in reality, it's more than that. There's a bond, like opponents shaking hands away from the arena. I've seen a lot of hardline coppers end up working for defence firms, working hard to keep the crooks free. There is one I know who works as a driver for a defence firm, acting like a taxi for criminals, picking them up and taking them to court.'

'That sounds demeaning,' Laura said.

'It is, but it's not about the money,' Joe said. 'It's just about finding a way to stay in the game, because as much as the cops like to fight the crooks, they love the game more than anything, and they miss it when they retire.'

'So you think Don Roberts might have received information about how Deborah Corley died and re-enacted it to pass the blame?'

'It's just one more possibility.'

Laura sat down and sighed. 'This could be never-ending.'

'Worse than that,' Joe said. 'We might only find out that Don Roberts isn't a copycat killer when someone else dies, because he would be stupid to repeat it, just for effect.'

'We could arrest him,' Laura said.

Joe shook his head. 'You'll get nothing from him. Even if he's innocent, he'll clam up.'

'So what now? A visit to the boyfriend?'

Joe checked his watch. 'In a couple of hours from now.'

'Why so long?'

'Because we've got a post-mortem to attend,' he said, and then pointed towards the door.

When Laura looked around, she saw Carson beckoning them over. She took a deep breath. The queasy feeling in her stomach told her that it was too early in the day to watch a young woman sliced open.

Chapter Eighteen

Jack threw his car keys onto the table. Bobby was safely at school, and so he headed to the kitchen to make a coffee, just pausing to switch on his laptop. He needed another kick-start, the booze still hanging heavy from the night before.

The steam from the cup bathed his face as he stood over his computer, and his hands paused over the wedding brochures that cluttered the table. Not today, he told himself, and pushed them to one side.

Once the computer had finished booting up, Jack started his day as he always did, by quickly surfing the newspaper websites, just to check for the headlines of the day. He was looking for something extra this time though, for the Jane Roberts story, trying to find anything that would shed light on what was in the emails from the night before. *Gorged on the floor* and *He'll stuff your jaws till you can't talk.*

He went to the nationals first, but it was what he expected: nothing much. The media had turned out for the press conference but it hadn't translated into column inches. It was the out-of-London syndrome, that it had to get really bad to be noticed by the London press, and so he trawled the northern dailies instead. The murder was featured more prominently, but it was still lacking in detail, and some had just lifted the report from the *Blackley Telegraph.*

Jack went to the *Blackley Telegraph* website again, checking for updates, but nothing had changed. The comments section had grown though, so that reading the news was like being caught in an argument. Some of the comments echoed the vitriol of the emails, hatred spewed out under the cover of anonymous usernames, and some criticised the police, saying that they couldn't catch a serial killer because they were too wrapped up in form-filling.

But no one mentioned anything about something being in the victim's mouth.

He brought up the second email and read the poem again.

He'll stuff your jaws till you can't talk,

He'll bind your legs till you can't walk,
He'll tie your hands till you can't claw,
And he'll close your eyes so you see no more.

Those words were specific. Jane must have been bound and gagged, there could be no other conclusion, but there had been nothing in any of the newspapers, no rumours or hints at the press conference the day before. So if the gorging reference had some truth, the emailer must be close to the investigation.

Then something occurred to him. There had been a niggle the night before, that there was something he wasn't seeing, but as he thought more about it, it revealed itself, and it made him sit back and stare at the screen. What if the emails were from the killer himself, trying to use the press as a platform?

He took another drink of coffee and thought about that. It wouldn't be the first time. Then, right on cue, he was interrupted by the arrival of another email. The title grabbed his attention: *Another one bites dust.*

Bites dust?

Jack clicked on the email, and then as he read he realized that it wasn't about the woman found yesterday, but about the victim from a few weeks earlier, the copper's daughter, Deborah Corley.

You're slow, Jack. I find the newspaper not writing all the details unamusing. I know those boys in blue think they have to keep secret all that goes on, that people will get scared, but I think people should know. How else do they catch the killer? Ha ha.

Think of charming little Deborah, blessed by life's opportunities. Sunday school, pony lessons, pretty in

108

the press picture, and so she should be, with every-thing life had given her. But no more. Deborah has smiled one last time, silenced forever, her laughs muffled. She tried to cry out but couldn't.

Write about it, Jack. Find the real story. Tell the world everything. Because if it's not you, it will be someone else.

He sat back and rubbed his eyes. That was strong stuff again. And what about *her laughs muffled?*

He took another sip of coffee and pondered on his reply. What if he was reading too much into it, and it was just some weirdo trying to make him print some untruths by hinting that he knows things? Jack wasn't going to wreck his reputation on anonymous hints.

He put his cup down and typed a reply.

I can write the stories if you have proof that you know things. What do you have? Jack.

Jack drummed his fingers on his knees as he waited, his eyes fixed on the screen, the house enveloped in silence. Then there was another ping. Another reply.

Ask them about Emma was all it said.

But who was Emma, and who was *them?*

Chapter Nineteen

Carson was first into the mortuary, pushing the door open with a thump, Laura and Joe trailing behind him. It was really just the basement of an old hospital building, lined by cracked green and cream tiles, with a sign over the door in Latin – *Hic locus est ubi mors gaudet succurrere vitae*. This is the place where death rejoices to help those who live.

She took a breath as she went in, the swinging door wafting the odour of cleaning fluids and stomach gases. She reached into her pocket for the small tub of Vicks she carried in her bag for moments like this, a quick smear under the nose taking away the worst. She could never get used to the smell of a freshly-opened stomach, like stale food mixed with vomit and gas.

Joe Kinsella was different. He was quiet, but there was an intellectual detachment about him, like he was there to spot something, not just get through the ordeal.

Laura could deal with post-mortems, but only just, because they were different to finding a body or being puked on by a drunk at the custody desk, where you deal with the moment, adrenaline driving the action. Post-mortems were cold and calculated, the exposure to death by appointment, and so there was too much time to think about it. She wasn't one of those who could eat their

110

sandwiches over the body, and it was the jokers that always made her wary. That was usually a front, their own way to deal with the difficulty of the situation.

Carson wasn't like that. He was uncomfortable, worried about keeling over or feeling faint but was too macho to admit it, although he seemed determined to get the job done and get out.

When they walked in, Jane Roberts was already on the table, which was nothing more than a sloping tray with raised edges, built so that the blood could be sluiced into the drains without dripping onto the floor. Jane was uncovered, although there were plastic evidence bags over her hands, and she bore little resemblance to the attractive young woman who had gone missing. Her stomach was distended, with her skin showing a green tint and her face swollen, the sharp cheekbones and pouting mouth Laura had seen in photographs now gone forever.

The pathologist, Doctor Pratt, was walking round the body, trying to form a snapshot view before he started slicing. He was in a green scrub suit and what looked liked a Perspex welding helmet, although the visor was still up and over his head. He played the fool and the flirt, wide around the stomach, with grey hair sticking up wildly on top of his head, but he was the best there was, and that was all that mattered.

He gave Laura a smile as he looked towards them. 'Ah, the cavalry. And McGanity. So good to see you. I heard they had you shoved into a uniform for a while.'

Laura smiled her greeting and went directly to

111

the head-end of the mortuary table. It was nearer to the action, but could be a grim spot to be at when the Stryker saw shrieks into the skull and the scalp gets peeled forward like a swimming cap. The only saving grace was that the cooling fans were always at the top of the table, so that the smells were blown down the body, not up. It was always the ones at the feet who fainted. And Laura knew that this was going to be a bad one because the body had been lying outdoors for a few days, with plenty of time for the gases to start bubbling inside.

'So you want to know what I think so far?' Doctor Pratt asked, as he pulled his pen from the pocket of his green smock. 'Step closer,' and when Carson was by his shoulder, he said, 'Look here,' and used the pen to point to Jane's wrists, just visible above the plastic evidence bags. Laura joined them, and saw brown marks on the edges of the forearms, the signs of abrasions. She knew what that meant: ligatures.

'Tied up, just like last time,' she said.

'Not tied,' the doctor said.

Carson frowned. 'What do you mean?'

'Cloth or leather ligatures would give a more even ring around the wrists,' Doctor Pratt said. 'These marks seem more abrasive, as if it was something rigid against her wrist bones.' He pointed to the right wrist. 'What do those grazes remind you of?'

Laura looked closer. The scrapes on the wrist bone were typical of post-arrest injuries, where the cuffs had to be tight to restrain, but some-times they caused grazes when they rubbed against the prisoner's skin.

'Handcuffs,' Laura said.

The doctor smiled. 'Just like handcuffs.'

'So something has changed,' Laura said. 'The first girl was bound using something softer. Maybe it is someone copying?'

'Possibly,' Joe said, pulling at his lip, 'but it will also make the killer harder to find.'

'What do you mean?' Laura said.

'If she was cuffed, there won't be much to find in those,' he said, and pointed towards the evidence bags placed around the hands, there to collect any debris that may have fallen out of the fingernails or from the palms as the body was transported. 'When people are strangled, both the killer's hands are being used, and so they can't fight off the victim, who will scratch and fight and gouge, and so you often get hairs in the victim's fingers. If some of the skin comes with the hair, you can get the DNA. Or there might be skin under the fingernails. But if she was cuffed, there will be none of that.'

'Was she strangled?' Carson asked, looking at Doctor Pratt.

'I can't be too sure just yet, not until I open her up, but that would be my guess,' he said. 'Look at her cheeks. Do you see those little black specks.'

Laura peered closer, trying to see through the discolouration and bloating from being left outdoors for a few days. Then she saw them, like tiny dots.

'They're called petechiae,' Doctor Pratt said.

'Burst blood vessels?' Laura said.

'Pretty much so,' the doctor agreed. 'The pressure around the neck increases pressure in the veins and capillaries, and so they just pop when they reach the surface. I haven't looked under the eyelids yet, or inside the nostrils, but there'll be some there, I can guarantee it. And do you see that dried blood around her nostril?'

Laura nodded.

'Again, more likely due to the strangulation than a punch.'

'Is it manual strangulation?' Carson asked.

Doctor Pratt breathed out noisily and then nodded. 'My first guess is that she was throttled by a left-handed person.'

Carson looked surprised. 'How can you tell?'

'Look at the bruising on her neck.'

They all took a step closer. Laura could see some brown marks just under the jaw.

'You can see her colour,' Doctor Pratt said. 'Lying outdoors since the weekend hasn't done much for the poor girl's looks, and so the marks could be due to putrefaction, that sometimes happens, that bruise-type marks are formed. Once I dissect the marks, I'll be able to tell whether they were bruises inflicted before death.'

'There are quite a few bruises,' Laura said.

'Yes, but they are mainly on her right side,' Doctor Pratt said. 'Or, as you might prefer it, the killer's left. There are only two bruises on the left side of the neck. Think of a left-hand around the throat. That would be where the thumb would go. There are a lot more on the other side, where the fingers go. That is a left-handed grip. There are a lot of bruises though, and so he must have changed his grip.'

'What if the killer was above her head when she was on the ground, looking down her body?' Carson said. 'That would make it a right-handed grip.'

Doctor Pratt shook his head. 'Look how the bruises are just under the jaw. That shows the pressure was towards the jaw. If he had been over her head, the pressure would have been away from the jaw. And it was a one-handed grip too. The hand ends up under the jaw when you use one hand, whereas a two-handed grip tends to go around the neck.'

'I don't agree with the part about him being left-handed,' Joe said.

Doctor Pratt looked round, surprised. 'What do you mean?'

'She will have cuts and bruises in the small of her back,' Joe said.

'Go on, Sergeant, enlighten me.'

'The cuffs,' Joe said. 'We didn't have those in the last murder. They are hard, uncomfortable, and if she was on her back, they would have dug into the skin as she struggled.'

'But why is that important?' Doctor Pratt asked.

'You are assuming that he used his left-hand because that is his preferred hand?'

The doctor nodded.

Joe raised an eyebrow. 'I'm thinking that he used his left hand because he was doing something else with his right. We thought at the scene that she was still alive when that debris was rammed between her legs, and so if he wasn't raping her when she died, I reckon he was satisfying himself as he throttled her. It would have been much easier if she had been on her back rather than pushed against a tree or something, as it would have been easier to push down.'

'And so the cuffs would dig into her back more,' the doctor said.

Joe nodded. 'That was my thinking.'

'There's only one way to find out,' Doctor Pratt said, and then he waved at his mortuary assistant, who had been skulking in the corner. 'Diener!' he shouted. 'Come here.'

Laura looked over to the young man sporting a ponytail and beard, his black T-shirt visible under his scrub suit. He looked like he spent his evenings on the internet fighting fantasy battles. And he didn't look happy.

Doctor Pratt leaned towards Laura and whispered, 'That's their job title, dieners, but it is really just German for servant. Those who know that hate it.'

'You could always call him by his name,' she said.

The doctor's eyes twinkled as he smiled. 'This is much more fun.'

As the diener joined them, Doctor Pratt pointed to the body. 'We just need to lift her, to check her back.'

The diener nodded but didn't say anything in response. He scowled at Doctor Pratt and then grabbed hold of Jane's arm and gave it a hard yank; there was no need to be gentle with her anymore. As Jane was rolled onto her side, Laura and Joe bent down to check her back.

Her shoulders and buttocks were pale, but the

116

small of her back was dark from the lividity, where blood had settled as she lay there, undiscovered. Laura knew that the pattern meant that Jane hadn't been moved recently to the spot where she was found. She had either been killed in that spot or been dumped there not long after her murder. There was an indentation in her back from the body block, a square piece of hard plastic placed under the body to make the chest jut out and the head tilt back, to make incisions easier. Just below that though, in the small of the back, just about visible in the purplish-blue of her skin, Laura could see the path of scrubbed and ragged skin, just as Joe had guessed.

'Looks like you were right,' Laura said to Joe, who just shrugged.

'And her shoulders there,' Doctor Pratt said, pointing to grazes and bruises on her shoulder blades. 'Another sign that she was throttled on her back, those being where she was in contact with the ground.'

'That doesn't mean that he was masturbating though,' Carson said. 'It could just be that the killer throttled her using his strongest hand. And what about Don Roberts? Is he left-handed?'

'Are you still going with that theory?' Joe said.

'Not as the main theory,' Carson said, 'but I'm not going to rule it out until we have to.'

Joe looked at Doctor Pratt. 'Can we be sure it was strangulation?' he said.

'As opposed to what?'

'Her mouth was jammed full of leaves and dirt,' Joe said. 'Perhaps she suffocated?'

The doctor pointed at the dead girl's neck

again. 'She was probably alive when those were inflicted, and so my best guess would be strangulation. Also, it would have looked worse when you found her, because her tongue and lips will have swollen as she rotted in the woods, and so it might not have been quite as jammed in there when she died. It's possible that the hand marks on the neck are from when he restrained her, but we won't know until we open the neck and check whether the hyoid bone is fractured. If not, then yes, she probably suffocated.'

'Does it make a difference, Joe?' Carson asked.

Joe thought about that. 'I think it makes it less likely to be a random sex attack if she suffocated,' he said. 'Throttling is an aggressive, sexual act. It isn't uncommon for it to be a turn on for sociopaths. Gorging? It doesn't have the same hands-on feel to it, if you know what I mean.'

Doctor Pratt chewed on his lip for a moment, and then he pointed at Laura. 'Could you just pop onto the spare table.'

Laura looked at the other steel table further along in the room. 'Do I have to?' she said.

'Will it help the investigation?' Carson asked.

'It could do,' the doctor replied.

'McGanity, get on the table,' Carson said, and moved towards it, waiting for the show.

Laura took a deep breath and closed her eyes. 'All right,' she said, and then gripped the side of the mortuary table as she clambered on. The table was cold through her suit and her feet clanged loudly. She tried not to think of all the others who had been there before her. As she put her head back, her hair spread out over the metal.

118

'If my left hand was my strongest, and the victim was on her back,' Doctor Pratt said, 'which side would I go to in order to throttle her?'

Carson looked at Joe before turning back to Doctor Pratt. 'McGanity's left, your right, so that your left arm is over her, pressing down.'

Doctor Pratt nodded and went to stand by Laura's side. Laura watched as his left hand went to her neck. She swallowed as his hands went around her throat, pressing gently.

'Look how even my hand is around the neck,' the doctor said. 'The curve of my hand, my index finger and thumb, are right under her jaw, and I could push right down, if I wanted to. She would find it hard to move her head.' He smiled down at Laura. 'Which, of course, I wouldn't do.'

Doctor Pratt stepped away and then went over to the other side. Laura closed her eyes for a moment as she felt his hand go around her neck once more.

'Look at my left hand now,' he said. 'I have to contort my arm to get it evenly around her neck, because my left arm is by her side, not over her. I could move her head towards me, I suppose, but the pressure would be different. I would be pushing the head back, not down, and so Laura would be able to move her head around, perhaps make it harder for me to throttle her. And so the most natural way for me to throttle someone from this side with my left hand is to have my hand tilted, so that the tips of my fingers are right under the jaw, more vertical, with my thumb lower down, so that the pressure comes from the base of the thumb, not the curve of the hand.'

119

'You could straddle her,' Carson said.

'I could,' Doctor Pratt said, 'but the killer didn't.' He pointed towards Jane Roberts. 'Look at the bruises from the killer's thumb. They are much lower down than the bruises from the fingers, which suggests that the killer was to her right side, to the left from the killer's angle.'

'Why make it difficult for himself?' Carson said.

Doctor Pratt pointed towards Joe. 'He got it right. It leaves his right hand free to relieve himself.'

As Doctor Pratt stepped away from the table, Laura slid off and back onto the floor. As she straightened herself, she saw the diener smirk at her, recognising her discomfort. She turned away.

'So once I've dissected the neck, I'll know for sure,' Doctor Pratt said.

'Will you do that first?' Carson asked.

The doctor tutted. 'Everything in its proper order, Inspector. Got to pop the skull and empty the chest cavity first. Are you going to wait around?'

Carson glanced towards the door and then back at Jane Roberts. 'How long will it take?'

'A couple of hours.'

Carson shook his head. 'No, thank you, Doctor, we'll keep on with our enquiries. Call me when you've come to your conclusion.'

Doctor Pratt nodded at Carson and then winked at Laura. 'Thank you, Inspector.'

Carson looked at Laura, then at Joe, and then he headed for the door. When he realised that no one was following him, he turned around and bellowed, 'Come on, we haven't got all day.'

Joe smiled at Laura. 'He's getting queasy in his old age,' he said, and then went to follow Carson.

Laura watched as Doctor Pratt pulled down his plastic visor and reached for a scalpel.

She turned away. Maybe Carson was right, that it was too early in the day to watch this.

Chapter Twenty

Jack went to the *Blackley Telegraph* office first. Dolby was in his room, a large cup of coffee in front of him.

'I should have made you buy me this,' Dolby said, chewing on a granola bar.

'What do you mean?'

'Because my idea worked,' Dolby said. 'The phone has been ringing all morning. It seems like your article about the police failing has touched a nerve. I've just had the press officer on the phone to me, asking why I'm attacking rather than helping.'

'It must give you a glow,' Jack said. 'But, yeah, I owe you one, for keeping my name off it. Just make sure the cheque is paid to the right person.'

Dolby tossed the granola wrapper into the bin and lifted the lid off his coffee. 'I don't know why I buy this crap,' he said, grimacing as he took a sip.

'Because it makes you feel big to talk Italian

when you buy a drink?'

He pointed and winked. 'You're on form today, but I know you're not here to talk about my brunch. What can I do for you?'

'Have we been asked by the police to hold anything back?' Jack said. 'Are you hearing any rumours?'

Dolby shook his head. 'The police don't speak to me anyway, and they always hold something back.' Then he frowned. 'Why do you ask? You're the one with access. The sweet nothings drying up?'

Jack smiled. 'Laura won't talk about stuff like that, because she knows that you'll print anything to sell a paper.'

'Okay, let's cut the sexual tension in here,' Dolby said, his hands held up in mock surrender. 'What have you got?'

Jack reached into his pocket and pulled out the emails. 'I've been getting these.'

Dolby took them and began to read, and Jack knew he had his attention when the polystyrene cup went onto the desk. Dolby looked up. 'Who are these from?'

'I don't know. They came last night, and then more this morning.'

Dolby's mouth opened as if to say something, but then he closed it and sat back in his chair, tapping his lip with his finger. 'It could just be bullshit, some crank wanting attention.'

'Possibly,' Jack said, nodding. 'But there is another possibility.'

'Go on.'

'They could be from the killer.'

Dolby looked at Jack, and then back at the emails. 'Murders attract attention-seekers.'

'I know, but could you rule it out?'

Dolby handed them back to Jack. 'I'm not going to run a story on them. If it is some crank, the publicity could backfire.'

'I'm not asking you to run it yet.'

'So what are you asking?'

'I'm going to speak to Laura, and if there's anything in it, see if they will give me exclusive access.'

'Okay, talk to them and let's see what we can do.'

'Provided they will work with us,' Jack said. 'The poison piece you got me to write won't make you popular.'

'So go in as freelance. Just make sure you sell the scoop to me.'

'It will mean that you'll have to work with the police. Can you do that, Dolby?'

'Jack, I will do anything that makes people buy this paper.'

'I thought as much. I'll get back to you,' Jack said, and walked out of the office, emails in hand.

Chapter Twenty-One

Laura checked her notes, just to make sure that she had the right address. She needed some fresh air, to take away the mortuary smells that had locked into her nostrils, and so she headed out to speak to Adam Carter, Jane's ex-boyfriend.

Adam's house surprised her. Jane Roberts had been brought up by a crook, and Laura had expected her background to guide her lifestyle choices. But this was suburbia, middle class, plain and ordinary, with a driveway for two cars, an open-plan lawn, and a white garage front, which was probably filled with tools and rubbish, waiting for a tip-run rather than a car. There were mock shutters around the windows and the bricks looked new and clean.

The front door opened before Laura got there, and as Laura reached into her pocket for her identification card, the woman who answered the door said, 'No need, we were wondering when you would call.' She seemed almost too young to have a son old enough to be Jane's boyfriend, with her hair flicked over her face and her figure trim in tight jeans and a T-shirt. She stood aside, and as Laura walked down the hall to the living room at the back of the house, the woman went to make a drink.

Laura didn't sit down at first. Instead, she tried to read the family from the surroundings. The house was clean and well-furnished, with flowers on the window sill that framed the small garden outside, the space consumed by a conservatory. Laura caught a glimpse of the dining room, through an archway from the room she was in, and the formal place settings and another vase of flowers showed how the occupant wished to be viewed: on the way up.

As the woman came in with a cup of tea, Laura said, 'Are you Adam's mother?'

'Yes,' she said. 'Call me Tracy.'

Laura took the drink from her, and as Tracy sat down, gesturing for Laura to join her, Laura saw sadness behind the politeness; a redness around the eyes, the nervous way her finger scratched at her cup, the flicking of her hair.

'Be gentle with Adam, he is really upset about all of this,' Tracy said.

'Why did they split up?'

'He didn't tell me,' and then she gave a small laugh. 'I'm his mother. I'll be the last one he'll tell.'

'I've got a little boy,' Laura said. 'Is that how it ends up?'

'How old?'

'Eight.'

'Enjoy it,' she said. 'You'll find it hard when another woman becomes more important, and the only thing you know about your son is that he won't tell you anything.' Then she seemed to remember who she was talking to. 'That isn't to say that he has done anything wrong. I mean, there's nothing sinister or anything.'

Laura didn't react. People who had something to hide usually revealed more when they tried to fill the gaps.

'Has Adam got a new girlfriend?' Laura said.

Tracy shook her head and gave a sad smile. 'It was only Jane,' she said. 'She brought trouble though. And I don't mean Jane herself. She was a sweet thing, but her family caused trouble for her and for Adam.' She sighed. 'He's a good-looking boy. It would be disrespectful to Jane right now, but he won't be single for ever.'

Before Laura could ask anything else, there was the rumble of feet on the stairs and then a tall slim young man came into the room.

Laura saw that Tracy's description wasn't motherly blinkers, and the camera hadn't lied. Adam was a good-looking young man. Just over six feet with tousled dark hair and soft brown eyes, Laura guessed that he wouldn't get lonely once the mourning period ended. Laura stole a quick glance at his hands, to see whether they showed any signs of worry, bitten fingernails or skin, but there were none.

'Are you the police?' he asked.

Laura nodded.

He looked down at his mother. 'You can leave us alone,' he said to her.

'No, I want to stay,' she said.

He shook his head. 'No,' he said, his voice firmer this time.

Tracy considered him for a moment, and then stood to leave the room. Adam waited until the door closed, and then he looked at Laura and said, 'You're here about Jane.'

Laura nodded. 'Yes, and I'm sorry to intrude, but we need to find out who killed her. Can you tell me when you last saw her?'

'We split up a month ago,' he said, but he looked away as he said it.

'You've no need to pretend, Adam,' she said. 'We know you were still an item. We've spoken to her friends.'

He looked down and nodded, and when he looked up again, Laura saw that his eyes were red.

'I wasn't supposed to see her anymore,' he said.

'Why not?'

'Her father.'

'What do you mean?'

Adam sat down and rested his head against the top of the sofa.

'I'd been threatened,' he said eventually.

'By Jane's father?'

He nodded. 'He doesn't like my career choice.'

'Which is?'

Adam looked at Laura. 'I've applied to join the police.'

Laura was surprised. 'Good choice.'

Adam scowled. 'Don didn't think so.' He sighed heavily. 'I got my degree in law, and my mother wanted me to be a lawyer, had bragged to all her friends, but there are no jobs anymore.'

'Law isn't the career it once was,' she said. 'And you chose the police because it was better than nothing?' When Adam didn't respond, Laura added, 'It's okay, I'm not on the recruitment panel. I joined because it's all I ever wanted to be, and I haven't been disappointed. You'll enjoy yourself.' As Adam nodded to himself, she asked, 'So how did Don Roberts take it?'

He looked up. 'Not well,' he said. 'He told Jane not to see me anymore.'

'So what did you do?'

Adam blushed. 'She was a grown woman, but her father made it difficult. She would say that she was going to a friend's house, and then we would meet up in town. But his friends would follow her, and so she had to make really complicated journeys to get there.' He shook his head.

'One of his apes threatened me, told me that if I saw Jane again, Don would hurt me so that no girl would ever look at me again.'

'Is Don that anti-police?'

'It seemed like a gut reaction at first,' he said, 'but then it became about disobeying him.'

'When was the last time you saw her?'

Adam looked down at his hands and then rubbed one palm with his thumb, as if he was wiping away a stain.

'Last Friday, the day before she went missing,' he said eventually, and his hand went to wipe away a tear. 'We went to the cinema and then came back here.' He blew out, tears running down his cheeks now. 'Mum and Dad were out, and so we had the place to ourselves.' He shrugged. 'Well, you can guess what happened.'

'Had you made any arrangements to meet up again?'

He nodded. 'The following night.'

The night she died, thought Laura, but she didn't say it. 'What happened?' she asked.

'Nothing,' he said. 'We had agreed to meet in the Black Bull in town. There's a door at the back that leads to a car park.'

Laura nodded that she knew it. She remembered it from her brief spell in uniform, when the young constables would shine torches in there after the pubs had closed, trying to frighten couples who preferred the convenience of the car park wall to the warmth of the bed.

'She was supposed to walk straight through the pub, and then we were going to jump in a taxi and go somewhere on our own.' He took a few

128

seconds to compose himself. 'I waited for more than an hour, and I tried her phone but she didn't answer.'

'Why didn't you call us?'

'What could I say,' he said. 'I just thought her father had caught her going out, or had followed her or something.'

'Did you try to call her again?'

'A few times,' he said. 'There was no answer, apart from just once, but no one said anything.'

That surprised Laura. 'When was that, the answered call, I mean?'

He reached into his pocket and pulled out his phone. He pressed the screen a few times, and then he looked up. 'Monday afternoon. Just before three.'

'We think Jane died on the way to meet you.'

Adam paused and took a deep breath to compose himself. 'I thought maybe she had left her phone at home and her father had answered,' he said. 'If he had known it was me, there would have been trouble.'

'But what about Jane's killer? He could have been the one who answered?'

'Maybe the killer and Jane's father are the same person?'

'Do you believe that?'

He shrugged. 'He's capable of it.'

'How do you know?'

'Just stuff Jane's told me.'

'Like what?'

He scratched the side of his mouth with his finger, and then looked to the ceiling when he heard the vacuum cleaner start upstairs. Adam's mother was being conspicuous despite not being in the room.

'He likes money and he likes power,' he said. 'He used to turn a blind eye to drug dealing in the clubs where his boys ran the doors, because he would get a cut. The agreement was that if they got caught, they'd keep their mouth shut and take the hit from the court. Except that some of them didn't like the idea of prison, and so they told the police all about the arrangements. Those that talked didn't work again. There was a rumour that one didn't walk again. Now, it's the protection rackets he likes, except that he calls it security. He's a big man in a small world. Those who won't pay the money get hassle from the local idiots, just juvenile stuff, like shit through the letterbox or eggs at the window, but a couple of people have had petrol poured into their hallways.'

'So he was worried about having a policeman's wife as a daughter?'

'It was worse than that,' he said. 'She was thinking of joining too.'

Laura was surprised. 'Did Don know about this?'

Adam nodded. 'Now you know why he told us to split up. He thought I was a bad influence.' He gave a small laugh. 'I don't think Don got the irony.'

'Do you have a picture of Jane that we can use?' Laura said. 'Her family isn't cooperating at all.'

Adam nodded and left the room. As she listened to the thumps of his feet on the stairs, Laura wondered whether everything she'd heard made Don Roberts more of a suspect. She glanced up when she heard movement in the hall, and saw that Tracy was watching her.

Adam bounded back into the room, holding a photograph. 'Is this okay?' he said, as he passed it over.

Laura looked down, and the corpse from an hour earlier was brought to life. She was laughing in this photograph, her hair thrown back, full of zest and life. It looked like a holiday shot, Ibiza or somewhere, her arms tanned in a pink vest, the sky bright blue behind her.

'Perfect,' Laura said, and for a moment she felt some of Adam's sadness, that someone so young and beautiful could end up like she did, abused and dumped in the woods. She tried to look convincing when she said, 'We'll find her killer. I promise.'

Chapter Twenty-Two

Jack was outside the court when he managed to speak to Laura. Her phone had been switched off, because he had been trying to get hold of her since his conversation with Dolby, and so he had gone to court, looking out for sidebar scraps. The clock had moved onto twelve and the court had emptied, so he tried again. When Laura answered, it sounded like she was outside.

'Jack? Look, I'm sorry I wasn't there this morning. How was Bobby?'

131

'He's fine,' Jack said, 'but I'm not calling about that. It's about the murder.'

'I can't tell you much.'

'At least answer this then: what did Jane Roberts have in her mouth, and Deborah Corley?'

There was a pause, and then, 'What do you mean?'

'It's okay, I'm not looking for a quote,' he said. 'Just call me curious.'

'Come on, Jack,' she said. 'Curious with you means more than just that. So tell me why you think there was something in her mouth?'

'If you'll give me a couple of minutes of your time, I'll come and show you,' he said.

'Okay,' she said, more softly now. 'It would be good to see you anyway. It seems like ages since we talked.'

'I know, but just business for now,' he said, and then hung up.

As the hum of the street took over, he felt that excitement again, something he hadn't felt in a while. Maybe he was finally going to write the story he wanted.

He headed for his car.

Laura looked at her phone.

She was outside the station, fresh from her trip to see Jane's boyfriend. How did Jack know that there had been something crammed into Jane's mouth?

She knew she needed to speak with Carson, as Jack would be gaining special access. At some point they might need to ask journalists to hold something back, but if they find out that someone is getting the inside track, they won't agree.

She walked quickly into the station, and when she went into the canteen she saw that Carson was sitting at a table. Joe was queuing for food.

'How did you get on with the ex-boyfriend?' Carson asked, as she sat down opposite.

'He wasn't so ex,' Laura said.

Carson looked interested at that.

'He had applied to become one of us, and Jane was thinking of joining too,' Laura said. 'Daddy didn't like that and so tried to split them up.'

'Jane was an adult,' Carson said.

'Yes, but he could make it difficult for them, and Jane still lived at home.'

'So Don is back in the frame?'

'He was never really out of it.'

'How does the boyfriend rate as a suspect?'

Laura thought about that. 'He can't be ruled out, but I believed him. We've got something else to think about now though.'

'Go on.'

'Jack has just called,' she said. 'He knows that there was something jammed into Jane's mouth.'

Carson looked surprised. 'How does he know?'

'He didn't say, but he'll tell me when he gets here.'

'He's not thinking of interfering, is he?'

'I don't know what he's doing,' she said.

'You know the force has never been comfortable with this.'

'I know, I know,' she said, her voice weary. 'But Jack must know something worth listening to. Hear him out.'

Carson's response was interrupted by the clatter

133

of a tray onto the table. Joe passed three plates around with limp white bread and crispy tongues of bacon, and then scattered some sauce sachets onto the table.

'I saw you and thought you looked hungry,' Joe said to Laura. 'I heard you mention Jack.'

'He knows about the mud jammed into Jane's mouth,' Laura said.

Carson took a bite of his sandwich. 'Do you talk in your sleep?' he said, mumbling through his food, and when Laura responded with an arched eyebrow, he added, 'the whispers were always going to start. And maybe it's no real secret. There's more than just us who know about it. There are the kids who found her, the uniforms who combed the scene. Someone will always talk. If we think that the rumours will end up in print, we'll ask the press for an embargo, which means that Jack doesn't get any special favours.'

'I think there's more to it than it seems,' Laura said.

Carson stopped chewing at that. 'How do you mean?'

'Because he's on his way here. He would have told me if it was just press rumours.'

Carson looked like he had lost his appetite. He put his sandwich back on the plate. 'I just hope he isn't using you to get closer than everyone else.'

'I wouldn't let him,' Laura said, but from the scowl that Carson flashed across the table, Laura realised that she would be frozen out of the case if he tried it.

Chapter Twenty-Three

Jack had texted Laura to let her know that he'd arrived, and as he walked through the station doors he checked his pockets for his tools: a voice recorder, paper pad and pen. He was in the glass-fronted reception area, the windows like ticket kiosks, the seats opposite filled with bored customers waiting to be seen, some holding vehicle documents, one or two looking like they were waiting for a relative to emerge from the cells. As he glanced along the chairs, Jack saw a grinning face at the end. It was David Hoyle, the brash young defence lawyer from the court.

'Mr Journo,' he shouted over, and then leaned back in his chair and put his hands behind his head, his legs outstretched, expensive-looking brown brogues on his feet, a fawn-coloured suit and pink shirt making up the ensemble. Hoyle looked a step up from the sale-rack suits and gelled hair of the police station runners who seemed to do most of the defence work.

'Whose life are you exposing today?' Hoyle said, his eyebrows raised.

'Oh, you know, sometimes it's good to get away from the routine,' Jack said, and grinned back at him. 'Like writing up your speeches.'

Hoyle's smile twitched, and then he waved away the dig. 'I know you don't mean that,' he said. 'I'm the best thing to happen to that court-

135

room in years.'

'The world is full of undiscovered geniuses, Mr Hoyle,' Jack said. 'It's good to finally meet one.'

Hoyle's smile waned. 'You know that none of this matters,' he muttered, leaning forward, so that Jack had to get closer to hear him properly.

'*This* is people's lives,' Jack said.

'But we're only passing through them,' Hoyle said, waving his hand dismissively. 'I talk like I make a difference, but I know that I don't, not really. When I've finished, and you've written it up, will anything have changed?' He shook his head. 'No, not one thing. They go back to their messy little lives and I see them the next time they fuck it up.'

Jack was surprised. 'You seem down today. A bad morning in court?'

Hoyle shrugged. 'Sitting around here makes me like that. So what brings you to this neck of the woods?'

'Just the usual journalist stuff. And how about you? Another cursed young innocent?'

'None of us are innocent, Mr Garrett.'

'Maybe so,' Jack said, 'but some are a lot more guilty. And the problem with lawyers is that guilt is just a verdict, and not a moral point.'

Hoyle smiled at that. 'If I worried about morals, I would be a bad criminal lawyer.'

'I'll save the ovation for later,' Jack said. 'So what have you got?'

'Just kids, doing what kids from the shifty part of Blackley do,' Hoyle said.

Jack was rescued from the conversation by a door opening behind him. It was Laura. She

136

tilted her head to tell him to follow her.

'Enjoy yourself,' Jack said to Hoyle, and then followed Laura further into the police station.

'What did he want?' Laura asked.

'To impress me with his greatness,' Jack said, and then he slowed as he saw Carson waiting for him.

'What kind of mood is he in?' Jack asked Laura in a whisper, nodding towards Carson.

'The usual.'

'Tetchy, then,' he said, watching as Carson turned around and walked away. Jack took it as a sign to follow.

They settled in some low chairs along the edge of the canteen, the air heavy with the smells of lunch. Laura went to get some drinks.

Carson eyed Jack with suspicion. 'Laura tells me that you're not really pursuing this story.'

'Like she said, not really.'

'But you were at the press conference, and it was your name by the story on the website.'

'It was just to give the local angle if the nationals became interested, and the local rag wanted to use it,' Jack said. 'I still need to put food on the table.'

Carson placed a newspaper in front of Jack, who looked down and saw the headline *How Many More?*

'Does this have anything to do with you?' he said.

Jack looked closer, just an excuse to avoid Carson's glare. It was his article under Dolby's byline and photograph.

Jack pointed at the picture. 'It doesn't look like

me,' he said. 'And aren't you more interested in why I'm here?'

Carson scowled. 'Go on, tell me what you've got.'

Laura appeared with coffees on a tray, and Jack delayed his answer as he took a sip from his cup.

'Just what I said on the phone to Laura,' Jack replied, 'that I was curious about what had been in the dead woman's mouth when she was found.'

'Who told you about that?' Carson said.

Jack took another sip and considered Carson over the lip of the cup. Carson was frowning.

'I have something to show you,' Jack said, and he reached into his pocket and handed Carson the emails he had printed off.

Carson looked down at the pieces of paper. 'What are these?'

'I received them last night. My email address was at the top of the story I did yesterday.'

As Carson took in the words on the page, Jack turned to Laura and whispered, 'Early start.' His hand drifted towards her leg.

'I know, I'm sorry,' she said, quietly, blushing slightly. 'It will settle down soon, don't worry.'

'Fuck!' Carson said, and he slammed the papers down on the table, spilling his coffee.

Laura looked surprised, and then she picked up the papers and began to read. When her eyes widened, Jack knew she had reached the poem.

He'll stuff your jaws till you can't talk,
He'll bind your legs till you can't walk,
He'll tie your hands till you can't claw,
And he'll close your eyes so you see no more.

She put the papers back on the table. 'So this is

how you know.'

'So what do you think?' Jack said. 'Could they be from the killer? Who else knows the details of the murder scene? Your squad and the killer, that's who.'

'And every one in uniform who was guarding the scene, and their families when they got home and spilled the news, and then their neighbours,' Carson said. 'These things don't stay secret for long, so don't get too excited.'

'What about this one then?' Jack said, and handed over the email that simply said *Ask them about Emma.*

Jack watched Carson as he read it. He looked confused now.

'Emma?' Carson said.

'Are you sure they're not from the killer now?'

Carson looked at Jack. 'What do you mean?'

'He is telling me that he knows something about why Deborah and Jane were killed, but my guess is that you have no clue what he's talking about, which means that he knows something you don't.'

Carson thought about that for a moment, and then said, 'It could just be an attention seeker. We get them all the time in murder cases.'

'So you're discounting the possibility that they're from the killer?'

'No, I'm not, but I've got to use my resources carefully. Do you remember that idiot who sent in the Yorkshire Ripper tape, Wearside Jack? And what do people remember about it? That more women died because the police wasted their time chasing him.'

139

'And if you write him off as some nutter and it turns out that they are from the killer?'

Carson didn't answer that, as the reality sunk in that whatever he did, it could be the wrong thing, and more women could die if he got it wrong.

'Could it be a leak from within the station?' Laura said.

Carson picked up the papers again and read through them carefully. 'It's pretty mean about Deborah Corley, and so if it is, someone has just got themselves a fucking problem.'

'I've got a different idea then,' Jack said, drinking his coffee. 'Whoever he is, he's said that he'll write to other reporters; so the information will get out there. So why don't you use me and take control?'

Carson scowled. 'What do you mean?'

'What do you gain now by keeping the facts back?' Jack said. 'Because that is what you are doing, keeping it back. If you go public, then at least you're back in control of the information, rather than leaving it to the internet.'

'If I need press advice, I'll speak to the press officer,' Carson said.

Laura turned to Jack. 'You're not thinking of writing this up, are you?'

He tilted his head as he thought about it. 'The local paper will want it,' he said. 'You know that they've run a few anti-police stories, and they haven't got many friends left to lose.' When Carson's lips tightened, he added, 'I'm not the guilty one here. There could be someone in this station blurting out secrets. The email said that he would know if I spoke to you.'

Carson put his head back and looked at the ceiling. He sighed and then looked back to Jack. 'So what are you proposing?'

'Go at him head on, turn him into a villain, spoiling murder investigations,' Jack said. 'Give more details about the murder and out him, whoever he is. Let him know that he's gone too far, and see if someone will give him up – a disgruntled ex-girlfriend or colleague.'

'But then he's dictating the investigation,' Carson said.

'He already is, because he's spilling what you're keeping back,' Jack said. 'You won't be in control of it.'

'What, make him the main figure?' Carson said.

'As a hate figure, not a hero,' Jack replied. 'Everyone likes a whistleblower, but not if it costs lives. This just gives you the initiative. If the local paper doesn't want it like that, then I reckon I can get one of the nationals interested. Make it about how he is risking lives, forcing you into giving more details.'

'You could always choose not to write anything,' Carson snapped. 'I thought you were freelance.'

'I am, but I have major customers, and the local paper is one. Think about it. It might make someone give him up, so you win both ways: if there's a leak, you get it plugged, and you get your revenge. If it's the killer, someone might know something from his letters, or even the email address.'

Carson nodded, although he was still scowling.

'Pitch it that way, as a leak,' he agreed quietly.

'Will you let me approve what you send in?'

Jack shook his head. 'It needs to be my story, not yours, but if you think I've fouled it up, fine, shut me out of the press conferences.'

That brought a smile from Carson. 'That would be a pleasure,' and then he sighed. 'If you want to know what was in their mouths, follow me,' and he got to his feet. Jack did as he was asked, Laura and Joe with him, and they made their way to the Incident Room. When they got inside, Carson pointed Jack to the wall at the front.

When Jack saw the photographs of Jane Roberts and Deborah Corley, his eyes widened and his mouth opened, but no words came out. *Gorged on the floor.* That's what it meant.

Jack turned to Carson with fresh resolve. Now it seemed like more than just a story. He just had to make Dolby stick to his promise.

The noise around him was like an echo, the movement just a blur. Case-builders and detectives moving around with papers in their hands, or sitting in huddles, whispers over lunch, gripes about Carson, the lead detective working them hard.

He glanced over to where Carson was sitting with Laura McGanity. She had queued for drinks next to him. She had touched him, just accidentally, a light brush, the soft swish of her trousers, her thigh against his thigh, a hint of perfume as her dark hair flicked past. Why had she done that? She could have stood further away, but she had invaded his space, as if she hadn't seen him.

And he remembered how she used to be. Her

142

accent had been filled with the south when she'd first moved to Blackley, all those rounded vowels, although it wasn't quite that London sound. It was more cultured, educated even, and now she was back in the suits, hanging around with the headquarters crew. She would have noticed him before, but not now.

He closed his eyes as the memory of her perfume returned. It was so hard to recapture a scent. He could recall Laura's smell though. There was the staleness of no sleep mixed in with the fabric conditioner on her clothes, fake and flowery, all lying underneath the musk of the perfume sprayed onto her neck. He could smell coffee on her, and just a hint of sweat from the morning's work. He swallowed as he thought of how she would smell at the end of the day, at home, intimate.

He opened his eyes and looked away. People would stare at the flush in his cheeks, at the shortness of his breaths.

His smile faded as he thought of the woman behind the counter. He had smiled at her when she'd asked him what he wanted. She hadn't smiled back. Just served him his food and saved her beam for the inspector standing behind him.

He heard the rumble of feet and he looked up. It was all movement now, the rooms that overlooked the atrium emptying as the staff hurried to the canteen for their lunch. The tables around him would fill up with the typists and administrative staff who prepared the files, who turned the footwork into something fit for court, and the detectives who'd worked out how to keep their working day from nine till five. He knew there'd be more uniforms soon, as they found an excuse to come back to the station, where they could eat without being pestered.

He heard a noise, an angry shout. It came from Carson's table. There was someone else there. A man. Then he recognised him from the photograph on the newspaper website. It was the reporter. He had told him to look for Emma, not to speak to the police. He saw a printed sheet pass between them. An email.

He felt the first growl of anger and took some deep breaths through his nose. He could hear the sounds in his head again. Like a constant song, the beat never leaving him, so that the only way to fight it was to sing along.

He looked up again. Think of something else. Not here. Stay calm. They were all eating their lunch, hadn't noticed him. That's how he liked it.

Then he saw something else. A touch on Laura's leg. Personal. Close. Had he missed something? The noise in his head grew louder, taunting him, and a flush crept over his body. He had known his work wasn't done. Now he knew why.

Chapter Twenty-Four

Laura sat at the back of the Incident Room as the rest of the squad filed in, all pulled in from their enquiries to listen to Carson's update. Or rather, to listen to his warning. Carson was at the front of the room, glowering, pacing, with Joe Kinsella sitting in a chair nearby, his legs crossed. Laura was there to check for reactions at the back.

There was some chatter as people found their places, just casual exchanges. Some people were holding sandwiches after being dragged out from their lunch. Everyone seemed tense, as if they sensed trouble, with nervous glances to the floor or their hands, or at pretty much anything that wasn't the prowling Carson.

Carson nodded to someone that they ought to close the door, and then once it had settled in the frame, he said, 'You all know why we held back details of the bodies from the press – to filter out the weirdos and so that *we* control the inform-ation, not the media.'

Laura watched for a nervous reaction, an extra shuffle of the feet, but everyone was static, as if they guessed that something had gone wrong.

Carson put his hands on his hips and looked around the room, and the gleam from the lights that reflected off his head matched the angry glare in his eyes. 'It's got out,' he said, trying to catch everyone's gaze. 'We have been contacted

145

by a reporter who knows about the condition of the body. He was told this by email, someone leaking details to him.'

'Which reporter?' someone asked.

'It was Jack,' Laura said, and she felt her cheeks flush as everyone turned around to look at her. 'And before you say or think it, it hasn't come from me. He came down because he found out, to make sure that we knew there was a problem.'

'So this is it,' Carson said. 'Confession time. Has anyone got anything they want to get off their chest?' No one moved. 'If you have told someone about this, for personal gain or just because you've got a loose tongue, head for that door. You'll be off the team, but I'll leave it at that. But if you don't confess and I find out about it, you are fucked.' He paced up and down, looking everyone in the eye. No one dared look away. 'Anyone?'

Still no one moved.

Carson stopped. 'Okay, thank you for your time,' he said. 'Go back to whatever you were doing. If anyone hears of a leak, I want to know. Squad loyalty comes before friendships, because if you cover for someone else, you both fall. Everyone got it?'

No one responded, but no one disagreed.

Carson headed for the door and nodded at Laura to follow. She felt everyone's eyes on her as she made her way through the room, and once she was out of the door, she heard the rumbles of conversation start up.

'You're in the clear on this one, McGanity, so don't worry what they think,' Carson said, and then he smiled, the colour in his face draining slightly. 'You worry about the killer. I'll catch the bastard who contacted Jack.'

'And if they are one and the same person?'

'Then people will blame me for getting it wrong. Either way I stand to lose.'

Jack called Dolby and told him that the police were willing to go with the story.

'I like it,' Dolby said. 'Dirty coppers leaking secrets. Let me have a look at it when you've finished, see if I can put my own special gloss onto it.'

'No. This one goes in as I write it,' Jack said. 'I'll be shut out from the police for ever if this gets messed up.'

Dolby sighed and then said, 'But I retain the right to not use it at all.'

'And it's going to the nationals too. I've still got a few contacts.'

'Come on, Jack, you know I can't promise to publish what I haven't seen. And this should be my exclusive.'

'Do you want it or not, Dolby?' Jack said 'Those are my conditions.'

There was a pause, as Dolby thought about it. Jack wasn't sure it was material for the nationals. The court stories from Blackley made it big sometimes: teachers caught in bed with their students, or asylum seekers breaking the law. Sex and immigration always invited outrage, and if it could be mixed with a crime, it got shoved forward a page or two. But he wasn't prepared to give it up.

'Okay, I'll go with it,' Dolby said eventually. 'But this is a one-off.'

'Whatever you say, Dolby,' Jack said. 'I'll have the story with you today,' and then he hung up.

Then he called Harry English.

Harry English was Jack's news-desk editor from his London days, when he worked on one of the nationals before he went freelance. Harry was a bear of a man who wore the smoke and stress of Fleet Street in the flush and broken veins in his cheeks. He was a good person to offer a decent story to, one that might interest the dailies, and he always gave a fair price if it was worth printing.

Harry answered his phone with a cough and then said, 'Jack, it's been a long time. I suppose you're calling about the murders up there?'

'You've heard of them then.'

'We keep an eye on the north, you know,' Harry said chuckling. 'We just don't feel like printing much of it.'

'The police want to release some extra information, but through me,' Jack said. 'Would you be interested? It's grisly stuff.'

'Sounds good.'

'You're all heart, Harry, but I need a guarantee that it will go in tomorrow's paper.'

'That depends on how good the story is.'

'Oh, it should be good.'

'How come, hotshot?'

Jack smiled, even though Harry couldn't see. 'We've got someone from the police leaking details of the crime and bad mouthing the family.'

148

There was a pause, and then, 'Sounds interesting.'

'It is,' Jack said. 'The police are having to change their tactics because of him. So you're interested?'

Harry coughed out a *yes*.

'Good,' Jack said. 'I'll have the story with you tonight,' and then he hung up.

The car was quiet again. Bobby had to be collected from school shortly, but Jack knew that he could write the story as Bobby watched television. He enjoyed the buzz of a deadline.

Jack closed his eyes to clear his head, because he had to plan what he was going to write. Start with the ending, that's always the way with newspaper stories, that you have to give away the cliffhanger to make the reader have a look at the story.

The story was for one of the tabloids and the local paper, so it had to be snappy, make people feel threatened. It would be *Cop Flops Secrets,* and then a shock-horror tale of how the leak could cost lives. The person who had sent the emails had to be the villain, not the anti-hero. Jack felt good to be writing something different from the court stories or whatever Dolby wanted to highlight. It was something he could control and he realised that he missed it, the buzz of creating something that people would enjoy reading, even if only for a few minutes on a crowded bus or train.

Jack's thoughts were interrupted by some shouting. Some kids strutted out of the station, in dark tracksuit bottoms and hoods, followed by David Hoyle. They shook his hand, street-style, making

Hoyle look clumsy, before they walked to a taxi, laughing as they went.

Jack waved at Hoyle, who gave him a salute. Another day, another win.

He followed the reporter outside, but he was distracted by a noise behind him. It was David Hoyle, his cologne drifting towards him, sweet and cloying. He knew how it worked – he was supposed to notice it, not enjoy it. Like the gaudy gold band on his wrist, and the diamond-studded ring he wore on his little finger. It was the show, just to say that he was winning, like the arrogance in his walk, bolt upright, feet apart, get out of my way. His clients bounced in front of him, another day of success for them. And he knew who they were, had seen them before.

He felt the first rumble of anger, so that the noises became louder as he got outside, his vision clouded, so that everything was on a time lag, the images blurring. He could see the reporter, but he was out of focus, just the red of his car visible. The sounds from the youths seemed to echo in his head. Anger turned to rage, starting as a tremor in his stomach, churning, hot. It spread quickly throughout his body, an urge he couldn't control. It was a need. No, it was more than that. It was a demand to hurt someone, like a scream of desire.

His cheeks glowed red as his arousal grew. He clenched his fists and looked down. He couldn't make it go away now, he knew that, but he could contain it, save it until he could use it, so that it was always there, the ticking bomb.

He heard a noise, the cough of an old engine, and through the blur he saw something red move away. The reporter's car. That would help, he knew that. To hurt those who betrayed him.

Chapter Twenty-Five

The Incident Room was still busy from the lecture Carson had given not long before, the detectives muttering between themselves. Joe had gone to the back of the room, paperwork growing into a pile by his keyboard. Laura walked over, ignoring the icy glance from Rachel Mason as she passed her.

Joe looked up as Laura got close. 'Did you see anything?' he said, leaning back, taking a breather, rubbing his eyes.

'No, nothing,' she said. 'If the leak was in here, he's cool. What are you doing back here?'

'So I'm near the printer,' he said, and lifted up the paperwork scattered on the desk. 'I'm looking for anything related to arsons or animal cruelty from twenty or thirty years ago.'

'Any joy?'

He shook his head. 'None whatsoever,' he said. 'It seems like the system purges itself every few years, and so the further back you go, the less there is, and go back more than fifteen years and it's like entering some world where computers didn't exist.' He tapped his pen on the desk, frustrated. 'If we had a name, we could do a better search, just to see if the suspect had anything relevant, but we don't, so we can't.'

'How come arson or animal cruelty are relevant?'

Joe stopped tapping his pen. 'Why do you think men kill pretty young women?'

Laura thought about that. 'Sex, I suppose. Lust. They want what they can't get, or maybe they get their kicks by killing, and prefer young women to older women.'

'But why do they get their kicks by killing? You have to know the why to find the suspect.'

'Power, would be my guess,' Laura said.

Joe smiled. 'You are nearly right, because it's about having *no* power and then striking back.'

'Isn't that the same thing?'

'Not quite,' Joe said. 'Some people kill because of the power trip, because they feel powerful, like predators, where it's all about picking on the little man, or woman, whatever the case may be. But killers who have a history of arson or being cruel to animals do it for the opposite reason, because they have no power.'

Laura sat down. She could tell that this was going to be a long conversation, and with Joe Kinsella, you had to have your mind clear to let it all sink in. 'Explain.'

Joe twirled his pen. 'Children burn things down or torture animals as a way of striking back,' he said. 'Imagine an abused child, or a bullied child, or even just an odd or insecure child, different from the rest. How can he protect himself?' Joe raised his eyebrows. 'He can't, is the answer. So he hits back secretly, at things that can't strike

152

back. Small animals, or buildings, where he can set the fire and retreat. It's cowardice, but borne from revenge, not anger.'

'But not all child arsonists turn into murderers,' Laura said.

Joe nodded in agreement. 'But most serial killers have arson or animal cruelty in their history. Something happens that takes them from the bud to the bloom. So it might be puberty, some misconnect of the wires, or an abnormally strong sex drive. All we have are generalities, not as good as neat forensics, but these best guesses are usually right.'

'So why would he choose these women?'

'That's an important part of the puzzle, the future victim,' Joe said. 'Killers rarely attack the source of their resentment. If they were humiliated or abused as children, you would expect them to go back and kill the people who did it. But they don't.' He paused, before continuing. 'Imagine spending your childhood as a victim of bullying, and the constant dreams of striking back, the satisfaction those dreams provide. So what happens when you hit puberty, and you are excited most by fantasies of revenge? They become something to masturbate to, something with more of a kick than watching the girl next door getting changed, and so hatred gets mixed up with sexual desire, and it becomes almost impossible to separate the two.'

'So the motivation is desire mixed up with revenge?' Laura said.

Joe nodded. 'Something like that.'

'Can we expect the next victim to be young and

attractive, like Jane and Deborah?' Laura asked.

'Probably,' Joe said, 'but still connected in some way. Remember what I said about the location of Jane's body. There is so much we don't know about Jane's movements. Deborah's family were more helpful, but Don Roberts has put up a wall.'

'Do you think it might be someone known to both of them?'

Joe thought about that. 'Probably not, but it's a close run thing. Just over half of killers like this attack strangers, and so we should try and root out the local psychopath, but we would be foolish to rule out a connection. It might be worthwhile going further back with Jane and Deborah. Were they friends at school, or at the youth club? Did they both know anyone called Emma? Or what about their parents? But this could just be about the weedy kid who was always humiliated by the pretty girls. Now he is all grown up, he sees the pretty girls as the cause of his problems, and so pretty girls are in his revenge fantasies.'

'Do we have someone going to the schools?'

He pointed towards Rachel, who glanced over. 'Rachel is doing the rounds. When I've finished trying to get something from the computer about grown-up child arsonists, I'm going to search Jane and Deborah, see if anything comes up from their past.'

'Why didn't you start there?' Laura said. 'You once told me that the victims are the most important thing to look at, because they help to identify the type of killer.'

'And that's still true, but I don't think the killer

is someone from Jane or Deborah's past, because that would mean that the killer is in his early twenties, maybe even younger,' he said. 'That seems too young, especially for a well-developed method like this, repeated both times. We have to consider everything, so I'm looking, but I would put the age of the attacker as being nearer forty, or maybe even older.'

'Because the young aren't as controlled?' Laura said, and when Joe smiled, she added, 'you've told me that before.' She pointed at the papers. 'So how long will you be doing this for?'

'Not much longer,' he said. 'I'm hitting too many blanks.'

'What sort of person are you looking for,' Laura said, 'apart from someone with arson or animal cruelty in their past?'

'Mr Invisible,' Joe said, and frowned. 'This person will not be immediately obvious. Think about the scenes. You mentioned control. That's how they were, well-ordered, with the bodies laid out, clothes gone, no forensic trail. This killer is no fool, and most importantly, the bodies weren't mutilated.'

'They had dirt and leaves jammed into their mouths and other orifices,' Laura said.

'I think that was part of the fantasy, because it happened before they were killed. If the killer is some oddball, unable to control himself, the body would have been badly mutilated. There would have been forensic trails everywhere, and we would have probably caught him pretty quickly. The fact that the bodies were not like that suggests that the whole killing was controlled and considered, which means that the life that he leads will be just like that, a façade, where no one knows what he really thinks. He may have built up the picture-perfect life. Steady job, local church. Maybe even marriage and children. His house and car will be neat, and everyone will comment, when he's caught, that he seemed such an ordinary man.'

Laura exhaled. 'So he won't be on the radar much then?'

Joe shook his head. 'This is a desperate trawl, nothing more, but we need to build up a suspect list.'

'Don't let Don Roberts see it,' Laura said. 'There'll be a bloodbath. He'll see it like a hit list.'

'And that's why we need to find whoever is sending the emails, in case there is a leak,' Joe said. 'So Don is still not cooperating?'

Laura shook her head. 'That's where I'm heading next, just for one more try,' she said. 'There are people working their way through Jane's friends, but it's all a mystery so far.'

'And what about Jack?'

Laura sighed at that. 'He's writing the leak story.'

'It's a risky business,' Joe said.

'What do you mean?'

'I'm worried that Jack's first instinct was right, that he might be something more than a leak, because there is one person who does know all the details, and that's the person who killed the two women. If the leak is the killer, we risk giving him a platform, because he thinks he can communicate with us through Jack.'

'Why do you think he'll do that?'

'Because that's what they do,' Joe said. 'Who-ever is killing these women, they're displaying power, maybe for the first time. One thing he will enjoy is the mayhem it creates. He will follow the news story and take pride in beating us, the police, because this whole thing is about flexing his muscles.'

'It's a calculated risk then,' Laura said, 'because if the description of the bodies makes someone think of a name, or decide not to shelter him any-more, it will be worth it.'

'That's the problem with risks,' Joe said, waving his pen at her. 'They can go wrong, and in this case, that will mean another dead woman.'

Chapter Twenty-Six

Laura glanced out of the car window and felt a tickle of nervousness. She took a couple of deep breaths and brushed the lint from the front of her suit.

She strode up to the door of Don Roberts and pressed the bell. The electronic chime echoed inside and she looked around as she waited, turn-ing back when she heard the click of the door latch. When the door opened, she saw that it was Don, wearing the same clothes as the day before, a plain black T-shirt with gold necklaces dripping across his chest. Tough guy caricature.

'Hello, Mr Roberts,' Laura said, trying to sound friendly, so that he might forget for a second that she was a police officer.

He considered her for a moment, his teeth clenched, and then, to Laura's surprise, he stepped to one side.

'Come in,' he said, although it was more of a command than a welcome.

As she walked past him, she saw things she hadn't noticed the day before, when her focus had been on breaking the bad news. There were reflective stones set into the stairs, so that each step shone like a glitter ball, and the wallpaper was thick black flock, but when the sunlight caught it, there was a red underlay to it, something more special than a roll from the local DIY shop. It was always the way with crooks, that they can't bank the money and so they spend it, usually on cars and chandeliers.

Laura was even more surprised when she went into the living room. The room was the same as the day before, bright red leather sofas in front of a large television, with white ornate dog figures in the corner, but this time it was filled with people, and it didn't look like the family had gathered to offer their condolences.

There were six men sitting down, every available piece of red leather taken up, and all of them looked to be from the same mould, with muscles stretching their T-shirts, the blue and black curls of tattoos stretching down their forearms. They wore their hair shaved or cropped short and their mouths were set into scowls.

Laura tried to stay relaxed, nothing was going to happen to her, although she felt her mouth go dry and her heart hammer in her chest.

'We need to speak in private,' she said to Don.

'Do you have a suspect?' he said.

'I would rather we discussed this alone.'

'I wouldn't,' he replied sharply.

'I didn't come here to be a sideshow, Mr Roberts.'

He nodded towards the door. 'That's the way home, sweetheart.'

She looked down for a moment, and then she sighed. 'Okay, if this is how you want it,' she said. 'No, we don't have a suspect, although it is more difficult when the victim's family won't help. Why won't you help? You've nothing to hide, I presume.'

She fought the urge to take a few steps back as Roberts clenched his jaw and took some deep breaths through his nose.

'You can call me many things, but I would not harm my daughter,' he said, his voice turning into a growl. He looked at the men on the sofa, and a quick glance from Laura told her that they were shocked. Roberts turned back to her. 'You think you are doing a great service, ticking your boxes. Spoken to bereaved family. Tick. Tried to find boyfriend. Tick. But you're wasting your time, because people won't want to talk to you.' His lips curled into a smile, but his eyes remained dark and cold. 'People *will* talk to me.'

'But how do you know you're going to get the right answers?' Laura said. 'People will just give you what you want because they're scared of you.'

'I'll know,' he said, speaking slowly now, 'because I'll make it clear that I'll be back if I get the first whiff of bullshit.'

Laura looked at the men sitting on the sofa. She noticed a few fists clench. 'You know that this house will be the first place we look if any of the local perverts wind up dead,' she said.

No one said anything.

'Did any of you see Jane on the night she went missing?' she asked.

Still silence.

Laura realized that if she was going to get a reaction, she was going to have to provoke it.

'Come on, fellahs,' she said. 'It's not a hard question. I bet some of you liked her. Pretty young woman, nice body, the key to Don's empire. Are you sure one of you didn't want her a little too much?'

'That's enough,' Roberts barked.

'And what about Deborah Corley?' she said, ignoring him. 'Did you see her around?'

Laura heard Roberts step closer to her. She could smell his breath, no sleep and cigarettes, and she noticed a few people shifting uncomfortably in their seats.

'Are you all going along with this to protect yourselves?' Laura continued. 'Perhaps you'll blame it on some local pervert?'

'Stop!'

It was a female voice.

Laura whirled around. It was Don's wife, Helen. Jane's mother. There were tears streaming down her face and her eyes were red.

'Stop, please,' she said, her voice quieter now, her hand gripping the door frame for support. 'This isn't about scoring points.'

'So help us then,' Laura said. She turned to

Don. 'You conduct your own enquiries, fine, but don't shut us out.'

Don Roberts looked at his wife, and then back at Laura. He pursed his lips a couple of times, and then said to Laura, 'Time to go.'

Laura looked at Mrs Roberts, who was staring at her husband.

'Tell me one thing,' Laura said. 'Does the name Emma mean anything to you, in connection with Mike Corley?'

Don blinked, but then he clenched his jaw and pointed towards the door. 'Like I said, you're done here.'

'Okay,' Laura said. 'I'll go now, but come and see me if you want to talk.' She was looking at Mrs Roberts as she said it.

Laura went towards the front door, and as she heard it slam behind her, she looked down at her hands. There was a tremble to her fingers. She wasn't sure how many friends she had made in there, although when she glanced back, she saw a face move quickly away from the glass in the door.

Chapter Twenty-Seven

Jack was at the table, hunched over his laptop, writing the leak article, his beer bottle almost empty, when Laura came through the door.

Bobby was watching television, and he turned around excitedly. She grinned and went to him.

161

She slumped on the sofa next to him, and Jack watched with a smile as Bobby told Laura about his day at school. The tiredness seemed to fade from her eyes and within a few minutes, she was laughing at something Bobby said about a teacher. They watched television for a few minutes together, Bobby leaning into her, until she kissed him on the top of his head and said she had to get a drink.

Jack held the bottle in the air as Laura walked past. 'One more from the fridge if you're going near it.'

'You're going to have to come and get it,' she said, and when he turned to look, Laura was beckoning for him to follow her, smiling.

Jack obeyed, and when he got into the kitchen, Laura stepped forward and put her arms around his neck. She pulled him close and kissed him on the lips, just briefly.

'A bit early for beer,' she said softly.

Jack didn't answer. Instead, he grinned and then pulled her into him again, kissing her harder this time. She responded at first, but then she whispered that Bobby might walk in on them and pulled away. She leaned against the counter. 'How's the story coming on?'

'It's getting there,' he said, opening the fridge and reaching for another beer. 'How's the investigation?'

Laura smiled. 'It's getting there.'

'And that's all I'm getting? I was shown the photographs of the bodies earlier, and now it's all secret again? I could pull the story.'

She sighed. 'Okay, okay, don't get like that. On

162

the record, we are pursuing some interesting lines of inquiry.'

'And off the record?'

'We're getting nowhere. Jane's boyfriend's in the clear, but we always thought he was. That's where Jane was going when she was killed, because Don didn't like him and so they had to sneak around. That's why she was on her own, which makes it really sad. Apart from that, we've nothing.'

'What about the reference to Emma?'

Laura shook her head. 'Nothing so far. It sounds like the emails could be from some attention-seeker.'

Jack took a drink of his beer. 'I've got the story in one of the nationals,' he said.

'Harry?'

'It's still good to have favours to call in.'

'He won't be there for ever,' she said.

Jack shrugged. 'Who is?' He took another drink of beer and then said, 'You're back early. We could have a night in.'

'We could, provided that you don't grill me any more about the case.'

'What is there to know? Is Don a suspect?'

'Should he be?'

'Maybe he's a copycat, covering up something he's done in the past by making Jane look like a second victim.'

Laura put her hand over her mouth, shock on her face. 'What, you mean a police officer might have leaked things about the first victim to him?' Then she grinned playfully. 'We thought of that, Sherlock. You're not the only sleuth in town, you know.'

Her head went back and she put her hands to her face before she swept back her hair.

'You need to get more rest,' Jack said.

'And you need to drink less.'

'Come on, Laura, you know what I mean. Stop feeling like you've got something to prove. You're a good detective, everyone knows that.'

Laura shook her head. 'There's always something to prove, you know that. I'm a woman, I'm from the wrong end of the country, the London upstart. There is always someone jostling for my position, and the handicaps mean that I've got to jostle a little bit harder than others.'

'Okay,' Jack said. 'Just don't forget about us two at home, waiting for you.'

Laura didn't respond at first, and for a moment Jack thought he had said too much, until she replied, 'You're both my family,' her voice slow and low. 'I could never forget that. We're getting married, for goodness' sake.'

Jack nodded, smiling. 'Thank you.'

'And that reminds me,' she said, pushing herself away from the counter and walking past Jack. 'I've got to fit into a dress, so I think I'd better go for a run.'

Chapter Twenty-Eight

Laura was looking down as she started the jog up the long hill. It would take her home eventually, but there was still over a mile of hard running first and it was getting dark. She worried about the traffic. She had already slipped the headphones out of her ears, but the steady pound of her feet on the footpath filled her head instead, and every slam of her shoes on the ground reminded her that she was getting closer to home.

She didn't enjoy running, never had. It made her knees hurt and too much moved around for it to be fun, but she knew that if the wedding day was ever going to come around, she had to do this. She would have the rest of her life to wind down, and so she pushed herself on, her water bottle gripped in one hand, sweat pouring down the end of her nose. It seemed like every step was an effort, her shoulders working hard to keep the rest of her body going, blowing heavily as she went. She told herself that it was about more than just getting trim for the wedding. It was about shaking off the memories of the day, about feeling alive as she felt the fading sun on her face and enjoying the rolling green hills she saw whenever she looked up. But she knew that was a lie. She hated every step, and she knew she would stop as soon as the small band of gold went around her finger.

Laura glanced ahead. The road climbed steadily, with the pavement petering out further on. She glanced back. She could hear an engine getting closer, straining. It would appear around the bend shortly, the beams of light just painting the wall ahead as it got closer. Her clothing was bright, with dayglo strips running down the arms and legs of her running gear, but she put in some extra effort to get ahead of whatever it was, to get away from the corner so that she didn't appear as a surprise, her arms pumping, her head down again.

Laura looked around as the engine got closer and then rounded the corner behind her. It was an old van, small, and the wind caught the scent of the fumes that were billowing from the exhaust. She couldn't see the driver because of the glare of the headlights.

Laura glanced up. The pavement was about to run out and so she knew that the van would catch her up when she was on the road. But there was no traffic ahead and so there was plenty of room for it to pass her.

She stepped onto the road as the pavement ended, and felt the harder ground jar at her knees, every step sending jabs of pain through her legs. The van was right behind her now, the sway of her body caught in silhouette on the road from the beam of the headlights. She waited for the van to go straight past, her mouth set firmly, not wanting to take in the blast of exhaust fumes as the van carried on up the hill, her breaths coming fast through her nose.

But it didn't go past. Something was wrong.

She looked back again. She was blinded by the glare of the lights. The van was only a couple of feet away now.

She tried to pick up her speed, worried, but the van stayed with her, the front bumper too close. She kept looking back, but she knew she couldn't stop because it was right behind her. It hugged the wall at the side of the road, so that she couldn't just move out of the way.

She ran faster, her breaths coming hard now, her lungs aching in her chest, the heat from the front grille on her calves. She gestured with her hand that the van should go past her, but it didn't. It stayed with her. It wasn't just another motorist.

Laura looked ahead, hoping for someone else to approach. There was nowhere to go on her left, the wall right up to the road. The engine seemed to pick up, trying to find some acceleration on the slope. She could leap for the wall, her only escape, but the van was too close. It would catch her ankles and drag her to the floor if she did anything to change her stride. Her legs were tight with effort, her heart was beating hard. She looked quickly over her shoulder again. The van was moving into the centre of the road, trying to get alongside her. She could feel the vibrations of the wheels under her feet. She could see a grass verge ahead, too steep for the van. Twenty yards away. She could dive onto that and then scramble for the wall.

She put her head down and tried to sprint, but her legs didn't respond. Her head went back. Almost there. Ten yards. Five yards.

The driver must have realised what she was going to do, because the van swerved towards her, the front wing heading straight for her legs. She let out a shout and made a leap for the verge.

She landed in a heap, banging her leg on a rock that jutted out of the grass, her hands breaking her fall, pain shooting to her shoulder. She felt a rush of air as the tyre brushed her foot and then there was a bang as the van ran into the verge.

Laura looked up angrily, her chest pumping hard. The van reversed quickly, the bumper dented, and then stayed there, smoke trailing from the exhaust at the back. She started to get to her feet when the driver door began to open. Laura got ready to shout, but then she stopped. The driver's actions were too deliberate. The door was fully open, but no one was moving. And then she noticed something else too: there was no registration plate.

Think, she told herself. He might have a weapon, whoever it is. She started to back away up the verge, towards the grey drystone wall at the top, and she felt trapped when her back hit the stones.

She tried to work out what to do when a car rounded the corner towards them, coming down the hill, going slow.

The driver's door slammed closed, and then Laura coughed as the van took off up the hill, her face shrouded in blue smoke, the noise of the engine loud.

As Laura watched the van go, the driver of the other car wound down his window.

'Are you all right?' he asked.

Laura nodded her thanks, her smile weak as she got up. 'I'm fine. Just took a tumble, that's all.'

The other driver smiled back at her and then pulled away slowly. Laura sat down on the grass again and listened to the noise of the other engine as it faded into the distance.

What was all that about? Was it because she was a lone woman, jogging along a dark country lane, or because she was a police officer, some kind of revenge?

Then she remembered the emails. Whoever had sent them knew about Jack. Did he also know about her? She looked up the hill again, the van gone now, but then she thought of what was at the top of the hill. Her home, with Bobby inside. Had he gone there?

She dragged herself to her feet and set off running again, except this time all she could think about was her son. It drove away the pain in her legs, her chest, her heart going too fast. She needed to get home.

Chapter Twenty-Nine

Nothing was clear anymore. He drove quickly in the van, too aroused, too angry. He couldn't go home. The noise in his head was loud now, like a scream that he knew he had to silence. The journey was just a stream of red lights, blurred, blending into one. He couldn't remember where he had driven.

He thought he could hear people mocking him, just quiet laughs, almost inaudible, but definitely there. He took deep breaths, sweat prickling across his body, his shirt sticking to his back.

He had to find someone. Blackley was too far. He headed back into Turners Fold on one of the back roads, so that he wouldn't pass her. She hadn't got a look at his face, he was sure of that, but he couldn't give her a second chance.

He was soon in the town centre, looking for a woman, any woman. This was different to Jane and Deborah. This was about the instant need, not revenge, and the rush of adrenaline blocked out the noises outside.

He saw a young woman coming out of a shop, a carton of milk in her hand, looking down, her car keys with her. He slowed down. He liked her. She wore a tight T-shirt and he could see her titties bounce as she went back to her car. She shouldn't have worn that. Bad choice. But then he saw him, the boyfriend, waiting. She skipped as she got closer.

He drove on. He knew there'd be more. He thought about going where he said he would never go again, where the women roam in packs, their skirts short, handbags slung across their bodies, ready to laugh at him, fucks for money. Weak man. But it was a bad idea. They were in Blackley, a few miles away, and he needed release sooner than that. And anyway, the women who sold themselves looked out for each other, and they always fought him off whenever his hands went around their throat, just for a tease.

He carried on driving in a loop around the

small town centre and then onto some suburban curves. And then he saw her. The noises got louder.

She was young, in her twenties, walking on her own, head down, her arms folded across her chest, wrapped up in her thoughts, a cigarette jammed between her fingers. Perhaps on her way home from an argument, so it was possible that she wouldn't really hear him.

He drove past her and pulled into a side street. He got out of the van and waited, leaning against the driver's door. He would have to be quick, there were houses nearby, tall Victorian buildings that had been converted into flats and bedsits. Practice meant he could do it quickly. The snap of the cuffs, the hands around the throat.

The noises in his head receded. They always did when it was time, as if they didn't want to put him off. He had to be perfect. The timing of the grab, the threat. All he could hear was the stillness of the night, and like always, it seemed like sound had been magnified, so that her footsteps were loud slaps on the tarmac. He could hear her clothes rubbing together as she walked, the suck of her lips on the cigarette. Traffic sounds were distant. It had to be now.

She was there, crossing his side street, her head still down, the grey-blue cigarette smoke curling behind her. Why had she chosen that route? Choices again. She had made that choice, put herself in danger.

He set off walking, falling into step behind her. He was wearing soft soles, so that he could get close before she heard him. He tried to keep to the left, to keep out of the shadow of the street lights.

And then he was within grabbing distance.

He reached behind, for the cuffs that were attached to his belt. He took a deep breath through his nose. It made her turn around. She looked startled and was about to scream, when his arm snapped forward, his hand went around her throat, squeezing hard, his free hand snapping the cuff around one wrist, his legs moving quickly, pushing her towards an alleyway he could see ahead.

Chapter Thirty

Jack had finished the article for Dolby and was drinking another beer when Laura burst into the house. She was limping, panting hard, her cheeks streaked with tears. When he looked round, she went to her knees, her face in her hands.

Jack ran to the door and looked along the road, tried to see what had frightened her. There was nothing there. 'What's wrong?' he said, kneeling down, his arms going round her. Her back was sodden with sweat and she was sucking in huge lungfuls of air.

'Someone in a van just tried to run me over,' she said.

'Shit! Are you okay?' He pulled away and looked for injuries.

She shook her head, and then gave a small sob.

'No, I'm not. I've hurt my leg.'

He saw a rip in her running gear and a graze on her leg.

'You shouldn't run on these country roads at night,' he said. 'They're dangerous.'

'Don't make it my fault!' she shouted, a hand wiping tears from her cheeks. 'He was doing it on purpose.'

'What do you mean, on purpose? Are you sure? I mean, how do you know?'

'I just know, because I saw how it happened.'

'But why you?'

Laura got to her feet, grimacing in pain. 'I don't know. I'm a police officer. I've made enemies.'

'But why now?'

She was leaning forward, her hands on her knees, still out of breath. 'That's what worries me.'

'What do you mean?'

'Come on, Jack, think about it. Someone gets in touch with you who might be a killer, and then this,' and she gestured to the blood on her knee.

'He threatened this,' Jack said quietly. *If you tell the police, I'll know.* That's what he said.'

Laura straightened and looked over at Jack's computer. He saw the look in her eyes and knew what it meant: that this was Jack's fault.

She pointed upstairs. 'We need to get Bobby away from here. This person must know where we live, and so Bobby cannot be in the house if he comes back.'

Jack nodded. He understood. He went to put his arms round her again, but she brushed him away.

'I've got to go in,' Laura said, but as she moved,

her knee gave way, making her take all her weight on one leg. She looked at Jack, angry now. 'Bobby needs to go somewhere tonight.'

Jack agreed and watched as Laura hobbled upstairs.

He didn't do anything at first, except look towards the window and wonder what danger his article had brought to them as he listened to the sound of drawers opening, of her showering quickly, and then the sound of chatter as she spoke to Bobby, cajoling him, making out like it was an adventure, not wanting to frighten him.

Jack went to the window again and looked out. There was nothing but darkness. Was someone else looking in?

He turned around at the shuffle of feet. Laura was in a suit, Bobby in pyjamas and a dressing gown. Laura was holding a small suitcase.

'He's staying at Martha's tonight,' Laura said, and Jack nodded his approval. She was an old family friend. Laura ruffled Bobby's hair, making him smile. 'And your daddy is going to collect you from school. Isn't that exciting?'

Bobby's smile faltered, and Jack could tell that Bobby sensed that something was wrong. His father didn't often travel all the way north to collect him. The handover normally took place at a motorway service station on the M6.

Jack went to Bobby and wrapped him up in his arms. 'Have fun with Martha,' he said. 'Remember she's an old lady. Don't be a rascal.'

Bobby giggled at that, and as Jack straightened himself Laura grabbed Bobby's hand.

'I'll be back later,' she said, and then she was

gone. The peace of the night was broken by her car engine, the dark fields briefly illuminated, and he watched as her car disappeared out of sight. Then it was quiet again.

He stepped back inside and closed the door, checking the locks. It was going to be a long night.

Chapter Thirty-One

Jack looked out of the window. He was standing a few feet away from the glass, hoping to sink into the shadows.

It was nearly eleven now and Laura had been gone for a couple of hours. All the lights were off in the house. He wanted to see out without anyone else seeing in. He didn't know what to expect, but if whoever was in the van was going to come calling, he was going to be the one with the surprise.

What if they had got it wrong though? Perhaps it was just a bad driver, or someone who wanted to scare Laura for kicks.

The answer came sooner than he expected.

The only source of brightness in the room was Jack's laptop. It displayed a screensaver of family pictures. He went to it and idly tapped a key. When the screen returned to normal he saw that he had a new email from the same sender as before. The message title was just one word: *Why?*

Jack clicked on the message.

Why the fuck didn't you speak to Emma? If you want to know the full story, that's where you need to go. Find her. Go there. I know you can. Or is it because you're too busy with the police? I told you not to go to them, and now Laura has had a little accident, but it could have been so much worse.

It's not part of the story, just a random frustration, but someone else took the brunt.

Jack sat down to read it again.

There were no doubts now, or else how would the sender know that Laura had almost been run over by a van, and that he had been to the police? Was he watching?

He looked at the screen again, and the words seemed to swim in front of him. He had to calm down though. Just because it had been the person who sent the emails, it didn't mean that he was a killer. Carson might be right, that it was just a leak, someone in the force spilling secrets, and that he was just trying to frighten Laura, to let Jack realise that he knew the messages had been passed on to the police. After all, if he had wanted to run her over, he could have done.

Jack typed quickly. *Have you been watching? And what do you mean that it could have been worse for Laura? Who are you?*

His eyes didn't leave the screen as he waited for a response, his head filled with thoughts of Laura alone on a country lane, an anonymous van stalking her.

When the message came through, its title was: *Just a hint, Jack. A little present.*

There was an attachment. A photograph.

176

It seemed to take an age to load, the image slowly unfurling itself along the screen, every pause revealing another tantalising glimpse. Except that when it had finished loading, Jack felt his heart pound. Laura needed to see this.

He called Laura. She answered on the second ring.

'Tell me about Jane,' Jack said. 'Was she naked when she was found?'

'You know she was,' she said. 'We released that information, and you've seen the photographs.'

'But I know the police sometimes mislead the press, if it helps the investigation,' he said. 'Is that how she really was, or had someone removed the clothes for some forensic analysis?'

'Jack, I'm not in the mood,' she said, exasperated now.

'I've had a new email,' he said. 'From the same person as last night. Except this time he's sent a photograph.'

'What!'

'I'm no expert on forensics or decomposition,' Jack continued, 'but Jane looks pretty fresh in the picture.'

'Tell me,' she snapped.

Jack looked at the picture again, so he could describe it.

'Pale skin, her blonde hair against the ground, but her face looks flushed. There are pinpricks of blood across her cheeks and a thin red trickle from her nose. And I can see the debris in her mouth.' He peered closer. 'Her cheeks look full, pushed out, with leaves and dirt sticking out, as if she had choked on it.'

'You mentioned clothes,' Laura said urgently.

Jack looked at the picture again.

'I can see her torso,' he said, 'but her shirt is pulled open, her bra pushed up, so that her breasts are visible.'

'We need that picture,' Laura said.

'So she *was* naked when you found her,' Jack said.

'Jack, the picture!'

He typed in Laura's police email address and forwarded it to her. After a few seconds, he heard a ping down the phone as the email landed in Laura's inbox, and then she gasped as she opened it.

'He was the person in the van,' she said, her voice quieter now. 'He knows where we live. Bobby isn't coming home until we catch this bastard.'

'You'll catch him,' Jack said.

'I hope so,' she said, and he could hear the tension in her voice.

He was about to hang up when she said, 'I love you, Jack. Protect yourself. Don't let anyone near the house.'

'I will,' he said. 'And I love you too.'

He clicked off the phone, and as he put it back into his pocket, he became aware of the silence again.

Chapter Thirty-Two

The morning arrived as a stream of sunlight through the open curtains.

Jack squinted as he opened his eyes. He had slept downstairs, curled up under a blanket on the sofa so that he would hear the noise of anyone trying to break in. There was someone in front of him. Dark hair, dimples, a smile, holding a cup of coffee towards him.

He sat up and rubbed his face back to life. He took the coffee. 'Thank you.'

'You make a poor guard dog,' Laura said. 'I came in last night and you didn't budge.'

Jack grunted. It still felt too early. He checked his watch. Nine o'clock.

'How's Bobby?' he said, the coffee bringing him to life.

'I've just been to Martha's so that I could take him to school, and he's fine, but we need to be careful. We don't want him to be scared when he's here.'

Jack nodded.

'And I brought you a paper,' she said, and handed him the *Blackley Telegraph*.

He looked at the headline, large and bold, next to a photograph of Jane Roberts. *Cop Flops Secrets*.

He threw it onto the coffee table. 'Things have changed now,' he said.

'I know, but thank you for the photograph,'

Laura said. 'He might have revealed too much of himself now, because we can focus on the emails. We can chase the IP addresses, see where he accessed the email account, and the photograph has been sent to the technical people. Digital photographs have hidden attributes. Time and date. Make and model of camera. If he registered the camera, it might even have his name.'

Jack smiled. At least some good might come out of the messages.

'I'm going in now,' Laura said, and she bent down to kiss him.

Her lips felt soft on his, and for a moment he wished that she didn't have to go, so that they could do what they used to do before she went back onto the murder team: just relax, spend lazy days together when she was between shifts, with Bobby at school. It wasn't like that anymore.

Then he remembered the photograph of Jane Roberts, and the ones he had seen pinned up in the Incident Room, and Laura's near miss with the van.

'Go catch the bastard,' he said, and he watched as Laura left the house.

Once the sound of her car had faded into the distance, he picked up the copy of the newspaper and looked at the front page again. As he read the story, he saw Dolby had stuck to his part of the deal – that it would go in unaltered. Harry English will have made some alterations with the version in the *London Star,* and it will be tucked away inside somewhere, but anything might help.

Jack's knees creaked as he got to his feet and he hobbled over to his laptop. He jabbed at the power button, frustrated, not in the mood to look through the online newspapers, but he wanted to know how far the article had spread onto the internet.

It seemed like a long wait, but eventually the whirring of the computer stopped and he skimmed through the usual sites. There was nothing new so far.

He clicked on the email software, and he saw that there was a new message. He took a deep breath as he leaned forward to read.

You've done some good work, Jack Garrett, but you know now that you've got it wrong. So wrong. And remember: I know your name. You don't know mine. Knowledge is power. Remember Emma.

Jack slumped onto a chair and glanced towards the window. There were green hills and nothing else. And he knew that at night there was nothing but unrelenting darkness, easy shelter for anyone who wanted to approach.

Rupert Barker looked along the hallway when he heard his newspapers flop onto the mat.

He had taken *The Times* ever since university. It had changed over the years, with more celebrity and sports news, and the large sheets had shrunk to tabloid size, but he still enjoyed reading it with his morning coffee. Since his retirement though, he had added one of the red tops, just for fun, a bit of light relief. He would skim the headlines and smile, and then he would relax in his chair with *The Times*, and watch the morning slide away.

Retirement was hard. Thirty years as a child psychologist, speaking to the frightened and vulnerable all over Lancashire. But then it eventually caught up with him, the relentless plough through childhood problems, and so he gave it up, to spend his days reading or dozing in front of his fire.

He went into the kitchen and flicked on the coffee machine, almost tripping over his cat, a scruffy black-and-white thing with a gnarled right ear. The water started to gurgle through the ground beans and he took a deep breath and smiled. The smell of fresh coffee always signalled a good morning. The problem and the pleasure of retirement was this: so much time to fill, but so much enjoyment in trying to fill it.

He groaned as he picked up the papers from the mat and then shuffled back to his living room, a jumble of books and old memories, so dusty that it made the noses of visitors twitch. But it was his sanctuary, where he knew he would see out his life, reading and remembering in a high-backed chair in front of the fire. It had been a few weeks since he'd had to light it, the summer just starting now, but he still pointed his chair towards it. He glanced over to the garden, and saw that the cherry blossom from his neighbour's tree was tumbling across the lawn and the flower-beds were starting to explode with colour. The only sounds were the chirp of garden birds eating from a nut feeder hanging from one of his trees and the creak of the weather vane on the church tower behind his house.

He reached down for his glasses and lifted them onto his nose, and then started to flick through the red top.

He chuckled at the first few stories, footballers' tales, massage parlours and mistresses, the press getting all vexed at overpaid young men enjoying themselves too much. He was flicking quickly, the pages making him smile, just as he'd hoped. Then he saw a headline, *Cop Flops Secrets.*

He started to read it, a story of an anonymous police officer sending emails to the press about a murder on the other side of the county. He shook his head. Someone was going to lose their job, and for what? Some work-place grievance?

Then he stopped. He felt a jolt in his chest, winded, and his fingers gripped the side of the newspaper. His mind flashed back through the years, like a video on fast rewind.

He put the paper down on his lap and looked out of the window again.

The story had taken him back to just one boy, the one who had always troubled him. The abuse-driven anger he had always understood, but it had seemed to be more than that in his case. It was his coldness that stuck with him, the matter-of-fact way he talked about what he had done. A direct stare, a tilt of the head.

He looked at the story again, and the memories from twenty years earlier became louder. The coffee machine bleeped that it had finished, but Rupert ignored it. He was thinking of something else now. Or rather, someone else. A quiet and withdrawn child, his hands on his lap, a flick of light hair, no emotions on his face.

Jane Roberts was found strangled, with her mouth and other orifices filled with dirt and leaves.

He glanced out of the window once more, but

he thought the garden looked untidy this time, the cherry blossom cluttering his lawn and weeds emerging in the gaps between the flowers.

Chapter Thirty-Three

Jack had been distracted by the emails, because the first time he realised he had unwelcome visitors was when the front door flew open. He hadn't heard a car outside.

Jack turned around, shocked, and then he looked for a weapon, a knife lying around, anything, but there was nothing to hand. Three men walked in, wearing black jeans and black T-shirts, hair cropped short, two of them with scars on their faces, memories of past conflicts etched into their skin. One of them was holding a dog, one of those muscled breeds, with menace in its eyes, straining at a leash. The man holding it was older than the other two, tall and angry-looking, his cheeks flushed booze-red. Don Roberts, Jack guessed.

Jack tried to weigh up the situation. People like Roberts were all about intimidation, mean dogs and scowls, but Jack's first guess was that Don wouldn't attack him in his own home. They ruled by reputation, big men in a grim pond, self-crowned kings of a part of Blackley that most people aspired to leave, but Jack was not one of their subjects, and so was more likely to report them. Don was there to frighten, not harm.

But Jack had written about Don's daughter,

about how she had been found. That would make him unpredictable.

Jack tried to look relaxed. He crossed his ankles and waited for Don to speak first.

It was a long and uncomfortable minute.

Eventually, Don Roberts said, 'You know who I am?'

Jack nodded. 'Jane's father.'

Don faltered at that. Normally people deferred to him, the big man, but Jack had referred to him in relation to his dead daughter.

Don tensed and recovered. 'So you know why I'm here.'

'The article about the police leak.'

Don scowled and moved forward, so that the dog was by Jack's feet, its mouth open, panting slightly. 'You wrote some disgusting things about my daughter.'

Jack heard the break in his voice and saw how his eyes were rimmed red. He tried to remember that Don had lost a child. And Don wasn't wrong, because Jack had mentioned what had happened to Jane.

'If you read the story, you'd know it was about a police leak, not your daughter,' Jack said.

Don handed the dog to one of the other men and then bent down to put his face close to Jack's. 'You didn't have to write it.' He was so close that Jack could see the spittle on his lips and smell the lack of sleep on his breath.

'It's what I do.'

'Not good enough,' Don said, glaring at him.

'Be angry at whoever is spreading stories, not me,' Jack said, and tried to hide the nervousness

185

in his voice.

'I just want the fucker caught,' Don said in a growl. There were the beginnings of a loss of control. His fingers shook and his breathing seemed laboured, as if he was struggling to hold onto his emotions.

'So work with the police,' Jack said.

'What, so they can put him in a cell and give him a television, let him taunt me from prison with his Facebook page? Let him out in fifteen years' time when he promises to be a good boy, and all the time my daughter stays dead?' Don took some deep breaths and looked down. When he looked up again, his mouth was screwed up into a snarl, his fists clenched tightly. 'That isn't going to happen.'

'So what is coming to Jane's killer?'

'Justice,' Don said. 'My brand, not the official version, and you're going to help me.'

Jack's tongue flicked across his lips, his mouth dry. 'How?'

Don reached into his pocket and pulled out a small craft knife. He turned it in front of Jack's eye, the blade glinting in the light that filtered in through the window. 'I'm not going to hurt you right now, but I just want you to know how dangerous it is to say no.'

Jack swallowed. 'I don't know how I can help you.'

'It's easy,' Don said. 'There is someone in the police contacting you, because that is what your story is all about.' Don pressed the flat of the blade against Jack's face, the tip pointing towards his eye. 'Get him on your side and tell me what

186

he says.'

Jack didn't respond. He wanted to shake his head, but the blade was too close.

'What's wrong?' Don said. 'Got a pang of conscience?'

'It's more than a pang,' Jack said, his voice hoarse. 'It would just be wrong.'

Don Roberts smiled, just a flicker, and then he pressed the blade down more firmly against Jack's skin. 'I didn't give you a choice.'

Jack struggled to keep his face still, not wanting a grimace or twitch to send the blade into his eye. 'What if I don't accept?'

'Anybody who stands in my way is my enemy, and you do not want to be that person.'

Jack's gaze flitted between the blade and Don's face. He could hear the dog growling, like a low rumble, his paws making light clicking sounds as he tried to get closer.

Don stepped away and put the blade back into his pocket. Jack let out a long breath and looked towards the two apes standing behind Don. They were smirking.

'So do you agree, Mr Garrett?' Don asked.

Jack chewed on his lip and then looked down as he shook his head. 'I can't do it,' he said, trying to keep his voice calm. 'It would be illegal, and if you caused the murderer any harm, I would be implicated. So no, I won't do it.'

Don stared at him, his hand inside his pocket. Jack thought he was going to go for the blade again, but the silence grew, and then Don snarled, 'I expected that response, but I'll persuade you eventually.'

With that, Don turned to leave, his two henchmen in his wake. When the door clicked closed and he was alone again, Jack let out a long breath and cursed the leak story. Now he was really getting attention he didn't want.

Chapter Thirty-Four

Rupert glanced towards the building that had been his practice until a few years ago. A building at the end of a long row of shops, painted white and with vertical blinds blocking the view inside, a small brass plaque by the front door, Barker and Holmes. He knew it would be quiet, because it wasn't even ten o'clock. Most appointments were in the afternoon. The morning was for writing reports.

He pressed the small silver button on the intercom, and after a click, heard a familiar voice ask him what he wanted.

'Hello, Anne,' he said, clearing his throat. 'It's Rupert. Can I come in?'

There was a laugh and then a buzz as the security lock allowed him in. He gave the heavy wooden door a push and then he was inside the building he thought he would never enter again.

The smell was familiar, polish and air-freshener, the heating on too high, as always. A corridor stretched ahead, leading to some of the small rooms where he had tried to put right some of the disturbed young minds that had walked through the door. All Rupert could hope for was that some walked back along the same carpet tiles with healthier minds than when they first entered.

He turned towards the reception area, the low table covered with back copies of *Lancashire Life,* and saw a smile that had aged since he'd last seen it, but was still as welcoming.

'I hope you don't mind me calling round,' he said.

'How can you say that?' Anne said. 'This is your practice.'

'It *was* my practice,' he said, smiling. 'I'm glad to be where I am.'

'How is retirement?'

'Quiet, but that's how I wanted it.'

'Good, good,' Anne said, fast running out of conversation. She smoothed down her cream blouse and toyed with her fringe, her hair grey and brittle. He remembered her when she had first worked for him, an attractive brunette fresh out of a bad marriage. Twenty years later, Anne was moving towards old age. 'Can I get you a drink, Doctor Barker?' she said.

'It's just Rupert now,' he answered. 'I'm here to look at an old file.'

Anne looked surprised at that. 'Why? And how old?'

'One of my former patients has looked me up,' he said, lying to her. 'He might want some more help, but I can't remember enough about him. I'll be able to refer him to the right place if I can remember the specifics.'

'Is he still young enough to come here?'

Rupert shook his head. 'He's a really old client. Maybe even before you joined.'

Anne looked towards the back room, looking unsure. Rupert glanced the same way, towards the new partners of the practice, some young blood he had recruited not long before he retired to make sure that there was someone to buy him out. They were her bosses now.

'What's his name?' she asked.

'He wouldn't say. He came to my house, became really agitated, and then left. I think he'll come back.'

Anne swallowed, nervous now.

'He was my patient,' Rupert said.

Anne nodded, looking embarrassed. 'Okay, I'm sorry. You know where they are. Promise you won't take anything.'

Rupert smiled. 'I won't.'

He turned to leave the reception area and go through the fire door, but then he turned to see Anne holding up a small key. 'You'll need this.'

Rupert took the key from her and thanked her, and then went back into the hallway.

He walked quickly and quietly. He didn't think the new partners would mind, because he was one of *them,* a fellow professional, not a rival, but still he was hoping to slip in and leave unnoticed.

He unlocked the door to the cellar and then clicked on the light, squinting to make out what lay below in the mute glare of a naked bulb. There were wooden shelves lined with boxes, divided into years in accordance with a patient's final consultation, each box packed alphabetically.

As he thought of the boy, his mind flashed back to the end of the eighties. New age travellers and the Manchester scene. The 1985 box was on the middle shelf at the end of the row, the brown cardboard faded now. It was a good place to start. The lid had a film of grey dust and he sneezed as he lifted it down.

As he raised the lid, the names on the files were like small nudges to his memory, just flashes of frightened young children, made angry by the big kicks life had given them. Yet none of them were the one that he'd had in his mind since he'd read the newspaper that morning.

He pulled down the box for 1986. Still nothing.

He grunted with exertion as he put a box back, and then worked his way through the late eighties. He felt a tremble of excitement when he pulled out the box for 1990.

It took him a few seconds to work out the reason, but then he realised that it was the colour of the files. They had been buff-coloured before 1990, but as soon as he saw the blue files, he knew that he was closer.

He flicked through the files slowly, the faces coming to him now as if he was flicking through photographs. Then his fingers stopped at a name. Grix. Shane Grix.

Rupert's fingers trembled as he reached into the box and contents, speckles of mould soiling some of the pages, and started to read, the scribbled notes from two decades ago jogging his memory.

He put the file down and looked up at the cellar door. He had been right, but that didn't make him feel better. People had died. The question now was whether he was prepared to stop it from happening again.

Chapter Thirty-Five

Jack trotted across the road to the court building. He was still angry from Don's visit, and when he saw a police car further along the road, he remembered the emails again. Was he being watched? Was the killer a police officer, in that very car? Except that he also knew that police cars were often outside the court, waiting for police witnesses to finish giving their evidence.

He wanted to get back to his routine though, but he saw that it was another slow news day as he climbed the steps – just the usual collection of deadbeats and villains mixed up with nervous first-timers. He headed for the courtroom, hoping for a hint from the prosecutor, and he walked quickly past the ushers' kiosk, where they were clustered in their black gowns like caged rooks, waiting for the call to let them know which name they had to bellow out next. He got close to the courtroom door when he felt a tug on his arm. He looked round. It was David Hoyle.

'I was looking for you,' Hoyle said.

Jack gave a small laugh. 'I thought you were too good for this place, and now you need the publicity?'

Hoyle shook his head slowly. 'Come into a

room. We need to talk privately.'

Jack was curious, and so he nodded his agreement and then followed, but there was something about Hoyle's attitude that made Jack decide that private didn't mean off the record, and so he reached into his pocket to switch on his voice recorder.

Hoyle led Jack to a small square room, fitted out with a square table and four chairs, the seat pads worn out by years of bored lawyers listening to tired old excuses. He put his files on the desk. 'I saw the article in the paper this morning,' he said.

'Do you want me to sign it for you?'

Hoyle frowned and put his hands on his hips. 'You really are a smart arse, aren't you,' he said. 'This is for your own good.'

'Enlighten me.'

Hoyle stepped closer, so that Jack felt the air around him fill with the cloying smell of old cigarettes. 'I act for Don Roberts,' Hoyle said, his voice almost a whisper, as if the news was supposed to elevate his status.

Jack felt a ripple of anger when he heard Don's name. 'Which case is that?' he said, his voice dripping with sarcasm. 'Because Don hasn't been in trouble for a long time, so I'm told, and you haven't been around that long. No, what you mean is that he sends all his cronies and runners to you, and although you think it gives you the power, so you can play your game, it's really the other way around. It makes you one of his lackeys now, except that you don't see it like that, because you wear a suit and carry a file.' Hoyle's cheeks were starting to flush red, but Jack wasn't going to stop. 'I had a visit this morning from Roberts and his goons, unhappy with my story, and I got too close to a blade for my liking,' he said. 'Well, tough shit, because writing stories is what I do, and so I'll tell you what I told him, that I'll keep on writing what I want to write, and I will not pass on information to him.'

Hoyle took a deep breath, and the glare in his eyes said that he was trying to stay calm. 'I'm not interested in your fucking artistic fulfilment, or whatever it is that drives you,' Hoyle hissed angrily. 'I'm telling you for your own good. I know what Don Roberts and his cronies can do. Remember, I've helped them get away with plenty, and there are cases that you don't hear about, because I helped to keep them away from the court.'

'Bully for you,' Jack snapped back. 'The difference between you and me is that I can pick and choose what I do, but you can't, because you're on the payroll.'

'What if I can get you access?' Hoyle said.

Jack laughed bitterly. 'Access? To what?'

'To Don, to write his story,' Hoyle said. 'Don wants you to contact the leak, to send information to him, but there is another way. You could write about Don Roberts, but just write it up how Don wants it, not how the police do. It might bring people forward.'

'Why should I want to? I'm not sure anyone would be that interested.'

Hoyle considered Jack for a few moments, and then he sighed. 'Let's not talk around it, okay.

194

This is off the record.'

Jack thought about that and then nodded, and Hoyle's eyes widened as Jack reached into his pocket to turn off the voice recorder. 'It must have switched itself on,' he said, as Hoyle shook his head, disbelievingly.

'We both know that Don Roberts doesn't exactly lead a regular nine-to-five,' Hoyle said, once he saw that the red light was no longer on. 'In one sense, he's a businessman, except that he likes to keep his methods and profits to himself. Fine, that's his problem. I don't give him tax and business advice. I just help his casual employees when they get into trouble.'

'Why you?'

'Because he thinks I'm good, and because I work from home. I know I've got a big firm's name on the letterhead, but I'm left alone to do the work in Blackley. Provided that I bill properly, the firm is happy, and Don Roberts doesn't want a building full of clerks and secretaries in Blackley knowing his business. And he needs me handy. He pays me privately for those special friends of his, and so I don't have to do all the Legal Services Commission bullshit with him.'

'But why the turn around?' Jack said. 'Roberts was snarling threats this morning, and now he's offering the exclusive. I don't understand.'

'It's not that complicated,' Hoyle said. 'He knows which battles to fight, and which ones to back away from. He's hurt about the story in the paper this morning. He called me and wanted to know whether he could sue anyone, but I told him that there was nothing untrue in there. I also told him that there are more ways to play the same tune. He's not happy, but he wants to find Jane's killer. If using you does that, he's prepared to work with you.'

Jack shook his head. 'The deal works both ways though.' Hoyle looked confused, so Jack added, 'I've got to want to work with him. I told Roberts this morning that I wasn't interested in helping him out, and nothing has changed. Besides, your angle doesn't work. People who know Don will know why he wants the information, and won't be sucked in by some father's cry. Those who don't know him won't call him, because no one is interested in Don Roberts, because he hasn't paraded himself at the police press conferences with a tissue in his hand. The public have got to like him to help him. That's not fair, but that's the world. And so the answer is no, I'm not interested. If I change my mind, I'll get in touch.'

Jack went to leave the room, but Hoyle gripped his arm and said, 'Don't mess with Roberts. You can hide behind your pen, but it is still only a pen, and Roberts has got more dangerous weapons than that, and a very long memory.'

Jack looked down at Hoyle's hand around his arm and then yanked it away. 'Good to hear it.'

Hoyle stared at Jack for a few seconds, and then he picked up his files and marched out of the room.

When Jack was alone again, his teeth chewed a furrow into his lip. He was freelance so that he could do things his way, and when he thought of Don Roberts, he knew there was only one way, and that was Don's way. But Jack knew that he had just created a very powerful enemy.

Laura watched the squad look up as Carson barged in. Her eyes felt heavy from her midnight meeting with Carson. Rachel Mason tracked Joe Kinsella as he followed Carson into the room, and then she glanced at Laura, before turning away and looking back at her computer screen.

The meeting had the same format as the day before. Joe was at the front, just behind a silent Carson, keeping an eye on people's faces. Laura sat at the back to listen out for the whispers.

There was a sense of frustration that they were getting nowhere with the investigation. It had been forty-eight hours since Jane had been found and nothing had turned up so far. They had knocked on doors, spoken to the town's peepers and perverts, pestered the forensic science lab for results, but still they had no leads. The mood in the room was tetchy and Carson wasn't about to improve things. He slammed the door shut when everyone was in, making the newspaper on the desk flutter. It was folded in half so that Carson could reveal it as a surprise for those who hadn't seen it.

Carson folded his arms and spoke to the group.

'Has anyone thought of anything that will bring us closer to the killer?' he asked, the words coming out with a growl.

Some people exchanged glances, the occasional shrug, but no one spoke.

Carson nodded to himself and then turned to the desk behind him. He lifted the newspaper and opened it out, showing the headline over the photograph of Jane Roberts.

'Remember this?' he said. 'A leak, disclosing squad secrets. We had to release a story to try and expose him, and that meant giving details of how Jane Roberts was found.' He looked at all the faces in the room. No one was averting his gaze. 'I said yesterday that whoever was leaking secrets to reporters had a chance to leave the squad, no questions asked.' He threw the newspaper back onto the desk. 'I'm glad to see that you're all still here, because something happened last night that changed things.' He reached for an A3 piece of paper that had been face down on the desk. When he lifted it up, there were murmurs around the room.

Carson was holding up the photograph of Jane Roberts that had been emailed the night before.

'The more observant amongst you will notice that Jane looks a little fresher than when we found her, and she's wearing clothes. It was sent to Jack Garrett last night, McGanity's paramour. So this means one thing: whoever sent those emails is the killer because she was naked when she was found and so the killer must have taken the photograph.' He banged his hand hard onto the desk. 'We've lost a day already, by not looking at them hard enough. The emails are the key now. We have direct contact.'

Carson let that hang in the air for a few seconds, and then he said, 'McGanity was almost run down last night, and we think it was our man, because the emails mention it. He referred to Laura by name, and so he knows who is on the squad. He knew that Jack Garrett had been here yesterday. We need to be vigilant. Keep an eye on your mirrors. Watch out for people hanging around near your house. Make sure you know where your family is.' He paused, and was met with silence again. No one seemed cowed. 'The email also said that there was another victim last night.' That sent a buzz of whispers around the room. He pointed to two detectives sitting alongside Laura. 'You two. Compile a list of all Escort or Astra vans, light brown in colour.' He pointed to two more. 'Get in touch with Google. Find out which IP address was used to send these emails. Don't let them fob you off.'

'Sir, we've got something,' a voice said at the back. When everyone turned to look, Rachel Mason pointed at the computer screen. 'I skimmed through the logs from last night while you were talking. Someone reported that his girl-friend hadn't come home.'

There were murmurs around the room as Carson said, 'What does it say?'

'A twenty-four-year old woman, Caroline Holt,' Rachel said, reading from an Incident Report. 'She'd been to visit her cousin along the road. She hadn't come home by midnight, and when he called her cousin, she said that she'd left a few hours earlier.'

'That's him,' Carson said, a gleam in his eyes. He nodded at Rachel. 'Go speak to her boy-friend. Get photographs. See if there is any link to the other two victims.'

The rumbles of conversation carried on until Carson clapped his hands. 'Right, that's it. Back to work. You know what you're doing.'

Laura stayed where she was as the officers who had enquiries to make filed out, and then she went to the front to speak to Joe and Carson. As she got there, she caught Rachel Mason looking back as she left the room, those icy-blue eyes watching her.

'There was nothing going on back there,' Laura said to Joe.

'Same here,' Joe said, scratching his lip with his finger. 'If the killer was in the room he'd make a good poker player.'

'So what are we doing?' Laura said.

'The emails said that Emma was the key,' Carson said. 'That has to be what we look for now, a connection to Emma. Let's go back to their friends and parents and find out who she is. They need to think harder.'

'And if it still comes up blank,' Joe said, 'we just wait for him to do something else that shocks us. Except that I don't really want to wait for that, because if it involves another dead body, the attack on Laura is a sign that it might be one of us that gets found.'

Chapter Thirty-Six

Rupert checked his watch, nearly eleven-thirty, and looked up at the police station.

Blackley. He had never been here before. He had always lived where he had practised – in Cleveleys, a small seaside town on the Lancashire coast forty miles away, so different to Blackley, where the skyline of terraced streets was broken by old stone chimneys and giant blocks of empty mills, the windows in darkness, shadows of dereliction.

The police station looked new though, all giant glass panels and wooden surrounds, rising high amongst the office complexes and out-of-town superstores. The doors to the station were built for impact, not use, large and made from heavy wood, and as he walked towards them, he tried to blink away his doubts. He was sworn to confidentiality, his patients had been troubled kids through the years who had needed guidance to help them back on the path to a successful adult life. He'd lost more than he'd saved, but for everyone he did help to straighten up, it was worth all the effort of the failures.

Confidentiality. It was that word again, the one that he had stood by throughout his working life, and sometimes hidden behind when the police wanted information, or when social services were looking to apply their own brand of care. He would disclose what he was required to disclose, by court order, or when he was engaged to help the system, but when he saw a child as a patient, his first duty was to keep their secrets.

But did he owe a greater duty to the public now, to tell them what he knew?

He pulled on the door and went into the reception area of the police station, a line of chairs opposite a bank of glass counters. There was a large window behind him, so that it was like being in a glass tank. He could only see movement behind one of the counters, the rest shielded by blinds, where a grey-haired woman bent down in hushed conversation with a young man holding driving documents. Just routine.

Rupert looked along the chairs. There were only three people there: a young man in a tracksuit, his jaw set, his stare fixed at a point on the ceiling, and a middle-aged man sitting alongside a woman in a suit, who was checking her hair in the glass opposite. Solicitor and client was Rupert's guess.

He sat down and waited his turn.

The door that went into the main body of the station was busy with police officers heading in and out, talking into radios or laughing and joking.

Not long after, the young man with the driving documents stepped away from the counter and the woman behind the glass shouted, 'Next'. Rupert looked along the row and gestured towards the others. The solicitor smiled and shook her head, said that she was waiting to see someone, and the young man in the tracksuit simply ignored him.

Rupert looked up at the glass counter. The woman in a clean white shirt with red and black shoulder flashes beckoned him forward, although she looked impatient rather than helpful. Rupert took another look along the row and saw that it was he who was expected to be next.

He creaked to his feet and walked slowly over to the window.

'Yes, love?' the woman asked, her tone patronising.

He thought about leaving. This was it, his last chance to stick to his vows of confidentiality. Then he remembered the description of the dead girl, of how she was found, along with her picture.

'I'm here about the murder,' he whispered into the glass. 'Jane Roberts. I want to speak to the detective in charge.'

Rupert saw her eyes flicker wide, and then she nodded.

'What's your name?'

'Rupert Barker.'

'And you want to speak to Inspector Carson?'

Rupert nodded. He remembered the name from the news report.

'Wait there,' she said, and she pointed to the chair he had been sitting in before.

Rupert went back to his chair. His hands were wet. His mouth was dry. What if his thoughts meant nothing? He would have broken his vow and it would all have been in vain. He might as well give away the key to his old filing cabinet, childhood confidences betrayed. What would happen to his former patient, Shane Grix? Would the police be kicking his door down later on, based on confidences he had disclosed years ago? Maybe the killer and the patient he had in mind were different people? He had slowed down now, retirement bringing a different gear. Should he ruin his reputation based on a decades-old hunch?

He looked up when the door banged open, his heart thumping hard in his chest. It was a uniformed officer, heading out on a patrol. There was a police driver just behind him, taking bags towards a van parked just outside.

Rupert closed his eyes and took a deep breath. He wasn't ready to do this, he knew that from the relief he felt when the officer kept on walking. He opened his eyes and waited for some suits to come rushing towards him, and he knew that once they got him in one of the rooms on the other side of the doors, he would find it hard to resist their questions. He felt the urge to go.

Rupert stood up quickly and marched to the exit. He couldn't do this. When he got outside and felt the soft caress of summer again, he let out a long sigh and let the breeze dry the sweat that had spread across his forehead. It was time to go back to his life. He wasn't prepared to give up the one thing he still had: his reputation.

He walked quickly to his car and climbed in. He felt his pulse slow down when he heard the engine rumble to life, and as he pulled out of the car park, the police station fading in his rear view mirror, he gave a relieved smile.

He had done the right thing.

Everyone looked round when there was a knock on the door of the Incident Room. It was one of the civilian workers from the front desk.

'Yes?' Carson said.

'There's a man at the desk wanting to speak to someone about your murder case.'

Laura exchanged glances with Carson and Joe. 'Who is he?' she asked.

'Someone called Rupert Barker. He seems nervous.'

Carson looked at Laura. 'Sounds like he needs your gentle touch.'

'Or maybe any touch but yours,' she said, and then stood to follow the civilian worker back through the police station.

Laura walked out of the Incident Room and towards the doors that separated the waiting room from the main body of the station. As she looked through the doors, Laura could see one of the local solicitors, a wannabe glamour-puss, sitting next to her client and preening in the glass, and there was someone in a tracksuit, but he didn't look much like a Rupert.

There was a room behind the glass kiosks, where the counter staff went when they had to make some enquiries they were trying to keep secret from the customer. Laura put her head round the door. 'Where did he go?'

The counter assistant looked up from the note she was writing and then back out through the glass.

'He was here a minute ago.'

Laura looked through the glass in the door again. 'He's not here now,' she muttered under her breath, and then gave the door a push and went into the foyer. She was met with a couple of blank glances, apart from the solicitor, who was still flicking at her long hair and smiling at her reflection.

Laura went towards the exit doors and then out into the sunshine. She looked along the line of parked vehicles just outside the front doors and saw a car starting to pull away. She tried to make out a number plate, but he was too far away. A departing police van then blocked her view.

Laura pointed at the camera in the corner of

the foyer as she rushed through. 'How can I view what has just been recorded?'

The woman behind the counter shrugged and then pointed upwards. 'In the CCTV room, I expect.'

Laura walked quickly through the station and headed for the stairs, avoiding the lift, a confined space. Laura got nervous whenever she felt closed in. She hadn't always been that way, but a bad experience a year earlier, when a case had ended up with her being trapped in a small space, had made her this way. If there was a way to avoid them, she would take it.

She headed for the top floor as quickly as she could, her legs aching from her efforts the night before. She was out of breath when she burst into a small room that was dominated by a bank of television screens. There were images from around Blackley, the town centre and Saturday night flash points, along with some of the major traffic routes out of town. The CCTV operator looked up, his eyes taking a second to re-adjust from focussing on the screens.

'Do you have the foyer downstairs monitored?' she asked.

He shrugged and nodded, then pressed a couple of keys. An image of the entrance downstairs was displayed on one of the centre screens.

'Can you wind it back ten minutes?' she asked.

His tut was barely audible, but Laura heard it, although she focussed on the screen instead as the footage was rewound.

'There!' she said quickly, as a figure seemed to walk backwards out of the station. When the operator pressed the play button, Laura watched as the figure walked in.

He seemed old and small, his head bald, his features pointed. He seemed uncomfortable, nervous, as if he wanted to say something but would be quite pleased if he never got the chance. As he sat down, Laura watched as he shifted in his chair, crossing and uncrossing his legs, biting his lip, his hand running over his scalp as if he was brushing hair that had long since lost the battle with time, glancing up as two police officers strode through on their way out of the station. When it was his turn to go to the counter, he seemed to hold back, and although he held his nerve long enough to speak to the lady at the counter, he stepped away quickly after that and looked at the floor. He sat down for a short period and then he left, as if he was no longer uncertain, more determined to get away than he had been to enter.

'Have you got any external footage?'

He tutted and pressed a couple of keys, and then a view of the car park appeared on one of the screens. Laura watched as the man walked quickly to a car. As he climbed in and reversed, there was a good shot of the number plate. She jotted it down and said, 'Save that footage,' and then ran out of the room. The CCTV operator barely acknowledged her demand.

She went into the room next door and found a spare computer terminal. Once she had logged in, she did a check on the number plate. Rupert Barker. The same name as given by the man who came in.

Laura headed for the stairs again. She knew where she was heading next: to see Rupert Barker.

Chapter Thirty-Seven

Some kids looked at Jack's car as he drove onto the Whitcroft estate. They had the usual hoods and loose fits, with more menace than the black hair and pale faces of teenagers seen in the better parts of town, where rebellion was just a phase. Jack knew that they were trying to work out how to spoil someone's day, and their eyes had settled on Jack's relic from the seventies, the Calypso Red paint blistering on the front wings and the windscreen covered in dust and squashed flies.

Jack hadn't stayed long at the court. There wasn't much going on, and he wasn't in the mood to write up any of Hoyle's speeches. Instead, Jack decided to return to the estate, to find out more for the feature Dolby had pencilled in for the weekend edition.

He was sorting out his voice recorder, deleting old interviews to clear some space, when the security van drove up to the front of his car, stopping inches short. Another car pulled up close behind.

Jack put down his dictaphone and watched as the two security guards got out of the van, their arms hanging away from their body. It wasn't a friendly visit. They walked towards his car, and then stopped and folded their arms. Then Jack's passenger door flew open and someone jumped into the seat. Don Roberts.

Jack was shocked. He looked back to the security guards, who were both grinning at him now. DR Security. Don Roberts. He should have guessed.

'Let's get this over with,' Don said, turning towards him.

'There is no *this*,' Jack said, trying to hide the nerves in his voice.

'Have you reconsidered?' Don said.

'About writing an appeal for information?' Jack said, and then shook his head. 'No, I haven't.' He tapped his finger nervously on the steering wheel.

'Why won't you help me find Jane's killer?'

'Because of what you will do when you catch him?'

'Which is what?'

Jack looked at Don. He saw the clenched fists, the scar that ran from one corner of his mouth. But then he saw something else. It was confusion. In Don's eyes, Jack could see that he didn't know why his daughter had died, why something so awful had visited him. There was pain and grief and anger, and the determination to avenge his daughter's death in the only way he knew how: through violence.

'You would do exactly what any father would want to do,' Jack said. 'Kill the bastard who murdered your daughter. But I'm sorry, I can't help you do that.'

Don looked down, and Jack wanted to look

away when he saw the tremble to Don's lip.

'Would that be so wrong?'

'Yes, in my world.'

Don clenched his jaw but didn't respond.

'Go to the police,' Jack said.

Don shook his head.

'You don't want the police poking around your life,' Jack said. 'That's your choice. But as bad as it sounds, you need to get the sympathy of the public to get the information you want, and so stand with the police, as a grieving parent.'

Don put his hands on his knees and clenched his fingers around the kneecaps, his knuckles turning white. Jack became aware of the silence. He could hear the gentle crackle of the branches on a silver birch. The soft creak of springs as Don moved in his seat. The rhythm of leather heels as an old man in a grey suit walked towards the shops.

Don's shoulders slumped and the clench in his jaw softened. He looked at Jack, and there were tears in his eyes.

'I've never had to do anything like this before,' Don said, and for the first time Jack saw the anger slip away, leaving just grief, and it looked deep and raw.

Jack looked out of his windscreen at the two security men. They were looking away, oblivious to Don's distress. Jack turned round to face him and said gently, 'Tell me about Jane.'

Don didn't wipe away the tears. They rolled down his cheeks as he took a deep breath to compose himself. 'What can a father say about his daughter?' he said. 'Loyal, loving, beautiful.'

'What about the last time you saw her?'

Don looked at Jack for a moment before answering. 'It was just an ordinary night. Jane was going out, and so was I, just to my old local.' He shook his head in disbelief. 'Quiz night. How fucking mundane is that?'

Jack didn't interrupt. He wanted Don to talk it out. He wasn't planning on using it, but he wanted to find out more, so he could pass it on to Laura. Don may be unwilling to help the police, but Jack thought differently.

'I was getting ready upstairs and so I never got chance to say goodbye,' Don continued, 'but why would I make a point of it anyway, because it was just a routine Saturday? I thought I would see her the next day.' He paused, and then said, 'She had a boyfriend, you know.'

'What about him?' Jack said, trying not to let on that he already knew.

'I wasn't supposed to know. Jane told me they'd finished.'

'Why did she lie to you? Did you have a problem with him?'

'He wasn't good enough for her.'

'So how did you know they were still together?'

'Because people report back to me,' Don said.

'She was a grown woman. Why couldn't she choose her own boyfriend?'

'She could, but there is a thing called family.'

'But you stopped her from seeing someone, and so she had to creep around, which made her walk alone that night.' Jack watched carefully for a reaction.

Don's fists went pale as he clenched them hard

around his knees. 'You make it sound like it was my fault.'

Jack shook his head. 'You weren't to know. But tell me this: why don't you want the police involved? That is the question everyone will be asking. Why aren't the parents at the news conference? Why wasn't she reported missing earlier?'

'Why should I be scared of the police?' Don said. 'You tell me, before you put it into print: what is it that I do?'

Jack realised then that he didn't know too much about Don Roberts, apart from the rumours that he was the one to be feared.

Don nodded angrily at Jack when he didn't respond. 'So you don't know much?' he said, with a sneer. 'Be careful what you print.'

'How much have you read about Jane's death?' Jack said. 'Some people have said some pretty cruel things on the internet.'

Don chewed his lip for a moment, and then he nodded slowly. 'They're sick,' he said, 'but let me say just one thing: say it to my face, because that's the thing with the internet. Everyone's a fucking hero when they're at the keyboard, talking up the fight, but it hurts just the same whether it's said to your face or from behind a screen. So if you print any of this, that's my message to whoever they are: say it to my face.'

'What have you found out so far?' Jack said. He tried to make it sound innocent, a throwaway question, but he overplayed it, and Don spotted it.

'That is for me,' Don said, and he leaned closer. 'I know who you are, I asked around, and so I

212

know who you live with. Do not underestimate me.'

Jack tried to meet his stare, but in his eyes he saw the look he recognised from the faces of the hardcore criminals who turned up in court sometimes. Not the thieves or the Saturday night fighters, but the career ones, the ones who played for high stakes. It was a look that told him that there were no limits.

They were interrupted by the security guards turning round to talk to someone who had grabbed their attention. It was a man with lank, greasy hair and stubble on his cheeks. He looked around furtively, his hands in his jacket pockets, his shoulders hunched. He was edgy, the paleness to his skin giving away the tell-tale signs of drug dependency. He was talking fast, making the security guards look towards Don, who opened the car door and stepped onto the pavement.

As Don slammed the car door shut, Jack wound his window down to listen to what was being said. He heard the word *paedo* and *weirdo*, and then part of an address.

Jack leaned out of his window. 'I need to go. Could you move your van?'

Don gestured for one of the security guards to move it, and as he reversed Jack watched Don reach into his pocket and produce a roll of twenties. He peeled two off and gave them to the informant, but before he was able to scuttle away Don reached out and grabbed him by the back of the neck. There was some finger pointing, and Jack could hear the angry hiss of Don's temper. The addict nodded quickly, and then Don

213

pushed him, making him stumble to the floor. He picked himself up and walked off quickly.

He was around the corner as Jack pulled away. Don was in deep conversation with the two security guards as he went.

Jack caught up with the informant, who was walking quickly, looking back as he went. Jack pulled alongside and wound his window down.

'I've just been talking to Don,' Jack shouted at him. 'Where does this weirdo live?'

He looked suspicious and kept on walking, but then Jack saw the memory of his car click into place. 'Rockley Drive. Number 19,' he said. 'Are you going to sort him?'

'Where's that?'

'At the top of the hill, on the right.'

'And you think that the guy from number 19 did it?'

He shrugged. 'He's a fucking weirdo, is what I know. He's always at his window when the school kids go past, looking through his nets.'

'And that's enough for you, is it?'

The visitor slowed down and licked his lips, his tongue flicking over the brown stumps of his teeth. 'If it was your kid, you'd be bothered,' he said. 'It's not right, that's all, what happened to Jane.'

'What's your name?'

'Don knows my name.'

Jack watched him go and then realised that he had another visit to make, if only to save a life.

Chapter Thirty-Eight

The noise in his head was like a drum-roll as he entered Cleveleys, tense and fast, almost drowning out the shouts.

He had followed Rupert Barker all the way, always two cars between them. When Rupert stopped at a small grocer, he asked people on the street if they knew where Rupert lived. The police crest on his vehicle made someone give him up eventually.

He got out of the car and walked quickly to the doctor's house, his lips moving in time with the words in his head. He went up the short path and then straight round the back, not looking up to see whether he had been seen or not. Once he was at the back of the house, he saw that the back door was wooden, with small panes of glass in the top half, so that he could see into the kitchen on the other side. He saw that there was an old-fashioned keyhole, and as he went to his knees, he smiled when he saw that the key was still in the door on the other side.

He took his jacket off and placed it over the small pane nearest the keyhole, and then he rammed it with his elbow. The cloth cushioned the noise, and he heard the soft tinkle of glass as it fell onto the floor on the other side. Once he'd reached in to turn the key, he stepped inside.

He closed the door behind him. He was in the

kitchen. Then he stopped. There was a radio on. He moved slowly, trying to work out where it was playing. No one shouted out. There was just the soft crunch of broken glass under his feet as he moved through the kitchen. He got to the hall and saw there were two other doors going from the hallway. He looked inside the room nearest to him and saw what looked like Doctor Barker's snug room, lined by books and photographs. The radio was on a bookcase by the window. He rushed over and clicked it off. All he heard then were the sounds of an empty house. The tick of the clock, the hum of the fridge, the soft pats of water from a dripping tap.

As he moved towards the hall, he paused by a photograph in a dusty silver frame. It was Doctor Barker from twenty years earlier. His hair wasn't as grey, and he seemed to stand a bit taller. He felt some of the years slide away as he looked at the picture. He looked down to his hands, and they seemed smaller, thinner. He heard small cries, felt the movement between his fingers as tears of rage ran down his face.

He shook the thoughts away and walked quickly out of the room. He knew where to wait. If he stayed by the door, the doctor might be able to get away, or shout into the street. Once he was upstairs though, it would be hard for him to run.

He smiled as the stairs creaked under his shoes.

Jack looked up at Number 19, the house mentioned by Don's informant. It was a dirty semi-detached house, the windows covered in dust and paint flaking from the door. The net curtains

216

in the front window looked dirty and brown, and the grass in the small square garden was long and unkempt. Jack paused at the gate, worried that the informant might be right and that he would be helping a killer to escape, but something about the house told him that the occupant was not much more than the local oddball.

The curtain twitched as he approached the house, the occupant must have been looking out, and then the door opened before he reached it. A skeletal man looked Jack up and down. He looked like he was on life's final lap, with grey stubble and purple bags under his eyes, dressed in a baggy grey T-shirt and hair that stood upright like he had just woken up. But the smoothness of his hands and the dart of his eyes told Jack that he wasn't quite as worn out as he looked.

'Are you from the council?' he said. His voice was muffled, as if his tongue was getting in the way.

'No, I'm a reporter,' Jack said.

He looked up and down the street, his eyes scared now. 'What do you want?'

Jack wanted to tell him to leave his house because his name had been given to Don Roberts, but he faltered. Instead, he said, 'I'm just trying to get a reaction from the neighbourhood about the death of Jane Roberts. Did you know her?'

The man nodded but looked at Jack with suspicion. 'I know Don,' he said. 'Everyone knows Don.' Before Jack could respond, he said, 'You haven't been to any other houses.'

'You seemed a good place to start.'

'What do you want?' the man said again, but he sounded angrier now.

Jack held out his hands in apology. 'Look, I'm sorry, but your name has been passed to Don Roberts as a suspect.'

The man went pale. 'What, for Jane's death? Why would anyone do that?' His voice was quieter than before.

'Because it makes the informant look good in front of Don,' Jack said. 'I had to let you know.'

The man started to back into the doorway. 'I'm not going,' he said, some of his composure coming back. 'I live here.'

'I know that. You do what you want. Tell the police. I just wanted to warn you.'

The man pursed his lips and then nodded at Jack, before slamming the door.

Jack didn't move straight away. He looked at the door, the numbers in white plastic, the bottom of the '9' broken off, paint blistering around the edges.

Then he turned away. He had done what he could.

Rupert Barker walked into his house, feeling foolish after his trip to Blackley. He walked through to his kitchen and put the bag of groceries on the counter, the outcome of a detour to the local shop. He bent down to stroke his cat and then rummaged for the tin of sardines, a lunchtime treat for his sole companion. The cat purred softly as it rubbed his leg, and Rupert smiled. Life was normal again.

Once the cat was nose-deep in the fish, Rupert

stepped away and felt the crunch of glass underfoot. He looked to the door. A pane of glass was missing. And the key was missing too. Then he realised that the house was too quiet. He'd left the radio playing when he went out, just to deter burglars. But there was just silence.

He looked around quickly, checking for any sign that things had been moved, the nerves prickling again, like they had ever since he'd rushed out of the police station. He had left for professional reasons, to protect his client's confidentiality, but the feelings of disquiet hadn't gone away.

He backed out of the kitchen and pushed at the door of the room at the back. He waited for a shout, but there was nothing. He could hear the creak of the weather vane on the church behind his house, flicking at the clouds as it twitched in the breeze. His finger tapped nervously against his lip. It was still too quiet.

His mind flashed back to the file he had read earlier in the day. Shane Grix. It had all come back to him as soon as he'd seen the name. The tilt of the head, the flit of his eyes, his hands always still on his knees, quiet, withdrawn. He remembered the photographs Shane's mother had brought in. He never seemed to be joining in. His friends would be joking, grinning, pushing and pulling at each other, but Shane always seemed detached, stood to one side, more of a half-smile on his lips.

No, it wasn't a half-smile. It was a knowing smile, an 'if only you knew' sneer, a deep enjoyment of his secrets. Rupert remembered the

219

struggle to get him to open up, and Rupert felt that he never really had. Shane Grix disclosed what he wanted to disclose, nothing more, and so Rupert could only advise his parents to try and be open with him, to discuss their problems with him, to encourage him to share his thoughts with them.

The sessions had stopped too soon. Shane wasn't from a problem family, and so there was no need to involve the authorities. They had been private consultations sought by worried parents. He had given them advice until they couldn't afford it anymore.

He whirled around as he thought he heard something, like faint knocks. He looked through the window, but all he saw was the bamboo as it swished against the fence. Was it the wind, or had it been disturbed?

He stepped back, tried to sink into the shadows of his living room. There was movement outside, he was sure of it. He thought about dialling 999, but he wanted to check that the house was clear first.

But the nerves were making him feel nauseous. His heart seemed to beat too fast, making him gulp down air, his stomach turning.

There was another noise. It was from upstairs. Just a bang, like something had been knocked over. Perhaps it was his cat, but it had been too heavy for that. He peered round the corner into the kitchen. His cat was still eating.

Rupert backed up against the wall. Someone was inside the house, he was sure of that. He thought about the telephone in the hall. He knew he should call the police, but he didn't want to. Not yet anyway. He worried about the confidences he might end up breaking.

His eyes shot to the ceiling again. There was another noise. The creak of a floorboard. Or was it a door?

Rupert stepped away from the wall and moved slowly towards the door that led back into the hallway, the stairs just on the other side. He tried to move silently, so that he could back away quickly if he saw real danger, make a call and get the police there.

He pulled on the door and the light from the hallway fanned into the living room, just making more shadows. He held his breath, waiting for whoever was in the house to rush at him. But there was no one there.

He exhaled loudly. He looked down at his hands. They were trembling. He thought about how he could protect himself, but he didn't have any weapons in the house.

He looked towards the stairs and moved slowly towards them, expecting to see Shane there, and then almost laughed to himself as he cursed his overactive imagination. He looked up but the landing was empty.

He put a foot on a step and began to climb. Memories of Shane went through his mind, but he knew he had no reason to be fearful. Shane was a long time ago.

But what about the young woman killed in Blackley?

The stairs went straight upwards with a landing to his left, but the landing was bordered by solid wooden panels, so he couldn't see whether anyone was hiding there, crouching behind, waiting to pounce. Rupert kept his back against the wall, only the occasional creak of a step or the brush of his clothes interrupting the silence.

He reached the top of the stairs and looked around. He exhaled loudly. No one there.

Then he heard the creak of a door, the sound of someone moving on carpet.

'Who's there?' he said, his voice weak. 'Shane? Is that you?' He heard something behind him, the fast rumble of feet along the landing. He turned around quickly, a shout caught in his throat. He went to scream, but suddenly an arm went around his neck.

He fell backwards, pulled down. There was stale breath on his cheek, coming at him in short bursts. He ended up on the floor. Then Rupert gagged as something was rammed into his mouth. A cloth, he could feel it in his throat, his cheeks pushed out. There was someone on top of him, hands around his neck. Rupert tried to push him off, but his opponent was heavy and strong. Rupert reached up and tried to scratch at his face, but there was a scarf there, tight around his attacker's face. He tried to get more breaths through the cloth, but it was impossible, his attacker's hands squeezing hard.

As he looked up, the last thing Rupert saw were his attacker's eyes, calm, cold, his head tilted slightly to one side.

Chapter Thirty-Nine

Laura checked her watch as Joe drove along the Cleveleys seafront, her side window open, the salt on the breeze making her lick her lips. It was almost two o'clock.

Laura turned her engagement ring on her finger absent-mindedly as she thought about how different Cleveleys was to her home, Turners Fold, even though it was only an hour away. And that was how she thought of Turners Fold now, as home. It had taken a long time before she'd been able to think of it in those terms.

Cleveleys seemed a world away from the dark green of the hills around her cottage. Here, the sky seemed brighter, as it soaked up some of the sunshine that glimmered on the sea, vivid blue to the horizon, not the stone-grey of the Pennines. Turners Fold was like all the other cotton towns in the country, characterised by lost industry and grand civic gestures, where old millstone buildings stood alongside imposing Town Halls and theatres, proud emblems of a prosperous past. The buildings in Cleveleys didn't brag or boast. They were either small redbrick or whitewashed seaside houses, with stained glass awnings over shop windows held up by ornate pale-green iron pillars. The seafront stretched into the distance, the beach below a mix of pebbles and sand, the sea a distant shimmer.

Laura had taken Bobby to the seaside since her move north, but it had been to Blackpool, and so it had been all noise and tack and lights, and then a dash for the car before the stag and hen night parties took over the streets. She imagined that it would be fun if she was a teenager, or with a gang of friends on a pub crawl, but the pavement stands selling cock-shaped rock told her that it was no place for children. She hadn't taken Bobby back a second time.

Cleveleys seemed different though. This was tea-room seaside, all buttered bread and after-noon dances. Even though she could see Black-pool Tower in the distance, it seemed like a whole different experience.

'Something on your mind?' Joe said.

'Uh-huh?' Laura said, and when Joe nodded down to her ring finger, she blushed and smiled. 'I do it a lot. It still seems strange, being involved in wedding plans again.'

'Strange?' he said. 'I thought it was supposed to be exciting.'

'It is, I suppose, but it feels different to the first time.'

'*I suppose* isn't giving it much of a billing,' he said. 'How is it different?'

Laura looked out of the window again as she mulled over her answer. 'My first wedding was the usual glitzy thing. Lots of frills and white, with bridesmaids and flowers, every girl's dream.'

'And the marriage?'

Laura gave a small laugh. 'Not as good as the day, and maybe that's the problem. It's hard to see it as a big new thing, because I've been there before, and that's why we're doing it much more quietly. But I can't say that to Jack.'

'Why not?'

'Come on, Joe, you're the one who understands how people tick. For Jack, it's his first wedding, but for me it's not, and the last time I went through it, the life afterwards turned sour pretty quickly. What if it happens the same with Jack?'

'Do you think it will go the same way?'

Laura thought about that, her fingers playing with her engagement ring again. 'No, I don't think so.'

'That took a while to come.'

Laura smiled. 'No, I'm sure,' she said. 'It will work out.'

'So what's the problem?'

'It's this, all of this,' she said, waving her hand to the window.

'What, the north?' he said, an eyebrow raised. 'Is it that bad up here?'

'No, no, you don't understand,' she said, laughing now. 'It's not as simple as that. I like it up here. It's my home. It's Bobby's home. I love London, but I like the open spaces, the slower pace of life here, but the wedding makes it all so damn final. I don't think Jack will ever move back to London, and once we are married this will be it.'

'If you like it here, what's the problem?'

'Because for every day we stay up here, it makes it less likely we'll ever go south again, and I'm a long way from my own family. From Bobby's family. And Bobby will get settled, and he'll meet a northern girl, and then that's it. Leaving the north will mean leaving Bobby, and I'll never do that. And what if me and Jack don't work out? I'll be stuck up here, on my own, just waiting for the occasional visit from my son.'

'Jesus Christ, Laura,' he said, laughing. 'You're thinking too far ahead and waiting for it to go wrong. This could be it, happy ever after.'

Laura didn't reply.

'It's just pre-commitment nerves, that's all,' Joe said.

'Yeah, maybe,' she said, then she turned to look at Joe. 'Do you know when we got together?'

Joe shook his head.

'It was right after his father died,' she said. 'Was I just a crutch? I'm older than Jack. Not by much, just a couple of years, but I come with a child and baggage, and sometimes I think he could have done better.'

'You're quite a catch, Laura McGanity,' he said, his voice softer now.

Laura blushed quickly. 'I wasn't fishing for that,' she said.

He smiled, his eyes warm. 'I know, but you shouldn't go into your marriage thinking that you are not worthy of your husband. You're an attractive woman, intelligent and funny, and your age makes you even more so.'

Laura felt her cheeks burn red. 'I was lonely though, back then, I'll admit it. I'd had a couple of boyfriends, but they didn't go anywhere. They were just someone to wake up to for a while. So was it the other way round? Was Jack *my* crutch?' She laughed. 'You know, this makes us sound just a little needy.'

'I've never heard you talk like this before,' Joe said. 'You've got the jitters, that's all. If you and Jack were not meant to be, he would have been just another boyfriend. Love is like that, complicated and messy. It's not all star-crossed fate. It's just two people meeting at the right time, and if you click, feel that spark, well, that's love. What was it like the first time you got together?'

Laura turned to look out of the window and thought back to their first kiss. Comforting Jack at his father's house, the death still raw. She was holding him, and then there was the touch, and the kiss, and yes, the spark. She remembered the excitement, nervous and lightheaded, and then the ecstasy as they made love, like a dizziness that made her want to cling onto him.

'Maybe you're right,' she said, her voice softer now, the memories giving her a glow that had been missing for most of the journey. 'I'm thinking about it too much.' Then she looked at Joe. 'What about you?'

'What about me?'

'Are you with someone?'

He pursed his lips, noncommittal. 'Nothing serious,' he said.

Laura was surprised. 'Why do you keep it quiet?'

'It's easier that way,' he said, and the way that he concentrated harder on the road told Laura that the conversation about Joe's private life had just ended.

Laura joined him in the silence and saw that the town was starting to peter out, but then Joe pulled to a stop in front of an old detached.

house, with a wooden bay window painted white at the front, next to a sea-green front door, art deco in style. The bottom half was redbrick, but the upper floor was rendered and painted white. The front bedroom window was large and gave views over the beach, and as she looked up, she saw the reflections of gulls as they floated over the sea.

'Rupert Barker's house?' she asked.

'If he has kept his driving documents up to date,' Joe said, reaching for the car door handle. 'It's Doctor Barker, remember. You don't want to offend him.'

Laura had made some calls on the way, to get some background on their reluctant witness. As they stepped onto the pavement, Laura said, 'His feelings don't matter. I need to be quick,' and when Joe looked at her, she added, 'We're sending Bobby to London, because of the van that tried to run me down. I want to get back to say goodbye.'

'Well, we're here now, so let's hope he doesn't waste our time,' Joe said. 'He could easily pretend he knows nothing, and then we get nothing.'

'I've got the touch,' she said, smiling. The coastal freshness landed deep into her nostrils as she took a deep breath, the sea giving the breeze some extra bite. It felt good though, a different air to the dampness of Turners Fold, and a long way from the fume-clogged oppression of London.

She made it first to the gate, and she reached into her pocket for her identification as she approached the front door and gave the door bell a jab. As it rang loudly inside, she turned back to the sea view again. She made a mental note to

228

bring Bobby to Cleveleys. They had passed a small fairground earlier on, and the shops sold the right mix of ice-creams and toys. He could ride his bike along the seafront.

Joe joined her at the door.

'No reply?' he asked.

'His car's here,' she said, and pointed towards the Volvo parked on the driveway. Laura turned and gave the bell another push.

'He may have realised who we are and is hiding in the kitchen,' she said.

Joe stepped back and looked up. 'There's no one peeping out behind the curtains. See if you can hear anything through the letter box, like a television or something.'

Laura bent forward and creaked open the flap of the letter box. She listened carefully but couldn't hear anything, apart from the mewing of a cat.

'No, nothing,' she said, and then turned to let it close. As she did so, she paused. She had sensed something, although she wasn't sure what. Just a hint that something wasn't right. She opened the flap again.

'What is it?' Joe said.

'I don't know,' she said, looking around, trying to work out what had flicked the switch in her mind. Then she saw it. 'There's a grocery bag on the side, only half-unpacked, and I can see a carton of milk. It's a warm day. You wouldn't leave that out. And a cat keeps on coming into the hall, looking skittish.'

'Is that it?'

Laura straightened and looked at Joe. 'No, it's

229

not just that. It's a feeling, intuition, call it what you want.'

Joe chewed on his lip. 'Try the door.'

Laura reached up for the door knob, and when she turned it and pushed, the door swung open slowly.

Laura looked at Joe and raised her eyebrows.

'If he's hiding, we might as well find him,' Joe said, and stepped into the hallway.

As Laura followed him, she thought she could hear the drip of a tap. The cat bounded into the hall again, its tail thick.

The hallway went past the stairs and towards the kitchen at the back of the house, with two doors going off to the left. As Joe went past the living room, he gave the door a push, and as it swung open, Laura saw that there was no one inside. There was just a sofa and a television, bookshelves lining the alcove formed by the chimney breast, filled with the orange spines of Penguin first editions.

Laura stepped around Joe and went towards the kitchen. She looked inside the bag. 'There's some meat in here too,' she said. 'Why didn't it go in the fridge?' She stepped out of the kitchen. 'Doctor Barker?' she shouted, but there was no response.

Joe stepped past her, and then he pointed towards the back door. 'There's a broken pane there,' he said, and then pointed downwards. 'There's glass on the floor.'

'We need to be careful where we go then,' she said. 'If something has happened here, we don't want to mess up the forensics.' She saw that the door to the second room was slightly ajar, and so she tapped the bottom of the door with her foot. It swung open with a creak, and the room came into view. No one there.

She retreated along the hall. 'Doctor Barker?' she shouted again, and then she turned towards the stairs. As she looked up, she said, 'Oh shit!'

'What is it?'

Laura pointed upwards.

Rupert Barker was lying across the landing, his face looking down the stairs, clearly dead. And there was a piece of cloth sticking out between his bloated cheeks.

Chapter Forty

As Jack arrived home, he saw that there was someone waiting for him, pacing up and down. He was young, early twenties perhaps, dressed in a cream shirt hanging loose over denims. He watched Jack as he stepped out of the car.

Jack approached the visitor carefully, who seemed nervous, with some bruising around his cheek, his nose lopsided, as if it had been knocked to one side. 'Can I help you?' Jack said, as he got closer.

'Jack Garrett?' he said.

Jack nodded.

'I'm Adam Carter, Jane Roberts' boyfriend,' he said, and then his eyes filmed over as he corrected himself. 'Ex-boyfriend, that is.'

Jack studied him for a few seconds, and from

the way that he looked at the floor to compose himself, he guessed that he wasn't there to cause trouble.

'Look, if you're here to cause a scene, I just write stories,' Jack said. 'I'm not the villain.'

Adam nodded. 'I understand,' he said, and then held out his hands. 'Don't worry, that's not why I'm here. I've had enough trouble already.'

Jack pointed towards the bruising. 'Jane's father?'

He nodded. 'How did you know?'

'It seems like his style, and he's not exactly your biggest fan,' Jack said. 'When did it happen?'

Adam's shoulders slumped. 'Last night.'

'What did he say?'

'Does it matter?'

'It made you come here.'

Adam thought about that for a few seconds, and then said, 'He wanted to know what I'd told the police. I told him that I'd answered their questions.'

'And that got you a black eye and a bust nose?'

Adam shrugged. 'He asked me to prove where I was on the night she disappeared, and so I told him, that I was waiting behind the Black Bull for her to turn up, because we had to do this subterfuge thing, where she had to slink around trying to get to me without being caught. He didn't like it when I said that if he had been less strict with her, she would still be alive, because she wouldn't have been out on her own.' He rubbed his cheek. 'That's when the punch came.'

'Don is hurting,' Jack said.

'What, so I should cut him some slack?' Adam

said, his voice rising a notch. 'Why the hell should I? What have I done wrong, except love his daughter? And what is he doing to help find her killer?' He stepped closer. 'Nothing, that's what, except attack me. What good will that do?'

'And what do you want from me?'

'I want to tell Jane's story, so that everyone knows about her,' he said. 'I can tell you about Don, if you want. How he makes his money, and why he won't go to the police.'

'How will that help find Jane's killer?'

'That depends on how you write it.' Adam pointed towards the door. 'If we go inside, I'll tell you all you need to know.'

Jack checked his watch. Two thirty. He wanted to go to Bobby's school to make sure his father turned up. But then he thought of the story, and reckoned he had enough time. Just.

Jack pushed open the door and smiled. 'Okay, Adam, let's talk. But make it quick.'

'So when will this end?' Laura said to Joe.

They were both pacing up and down, looking at the house. There was a police officer stationed by the gate and two white vans outside. Laura could see the white forensic suits moving around in the house through the glass in the door.

'When we catch him,' Joe said. 'This is no spree killer, who'll end it with a suicide. This one is killing for thrills, and so we will have to stop him ourselves.' He looked at Laura as he said, 'There is one glimmer of hope.'

'Go on.'

'Killers like this get bored, because they spend

233

all their time chasing the next high, or at least one as good as the first time, but there never is a high like the first time.'

'Why is that good?' Laura asked, confused. 'It sounds like he'll do something worse.'

'No, they don't, and that's their problem, because how much worse can you do? So they taunt.'

'What do you mean?'

'Like it sounds,' he said. 'They spice up the game by taunting, or doing something to raise their own profile. It adds an extra element to the game, and makes them feel like they are getting away with something.'

'He's done that already,' she said.

'And he'll reveal more of himself with every message,' Joe said. 'Have you ever heard of Dennis Rader?'

Laura shook her head.

'He called himself the BTK killer.'

Laura looked confused. 'BTK?'

'It was a title he gave himself,' Joe said. 'Bind them. Torture them. Kill them.'

Laura shuddered. 'Sounds like a nice guy.'

'By all accounts, that's how he came across,' Joe said. 'Except that he got his kicks from going into people's houses and killing them. When he tired of the simple thrill, he started writing to the police, wanting more fame. That's why he came up with the name, BTK.'

'Do killers do it for such simplistic reasons, just for the glory?'

Joe shrugged. 'There are so many complex reasons that no one can ever be truly sure. All we can do is look at patterns and make predictions. Take Andrei Chikatilo, a Russian maniac. He killed more than fifty women and children. He was given names, like the Butcher of Rostov or the Red Ripper, but his motivation was sexual, nothing more. But then compare him to Alexander Pichushkin, another Russian. His motivation was notoriety, nothing more than that. It wasn't sex at all, which is what motivates most killers. No, he just wanted to beat Chikatilo's record, boasted that he wanted to kill one person for every square on a chess board.' Joe allowed himself a smile. 'He was convicted of forty-eight, and caused a real stink when he was told that, because it meant that he didn't beat the record.'

'So if killers are so unpredictable, why are you sure this person will change his tempo?' Laura said.

'Because it is all about patterns, and generalities, and best guesses, and he's already started with the emails.'

'So for him to carry on emailing Jack is a good thing?'

'It's the only link we have to him.'

Laura sighed and closed her eyes for a moment.

'You sound tired,' Joe said.

Laura opened her eyes. 'I'm not going to see Bobby now, because I can't leave here.'

'Bobby will be okay,' Joe said.

Laura didn't respond.

Joe turned to look at the house again. 'What do you think Doctor Barker knew that scared the killer so much?'

'There is another more important question,'

235

Laura said.

Joe turned to her. 'Go on then.'

'Why today?' she said. 'What's so special about today that made Doctor Barker act?'

'Jack's story,' Joe said. 'There must have been something in that story that spooked him.'

'The one that we told him to write.' Joe didn't respond, so Laura added, 'But the only detail that was really added was that Jane had debris jammed into her.'

'Which means that I was right, that the method is not new,' Joe said. 'Doctor Barker was a child psychologist. He must be one of Doctor Barker's former patients. If the detail about the debris was enough to make him drive over to Blackley, it must be something that the killer used as a child.'

'And from around here,' Laura said. 'The killer knew that Doctor Barker would recognise it, and so he silenced him.'

Joe nodded. 'It looks that way.'

Laura paused as she thought of that, before saying, 'Do you think that the killer knew the doctor had been to Blackley?'

'What makes you say that?'

'It just seems such a coincidence, that the killer is operating in Blackley but suddenly he panics and kills a doctor forty miles away. For all he knew, Doctor Barker may not have even seen the article, or even if he had, might have chosen to do nothing about it.'

Joe thought about that and then said, 'What do you think?'

'Doctor Barker was at the police station,' Laura said. 'The emails boasted that he would know if

Jack spoke to the police. He knew about me and where to find me. There was something jammed into Doctor Barker's mouth, and so we know that it was the same killer.' Laura grimaced. 'Do you really think the murderer might be a police officer?'

Joe looked at Laura for a few moments, and then he said, 'I don't want to think about that. I'll go see if they've found anything.'

Laura watched as Joe walked towards Rupert's front door. He spoke to someone inside, and when he walked back towards her, he was pulling at his lip.

'What is it?' Laura asked.

Joe looked up. 'I think we both need a drink,' he said. 'There is no doubt about the connection now.'

'Why?'

'Because I know what was jammed into Doctor Barker's mouth.'

'Go on.'

'A pair of knickers,' he said. 'A young woman's knickers, from my guess. Small and with a pink bow on one of the hips.'

'They sound like the pair worn by Jane Roberts,' she said, and then Laura realised why Joe was scowling. 'They *are* Jane's knickers.'

Joe nodded. 'At least I was right about something, because if he decided to use them to gag Doctor Barker, he did it for one reason: to taunt us.'

Chapter Forty-One

Adam Carter glanced around the house when he went inside, his hands thrust into his jeans pockets. He looked uncomfortable, his hands on his knees when he sat down, self-conscious.

Jack sat in a chair opposite. 'Are you sure you're okay about this?' Jack said. 'You've taken a beating already. If Don finds out, you might get another.'

He paused for a moment, and then said, 'Yes, because I want Jane's killer caught, and Don made it clear that he wasn't going to the police. I've got to do this.'

Jack smiled at the resolve that crept into Adam's voice as he spoke. 'Tell me about Don Roberts.'

'Not too much to say,' Adam replied, and Jack could hear the bitterness in his voice. 'He's just a small town bully who fancies a shot at the big time.'

'What do you mean, the big time?'

Adam scowled. 'So you don't know too much about him.'

'It's not what I know that's important, it's what you can tell me,' Jack said. 'I'm not going to go public with rumours. I need a source to quote.' When Adam's eyes flashed with alarm, he added, 'I can leave it as *unnamed,* if you prefer.'

Adam considered that and then said, 'He's in

the security business. You know that, right?'

Jack nodded. 'I'm doing a piece on the rough edges of Blackley. Don's name comes up a lot.'

'And what are people saying?'

'Not much,' Jack said. 'I know that Don runs a security firm, but no one wants to talk.'

'Well, that doesn't surprise me,' Adam said. 'It's all a sham, just a front for extortion.'

Jack tried to hide his smile. 'How do you know this?'

'Because Jane told me.'

'Did Jane tell you a lot about Don?'

Adam took a deep breath and said, 'Yes, everything. I don't like Don because of the sort of person he is, but he was protective of Jane, tried to look after her. He had money, he could give her the things she wanted. He wanted her to do well at school, and so he paid for extra tuition, things like that. So she was no rough girl from a criminal family. She was well-balanced, educated, clever, and Don didn't want her to know how he really made his money, but she found out anyway, from things that she heard. She didn't like it, but he was her father and she loved him, and so it made it hard for her, being well brought up but knowing that her father was just the local thug. I suppose you can imagine how it went down when she wanted to join the police?'

'Was her career choice such a bad thing for Don?' Jack said.

'To Don, yes. He was expanding his business, building up his retirement fund. He thought he was about to hit the big money, had his sights set on one of the big houses on the top road that

239

overlooks the town. Her timing couldn't have been worse.'

'How?'

'Because he knew that Jane would do the right thing if she came across one of his henchmen, because she knew her career would be short if she covered up for him. It would only take one whiff of a leak and she would be out.'

'Isn't that what he'd want?' Jack said.

Adam smiled and shook his head. 'Don loved his daughter, there is no doubt about that, and I reckon he would give it all up to give her the life she wanted. He was just hoping she would change her mind so he could carry on.'

'And he thought you were the bad influence, for making her think of the police?'

Adam nodded. 'Something like that.'

'So how does he make his money?'

'Same way as always: intimidation.' Adam leaned forward. 'Tell me: what do you think Don's business interests are?'

Jack thought about that. 'Working the doors is what comes to mind, running a team of bouncers. He's trying to squeeze into neighbourhood security.'

Adam nodded. 'That's right, he's got to keep on moving, because the government took the money out of door work, made him go all legit.'

'I don't understand.'

'Go back a few years,' Adam said. 'It was easy for Don to take charge of the doors. He had a bunch of thugs he would offer out to the local pubs and clubs. Except that it wasn't really an offer, because if someone refused, they would just create mayhem inside. Fights would get started on Saturday nights, chairs thrown, tables going over, the police running in. They always seemed like cases of random drunkenness, but they weren't. They were Don's men getting frisky. And so Don's men ended up on all the doors in town, the clubs paying over the odds just to stop their premises from getting trashed. Remember, this is Blackley, not Manchester, easy to take over with a bit of muscle. And then there were the extras.'

'Extras?'

'Drug profits mainly. Don Roberts didn't touch drugs, but he touched money. The doormen knew who was dealing in their clubs, and they turned a blind eye provided that they got a slice of the profits. And if they got a slice, Don got a slice of that, so that Don controlled the club drug scene for a while.'

'So what's going wrong?'

'The SIA,' Adam said. 'The Security Industry Authority. To be a doorman now, you've got to be accredited, and that means criminal record checks and courses. That ruled out a lot of Don's men, and so Don's influence on the doors weakened. He runs an agency now. If the clubs need a few extra bodies, they call Don and he sorts them out.'

'So he's hit hard times?'

'Not straight away,' Adam said. 'He was into car clamping as well, and he stepped it up when the door staff went legal. Don's men would hang out where they had put up their crappy signs and wait for someone to leave their car. As soon as they were out of sight, the clamp would come out.

When they went down to release the clamp, the poor sod in the car had a bill of whatever was the maximum withdrawal on the nearest cash machine. It was legalised blackmail.' Adam smiled. 'The same problem again. The government is going to take the money out of that soon, and so now clamping isn't the racket it used to be.'

'And wayward shoppers aren't going to be mugged for their money anymore,' Jack said. 'So how is he expanding when the government has forced him to cut back?'

Adam looked nervous for a moment. 'You have to be careful what you print, is that right?'

'The papers won't print it if it's libel, but if you tell me, I can decide that.'

'Okay, if you're sure,' he said, wringing his hands, his tongue flicking onto his lip. 'It's footballer burglaries and estate security.'

'Hang on, you've lost me now.'

'It's the same thing really,' Adam said. 'Take the footballer burglaries. It's easy to figure out when the man of the house will be out, because you just have to look at the fixture list. So Don's men make out like they are burglars and pay the footballers' houses a visit, particularly during a winter evening game or when they are abroad. If you scare the lady of the house enough, she'll want security, at any cost. Don would pretend that he'd read about the burglary and would offer his services. He didn't do too well with the top players, but if you drop a couple of football divisions, you get the cheaper players who like the status symbols, like private security.'

'What about the estate security?' Jack said. He

knew some of the answer, but he wanted to hear Adam's take on it.

Adam sighed. 'This is the thing I liked least, because it's just squeezing money out of people who've got nothing, just an old-fashioned protection racket. You've read all the stories about the police not being on the beat as much? Or at least, that's what the politicians say. People feel frightened, that the police are no longer protecting them, that it's all about targets and paperwork.'

'It can't be that bad,' Jack said. 'Most anti-police stories are just headline-grabbers.'

'Maybe, but people feed off those stories. How do they know that the stories aren't accurate, because they're certainly written up to sound accurate? What do you do when you've got the local idiots outside your window, taunting you, those rat-faced kids, all dressed in black, who never go home because their parents are rounding off a day of doing nothing with the contents of a stolen bottle of vodka, and the police don't take you seriously?' Adam gave Jack a sneer. 'Unless, of course, Uncle Don Roberts is there to provide some neighbourhood security, with his thugs wandering the streets, checking on those homes who have signed up, chasing the kids from outside, all for a modest fee, of course.'

'Isn't that just the free market?' Jack said. 'He fulfils a need.'

Adam laughed bitterly and shook his head. 'Do you think it's that innocent? He creates the need. Who do you think is getting the kids to act like that? You see, there's never a confrontation with the private security, because they know who is paying and who isn't, and the ones who are not paying get it. Eggs at the windows, beer cans, shouting, tyres slashed. If someone gets CCTV, the cables get snipped. It's fucking warfare out there, and it will only get quiet again when everyone has signed up to Don's private security. Everyone thinks that he's doing a good job, so even when the prices go up, families with no spare cash don't mind putting some Don's way.'

Jack sighed. This was heavy stuff, but he was wary, because he could see the bitterness in Adam's eyes, and journalists had to be careful of one-sided vendettas.

'And you know all of this through Jane?' Jack said.

Adam nodded. 'Jane used to talk about him all the time. She loved him, and felt protected by him, but she could never be proud of him.'

'So what do you want me to do?'

'I want you to write about Don Roberts, to expose him,' Adam said.

'Don's lawyer has already asked me to do the same, but a sympathy piece to help Don track down Jane's killer.'

'So he can kill Jane's murderer,' Adam said.

Jack shrugged. He had already worked that one out. 'I need proof to write an exposé,' he said.

'So get it,' Adam said. 'Walk around the estate. Find the houses with graffiti, or where the kids are hanging out. Ask them what life is like. Speak to those who are paying Don, if you want to make it balanced.'

'And what's in it for you, apart from revenge?' Jack said.

'It's about Jane,' Adam replied. 'Jane would not have been on her own if Don had treated us like a normal couple. I would have picked her up, or Don could have driven her down. But no, we had to run around and keep our secret, and so Jane was walking somewhere on her own. How do you think that makes me feel?'

'My story won't bring her back.'

'No, it won't,' he said. 'But it might just make a lot of other people's lives a bit brighter.'

Jack nodded and smiled, although as he thought about how Don would react, it seemed that with every interview he did, his own life got a little more dangerous.

Chapter Forty-Two

Joe was on the phone to Carson, updating him, when Laura saw her.

She was middle-aged, with neat grey hair and a plain wine-coloured skirt. She had been walking along the street towards Doctor Barker's house, and, as usual, the crime scene tape had an effect. It had been draped around lampposts, blue and white stripes, and for most people, it was curiosity, a chance to gawp at something out of the ordinary, maybe a word or two with the officer standing nearest. This woman was different. Her hand went to her mouth, shocked, her eyes wide, and then she looked around, as if she was unsure what to do.

Laura went with her gut instinct. She tapped Joe on the arm and pointed towards her. 'She knows something.'

Joe stopped talking to Carson for a moment and nodded.

Laura set off to walk towards her, and as Laura got closer, she saw tears forming in the woman's eyes.

'I'm Detective Sergeant McGanity,' Laura said, smiling, trying to reassure the woman. 'Are you okay?'

The woman took a few seconds to respond, as if she had barely heard the words. 'Is it Doctor Barker?'

'Did you know him?'

The woman looked at Laura, confused. 'Did? I don't understand.'

Laura cursed herself. She had given away that he'd died and she did not know who the woman was, although as Laura looked back towards the house, at the forensic suits and police vehicles, it was obvious that something serious had happened.

'Yes, I'm sorry,' Laura whispered, trying to keep her voice low. 'Doctor Barker has died. Did you know him?'

The woman looked at the house, and then back at Laura. 'I heard the police were down here and I was worried, but I didn't expect all of this.' She took a tissue out of her handbag and ran it under her eyes. 'How did he die?'

'I can't tell you, I'm sorry,' Laura said. 'Tell me how you knew him.'

'I used to work for him, before he retired, I

mean,' she said. 'I'm Anne. His practice is still there.'

'So who works there now?'

'Some new doctors. Just younger versions of Doctor Barker really.'

'When was the last time you saw him?' Laura asked.

Anne dabbed at her eye again. 'That's the weird thing,' she said, sniffling. 'He came to the practice this morning.'

'Today?' Laura asked, surprised.

Anne nodded. 'He said he was tracking a former patient down.'

Laura tried to hide her eagerness, but she knew this was important. 'Did he give a name?'

Anne shook her head. 'He said a former patient had sought him out and asked for his help, but he couldn't remember anything about the case.'

'How did he seem?'

Anne thought about that, and then said, 'Now that you mention it, he did seem a bit jumpy and nervous. More than usual, anyway, because he was normally very calm.'

'Did he find what he wanted?' Laura said.

'I don't know,' Anne replied. 'I didn't see him with anything, but I was talking to someone else at the time. He just said goodbye and then he went.'

'What time was this?'

'Not long after we opened up,' Anne said. 'Nearly ten, I think.'

And then he went straight to the police, Laura thought, before saying, 'Come with me.'

Anne looked suddenly scared. 'I don't want to

247

see him,' she said. 'Not if he's dead.'

'No, not that,' Laura said. 'I want to go to the office with you, because if Doctor Barker didn't take anything with him, whatever he was looking for must still be there. Come to the car.'

Anne thought about that, and then nodded her agreement. Laura could feel Anne's nervousness as they walked to Joe's car. Once Anne had climbed into the back, Laura gestured for Joe to join her.

'What is it?' he asked, once he reached her.

'We've got a lead,' Laura whispered, talking over the roof of the car and pointing towards the back seat. 'Barker was at his old office this morning, looking for details of a former patient, just before he came to Blackley.'

'Sounds promising,' Joe said, and climbed into the driver's seat, turning around just to smile a hello.

The journey was a short one, Anne taking them through side streets lined by shops selling seaside buckets and metallic balloons. As they followed her into the building where she worked, Laura wondered what her new employers would think about her bringing the police with her. She didn't have to wait long to get her answer, because as Anne took them along a corridor lined by cheap carpet tiles, a door opened further along and a man with skeletal features and greying hair cropped right down to his skull appeared in front of them.

'Can I help you?' he asked, his smile polite but firm, stretching his skin further. It seemed to Laura that his intention was to stop them rather

248

than help them.

Laura introduced herself, but before Joe could join in, the man said, 'I guessed what you were as soon as I saw you. The question was how I could help you. What is the answer to that?'

'Doctor Barker came here this morning, looking for something,' Laura said, fighting to keep the irritation out of her voice. 'We need to know what he was looking for.'

'Doctor Barker?' He looked at Anne, confused, and when she nodded, her eyes down, the man smirked. 'Why don't you just ask him?'

Laura glanced at Joe, who nodded. The secret was already out. 'He's dead,' Laura said bluntly. 'Killed, we think, because of whatever he found here this morning.'

The smirk disappeared as the man glanced over at Anne, who nodded tearfully and then cast her eyes to the ground again.

'Why didn't you tell us Rupert was here?' he whispered to Anne.

'I'm sorry, we haven't got much time,' Laura said, stepping closer. 'I just want to stop this happening to someone else.' She turned to Anne. 'Show me what he was looking at.'

'He went to the archive files,' Anne said.

The man didn't move. 'Those are still confidential files. I can't just turn them over.'

'We don't want the files. We just want to know which file he was looking at,' Laura said, as she stared him down.

'I can't see the difference,' he said.

'What about this then?' Laura said. 'If Doctor Barker was killed because of what he knew, then how do we know that other people here won't be next? Because the murderer will kill again.' She pointed at Anne. 'Maybe her, and perhaps even you.' Laura stepped closer. 'It's just the name. Nothing more. Which file did a murdered man look at just before he was killed? Or is your own personal pride worth more than someone's life?'

'It's a professional obligation,' he said, some uncertainty creeping into his voice.

'What about risking that to save some lives? Or is your professional obligation more important than saving a life?' Laura persisted.

The man considered that for a few seconds longer, and then stepped to one side. Anne walked towards a panelled wooden door halfway along the corridor, thick with decades of paint. Laura could see her hands trembling.

'The archives are down here,' Anne said, and she dug into her purse for the key. She pushed at the door and stepped inside to turn on the light. 'Everything is down there.'

'Come with us,' Laura said. When Anne flashed an uncertain look at her boss, Laura added, 'you will be able to tell us if anything has been moved.'

When Anne got the nod that she should co-operate, they all descended into the damp and cold of the cellar.

It was lined by wooden racks and piled high with boxes. The dust made Laura's nose itch, and then she exhaled loudly. Where should they start?

Joe stepped past her and began to read the dates on the boxes. 'You only treat children here?' he asked Anne, and when she nodded, he said, 'We'll need to go back a few years, as the newest boxes will make the patients too young.' He began to walk along, examining the outside of the boxes, not the contents. Then he stopped and reached for a box from the top shelf, just at his eye-level. He grunted with effort as he put it onto the floor. 'Nineteen eighty-five,' he said. 'The dust has been disturbed on the lid, and that would make him about the right age.'

Joe removed the lid and put it on the floor before he groaned. The box was filled with files, all lined up neatly.

'There are some more boxes here with marks in the dust,' Laura said, and grabbed the next one along.

'Get down all the boxes where the dust has been disturbed,' Joe said, and as he and Laura looked along the shelves, they saw there six boxes with marks on the lids. Laura watched as Joe popped the lid on each one in turn, they were all filled to bursting with files.

But the final box was different.

Joe looked into the box and then at Laura, before he got to his feet.

'There's your answer,' he said.

Laura had to agree. In all the other boxes, the files were lined up, filed away. In this box, however, one file had been removed and placed on top of the others.

Joe picked up the file. 'Shane Grix,' he said, as he read the name on the cover. Then he opened it and began to flick through the contents. Laura watched as his eyes widened.

Anne looked at Laura, uncertainty in her eyes. Laura raised a finger to her lips to ask her not to say anything.

Anne looked at the floor, her hands clasped in front of her, as Joe read. He flicked through the pages, sometimes pausing to consider something in more detail. After a few minutes, he handed the file back to Anne, who looked nervously at the cover.

'Thank you,' Joe said. 'You might have helped us catch a killer,' and as he rushed for the stairs, Laura followed quickly behind.

Chapter Forty-Three

As the sound of Adam's car disappeared into the hills, Jack grabbed his own car keys and headed outside. He needed to be at Bobby's school, in case his father was late. As he climbed into his car, he wondered what to do with the information he had been given. He wanted to write about Jane, but what Adam had told him fitted in with the piece he had partly finished for Dolby on the Whitcroft estate. Dolby wanted it to sneer at those who always came up against the tougher side of life, but Adam's version gave the story a villain: Don Roberts.

He went to turn on the engine, but then paused and reached for his phone. He dialled Dolby's number, who answered on the second ring.

'How late can I leave the Whitcroft story?' Jack said.

There was a pause, and then Dolby said, 'I

thought it was almost done.'

'It is, but I've got another angle,' Jack said.

'I don't want another angle.'

'This ties in with Jane Roberts, the dead woman.'

Jack could almost hear Dolby's thoughts as he pondered on whether to allow Jack extra time. Eventually, Dolby said, 'How so?'

'The security on the estate is managed by Jane's father,' Jack said.

'That's a tenuous link.'

'Not really. Jane had a good upbringing, much more affluent than those people on the estate, but it was partly paid for by them.'

'And with a tragic postscript, because Jane was killed,' Dolby said, and Jack could hear him thinking. 'Write it up, see how it comes out.'

'Will do.'

'It needs to go in tomorrow though. Two pages.'

'I know, I know, but this will add something to it.'

Dolby sighed at the other end, and Jack knew he had just earned himself a late night.

The car started on the first turn of the keys. It was a good omen. Bobby first, and then it was back to the Whitcroft estate.

Laura put her phone into her pocket. They were heading towards the last known address of Shane Grix.

'He doesn't appear on the system,' she said. 'If Shane Grix is dangerous, he's avoided detection.'

'For the last few years anyway,' Joe said. 'Remember there was a time when our computer records were not that good, and so if he's been off the radar for more than fifteen years, he might not appear.'

'And he might have changed his name,' she said. 'So if the name isn't known to us, what did you see in the file that got you so interested?'

Joe glanced over. 'Shane Grix,' he said. 'A quiet kid from a nice family. Adopted. It's a bit of the old nature versus nurture thing, I suppose, but it seems that in this case quiet also meant withdrawn, and bullied.'

'There's a child in every school who is bullied,' Laura said. 'It doesn't make it right, but it doesn't make it exceptional either.'

Joe smiled. 'Do you remember what I told you about why some children are cruel to animals, or set fires?'

'Power,' she said. 'Or, at least, how they react to feeling powerless. They strike back at things weaker than themselves.'

'Exactly, and that's why young Shane went to see a child psychologist. He was mistreating small animals.'

Laura could see the gleam in Joe's eyes, the academic side of him taking over, relishing the chance to chase a theory rather than a killer. She turned away and watched the seascape flash into view as they passed the ends of those streets that ran towards it, just glimpses of bright blue.

'But what was it about Shane that made Doctor Barker go looking for his file?' she asked eventually.

'It was the way he was mistreating them,' Joe said, as he turned onto a street of semi-detached houses, with large bay windows and glass porches. He looked out of his window as his car crept along, and then he stopped alongside a grass verge that separated the path from the road. 'This is Shane's address. Or at least it was all those years ago.'

Laura looked out of the car and saw dusty windows and net curtains. She could see the outline of china ornaments on the window sill, and there was a flower basket hanging from a hook by the front door, although the flowers looked tired and sagging.

They both climbed out of the car, and looked up at the house. There was no car in the driveway and Laura wondered whether anyone was home.

'Shane was a boy when he lived here,' Laura said. 'He will be long gone.'

'But we might get the local gossip,' he said. 'Look at these houses. These are not new-build starter homes. These are old-fashioned houses, where people bring up children and then stay in when they've retired. I didn't see a single *for sale* sign as we drove here. Even if Shane has moved, someone around here will remember him.'

Laura sighed. She had stopped questioning Joe's methods, because he usually had a plan. So she walked towards the front door and rang the bell.

As they waited, she looked down at the lawn and rose bushes. They were untidy, but there was some sign of maintenance. The grass had been cut recently, although the branches on the rose bushes looked like they'd never been pruned.

No one came for a while, and they were about

to turn around, when Laura saw a white shimmer behind the frosted glass in the porthole in the door. Someone was coming.

The door was opened on a chain, milky-blue eyes and pale mottled skin peering at them through the gap in the door. Laura pulled out her identification, and for a moment, the old woman's eyes widened.

'Is it Mrs Grix?' Laura asked.

The woman on the other side of the door slammed it shut, but as Laura and Joe exchanged glances, Laura heard the jangle of the chain and realised that she was just taking it off its clasp.

'Is it Amanda?' the old woman asked as the door opened, panic in her eyes. 'Is she all right?'

'Amanda?'

'My daughter, Amanda,' she said. 'Is that why you are here?'

'Is it Mrs Grix?' Joe repeated, stepping forward.

The woman nodded. 'Call me Ida.'

'Can we come in?' Joe asked. 'It's about your son, Shane.'

The woman reacted like she had been punched in the stomach, her hand going across her midriff as she let out a yelp. Then she stepped to one side and asked Joe and Laura to go into the room at the front.

As Joe went into the living room, Ida shuffled along the hall. Laura followed and saw Ida rest her hands against the kitchen counter, her head down. Her fingers were trembling. Laura was about to go to her, but Ida straightened and clicked on the kettle, her hands going to a cupboard for some cups.

Laura backed along the hallway and into the living room. Joe was in front of a large photograph over the fireplace. It was two teenagers, the girl a few years older than the boy, both in identical school uniforms – bright white shirts and purple ties. The boy was staring at the camera, blond hair, his mouth pulled into a half-smile, but he looked more like he was sneering at the camera, not smiling at it. There were other photographs of the girl. More glamorous shots of her in her late teens, and then she was holding a baby, a young mother in her twenties. There were more pictures on the window sill, and Laura saw how the teenage girl blossomed into a woman as she looked around the room. There were no more pictures of the teenage boy.

'Shane?' Laura said, pointing at the photograph.

'Probably,' Joe said. 'What is the old lady doing?'

'Making a drink, but something isn't right. She didn't ask about Shane once she knew it wasn't about Amanda.'

Laura stopped talking as Ida came in, holding a tray with three cups on it, along with a small sugar bowl and a plate of cakes. The cups jangled slightly as her hands shook.

'I hope tea is all right for you both. And please help yourself to something to eat,' Ida said, although she didn't look at either Laura or Joe as she said it.

Joe reached over to take a cup and an almond slice, although from the way that he took a small bite and then put it onto his saucer, Laura guessed it was all about keeping Ida onside.

257

'What can you tell us about Shane?' Laura asked.

Ida took a deep breath, and then she smiled, before reaching for the handkerchief that had been tucked into the sleeve of her cardigan.

'Just what you probably already know,' she said. 'He was a quiet boy, and we thought that it was just his way. He was secretive, and a bit of a loner. He could be sweet though, when he wanted to be.' She gave a small laugh. 'Usually when he wanted something.'

'Why did you take him to Doctor Barker?' Joe said.

Ida looked surprised. 'How do you know that?'

'We've just come from his surgery.'

Ida scratched at her cup with her fingernail, and then said, 'He became too withdrawn and quiet. When he did say things, they were cruel and hurtful. We did what we could, but it seemed like he hated us both. Then we bought him a hamster for a pet. He seemed pleased at first, but then it disappeared. Shane said that he had left the cage open, so we got him another one,' Ida took a deep breath and dabbed her nose with her handkerchief. 'I was tidying Shane's room one day and I found the first hamster under his bed. It was dead, but we knew that it hadn't died naturally.'

'Why?'

'Its head was twisted, and it had dust from its cage in its mouth.'

Laura and Joe exchanged glances.

'We were so worried,' Ida continued. 'He didn't have any friends and spent all his time in his

258

room. We didn't know what he was doing, because he wasn't playing music, and if we went in he was usually just sitting on his bed, looking ahead. That's why we bought him the hamster, because we thought it would help to draw him out. But look what happened. Then a friend recommended Doctor Barker. We took him along for a few sessions, but it was hard to get anything out of Shane, so we gave up. We couldn't afford the fees.'

Laura saw Joe's interest, his fingers drumming hard on his knees.

'How old was he when you adopted him?' Joe asked.

Ida looked shocked for a second, and then her fingers toyed with her handkerchief before she spoke. When she said, 'From birth,' her voice seemed more hostile than before. 'We'd tried for our own children, Ted and me, but we had just one. Amanda. We wanted more, and it was hard, knowing that she would grow up an only child. So we adopted.' Ida wrung her hands and her voice trembled when she said, 'But it didn't work out, and I felt like I was to blame.'

'Why do you say that?' Joe asked.

Ida's cheeks went red. 'I turned his real mother away,' she said. 'I shouldn't have done, but she wasn't a mother to him. She had abandoned him, and we were the ones who'd brought him up.'

Laura sat forward and lowered her head so that she could catch Ida's gaze. 'Shane was always going to want to know about his birth mother.' she said softly.

Ida flashed her a steely look that didn't fit with

her gentle appearance. 'It was wrong, I know that, but she wasn't good for him.' She twisted her handkerchief between her fingers. 'I know what you are thinking, that we were thinking just of ourselves. And maybe we were. Is there anything wrong with that? Have you got children?'

Laura toyed with her engagement ring and thought of Bobby for a moment, and how he was an only child.

'I've got a child,' Laura said. 'A boy.'

Ida softened for a moment and smiled. 'I can tell. I can see it in you. Contented but tired. If I see women your age without children, they usually look really relaxed because they've got easy lives, or else they look hungry somehow, as if they are chasing something to make up for not having children. But how would you feel if someone came along who wanted to take him away? You would fight for him, and that's what I did with Shane. So I wouldn't let her close.'

Laura reached out and took one of Ida's hands in hers. It was cold, and her skin felt delicate. 'You're right, I would fight it, just like you,' she said.

Ida squeezed Laura's hand for a moment. 'Being a mother isn't just about giving birth, you know that,' Ida said. 'It's everything else. The hugs, the teaching, the loving. Those midnight illnesses, holding the bowl as he was sick. His first day at school. Helping him with his homework. Reading to him at night. Just holding him and trying to make him feel safe. That's what being a mother is all about, and then *she* came along, wanting to take over.'

'But you could have let her have some access, because you knew that Shane would have wanted to know about her when he was older. It wouldn't have meant he cared for you any less.'

'You make me sound selfish,' Ida said, dropping Laura's hand. 'It wasn't like that. She was just a child really, and everything about her would have been bad for Shane.'

'What do you mean, bad?' Laura said.

Ida sighed. 'She was young when she had Shane, and perhaps that wasn't her fault, but she turned bad as she got older. She was drinking a lot, and taking drugs.'

'How do you know?'

Ida paused as she thought about that, and said, 'We just knew.' She looked down as she spoke.

Laura looked at Joe and raised an eyebrow. His eyes narrowed, and Laura knew that he was thinking the same thing – that there was something they weren't being told.

'And she was a prostitute,' Ida said, looking up now. 'She went to court a few times, we read about that. No, it was better that Shane didn't see her. When she turned up at the house, we wouldn't let her see him. She carried on though, and so we had to get the police involved. And then she stopped coming.'

'How did Shane take this?' Joe asked.

'He didn't know at first, but then one night she turned up, and Shane must have heard the argument. When I went into the hallway, Shane was looking through the stairs. He just looked angry, scowling, but he didn't say much.' A tear rolled down Ida's cheek. 'It was my fault Shane ended up like he did. He became even quieter after that, and more spiteful.'

Laura was about to ask a question, but Ida cut her off with a raised hand.

'I'm sorry for telling you that, but it was part of what made Shane the boy he was,' Ida said. Then she straightened herself, as if confession time was over. 'So what have you come to tell me? Have you caught whoever did it?'

Laura looked at Joe, confused. 'Did what?' she said.

It was Ida's turn to look bewildered. 'That's why you're here, isn't it? Have you got a lead in the case?'

'Which case?'

'Shane's death,' Ida said. 'Isn't that why you're here, to tell me you've got a suspect?'

Laura exchanged glances with Joe, and then said gently, 'No, I'm sorry, it's not why we're here.'

Ida looked hurt. 'It's a long time ago now, but if you are not here about that, why are you interested in Shane?'

'It's about Doctor Barker,' Laura said. 'I'm so sorry, but he's been found dead in his house. We're tracing his former patients, in case there's a connection.'

Ida's hand went to her mouth. 'Doctor Barker? How? When?'

'This lunchtime. I'm sorry, this must be quite a shock,' Laura looked at Joe, who was staring at the photograph over the fireplace.

'How did Shane die?' Joe asked.

Ida looked at Joe, surprised. 'Why don't you

know about this?'

'What do you mean?'

'Shane was murdered,' Ida said, and then took a deep breath before a tear tumbled down her cheek. 'Have the police forgotten about it already?'

Joe leaned forward. 'Could you tell me more,' he said.

Ida wiped her cheek and then sat back. She was looking at her hands when she started to speak.

'Shane wasn't an easy teenager,' she said. 'Some of the boys around here used to pick on him. We did what we could, tried to keep him safe, but boys want to do boy things, like youth clubs and school discos. And why shouldn't they? You can't let the bullies win. But those things attract some of the wrong sort, and so Shane would come home upset, and Shane being upset was different to most people, because he wouldn't cry or shout; he would go quiet, and he would be like that for a few days.'

'Did he do well at school?' Joe said. 'Sometimes quiet boys find an outlet in getting good marks at school.'

Ida smiled. 'Those are the boys who do well in the end,' she said. 'My husband used to tell Shane that. Be patient, he used to say, because all these bullies and thugs fail when they go into the world. They end up in court and then prison, or in dull jobs. Work hard, try hard, he used to say, and you will overtake them all, and then one day you'll see them pushing a line of supermarket trolleys or delivering your pizzas. But Shane didn't do that.' She looked at Laura, and then at Joe. 'He ran away,' she said.

'Where to?' Joe said.

'London,' Ida said. 'He called me once, just to let me know where he was. He said that I wasn't to worry, that he was doing well, and that he would come back one day and he would show us how well he was doing. I asked him why he went, and he said he just wanted the bright lights, away from his boring, northern life, where no one would know him and he could start again.' Ida shook her head and her fingers gripped the handkerchief tighter. 'It wasn't that. He just needed to be far enough away so that he couldn't get back easily.'

'So what did he do in London?' Laura asked.

'What most runaways end up doing when they go down there,' she said. 'The police said that the kids find it exciting at first, the big busy city, but then they end up sleeping in squats and dosshouses. It was the same for Shane. He must have been so frightened. And then drink becomes a thing, because it gives them something to do, and then it's drugs. Maybe it was always there, something that he got from his mother.' She wiped away her tears, and looked ashamed now, and when she spoke again, her voice was breaking, wretched and filled with emotion. She could barely finish her sentence. 'The police told me he was a prostitute for a while, because he looked younger than his age, and some men like that kind of thing.'

'How old was he?' Laura asked gently.

'When he ran away? Sixteen. As soon as he left school. He was nineteen when he died.'

Laura knew then why Shane's death hadn't cropped up when they'd run some checks on him on their way to the house. Police forces didn't share information back then, and the details of victims wouldn't have got a mention on the database.

'What theory were the police working on?' Joe asked. 'A client?'

Ida shook her head. 'No one knows. He was found dead in an alley behind King's Cross. He had been strangled, but this is the really cruel thing, that he had been set alight, so that I never really got a chance to make him look nice for his funeral.' She sighed. 'There wasn't much left to identify him from. Just the boots he always wore, old Doctor Martens with red and green laces, and an old donkey jacket. There were some papers in his back pocket, all charred. Turned out to be Shane's dole card. The police looked out for him at the benefits office, just in case it was someone else and Shane needed to make another claim, but he never showed again.'

'How can you be certain it was Shane?' Joe said.

Ida smiled at him with teary eyes. 'Because if Shane was alive, he would have got in touch, because even though he had problems, he loved us. I know it was Shane, and I know he has gone.' She dabbed her eyes with her handkerchief and said, 'I'm sorry this won't help you finding out who killed Doctor Barker. He tried his best for Shane, but we couldn't afford to keep going. It wasn't the doctor's fault things turned out like they did. Did you think Shane might have been

265

involved?'

Joe shook his head. 'We are going through his old patients, that's all, just to check that it isn't related. Shane was on the list.' He reached out and held her hand. 'I'm sorry we disturbed you, Ida. I know this must all be very painful for you. Thank you for the tea.'

She nodded to herself. 'Doctor Barker was a nice man. I hope you catch whoever killed him.'

Joe nodded and pumped her hand. 'So do I,' he said. 'So do I.'

They made their exit, and once they were outside, Laura whispered, 'What do you think?'

Joe waited until they were back in the car before he said anything. 'There are two possibilities. One is that Doctor Barker got it wrong.'

'And the other?'

'That he didn't.'

Laura smiled at that. 'That would be some trick, coming back from the dead.'

'The identification of the body was based on assumptions,' Joe said. 'It was burnt out, and so there was no fingerprint evidence. If Ida is right, the police assumed it was Shane Grix because of the clothes and his dole card, and because no one challenged it. It went into history as fact and Ida thinks she has lost her son. But what if it was wrong? Doctor Barker thought it was Shane Grix, and he was going to tell us that today. He died not long after. That is one hell of a coincidence.'

'Perhaps he took the file he wanted,' Laura said. 'How do we know he didn't look at the Shane Grix file, realise that he'd got it wrong, and then take the one he really wanted?'

266

'We don't, I suppose, but it seems strange that the one file he leaves untidy involves a young boy who died in questionable circumstances, a boy with serious psychological problems, and the personality traits I would expect in a killer.'

'So what do we do now?'

Joe checked his watch. Five o'clock. 'Why don't you call some of your old friends in the London Met and see whether they can find out anything about Shane's murder? It will still be a live file, as the killer wasn't caught.'

'We won't find out much tonight.'

'I know, but if they start tonight, we might have it for the morning.'

Chapter Forty-Four

The streets of Whitcroft seemed quiet as Jack drove onto the estate. It was creeping towards eight o'clock, and the estate was slipping towards darkness. The street lights were coming to life, but not many seemed to be working. There was a playground ahead, just visible from the silhouettes of climbing frames, and Jack thought he could see dark shapes moving between them, the night rats getting ready to take over.

Jack went first to Number 19, the house he'd visited earlier in the day. He wanted to see whether Don had paid the occupant a visit, and he got his answer straight away. The net curtain in front of the window had been pulled down, and there was a crack in one of the window panes that hadn't been there earlier.

He walked slowly up the path, worried about what he might find when he got inside. He pushed at the door and it swung open slowly. It was dark.

'Hello?' he shouted. There was no answer.

He stepped in further and flicked on a light. Furniture had been turned over. A small table lay broken against the wall and the glass shade from a lamp was smashed on the floor.

Jack whirled around when he heard a knock on the door. There was a man. He looked over seventy, his shoulders skinny in a blue nylon shirt, just grey wisps of hair over his ears.

'What are you doing, lad?' he said. Despite his years, his voice was strong.

'Writing a story on the estate,' Jack said as he backed out of the house.

'You a reporter?' and when Jack nodded, he added, 'be careful what you say.' He turned to walk back to the house next door.

'What do you mean?'

'There are some who don't like what's happening to this place.'

'Do you?' Jack shouted after him.

The old man stopped and turned round. 'No, but it's not for me to speak up.'

'Why not?'

'Because I'll get trouble, and I'm too old to want it.'

'What about here?' Jack said, nodding back towards the empty house.

'Probably won't pay the security fees,' the old

man said.

'Did you hear what happened?'

The man nodded. 'A couple of hours ago.'

'Is he all right, the man who lives here?'

'I saw him walk out, if that's what you mean, but I don't think he will be coming back.'

'What makes you think that?'

'He had a bag with him, and I could tell from the way he looked back at the house.'

'Does it bother you, that you might be the next one to be forced out?'

The old man smiled and shook his head. 'No, lad, because I pay my dues.'

'Who to?'

'Who do you think?' he said. 'The security firm that you see driving around the estate.' He stepped closer. 'I wasn't old enough to fight in the war, but I knew people who did, and compared to those men, these thugs aren't brave. Just bullies.'

'So why do you pay?'

He gave a rueful smile. 'I'm old, not long left. I don't want to spend it cleaning paint off my walls or dodging flying glass.'

'But that means giving into them.'

'The price of a quiet life.'

'Would you be prepared to go in my story?' Jack said.

The old man shook his head. 'That wouldn't make my life easier, would it?' he replied. 'But good luck with it, because I wish they weren't there.'

'What about the police? Can't they help out?'

'Oh, they do, when they come around. I've seen the van driving around sometimes, but it's got orange bloody stripes all over it. The kids and drunks see it and hide. Once it's gone, it's back to normal.'

Jack scribbled some notes and thanked him. Just before he was about to leave, Jack said, 'Just give me a quote. What is it like to live on Whitcroft?'

'Like the country,' he said. 'Turned to shit.'

And with that, he turned and went back into his house.

The Incident Room bore the scars of a hard day's investigation. There was a dirty cup on every desk, alongside mounds of papers, print-outs of incident logs and crime reports and intelligence sheets. People were leaning back in their chairs, their top buttons undone, ties hanging slack halfway down their shirts.

Carson was at the back of the room, looking over someone's shoulder at a computer screen. Rachel Mason was in the middle of three male detectives, her stream of blonde hair standing out against the strident blue of her blouse. She was going through some papers on her knee, separating them into three piles on the floor. To Laura, it looked like she was sifting through suspects, because she had made three piles: possible, maybe and unlikely. She didn't look up as Laura moved through the room, but when Joe appeared in the doorway, she sat up more attentively.

There was a new photograph stuck to the notice board at the front. Laura turned to Carson, shocked. 'Is that the woman who didn't arrive home last night?' she asked.

Carson straightened himself. 'Caroline Holt. She hasn't turned up yet, which is out of character for her. It's not looking good.'

Laura went closer to it. If she was a victim, it was because Laura had escaped, which made her feel responsible. Caroline was smiling in the photograph, a glass of wine in one hand, her mousy hair pulled back into a high ponytail.

'What's the news from Cleveleys?' Carson asked.

Laura took hold of his arm and pulled him over to the side of the room. 'It's the same killer,' she whispered. 'Doctor Barker, the man who was at the station this morning, was found strangled, with Jane Roberts' knickers jammed into his mouth. Which means that it must be someone who knew he was here. It's too much of a coincidence.'

Carson looked around the room and put his hands on his hips. 'We've got to trust the team. We can't operate if we don't. Is there anything to get excited about from the scene?'

'Nothing obvious, but he might have left some trace behind. We'll find out tomorrow hopefully. The panties are the best chance, because my guess is that he didn't plan on leaving those somewhere else when he first took them from Jane.'

Carson thought about that, and then said, 'Anything else? When we spoke earlier, you said that Doctor Barker had gone to his office before he came here.'

'He came here to tell us something, but then changed his mind,' Laura said. 'When he got home, he was killed. The file we thought he had

271

been looking at related to someone called Shane Grix.'

'So we've got a name,' Carson said, surprised.

Laura grimaced. 'Shane is dead. Murdered in London. I've called a friend in the Met to see what they've got. He's going to have a dig around and get back to me in the morning.'

'Why are we bothered, if he's dead?' Carson said, turning to look at Joe, who had joined them.

'Because it bothered Doctor Barker, and now he's dead,' Joe replied. 'And I know why it bothered him.'

'Go on.'

'Because Shane used to torture animals. His own pet hamster, the school guinea pigs, kittens that belonged to a neighbour. I had a good read of his file, and this is the thing: he would jam sawdust and dirt into their mouths and backsides.'

There were murmurs of surprise. Carson's eyes widened. 'Why the hell would he do that?'

'Doctor Barker asked him the same question, and it was all down to squeamishness. Can you believe that? Young Shane Grix couldn't stand the noise and mess, because when the animals got scared, they would squeal and shit and piss all over him. So he jammed things in their mouths and elsewhere.'

Carson shook his head. 'He tortured animals and he was fucking squeamish?'

'It seems that way,' Joe said, nodding. 'But you have to remember why he was doing it. He was hitting back.'

'At what?'

272

'The local bullies, all those kids who taunted him for being different. His mother tried to help, in her own way, by giving him too much love, but he wasn't the loving type. He hurt animals because it gave him some satisfaction, as if he was hitting out at those who hurt him.'

'But animals are not inanimate,' Carson said, picking up on the theme. 'They get frightened and screech and crap on your clothes.' He shook his head. 'There are some really weird ones out there.'

'There always have been, but then things happen to them that change them,' Joe said. 'If he'd grown up somewhere different, where the kids were less cruel, or if his parents had taught him how to deal with bullies better…'

'Or karate,' Carson said.

'Yes, or taught him karate,' Joe agreed. 'People find ways to deal with the crowd. Some people learn to be funny, or choose to run with the pack rather than against it. Some even form their own little clique, like minds together, the chess club types, but they're all just trying to cope with life. Except that some don't do it as well as others, and so they end up like Shane Grix. Miserable, lonely and resentful.'

'And dead,' Carson said. 'The families don't know anything about Emma.'

'So we think. If Doctor Barker was still alive, I would tell him that he'd just got it wrong, but now he's dead too, with underwear from the second victim jammed into his mouth.'

'So what now?' Carson said.

'We wait to hear back from the Met,' Joe said.

'Or else we hope that he made a mistake with Doctor Barker. It was more spontaneous, and so we have a higher chance of getting a forensic result.'

As Carson thought about that, Joe went to sit next to Rachel Mason. As Laura watched them, she spotted something. A look that passed between them. A flirt. A smile.

Laura smiled to herself. Now she knew why Joe was cagey about his private life, and why Rachel was frosty whenever Laura got too close to Joe, because it seemed like Joe and Rachel were more than just colleagues.

Joe must have caught her looking, because he returned the smile and looked embarrassed. Laura was about to say something when someone shouted 'Shit!' from the back of the room.

'What is it?' Carson asked, walking over.

Laura and Joe lost their smiles as they watched Carson's expression change as he read something from a computer screen. Then he stood up and stroked his cheek, a puzzled look on his face.

'We have a problem,' he said. 'We've got the results back from Google and it looks like the emailer used proxy servers.' There were some confused looks. 'He went to proxy websites and accessed the web-based email through those, as the proxy websites provide internet addresses that are random and not recorded. People use proxy servers when they've got something to hide – like people who look at kiddie porn, or fraudsters.'

'So we've hit a dead end?' Laura asked. 'Like with Emma.'

Carson shook his head. 'Not quite. Remember

the two emails he sent yesterday morning, the one about finding *the newspaper not writing all the details unamusing* and *Ask them about Emma?* Well, they came from an internet address that is very close to home.' He pointed downwards. 'Right here.'

There were gasps.

'He accessed his email from a police computer,' Carson said, looking around the room.

'So he is a police officer then,' Laura said.

'It was just possible before,' Carson said. 'Now it's a definite, which means that he can find out about the investigation. Leads. Witnesses. Forensic results. So we are going back to pen and paper. Don't put any witness details on the computer. Everything stays in this room. No one must talk about the case outside this room. The squad has got to be locked down. He must not know how we are getting on.'

People looked serious, but Carson broke the mood by smiling and saying, 'He might have just made his first mistake.'

Chapter Forty-Five

Jack continued to drive around the estate, looking for something that would define the story. The differences in the houses were stark. Many were pristine, with well-tended gardens and shiny double-glazing brightened by his headlights, but they sat next to houses that seemed just the opposite, with cracked or broken windows, the walls splattered with paint and eggs. Graffiti covered many doors, with words like *paedo* or *nonce* sprayed in black. On others, the letters *WYD* were sprayed in large letters.

As he drove, the darkness seemed like a cloak, as whole groups of houses seemed to fade into the night, with street lights broken, and the further he went, the more obvious it became that the lights were broken where the damage was being caused, so that it seemed deliberate, to create a dark space for people to do what they would rather not be seen doing.

He turned into another street, a long stretch of townhouses and three-storey blocks of flats, when his lights caught a group outside a house. He heard shouts and laughter, but it was mocking, not fun. They were dressed in black, although he caught the glimmer of a bike wheel. They must have known he was there, but they didn't look round. He heard shouts of encouragement, and then something crashed on the floor, like a garden pot being broken.

Jack stopped and climbed out of his car. He was wary, but he knew that Dolby would want this in the story. He pulled out his camera and pointed it towards the group. There was a shout when the flash went off, the burst of light showing up a group of teenagers, pale faces in dark hoods. Some had scarves over their mouths, so all Jack saw was the gleam in their eyes.

'What the fuck are you doing?' someone shouted, with the deep burr of a man's voice in a wiry adolescent body.

Jack heard the group move closer to him, the movement just shifting shadows. 'Do you want to be in the paper?' Jack said, trying to keep the edginess out of his voice.

'Fuck, no,' the same voice said, behind Jack now.

Jack was in darkness, the street light above him not working. He could hear them bouncing around him, muttering, cursing.

'Which paper?' someone else asked, the voice higher-pitched this time.

'Just the local one. I'm writing about the estate.'

They all laughed but Jack stayed still. He wasn't sure how this would go. He knew he could deal with them one-on-one, but he was outnumbered, in the dark, and he had written enough court stories to know that some teenagers didn't know when to stop hitting.

'Why are you throwing things at the house?' Jack said.

'Who said we were throwing things?' the deep voice countered.

Jack's eyes were becoming accustomed to the darkness now, and he saw that the leader was leaning forward across his handlebars, staring, just his eyes visible above his scarf.

'What does WYD stand for?' Jack said.

'Whitcroft Young Defenders,' someone said, making them all whoop with laughter, apart from the leader, who didn't move or say anything.

'Defending it from what?' Jack said.

The laughing subsided, and the leader edged forward with his bike, until Jack felt the tyre hit his shin. 'What the fuck has it got to do with you?'

Everyone else fell silent, and Jack felt the mood turn more hostile.

'Because I'm writing all about you,' Jack said. 'Don't you want a starring role? Be more famous than the other gangs, if that is what you are.'

'People know who we are.'

'So what about that house? Won't they pay their dues?'

'I don't know what you mean.'

'Come on, you don't seem like the stupid type. You all work for Don Roberts, I guessed that much, earning cigarette money by making people sign up for his security firm.'

The tyre jabbed against Jack's legs.

'You need to be more careful what you say.'

They were interrupted by a beam of light, and as he looked, Jack saw that it was the security van with the two security guards he had seen earlier. It came to a stop by the pavement, and the leader rolled towards it on his bike. He leaned in and exchanged whispers with the passenger, and then he looked back and gave Jack a slow salute.

'See you around,' he said, and started to ride off down the road, the other youths following.

Jack let out a long breath and then went over to the van.

'You boys work long hours,' Jack said. 'I hope he pays well.'

The small one scowled. 'It would be a shame to see your car get damaged.'

'Round here, with you boys on duty?' Jack said, and then shook his head. 'You keep the estate crime-free, don't you? For a fee.'

'Those who pay get the protection,' he said.

Jack nodded towards his car. 'Is this going to cost me?'

The security man shook his head, and Jack caught the gleam of his teeth. 'Call it a trial period.'

'How long will it last?'

He smiled at Jack, but there wasn't too much humour in it. 'Your car will be fine,' he said, and Jack guessed the hidden meaning, that there wouldn't be any problems as long as he didn't write about the security situation.

'Thanks for that,' Jack said. 'Back to work though,' and he stepped away from the van.

He expected them to follow as he approached the house that had been the target of the youths, but instead the van set off, the path bathed in darkness once more as the headlights went around the corner.

He went slowly along the path, knowing that there was debris. His feet caught the shards of a broken plant pot, and he felt the soil and flowers underfoot. There was the tinkle of broken glass as he reached the door. He rapped hard on the wood.

There was no reply at first, but he could see the soft glow of a bulb inside the house, and so he knocked again. He was about to walk away when he heard coughing from the other side of the door. When it swung open, he saw a tall woman, messy straw-coloured hair that was streaked with grey, her face in shadow from the hall light behind her head.

She didn't say anything. She swayed slightly, and Jack caught the smell of drink.

'I'm a reporter,' he said. 'I just want to ask you about the damage that's been caused to your house.'

She put her hand against the door frame to steady herself. 'I've got nothing to say,' she said, and the words came out with a deep slur.

'What, you want them to get away with it?' Jack said. 'Why don't you call the police?'

The woman shook her head. 'There's no point,' she said and went to close the door.

Jack put his hand out to stop it. 'I'm a journalist. I'm doing a piece on the estate. It might stop if you go public.' He pulled out a business card from his pocket. 'Call me if you want to talk about the estate,' he said.

She took it from him and stared at it for a few seconds, before she slammed the door shut, leaving Jack in complete darkness.

He turned away, thinking that he finally had the makings of an article.

David Hoyle's home was ahead of him, on the other side of the field. He tried to focus. Stick to the plan. No more diversions.

It was one house converted from a small row of almshouses, so it was like a long bungalow with lots of windows. He had watched Hoyle go out before, and so there would be only one person in the house: Angel, his girlfriend. He smiled. He'd done his research.

He stepped out of his van and took a deep breath, felt it force out the noises, so that he could hear just the rush of his blood, everything else on hold, waiting for the aftermath. There was a path along the field that hugged a high hedge and ended next to Hoyle's home. An escape route.

He walked nonchalantly and pulled on his gloves, tight latex so that he could still feel through them. He tried to look natural, aware that if someone looked out from the houses opposite he would appear suspicious to them. His mouth was dry though, and he was aroused, beads of sweat on his lips. He had to be careful. He didn't want to leave a trace of DNA.

The path took him onto the street and so he made straight for a gate that led to the back garden. He reached for the latch, careful to make sure it didn't creak.

As the gate swung open, the street light outside caught the bright colours of garden blooms. He closed the gate slowly and began to move along the stone wall, the edges sharp, making soft swishes against his clothes. He didn't want to trip a security light, but when he got a full view of the garden, he saw that there was a light shining over the lawn at the back of the house. He sidled to the corner and slowly peered round, letting the room come into view. It was the dining room, a long table stretching towards the back doors, with a kitchen to one side, filled with brushed aluminium and utensils hanging from racks. There was no one there, and as he moved closer, he realised that he could see right through into the living room.

He kneeled down to the flowerbed and scooped up some handfuls of dirt, jamming it into his pocket. His hand pressed on the door handle at the back. It was unlocked. She must be in. He felt

281

his excitement grow, and so he tried to stop his heavy breaths, coming faster now, his tongue flicking onto his lip. He wasn't wearing a mask. He didn't expect any witnesses.

The door creaked on its hinges and he paused, waited for the rumble of feet or for someone to call out, but there was nothing.

Why had she left the door unlocked? She had made a choice to put herself at risk.

As he slipped inside, he noticed that it was warm in the house, the air filled with the cloying smell of plug-in air fresheners and the remnants of a microwave meal. He smiled. Dining for one. He thought back to the house layout. Three almshouses knocked through into one. There was a dining room at the end of the house, next to the kitchen. The living room was in the middle, occupying the space of what would have been the next almshouse, and the bedrooms were further along.

He moved slowly through the dining room and headed for the living room. He listened out for the sound of the television, his breathing as quiet as he could make it. He could hear chatter further into the house, just small mumbles of conversation. He stopped. Did she have a friend over? Two people would be hard to take on. He stopped to listen out more, but then he realised that he could only hear one voice. She must be on the telephone.

The living room was empty, the television just a black screen.

He moved towards the archway that led into a corridor separating the three bedrooms. The silence in his head was too quiet, the voices stopped, waiting for him to act, the ecstasy of the release.

The sound of her voice got louder. If she was on the phone it would have to be quick, silently grabbing her before she could say anything, although he grinned when he thought of what the person on the other end might hear. Her cries, muffled, maybe a struggle.

The first bedroom door was ajar, and so he pressed his ear against it. The room seemed silent. He gave the door a gentle push. No one was in there, just paintings scattered around the room.

He backed out of the room and went to the next one along. The door looked closed, but he saw that it wasn't clicked shut. He put his ear to the door. He could hear that one voice again, but there was something else too. He stopped his breaths so he could work out what it was. It was a clicking, scratching sound, fast but irregular. Then it came to him. It was the sound of finger-nails on a keyboard, broken by the occasional laugh or murmur. She was on a computer. He patted his back pocket, felt the handcuffs, his knife in the belt of his trousers.

He pushed gently on the door, ready to rush to her if there was a creak. His mouth was open to keep up with his breaths as the room came slowly into view.

The walls were light, but coloured blue by the glow of the screen. The carpet was thick, so that as he stepped inside his footsteps were silent. The air seemed warm and moist, and he could smell lavender. She must have just come out of the bath.

He saw her. She was facing a computer screen, headphones on, an instant messaging program open. She was wearing a long T-shirt, and her legs were bare.

His back brushed lightly against the wall as he got closer. She was engrossed in the screen and so she didn't see him, wasn't aware of him. He held his breath, not wanting to give himself away, but he knew she would become aware soon, even through the headphones. His hands reached behind for the handcuffs. Her fingers were slender, her fingernails manicured, graceful as they flitted across the keys, the glare from the screen catching the whiteness of her teeth.

He moved across the room, away from the comfort of the wall, lightly stepping on the soft carpet. He was almost behind her now. He could reach out and touch her hair, long dark strands flowing down her back.

Then she stopped typing and stared at the monitor.

He stepped back quickly. He had seen someone else on the screen. A woman's face, the close-up distortion of a webcam. And she had seen him. He had come into view of the webcam. There was a witness. Why hadn't he thought of that?

The noises rushed back into his head. They had been waiting for this moment. The fail, the mistake. He clamped his ears. There were laughs and whispers and mocking jeers. Then there was a scream from the room. It was her. She was screaming, her legs up to her chest, her eyes wide with fear. People would hear.

He turned to run. This wasn't how it was supposed to be. The door flew back as he ran through it, his feet loud on the hardwood flooring in the living room. He was heading for the same way out when he saw the front door. It would be quicker.

The door had a Yale lock, and he gave it a quick turn. He felt the cool breath of the evening air as soon as he stepped outside, making his sweat turn cold.

He heard another scream, but the door was open now and it carried into the street. He imagined the curtains moving on the houses opposite, and so he ran for the track, his heart beating quickly. He was angry with himself. He should have thought about the webcam when he heard the clicks on the keyboard. Someone had seen him.

He tried to shut that thought out as he ran, concentrating only on his escape, his feet thumping against the grass, the jingle of the handcuffs loud in the dark.

If he could just get to his van before he was spotted, no one would ever know.

Chapter Forty-Six

Jack drove around the estate, feeling better about his article.

He glanced towards the playground he had seen earlier. He heard laughter and then the sound of a bottle breaking on the floor, provoking more laughter. Jack looked to the houses opposite, expecting to see the twitch of a curtain to see what was going on, but there was nothing.

He drove past a building that was in the middle of the estate, and the sign on the front told him that it was the Whitcroft Community Centre. It was like most community centres: a square brick building with aerosol artwork decorating the outside walls, the wheelchair ramp bordered by a rail with paint flaking from it. He didn't need to go inside to know that it would look like all the others – painted cream, with a wooden floor marked out for a basketball court and filled with flimsy metal chairs that packed away in high stacks.

It hadn't escaped the attention of the local kids though. The sign was broken in places, and two of the windows were boarded up.

Jack drove on, not understanding why someone would want to destroy so much around them. He headed for the road out of the estate, and once the broken lights of Whitcroft were left behind he thought about Don, and the contrast between his own life and the lives of the people who paid for his services.

Jack turned into the leafy street that took him towards Don's house. It curved gently, and the only things that obscured the street lights were the branches of the trees that swayed in the breeze. There were no cars on the road. They were all pulled onto driveways, two for each household, mostly new.

He drove close to the copse where Jane had been found, and so he stopped. He positioned his car so that the headlights illuminated the patch of trees. The light caught a piece of crime scene tape that was left tied to a silver birch, just fluttering. Apart from that, it had returned to what it had been before.

Jack resolved to visit it in the morning, because the small piece of tape would make for a good photograph if the killer stayed free, some kind of metaphor for how time was moving on and the victims would be forgotten. Except that the memories of Jane's murder would linger in the minds of those who looked at it every day, and for Don Roberts and Mike Corley, the memory would never go away.

Jack set off again, and as he got closer to Don's house he saw cars cluttering the road. It looked like there was a meeting.

Jack drove past and then turned round so that he could watch. He was curious. What were they planning? Was another suspect going to be driven from their home, or even worse?

He had only been there for a couple of minutes when the front door opened, throwing light onto the driveway. Someone came rushing out, animated, turning to shout something. Jack leaned forward to get a better view through the windscreen. He recognised the figure. David Hoyle. Then Jack saw his car parked further along. He should have spotted it, a Mercedes with a personalised plate. He had seen it parked outside court many times.

Jack was surprised. What was David Hoyle doing there?

Hoyle turned back to whoever was in the doorway. He was waving his arms, finger pointing, and then he walked away, heading for his car. Jack started his engine, making David Hoyle look around. Jack set off towards him, and as he drew alongside, he wound down his window.

'Good evening, Mr Hoyle,' Jack said. 'Must be a big pow-wow to bring you out here. Why are you rushing off?'

Hoyle looked surprised and glanced back towards Don's house. The front door was closed now.

'Mr Hoyle?'

'Leave me alone,' Hoyle said, his tone more fearful than angry.

'Something has happened, I can tell.'

He held Jack's gaze for a few seconds, and Jack thought he was about to say something, Hoyle's lips twitching and pursing, but instead he opened his car door and started his engine.

Hoyle pulled away quickly, and as Jack watched the rear lights disappear round the curve ahead, he knew that whatever had made Hoyle bolt out of Don's house wasn't good news.

He'd raced home and concealed his van under tarpaulin at the back of the house. He was back in the small space with his computer, the door closed tightly so that the rest of the house was shut out. But it wasn't enough, the noises still made their way in. His hands were clamped around his ears. The noise was a clamour. The taps had turned into screeches, like nails down blackboards, and there was laughter, mocking shrieks.

He felt unsettled, still too aroused. He had skipped through his photographs. Shots of Jane, of

Deborah, their faces pale and still. And the others from before he came to Blackley. The pictures took him back through his memories, and he relived the struggles, the fear. He thought of the girl from the night before. He hadn't taken a picture, he hadn't had time. There had been just the release and then a short drive to the canal, stones weighing down her pockets. There would be no discovery. Not yet anyway. It wasn't enough. He wanted a bigger high, his hands around someone else's neck, the feel of their pulse, a drumbeat against his outstretched palm.

He wanted to go out again, but he stopped himself. It wouldn't be right. No more mistakes. Wait for tomorrow.

There would be no sleep, he knew that. Not now. It was time to plan.

Chapter Forty-Seven

Jack held up the wine bottle to the light. Probably only a glass left in it. It was close to midnight now, and he was alone in the house. He hadn't heard from Laura for a few hours, and he remembered the incident from the night before, when she was almost run down. He wanted to know she was safe. There was a killer to catch, he knew that, but she didn't have to sacrifice herself to do it. The screen swam in front of him and his fingers roamed clumsily across the keyboard, the sound of his tapping fingernails echoing loudly in the house.

He had written the story on Jane, but Jack didn't expect Don to like it. It had been written as a lead-in to the Whitcroft article, speculating on whether there was a link between the estate and the murders. The quotes from some of the people Jack had spoken to earlier had made it in as unnamed sources, and a connection had started to emerge, but it seemed loose and vague, as if there was still something missing.

Jack was browsing the internet, looking at the newspapers and sport stories, when there was a ping from the email software. He poured himself another glass of wine, stumbling a little, dropping some onto the table top, and then he opened the email.

It was from the same source as before, except that this time it had the title *Hoyly Moyly*. Jack leaned forward to read it, took a long sip, and then he stopped and put his glass down. The email made no sense.

He read it again.

Oh Angel, why did you scream?
It was a perfect plan, an evening dream,
Deviance and pleasure,
Something to treasure,
Bold on a summer night,
Man was out,
Looking after wolves,
Angel was in,
Watching out for me,
Your cries fall on devil ears,
Mine mount to storm fury,
Oh Angel, why did you scream?

Jack sat back and ran his hands through his hair as he tried to shake off some of the alcohol fog. As poetry, it was poor, but there was a message there. The taunts, the spitefulness, they were all familiar.

He felt the effect of the wine subside as he thought about the message. He knew his mind needed to be clear to work it all out. He clicked *reply*, and when the dialogue box came up, he typed:

So how are they all connected? Don is into security. Mike Corley is a local copper. Where's the link? Who is Emma? And who is the Angel from your email? You want your story told. Talk to me.

Jack went to the window and noticed again how dark the hills were. He felt like he couldn't do anything until he got a reply. It didn't take long to arrive. He went to the computer nervously, and sat down when he saw the contents.

There is always a connection. I'm going faster than before and sometimes it feels like it is too fast. But I have spotted a female. You know her, ha ha. Just need to work out the details.

So now you know I'm real, what next. Do I deserve a name, a title? The papers always like that. What do you think? Can you think of a name?

And then Jack remembered the scene from earlier in the evening, the fear etched onto David Hoyle's face. *Hoyly Moyly.*

Jack took the wine bottle to the kitchen and poured the contents of his glass down the sink. He went to the doors and windows, checked that everything was locked. He had an early start the next day, and a very long night ahead.

Chapter Forty-Eight

The morning had been a long time coming.

He had been awake all night, his mind filled by memories of the night before. They ran through his mind as fast flickers. The woman in her bedroom, talking into the webcam, in her panties, one leg pulled up to her chest. Her frightened look when she saw him. He waited for the tremble of arousal, but it didn't come. He felt unfulfilled. He tried to recall the other two women. Deborah. Jane. Young. Perfect skin. Blonde streaks in Deborah's brunette hair. Arms folded. Angry. Self-contained. The look of surprise. Dragging her into the van. Then that knowledge, the awareness that she was going under. She surrendered.

He still didn't feel finished. He thought back to the other woman from earlier in the week, the one he had dragged into the alley. He didn't know her name. He tried to use that, but the memory was no good. It hadn't been right. Too spontaneous. Just another woman. He thought he was past that.

He stared up at the Artex ceiling. Daylight had spread across it now. He could see a spider in the corner, winding its silver tracks. He thought he could hear it, soft shuffles across the paintwork, but then as he concentrated, he realised it was something else. Faint murmurs. The whispers that came to him when he was unfulfilled.

He looked down. His hands were gripping the

sheets, his knuckles white. He wasn't going into work today. It wouldn't matter any more after today. He knew who he wanted. He was missing one last piece. The need that screamed to him when everything else was quiet.

His thoughts flashed back to the night before. Not even the fear in her eyes was enough to satisfy him. That was just a taster, and it had been a mistake. He hadn't thought it through.

He threw back the covers. He needed more. He wouldn't be distracted.

As the thought of his target for the day came to him, he smiled and felt himself grow hard. But no, not yet. Don't dampen the fire.

Chapter Forty-Nine

Jack woke up filled with determination, the emails fresh in his mind. Once again, Laura had come home after he'd gone to bed, and left before he'd woken up.

He showered, dressed and headed into Blackley. He drove straight to where Jane Roberts had been found. The drive helped to clear his head, the roof down on the Stag, the wind ruffling his hair, almost like a gentle massage.

When he got there, he saw that the crime scene tape was limp, the light breeze from the night before gone, so that the loose end trailed into the shrubs and weeds. The sound of his car door seemed to echo in the trees as he climbed out and wandered towards the patch of ground where Jane had been found. It had been trampled by the boots of the police, the greenery moved to one side, all the bark and branches from around her body collected and taken away. The area around was uneven and thick with leaves, large twigs and ivy trails that snagged at his feet as he walked. Jane's killer had chosen a difficult place to leave the body, a place where the chances of falling and hurting himself were high. It would only take a small piece of DNA, like a splash of blood on a leaf, to make any case easier to prove against him. The ground was hard, so it would have been very difficult to bury the body. And of course the killer didn't even try to do that.

He looked around. The location was just so ordinary, and in such public view. Jane's killer would have been spotted if someone had looked out. So why here?

He looked along the path that disappeared into the trees. There was a woman further along, a small terrier trotting in front of her. She was bending down, a plastic bag over her hand, picking up the dog's mess.

As Jack looked along the path, he saw that it pulled to the right just as it disappeared into the shroud of trees. It suddenly struck him that Don Roberts' house was only a few hundred yards to the right and there was a fair chance that the path may end up near there.

But it wasn't just that. It was the woman with the dog, who was now walking past quickly, her head down. Don Roberts had a dog. He remembered its snarl from Don's visit. Did Don use this path?

Jack scrambled back up to the path and started to walk along it. The sunlight disappeared as the shade of the trees took over and it became slightly cooler. The floating pollen was suddenly replaced by the buzz and flicks of midges and flies.

The path started off as tarmac and then turned into gravel as it followed the line of the stream. The small copse turned into woodland, with large sycamores and horse chestnut blotting out the noise from the nearby road, and so all he could hear was the trickle of the stream and the sing song of the birds in the trees, the peace broken only by the steady crunch of his shoes.

He stopped when he thought he heard something behind him, or saw something, just at the edge of his vision, but when he looked around there was no one there. He tried not to think about what had happened near here a few days ago.

As Jack looked ahead, he saw the trees thinning out, and the bright red of new bricks started to appear in thc gaps between the trees. He began to walk quicker. His guess had been right.

He jogged the last part, fast crunches on the gravel as he went up a small rise and then onto tarmac again, his feet stopping before a grass verge. He looked along the road and smiled. There it was, the home of Don Roberts, with its pillars and its cars. He looked back along the path. The shadows had taken hold again, the path made dark and quiet by the trees. He turned back to the road. It didn't deviate too far from the path. Jane had been going out for the night on her own, and Jack knew that she would have taken the road; she wouldn't have wanted to go into the pub with dog shit and gravel dust on her shoes. Then Jack thought of the first murder. Deborah Corley. Her body had been left hanging out of a pipe that protruded from a grass bank next to a reservoir. He thought about that location. Why had it been chosen? Jack reasoned that Jane Roberts had been left near where she was attacked, because it was near where she had walked, but Deborah Corley was different. She had last been seen walking from her college, along a quiet road that would have taken her straight home. It wasn't near the reservoir.

He started off down the path again, rushed back to his car and clambered in, breathless. He headed for the ring road, shooting past the car showrooms and electrical superstores that lined the dual carriageway. Once he turned off though, the neon lights and traffic noise soon faded, as the road climbed upwards towards the tall green banks of the reservoir. Overspill pipes jutted out, water dribbling gently into small concrete gulleys that ran towards the river.

It seemed a strange place to leave a body, because it involved effort. The sides of the reservoir were exposed, and as Jack parked and then climbed the concrete steps that took him to the top of the banking, he looked back and saw the stream of traffic on the ring road. It would be so easy to be seen. He looked along the water, lapping gently against the banks. There were some people fishing on the opposite side, reminding Jack that it was anglers who had found the body.

As Jack watched the fishing lines break the surface, the bright floats bobbing in the water, something niggled at him, a memory, something almost within reach. He thought back to the dog walker he had seen before, close to Don's house. It linked in with that somehow.

Then it came to him. When he had visited Mike Corley, there had been a bait box in the hallway, a fishing rod against the wall.

Jane and Deborah had been left in those places for another reason. He shivered. It meant that their deaths were more than just sex murders. They were acts of revenge. The path through the woods was the obvious place for Don to walk his dog, and so when he did, he was meant to find his decomposing daughter, perhaps sniffed out by his dog. Mike was a fisherman, and had probably fished at the reservoir. Perhaps it was his favourite spot. Jane and Deborah weren't meant to be found by a bunch of mischievous kids or anglers. They were supposed to be discovered by their fathers.

Now he just had to work out what Don and Mike had done that demanded such vicious revenge. But first, he had to see Laura.

Chapter Fifty

Laura leaned back in her chair and rubbed her eyes. It was only ten in the morning, but the long hours were taking their toll. She had managed to drag every shift manager into the station and had demanded a list of all those officers who'd been on duty when the emails had been sent from the police station. The technical people were trying to narrow it down to an individual terminal or log-in details, but it was slow going. There were countless computers being used at all times in the station, and they all went through one major server.

She was rescued from looking at the list of names when her phone vibrated on the desk next to her. When she looked at the screen, she saw that it was a London number.

'Sandy?' she said.

There was a laugh on the other end, and then the familiar rounded vowels of the south hit her ears. 'Hey, babe, it's been a long time. How is it up there? I've heard they've got colour television now.'

She laughed. 'How's life in the clogged up, smoggy streets?'

'It's all sushi and soft shoes now.'

'So, what have you got for me?' Laura asked.

'What you wanted,' he said. 'Your boy, Shane Grix, was found in an alleyway near King's

Cross. Typical young drifter stuff. Down to the bright lights, except that it just got him into drink and drugs, and so he paid his way with sexual favours. Do you know how hard it is to investigate these things?'

'I haven't been away that long,' she said lightly. And Laura did remember the problems – any witness who could provide background information seemed to be in a new place each night. Some of the street sleepers found their own slot amongst the cardboard, and would defend it aggressively, but as soon as the authorities came looking, they shuffled off somewhere else. And getting them as far as a courtroom was almost impossible.

'It's even worse now,' Sandy said, interrupting her thoughts. 'Eastern Europeans hog the soup queues, even if they are not homeless, and they get pretty violent if anyone objects.'

'So you didn't get much joy?'

Laura could almost hear the shake of the head. 'Maybe things would be different now,' he said, 'but it was the Thatcher years. We celebrated the winners. What did some minister say back then, that the homeless were just the people you trip over on the way to the opera? Shane ended up in a fight with someone just like him. Strangled to death and then set on fire.'

'Forensic cover-up?'

'That was the guess at the time,' he said.

'And what about since?' Laura heard the sigh, and she guessed the answer. 'There hasn't been a *since*, has there?' she said. 'No forensics, no eye witnesses, and a family who don't make trouble.

299

Just another young homeless death.'

'It's called priorities, Laura, you know how it works. The file's still open, but short of a confession, we're never going to solve it. It was years ago.'

'How sure are you that the body was identified correctly? It was all based on clothes, wasn't it?'

'We're not,' he said. 'We tried dental records, but life on the streets had taken their toll. He'd lost three at the front, a couple at the back, and when we asked Shane's mother she said that he'd stopped going to the dentist after he was told to wear braces when he was thirteen.'

'Was there anything unusual about the body?'

There was a pause as Sandy thought back on what he'd found out so far. 'Not really. Apart from the gag.'

The hairs rose on Laura's arms.

'Gag?'

'A cloth, jammed into his mouth. I suppose it muffled the screams, and because it soaked up plenty of petrol, the fire burned pretty badly around the face.'

Laura rubbed her eyes. Her mind was still moving slowly, but she could work out the significance of what she had been told.

'Laura, what is it?' she heard Sandy say, but she still left it a few more seconds.

'It might be that you have to prioritise again,' Laura said.

'What do you mean?'

'I don't think your corpse is Shane Grix,' she said. 'I think Shane Grix may be the person who killed him.'

Sandy whistled. 'At least we've got a name now.'

'You always had the name, except the wrong way round,' she said. 'And once you discover who was actually killed, you might have a family who'll make more problems for you than Shane's did.'

The drive to the police station took Jack through the centre of Blackley, and as he passed the courthouse, he spotted David Hoyle's car.

Jack didn't often go to court on Saturdays, as Saturday cases were overnighters only, and were either so serious that the end of the case was a long way off, or else so trivial, like late-night drunkenness, that they didn't really deserve any ink in the first place. He decided to make an exception, so he could corner Hoyle again.

He pulled into the space next to Hoyle's car and jammed the meter with whatever small change he had left, and then walked quickly up the court steps.

The corridor was quiet; it always was on Saturdays. The lawyers wanted to be in and out as quickly as possible, and so the only people who ever hung around were relatives of the prisoners. Except that it wasn't as quiet as normal, because David Hoyle was sitting at the end of the corridor, leaning forward, staring at the floor.

He didn't look up as Jack approached, although he must have realised who it was, because as Jack sat down next to him, he said, 'If you want a quote, you won't get one.' His voice was quiet and forlorn.

Jack remembered the email from the night

301

before. *Hoyly Moyly.* It was time for some guess-work, because the poem had to mean something. *Oh Angel, why did you scream?*

'How's Angel?' Jack said. 'Is she okay?'

Hoyle looked up, surprised. 'What do you mean?' He had none of the arrogance of their usual meetings.

'I heard that she had a close call last night.'

Hoyle said nothing at first, and so Jack wasn't sure if his bluff had worked, but then Hoyle looked down again and said, 'How did you know?'

'It's a small town, Mr Hoyle. Rumours spread quickly.'

'Well, nothing happened, okay. There's nothing to say, nothing to report, and if you write other-wise, I'll sue you.'

'Is Angel your girlfriend?'

Hoyle sat up and leaned back in his seat. He folded his arms.

Jack nodded his understanding. 'Okay, thank you, Mr Hoyle. But tell me this: why are you here, and not with her, telling the police all about it?'

Hoyle ground his teeth and didn't respond.

'Are you so far gone that you look to serve Don before you protect your girlfriend?' Jack said, shaking his head. 'You've lost your way, Mr Hoyle.'

'You don't know what you're talking about.'

'Don't I? What, that women are dying, and if your girlfriend saw something, she might help the police catch him? But you would rather look after your client than help prevent another murder. So

302

what don't I know, Mr Hoyle? You tell me.'

Hoyle let out a heavy sigh and rubbed his eyes. He looked tired. 'Where did you hear about Angel?' he said.

'Just something I heard, and I saw the look on your face last night, like you had been dragged too close to something that was out of your comfort zone.'

Hoyle clenched his jaw. 'What the fuck does that mean?'

'You're a courtroom player. You can control what happens in there, because you know the rules, the tricks. That's how you deal with Don, because when he has to come here, or his men get charged, they are visiting your world, and you're in charge.'

Jack waited for the smart response, but as he looked into Hoyle's eyes, Jack just saw fatigue and worry, the fear that the evil of the world had come to him.

Hoyle looked down again.

'Talk to the police, David,' Jack said. 'Don's got no loyalty towards you. If he didn't use you, he'd use someone else.'

There was a pause, and then Hoyle said, 'But I want him to do it, to catch the killer, and that's what I hate about it. I care about the rules. Do you know that?' Jack didn't respond, and so he carried on, his voice rising a notch. 'I know you think people like me just try to weasel our way out of the rules, but it is still about the rules. It gives everything order.'

'Except that you are not sure whether you want this person to have that chance,' Jack said.

Hoyle looked him straight in the eye. 'I know what he did to Don's daughter,' he said. 'Any gaps that Don left out were filled in by you in your article, and I can't stand the thought that he could have done that to Angel.'

'So why are you here?' Jack said.

He looked around and shrugged. 'Because it's what I know, this place,' he said.

'But who is looking after Angel now?'

'She's at home, alone,' Hoyle said. 'She insisted on it. Angel isn't weak.'

'If the police call, will she speak to them?' Jack said.

Hoyle didn't answer at first. Instead, he just chewed on his lip. Eventually, he said, 'I don't know.'

Jack spotted something in Hoyle's voice, it sounded like fear, and then it dawned on him. 'That's really why you're here, isn't it?' Jack said. 'You haven't told her who the intruder was, that it might be the same person who killed Jane Roberts, and you don't know how to deal with it.'

Jack knew he'd hit home, because Hoyle looked up at the ceiling and clenched his jaw. After a few moments of silence, he shook his head and then got to his feet. 'I'm going back into court,' he said and wearily made his way along the corridor.

Chapter Fifty-One

Jack paced up and down outside the entrance to the police station, the print-out of the emails from the night before in his hand.

He turned around when he heard the large wooden doors swing open and smiled when he saw Laura. She walked over to him, returning the smile, although Jack thought she looked tired, her eyes red, the skin under them dark and puffy.

'Are you okay?' he asked.

She ran her hands over her face. 'We're just chasing this thing hard,' she said. 'We need to catch him.'

'Look after yourself too.'

'I will. It's nice to see you. It seems like forever since we spent some real time together.'

'I was going to say the same thing,' he said.

'Is this what this is about, that you want to see me?'

'No, no, nothing to do with that,' he said, and then he grinned. 'It *is* good to see you though.'

She moved forward and kissed him softly on the lips. 'You can have the rest later,' she whispered. 'For now, just tell me what you're doing here.'

'The emails,' Jack said. 'I've had some more.'

Laura's eyes widened, alert now. 'When, last night?'

He nodded. 'You remember David Hoyle?'

305

She thought for a moment and then said, 'Smart-arse defence lawyer. Nice suits, bad attitude.'

Jack nodded. 'That's him. I saw him last night, rushing out of Don's house. He looked frightened, and when I got home, I received this,' and Jack held out the print-out of the *Hoyly Moyly* email to Laura. As she read it, her eyes widening, Jack continued, 'There was an intruder in his house, while his girlfriend was home alone. She's the *Angel* in the poem.'

Laura looked at Jack, surprised.

'There's something else you ought to know too,' Jack said.

'Go on.'

'The bodies weren't left in random places. Don and Mike were supposed to find their daughters. It was revenge. I went to both murder scenes. Jane was found on a path that takes you right to Don's house, a path that people use to walk their dogs. Don has a dog.'

'And Deborah?'

'Mike Corley is a fisherman. I saw his gear when I was at his house. I bet he uses that reservoir.'

'He never mentioned that,' Laura said.

'Perhaps it wasn't a big deal when it was just Deborah, but when Jane was murdered, a pattern emerged.'

Laura thought about that for a moment, and when he passed her the paper, she said, 'Follow me.'

She walked quickly into the police station, rushing Jack through the reception area and towards Carson, whose pink dome gleamed through the crowd of uniformed officers putting off the start of the day. He was sitting with Joe Kinsella, deep in conversation. Jack threaded his way through the uniforms, and as he got closer to Carson, Laura held up the print-out.

'You might want to see this,' she said, and handed the first email over.

Carson looked at Jack. 'Is this what I think it is?' he said.

'Another email, to me,' Jack said, nodding.

'Fuck!' Carson said, his voice tired, his breath a mix of no sleep and too much coffee. As he read, Carson's eyes started to widen.

'What the fuck is all this?' he said. 'Poetry? Angel?'

'Taunts,' Jack said, pointing down at the paper. 'Angel is David Hoyle's girlfriend. Look at the title, *Hoyly Moyly*. Hoyle was at Don's house last night, and he left looking pretty fraught. I saw him this morning and asked him how Angel was, and he looked like I had kicked him in the gut.'

Carson turned to Laura. 'We need to check the incident logs from last night, see if she called it in,' he said.

'She didn't,' Jack said. 'Don Roberts is trying to deal with it himself, and I reckon Hoyle has joined the gang.'

'But if Angel had a confrontation, she might be able to give a description. This could be the killer's second mistake.'

Joe Kinsella was reading the email now. 'And we need to know how she was able to frighten him away,' he said. 'The first two victims would have fought too, so what was different about Angel?'

'You find out,' Carson said. 'I've got to go to a meeting with the top brass. They're worried about the cost of this case.' He sighed heavily. 'If we lose some of our squad, he'll kill again, and that won't make anything easier.'

'You might want to see this then,' Jack said, and handed over the second email. 'It arrived later on last night.' He watched as Carson read. *And I have spotted a female. You know her, ha ha. Just got to work out the details.*

Carson lowered the print-out and passed it to Laura. 'This might be aimed at you,' he said. 'You can't be alone today.' Laura started to protest, but he held up his hand. 'This is non-negotiable.'

Laura read it, and Jack saw the blood drain from her face for a moment. Then she recovered and said, 'We better catch him then.'

Carson smiled at her, but then said, 'Just be careful. We've had too many corpses.'

Chapter Fifty-Two

Jack was still outside the police station, sitting in his car and worrying about what lay ahead for Laura, when his phone rang.

The number on the handset was unfamiliar. When he answered, a quiet voice said, 'Jack Garrett?' It was a woman's voice, indistinct, but familiar, yet he couldn't place it.

'Yes, this is Jack Garrett.'

'Did you come to my house last night?' she

said. 'I've found your card.'

Jack thought about the previous evening, and then he knew why her voice was familiar. It was the woman from the Whitcroft estate, being tormented by a teenage gang. 'Yes, I did.'

The line went silent for a while, and Jack thought he had lost the signal, but then she said, 'Why did you come to my house?'

'I'm writing about the estate. You seemed to be having some trouble. I was passing, that's all.'

'Was that the only reason?'

Jack was confused. 'Should there be another reason?' he said.

'I've read your stories in the paper.'

'About what?'

'The two dead women.'

That got Jack's attention. 'Do you know anything about them?'

She went silent again, and Jack realised he had stopped breathing. He was waiting for her to talk.

'Don Roberts,' she said eventually. 'I can tell you all about Don Roberts, and Mike Corley.'

Jack let out a long breath. He wasn't aware of anything else around him. It was just her voice on the phone. 'I'm listening,' he said.

There was another pause, and then, 'I can tell you exactly how the dead women are connected.'

His mouth went dry and he felt a tingle of anticipation. He scrambled in his pocket and then his glove compartment for a pencil, and then found a scrap of paper to scribble on. 'So tell me what you know.' His fingers gripped the pen tightly.

'It was wrong, all wrong,' she said, although her voice was fainter this time.

'What was wrong?'

There was no response.

'Are you there?' Still silence. 'What's your name?'

There was another pause, and then she said, 'Emma.'

'Wait there,' Jack said, throwing the paper and pencil to the floor. 'I'm two minutes away.'

'So what do we do when we get to David Hoyle's house?' Laura asked Joe, as he drove them through the town centre.

'We persuade Angel to talk to us, not Don Roberts,' Joe said.

'But if Hoyle is there, he'll stop us.'

Joe shook his head. 'I've spoken to the court ushers. Hoyle is still at court.'

'Jesus, does life always have to be about the money?' Laura said.

'I reckon it's more than that,' Joe replied. 'Don wants to catch the killer himself, and we can both guess what will happen to him if he does. Hoyle knows that too, and so he's making himself visible, giving himself alibis, so that if Don is arrested for the murder of his daughter's killer, Hoyle doesn't get dragged into it.'

Laura looked out of the window and thought about the email from earlier. Where was he? Was he watching her now? She turned to look at the cars following them, but the road was empty. She slumped back into her seat and said, 'Why have you kept it a secret about Rachel?'

Joe stayed silent for a moment, and then replied, 'Not secret, private, because it's my private life. I don't want to be work gossip.'

'But your secrecy makes it seem like you're ashamed. Rachel is a pretty woman.'

'I'm not ashamed,' he said. 'And I'm not sure we're an item either. We just sort of keep each other company when we need it.'

'So it's about the sex.'

He gave a small shrug.

'I think Rachel feels more strongly about it than you do,' Laura said.

'What makes you say that?'

Laura smiled. 'I've seen how she reacts to me whenever I'm with you. She sees me as a threat.'

'And are you a threat?'

Laura blushed. 'I'm getting married soon.'

'Okay, I'm sorry. I shouldn't have said that. I like Jack, and you and me, well, we're good colleagues.'

Laura looked out of her window. The car suddenly seemed suffocating, the silence uncomfortable. She brought the conversation back to the case.

'Would it bother you if Don got to the killer first?' she said.

Joe didn't answer straight away. 'Depends if they get it right,' he said eventually. 'The problem is that we'll never know, because they'll get rid of the body. All we'll know is that the gaps between the murders will get longer, and eventually we'll wind up the investigation, never quite knowing if the right man was caught.'

'Is that worse than watching him walk out on a technicality, or a bad jury?' Laura said. 'Remember, Ian Huntley was only convicted eleven to one. It only takes three loose cannons to throw a trial. Or maybe he'll get a walkout after twenty years, free to enjoy his final years, ones that Deborah or Jane will never see.'

'I know how you feel, but if you work in the system, you've got to work with the system. It's not about justice, it never has been. It's about keeping a lid on everything.'

Laura gave up the argument. She closed her eyes for a moment, the long hours catching up with her, but as soon as she did, she thought she'd seen something. No, not something. Someone.

Her eyes shot open and she looked back along the pavement. She could only see T-shirts and bags, people on phones. Then she saw it again, a shock of grey hair and a slow shuffle, just a glimpse through the crowd.

'Go back around,' she said.

'Go back where?'

'Round the block. I've just seen someone.'

'Who?'

'Ida Grix,' she said.

Joe looked surprised. 'Why would she be here now, forty miles from home?'

'Perhaps looking for Shane, because she recognised something in our faces that told her that her doubts were coming true, that Shane hadn't died in London.'

Joe turned quickly into a side street and doubled back to the main street, crawling along slowly as Laura scanned the crowd again until she saw the same hair.

'There,' she pointed. Joe looked.

'What, going into that shop?' he said.

312

'Yes. Pull over.'

Joe scraped his tyres against the kerb as he brought the car to a halt, and Laura jumped out and trotted down to where she had seen Ida walk into a department store. It was a long way down the street though, and by the time she got down there, Laura couldn't see her. The shop doors opened automatically and Laura rushed in, looking around quickly, but it seemed like most of the shop was a mass of tight grey curls bobbing between the perfume counters. She remembered that there were too many exits to the shop to be able to know where Ida had gone, if it had been her.

Laura turned away, frustrated and trudged back to Joe's car. When she got there, Joe had his elbow out of the car window, his eyebrows raised in query.

'No joy,' Laura said.

'How sure were you?' he said.

'Sure enough to jog down the street to try and catch up with her.'

'That's good enough for me. I'm supposed to be looking after you though, so get in.'

'So what now?'

'Same as before,' Joe said. 'We go to David Hoyle's house and speak to Angel.'

As Joe set off again, Laura scanned the street once more, because she knew that if Ida had travelled to Blackley, she was looking for her son. And Laura also knew that they had to find him before Ida did, because the memory of Doctor Barker told her that Ida might not survive the reunion.

Chapter Fifty-Three

Emma's gate didn't offer much security, Jack thought. Old wood, painted green, and it wobbled as he pushed at it. The security guards had followed him as soon as he drove onto the estate, and now they were hovering at the end of the street, watching.

The house looked dirty from the outside, with cobwebs around the window frames and the remains of eggs on the ground. He knocked on the door, and after a few seconds, Emma answered.

Now that he could see her in daylight, he saw that life had been rough on her. She was tall, but looked too thin, with prominent veins in her forearms, and her face was just skin tightly wrapped around bones, the paleness of her complexion broken only by the dark circles under her eyes.

'I'm Jack Garrett,' he said.

She squinted, the light outside too bright for her. The smell of booze drifted over the threshold. She looked him up and down and then walked back into the house, leaving the door open as an invitation to follow. There was a weave to her walk, and his suspicions were confirmed when he saw an open bottle of cider on the floor by the chair.

Emma caught Jack looking, so she said, 'It's just a small drink when it's a nice day.'

As he checked out the living room, it seemed

that there hadn't been too many nice days for a while. The carpet was threadbare and the house smelled of damp dogs, the floor and chairs thick with dark hairs. As he looked towards the open back door, past the paintwork scuffed by paw-marks, he saw two scruffy brown mongrels lying on the ground in a paved yard that was peppered with dog shit. There was the thump of loud music coming from the house next door.

'How do you cope with that coming through the walls?' Jack said, trying to be friendly.

Emma glanced towards her neighbour's house. 'You get used to to it,' she said, and then looked back towards Jack. 'That's not why you're here.'

'Okay,' Jack said. 'Tell me what you know.'

She seemed to flush and then shook her head. 'It's personal,' she said. 'Will it definitely go in the paper?'

'I'm a reporter. Do you want people to know about it?'

Emma looked at Jack, and then shook her head.

'Can I call you Emma?' he said, and when she nodded, he continued, 'people have been killed, Emma. Don's daughter has been killed. Mike Corley's too. If you know something about this, you might save someone else's life.'

Her hands shook slightly. 'Poor girls,' she said.

'Did you know them?'

Emma looked at him, her eyes ringed red now, a tremble to her chin. 'It's beginning to feel like I did.'

'Tell me,' he said. 'I don't have to quote you.'

Emma thought about that for a few seconds. 'You've got nice eyes,' she said. 'You can tell what a man is like by his eyes.' She gestured towards a sofa. 'Sit down please.'

Jack tried not to look at where he was sitting, knowing that a coat of dog hairs was about to attach itself to his back. 'So you know Don Roberts, and Mike Corley?'

Emma's hand went to the glass of cider on the floor. She took a drink, her hand shaking, and as she sat the glass in her lap, a tear ran down her cheek. 'There is a connection, and I suppose I'm it,' she said.

'How do you know them both?'

Emma's eyelids fluttered with nerves, and then she slumped back in her chair and used a grubby palm to wipe the tears from her cheeks.

'It was thirty-five years ago,' she said, and then looked down at herself. 'Look at me now. A mess, I know that, but it wasn't always like this. Nineteen seventy-six. I still remember the year.' She poured some more cider into the glass and took a long drink. 'Mike Corley and Don Roberts. They used to work in a club in town.'

'What, together?'

She nodded. 'Not for long though.'

'Are you sure about this?'

Emma's hand started to shake again, and Jack had to lean forward quickly to stop her from dropping the glass.

'What is it?' he said. 'Tell me about the club.'

Emma looked down when she spoke, her lank hair falling over her face. 'It was a disco club,' she said. 'Manero's. I used to go there. Don worked the door. Mike was a barman. They were just boys really.' She shrugged. 'Disco music. The owner was just trying to cash in, but the club was rubbish. It wasn't only about having a turntable and speakers, and Manero's was just another cellar bar with a sound system.'

'I remember it,' Jack said. 'I don't remember it as Manero's, but I know that it seemed to change its name every few years. What was it? The New Lounge, and then Mountbattens.'

Emma's mood lightened. 'And Golden Gloves, then Roots, and Kiss. Every time the trade went quiet, they just re-upholstered the seats and changed the name.'

'I remember it when it was Kiss,' he said. 'I went there a few times. A bit dingy, if I recall.'

'But it was all Blackley had at the time, and I wanted to go,' she said. 'All my friends were into punk, but punk didn't do it for me. I wanted to dance, so I'd practise in my room. I started to go to Manero's because it was the only place where I could hear the music I liked and dance.'

'How old were you?'

'Fifteen, but I looked older. I was tall, and had grown up early, if you know what I mean. And the club couldn't afford to turn me away, even if I didn't buy more than a couple of Cokes. It was licensing, you see. They had to stay open during the week, and so I used to sneak out on school nights, when it was quiet and they weren't bothered about asking your age. One of my friends used to come with me at first, but her parents found out and stopped her. But I carried on going.'

'So did you know Don and Mike before you started going to Manero's?' Jack said.

317

Emma shook her head. 'Don was only young, but he was mouthy and a fighter. He had long hair back then, and a moustache, and he thought he was some real catch.' She laughed, but it was bitter, not nostalgic. 'The problem was that I fell for him.'

'Did you ever go out with him?'

Tears trickled onto her cheek again.

'I wanted to, but I was under age. I don't know when he found out my age, whether it was before or after it happened.'

'What happened?'

Emma looked down at her lap, and then around her room, as if she was suddenly seeing how her life had ended up, so different from the promise she'd had as a young girl just wanting to dance to disco music.

'It doesn't matter now,' she said. 'It was so long ago.'

Jack leaned forward. 'It matters now. You called me, remember, and so you must think about it, even now.'

The tears were coming in floods now. 'I think about it all the time.'

'So tell me,' he said. 'Don's daughter has been killed, and Mike's. What you know might be important.' She nodded and wiped away her tears. 'Tell me about Don.'

'It wasn't just Don. It was Mike as well.' She took a deep breath. 'Okay, this is what happened. It was in there one night, just dancing, enjoying myself, but it was quiet. It was always quiet, but that night there were only two other people in there. Mike worked on the bar, just a student, and

I think that night my drinks got spiked, because I only ever drank Coke.' She looked towards her glass. 'Times change, I suppose, but I didn't go out then to get drunk. I went out to dance. That night was different though. I felt a buzz, like I was queen of the club or something, really pumped, getting into the music, but then later on I felt dizzy, and then ill. I was sick in the toilets.' She looked up at the ceiling, biting her lip, but she couldn't stop the tears from falling. 'I can remember Don carrying me. He was strong. He took me upstairs, to the owner's office. I thought he was just looking after me, but,' and she shrugged, 'it became more than that.' Emma looked at Jack, her eyes wide, appealing for understanding. 'You know what it's like when you're really out of it. You know what's going on but you can't stop it, because all you want to do is lie down and be left alone.'

Jack could tell which way her story was going, and he felt a growl of anger. He could see the hurt in her eyes, even after all these years. 'That doesn't mean you wanted it to happen,' he said.

Emma took a drink of cider, and the shake to her hand was stronger than before. When she had taken a few large sips, she put the glass down on the floor and carried on talking. 'Don undressed me. I tried to fight it at first, but he was too strong, and then I was naked on the floor. There was a couch in there. The room smelled of dope, and I could guess what usually went on. Don lifted me onto the couch. I remember kicking and pushing him, but he just laughed. He pawed me and groped me and did things that no one else had ever done to me, and I was trying to get him off me, crying, but I couldn't. He made me do things to him, but I didn't want to. I was only fifteen and didn't know what to do, but he made me do it anyway. I gagged on him, and then Mike came in.' She shook her head. 'I should have fought more, shouted louder. Perhaps it looked like I didn't mind, or I wanted it, but I didn't. And Mike, well, he just joined in. Someone turned off the light, and I was face down, held down. Then I felt a pain, down there, and I knew that one of them was having sex with me. Then the other one. They both had sex with me, and I couldn't stop them.'

'You were raped,' Jack said.

Emma nodded slowly. 'What could I do?' she said. 'I was fifteen, drunk in a nightclub, having sex with two men.'

'That doesn't matter,' Jack said. 'You were raped, Emma.'

'But I couldn't go home and tell anyone about it, could I? I knew what they would have thought. Things were different then. I was a drunk, silly little girl, out of my depth.'

'No, you were a child, being abused by two adults.'

'That's what Simon said.' When Jack looked confused, she added, 'He's a friend. I tell him things.'

'How do you know him?'

'He's a policeman. He came round one day, to see if I was getting any trouble from the local kids.'

Jack felt a creeping sense of unease. 'And you're

320

sure he's a policeman? What's his second name?'

'I've seen him in his uniform, although a lot of the time he works in plainclothes,' she said. 'Simon Abbott. He was here this morning. He went to the shop for me.'

'What do you know about him?'

'Not too much,' she said. 'He doesn't tell me much about himself. He just seems to like sitting with me. We watch television together, or he asks me about my life, as if he's really interested. We even talk about Don Roberts sometimes, because of his bully boys around here. Simon told me not to pay him, because we should stand up to people like him, that I shouldn't give in a second time.'

'Is Simon the only person you've ever told?'

Emma nodded.

'And is that all he is, a friend?'

Jack saw the first trace of a smile, but it was slow coming.

'I'm too old for him. I mean, look at me,' she said. 'Anyway, he's a policeman, and so he understands these things.' She waved her hand. 'Don and Mike would have got away with it even if I'd told someone. They knew afterwards that I was a virgin. There was blood, and I was hurting, but they just put some money in my hand and put me in a taxi.'

'Did you tell anyone else at the time?'

Emma shook her head.

Jack drummed his fingers on the arm of the sofa. Emma was the connection, the emails had told him that, but now he was hearing the story first-hand, he struggled to rein in his impatience. 'Are you sure you've told no one?'

Emma shook her head, and then she said. 'No one. Not even when I was pregnant.'

Jack was surprised at that. 'Pregnant? Which one made you pregnant?'

She shrugged again. 'I don't know.'

'Did you have the baby?'

She nodded, slowly and tearfully. 'Don told me to get rid of it, not to tell anyone, but I couldn't do it. I was fifteen. How would I know what to do?'

'And what did Mike say?'

'I don't think he knew what to say. He was just scared.'

'What about your parents?'

'I didn't tell them until it was too late, and when I did, I told them that it was a boy at a party, and I wouldn't tell them his name to keep him out of trouble. They sent me away to have the baby, so that no one would know, and I gave him up, just like that,' and she clicked her fingers.

'What happened to him?' Jack said.

'I tracked him down once, because he was given to a family friend, a couple who wanted more children. They adopted him, and my parents made me sign the papers. They said it was best that way, even gave me money, but how could it be right if he wasn't with his mother? I tried to find him, and I did, I went to their house, but they wouldn't let me see him. They told me they would have my parents arrested if I went there again, for making me sell my baby. And so I stayed away. I gave up my baby a second time.'

'Have you ever seen him?'

'Not since they took him from me when he was

born. I didn't even get the chance to hold him. They told me to just forget about him, but how do you do that? He was my baby. I was nothing more than a child myself, but it didn't make it hurt any less. You think you're going to get better, but then things remind you and it comes at you like a train. His birthday. A baby in blue. That Hot Chocolate song. "So You Win Again". It was number one when he was born, and all I could think of was my old school friends hanging out and listening to punk records, and there I was, having a baby, sixteen by then.'

'Did Don Roberts or Mike Corley ever find out that there had been no abortion?'

Emma shook her head. 'It was as if it had never happened. Manero's changed its name. Mike left Blackley to go to college, and I didn't see him again until he came back to join the police. And Don carried on working the doors.'

'So no one knows, apart from your family, and his adopted family?'

'And Simon, my friend,' she said.

Simon again.

'How did he take it?'

'He seemed to be as upset as I was, but friends are like that, I suppose. They share your pain.'

Jack's fingers tapped on his knee. He thought of what Emma had just said, and knew that Laura needed to know. It seemed more important than Dolby knowing, because when Jack thought of what had happened to Laura, and how it could have been worse, it seemed more than just a story.

'I hated them for what they did to me,' Emma said, interrupting his thoughts, 'but I feel sorry for them now, and especially the girls.'

'What do you mean?'

'Think about it,' Emma said. 'I don't know which of them was the father of my child, but one of them was, and so one of those poor dead girls was my son's sister, if you think about it, and so they were sort of connected to me.'

'What is Simon like?'

'Oh, he's kind and thoughtful.'

'No, what does he look like?' The question came out too forcefully, and Jack thought Emma looked scared for a moment, but she recovered as she thought about him, her eyes to the ceiling, her head cocked to one side.

'He's tall and slim,' she said. 'In his thirties. He's got a nice smile.'

'What do you mean, nice?'

'Well, he smiles with his eyes, and sort of cocks his head to one side.'

Like you, Jack thought. He thanked Emma for her time and said goodbye. He had a call to make. But he had somewhere to go first.

Chapter Fifty-Four

As Laura and Joe approached David Hoyle's home, Laura shook away the stab of envy she felt every time she saw where defence lawyer lived, because it always seemed like they reaped the reward while people like her did all the danger-ous work. Yet deep down, despite the long hours and hard graft, she was proud of her job. She wondered if David Hoyle felt the same about his.

As she climbed out of the car, she looked at the house, three small almshouses converted into one, with views towards the hills that separated the Lancashire cotton belt from the more cosmopolitan sprawl of Greater Manchester. Stone steps led to a solid wooden door, although it looked like the knocks and dents in the wood were affectations, trying to reclaim the age of the house. She banged hard on the door. It was a while before anyone answered, but then she heard the rattle of a key and a face peered through the door, from behind a small chain.

'We're the police,' Laura said. 'It's about your intruder from last night.'

There were some nervous blinks, and then, 'Do you have identification?'

Laura lifted the police identification. Joe did the same.

There was another pause, but then the door closed and there was a small rattle as the chain was removed. When the door opened, there was a slender woman standing there, barefoot but in tight leggings and a long cream jumper. Her hair was luxurious and dark, falling over her shoulders. Her face was pale and drawn through, as if she hadn't slept.

'Is it Angel?' Laura asked.

The woman nodded.

Laura and Joe exchanged quick glances and then said, 'We need to talk about last night.'

There was a pause, and then, 'I've got nothing to say.'

'We know about the man who came to your house last night,' Laura said. She noticed Angel's eyes flicker nervously and her hand take a firmer grip on the door.

'David said it was a client, some kind of revenge, because a case had gone wrong,' Angel said.

Laura shook her head slowly. 'He has killed people.' Angel's eyes grew wide. 'If we don't catch him, he will kill someone else. You can help stop that.'

Angel paused, with her hand on the door, before she let go and the door swung open.

She led them into a spacious living room with views over the lawn at the back, her bare feet padding quietly across the hardwood floor, in contrast to the loud clicks of Laura's heels. Set in front of the window was an easel, a large piece of paper on it, washed-out watercolours visible. As they followed her, Laura asked, 'Is Angel your real name?'

'It used to be Angela,' she said over her shoulder. 'My publisher thought Angel was more marketable.' Angel caught Laura looking and said, 'I illustrate children's books. That's why I like it here, because the light is so fantastic. The window is west-facing, and so is in the shade for a lot of the day, dark and brooding, but all the time the fields and hills are painted by brilliant sunshine or the mood of the clouds. When I get the light later on, it catches the dust and the pollen, like fairies dancing.' Angel looked down, embarrassed. 'Listen to me, going on about sunlight when people are dying.'

Laura smiled politely and waited for Angel to continue.

'So who has he killed, this person?' Angel said. 'And how do you know it was the same person who came here last night?'

'I can't tell you how we know, but you are an important witness. You can help save lives.'

Angel nodded weakly her face pale. 'Tell me about him.'

And so Laura did. She saw Angel's eyes widen when she mentioned Jane Roberts.

'Did you know her?' Laura asked.

Angel shook her head. 'David has mentioned Don, her father, and he told me that his daughter had been murdered.'

'What did he say?'

'I shouldn't say,' she said. 'David was probably revealing confidences, and if he told me things, then they should stay with me.'

Laura didn't push it, because she knew that she and Jack had a similar arrangement, that she was allowed to come home and moan and gripe, knowing that it wouldn't be repeated outside their home. She had to keep back the really sensitive stuff though, but everything else was legitimate pillow talk.

Joe sat down on the sofa on the other side of the room, and Laura could tell that he was leaving it up to her, that there was a woman-to-woman rapport going on that he didn't want to spoil.

'So tell me about last night,' Laura said.

Angel rubbed her eyes as if mentally preparing to bring back the sequence of events. 'David had gone out, to speak with a client,' Angel said, a slight quiver to her voice.

'A client?'

'I didn't ask him for details, because he often sees clients in their home. That's the problem with living with a defence lawyer – it feels like your life is always on call, your plans wrecked by some idiot who has got himself locked up. Anyway, so he went out.'

'He went to Don's house,' Laura said.

Angel shrugged. 'Like I said, a client.'

'David was out, you were alone, and I reckon your intruder must have known that.'

Angel looked thoughtful at that.

'I didn't hear him come in,' she said eventually. 'I'd finished drawing. I was in the spare bedroom, where we have the computer. I was on the webcam, talking to a friend. She lives in France and we keep in touch that way. My friend spotted him, not me. She said that there was someone there, and when I looked round, there he was.'

'What did he look like?' Laura said.

'I didn't get a good look. I was shocked, frightened.'

'But you saw him, and at this point anything you remember will help. How tall was he?'

'He was tall,' Angel said. 'I noticed that. And slim, like his height made him awkward. Long arms and legs.'

'Ethnicity?'

'He was in shadow, but I would say white.'

'Facial hair.'

Angel shook her head. 'I couldn't see that much detail. It was like a flash and he was gone. I think the webcam scared him.'

'Close your eyes,' Laura said. 'Get rid of all of this visual clutter and think just about last night.

Tell me what you see. Imagine you had to paint him.'

Angel sighed, and then she closed her eyes.

'Okay,' she said, after a few seconds. 'He didn't have a full beard, but he might have been unshaven. And his face was skinny, with pronounced cheekbones. His hair was short, but cut that way, not shaved. His jacket seemed to hang off his shoulders, as if he was all a bit weedy under his clothes.'

'What was he wearing?'

'It was all dark,' she said. 'Black top, black trousers, I think.' Then her eyes opened. 'There was one thing: his smell.'

'What do you mean?' Laura said.

'He smelled musty and dirty, like he didn't wash his clothes enough. That's what I could smell when he'd gone.'

'Anything else?'

Angel shook her head.

'What did David say to you last night that made you not report it?' Laura said.

'He said he thought it was work-related, and that he knew who it was. He said he would sort it out, that the guy was harmless.'

'But that is a lie.'

'So you say.'

Laura leaned forward and lowered her voice. 'There's something I need you to do for me.'

'Tell me.'

'Spy on David.'

Angel sat back and shook her head. 'I can't do that.'

'David is a good lawyer, we both know that, but

he is going along with Don Roberts just to keep the money flowing, and right now Don is looking to kill whoever he thinks murdered his daughter.'

'Is that a bad thing?'

'It is if he gets it wrong,' Laura said. 'And even if he doesn't, we would have to do something about it, because we can't allow summary executions. David will get dragged in like everyone else when we start kicking in doors. If you want to carry on living with David, you need to protect him from himself.'

Angel thought about that for a few seconds, and then said, 'What do you want me to do?'

'Just let me know if you find anything out, or hear anything,' Laura said, handing over one of her cards. 'Please, Angel, you need to do this.'

Angel took the card and looked at it for a long time. Laura could see her struggling – if she helped the police it could end David's legal career in Blackley, and what's more, it could end their relationship.

But then Laura saw Angel realise that she had no choice. Angel looked up at Laura and, with a tear running down her cheek, nodded her agreement.

Chapter Fifty-Five

Jack was spotted as soon as he approached Mike Corley's house.

He wanted confirmation of Emma's story before he did anything about it. He didn't want to get a police officer arrested because of some drunken ramblings.

Mike's wife appeared at the window straight away. Jack guessed that she had become used to having the press outside her house. He didn't expect to be made welcome, but it seemed like they were jumpier than last time. He tried a smile and a wave, but she just turned away. Then he saw Mike Corley walking towards him, his fists bunched, his cheeks flushed red with anger.

'I told you last time, we've nothing to say to you.'

Jack pulled out his voice recorder. 'Before you hit me,' he said, 'what about Manero's?'

He stopped and pursed his lips, his fists by his side now.

'What do you mean?'

'Come on, you must know the name,' Jack said. His sympathy for him as a father had waned after hearing Emma's story. 'Did you read my article, where I said that there was no real connection between you and Don Roberts?'

'Go on,' he said, his eyes darting about nervously.

'We know that's not true now,' Jack said. 'Why did you keep it secret, Mr Corley?'

He shook his head and stepped forward, trying to push Jack away from his house. 'I don't know what you're talking about.'

'Yes, you do, but I'll explain it, if you want,' Jack said, standing his ground. 'Manero's. It's a night club from the seventies. You worked there, with Don Roberts. You were a barman, he was a doorman.' Mike Corley paled. 'Why didn't you say anything?'

He shrugged and tried to look nonplussed, but Jack could tell from the widening of his eyes that Emma's story was hitting home. 'So, I might have once worked with him. It's years since I worked at that club. How am I supposed to remember every face? Christ, it was decades ago.'

'I thought you might have remembered going with a fifteen-year-old girl, you and Don together, taking turns with a child.'

The angry flush drained away, and Jack thought he saw a wobble. But Corley took a deep breath and straightened himself. 'I've nothing to say,' he said, and turned to walk back to the house.

'She was a child, Mr Corley, and you and Don fucked her, two on one. Are you denying it?'

He whirled round. 'That wasn't me. And you've no evidence of anything, so get away from my house.'

'No evidence at all?' Jack queried, and then shook his head, his lips drawn into a tight grimace. 'What about a walking, talking piece of your DNA? Or is it Don's?'

Corley paused and looked confused for a

moment. 'What do you mean?'

'She got pregnant, Mr Corley. The young girl you took turns on. Emma, she was called. She had a baby.' Jack raised his eyebrows. 'It was a boy, by the way, Mr Corley.'

Corley took a step back and reached out to his car to steady himself. He looked back towards his wife who was watching through the window. 'Don't be making trouble, Mr Garrett. People could get hurt.'

'I've got it all recorded, so if anything happens to Emma, Don will be the first suspect, with you next in the queue. You understand me?' Jack said, as calmly as he could.

'But you're a reporter. You're going to print something,' Mike replied. His tone was measured and cold.

Jack smiled, although his heart was beating wildly. 'I don't know what will get into print, I don't edit the paper, but you will get the chance to deny it. So go on, what's your quote, because at the moment it looks like you and Don Roberts treated a girl really badly, and you ruined her life? No, not a girl. A child.'

Corley stepped closer and lowered his voice to an angry hiss. 'Why would anyone care now?' he said. 'It's ancient history, a skeleton in the cupboard. I didn't know she'd gone on to have a baby, but so what? Young people do stupid things. That's life.'

'But most mistakes don't go on to cost lives,' Jack said. 'Your mistake has killed people, including your daughter.'

Corley looked confused again. 'You've lost me.'

'Whatever is happening now is connected with what you did all those years ago. So, Mr Corley, what about a quote, or your story on what happened in that club that night?'

He considered Jack for a moment, and then stepped away. 'You won't print it, because you've no proof. So there's no quote from me. And if I see you round here again, there will be trouble.'

Jack held his ground. 'Even no comment is sometimes worth printing,' he said, and then turned to walk back to his car. Jack could feel Corley watching him as he went. As Jack climbed behind the wheel, Corley's wife was still staring at him through the window. As Mike Corley turned to go inside, Jack wondered what he was going to tell her.

Jack called Laura. Corley was watching him from his window, glaring, his fingers gripped tightly around the curtain.

'If you want a link between Mike Corley and Don Roberts, I've got one,' Jack said.

'Tell me,' she said, and Laura didn't interrupt as he told her all about the meeting with Emma.

'Did you say her child was adopted?' Laura asked.

'Yes,' Jack said. 'Her son was taken from her and handed over to a family friend. She tracked him down once, but she wasn't allowed to see him.'

Laura went quiet for a few seconds, and then she said, 'When was this?'

'She was raped in seventy-six, so she had the baby in seventy-seven.'

'It fits,' Laura said, almost to herself.

'What fits?'

'I can't tell you, Jack, not yet, but thank you for this,' she said, and there was an urgency in her voice. 'Who else knows?'

'Just one other person. A policeman. Abbott. Simon Abbott.'

There was another pause.

'Laura?'

'Don't go near Abbott,' she said. 'I'll speak to you later.' And then the phone went dead.

Jack breathed out deeply as he put his phone back in his pocket. He knew exactly where he was going. As he pulled away, Jack took one last glance at Corley, just in time to see his hand fall away from the curtain.

Chapter Fifty-Six

When they arrived at the police station, Laura didn't head for the doors.

'Where are you going?' Joe said.

'I'm going to find Ida, Shane's mother,' she replied, and held up her phone. 'That was Jack. Remember the reference to Emma in the emails? She called him not long ago, and so he interviewed her.'

'Why didn't he come to us first?'

'Because he was doing his job,' Laura said. 'And perhaps she wouldn't have spoken to us. She hasn't been keen up to now.'

'And what did she say?'

'Mike Corley and Don Roberts once worked

together, back in the seventies,' she said. 'Jack got the full story from the woman, except back then she wasn't a woman. Emma was a fifteen-year-old kid when Corley and Roberts raped her.'

Joe's eyes widened. 'Rape? Mike Corley and Don Roberts? Is she sure?'

'One of them got her pregnant,' Laura said. 'Guess what happened to the baby?'

'She gave it up for adoption. Shane?'

'That's my guess, and it seems like she's had one confidante all along. A policeman. PC Simon Abbott. Maybe we were wrong after all. Maybe Shane did die in that London alleyway, but Simon Abbott is exacting some kind of revenge on behalf of Emma?'

'Simon Abbott?'

Laura nodded. 'That's what Jack said. Do you know him?'

'He's a beat bobby, on the town centre patrol, the shoplifters' circuit. He's the right height, I suppose, but why would he do that?'

'When you find him, you can ask him,' Laura said. 'And check the duty rosters on my desk. See if he was on duty when the emails were sent from the station.'

'What are you doing?' Joe said.

'I'm going to find Ida.'

'Carson said you weren't supposed to be alone.'

'I'm not a child,' she said. 'Now we've got a name, you should have him locked up pretty soon.'

Joe nodded and walked towards the station doors. Laura went to her car and set off towards the town centre, where she thought she had seen

Ida not long ago.

Her intention was to park her car and then walk. Ida wouldn't know much about Blackley, and so she would stick to the major roads, perhaps not even venture out of the shopping zone. Laura checked her watch. Five o'clock. She left her car in one of the multi-storeys and started wandering.

It was thirty minutes before Laura saw her, as the crowds thinned out and the shops started to close. Ida wasn't alone. There was another woman alongside her, taller, younger. They were walking slowly, Ida's eyes flitting around as she looked at people as they passed her. Laura followed them for a few minutes, and then she realised something else, that it was just men Ida was looking at, as if she was looking for traces of Shane, the adopted son she thought was dead.

They walked slowly until they got to the end of a line of shops. When they turned around to walk back the same way they had come, Ida stopped dead. She had seen Laura. She began to look around, as if an escape route was about to appear at her side. The woman with her looked confused, and then angry as Laura went to Ida and grabbed her gently by her elbow.

'Mrs Grix, we need to talk.'

'Who are you?' the other woman said angrily.

'It's all right,' Ida said, and then, 'what are you doing here?' Her expression was a mix of fear and confusion.

'I work here,' Laura said. 'The question is really what are you doing here?' When Ida looked away, Laura pulled her to one side and said, 'Come on, let me buy you both a drink.'

The other woman stepped forward. 'Please tell me, who are you?'

'I'm the detective who spoke to Mrs Grix yesterday about Shane,' Laura said, and as she studied the woman's face, she remembered her from the photographs in Ida's house. 'Is it Amanda, Shane's sister?'

Laura saw her anger fade. Amanda nodded but didn't say anything.

Ida allowed herself to be led to a small coffee bar in the precinct, Amanda following meekly behind. It was filled with shoppers making their slow way home, the passage through the tables made difficult by bags and boxes on the floor. They found a space at the back, and Laura went to buy the drinks. When she returned with three coffees, Laura said, 'Talk to me, Ida.'

Ida sighed and looked down for a few seconds, and when she looked up her eyes were watery. 'Is it Shane?' she said.

'What makes you say that?'

'Just the things I read in the paper,' she said. 'They said that Doctor Barker's murder was connected to someone over here, and so I read about them. They sounded like Shane, but it can't be him, because Shane is dead.'

'How certain did the police seem back then?' Laura said.

'They told me they were sure, and they showed me some of his things. And it seemed like they were right, because Shane never came home. Back then, I had no reason to think that they weren't right.'

'But now you're not so sure?'

Ida took a drink of her coffee before she answered. She kept looking down as she spoke. 'Doctor Barker thought it was Shane, I know that now, and he was a clever man, so if he thought it was Shane, well, maybe it is.'

'So that's why you are here,' Laura said.

Ida tapped the side of her cup, her expression lonely and morose. 'I want to find him,' she said. 'I know what you think he did to those women, and if he killed them, he should pay for that, but he's my son. He's not my flesh and blood, but I brought him up. I did all those things for him that a mother should do, and I think of him as my child.'

Amanda snorted angrily. 'And he threw it back in your face,' she said.

'Don't say that,' Ida said, sounding hurt.

'Oh, come on, you know it's true. He ran away as soon as he could, and it ruined everything.'

'He wasn't a bad boy,' Ida said. 'He was just different.'

Amanda sat back and scowled. 'He used to watch me getting changed,' she said. 'I didn't tell you then because it didn't seem important, because I used to hit him when I caught him. He used to push the door open and peep through the gap.'

'That's not a nice thing to say,' Ida said.

'But if he is alive and has killed these women, then he was always like that,' Amanda said bitterly, and then folded her arms. 'I just thought you ought to know.'

Laura saw the resentment of Ida's natural

child, that the cuckoo had got all the attention.

'What will you do if you see him?' Laura said.

Ida shrugged. 'I don't know.'

'Tell me how he was adopted.'

Laura saw a flash of panic in her eyes, some long forgotten fear resurfacing with a jolt.

'What do you mean?' Ida said.

'Just that,' Laura said.

Amanda looked at Laura, and then at her mother, confused.

Ida looked worried, and wrapped her hands around her cup even more tightly.

'I'm not interested in whether it was a crime,' Laura said. 'I just need you to tell me what happened.'

Ida looked at Amanda for a few seconds, her eyes filled with silent apology, and then she said, 'Shane's mother was a young girl, from here, Blackley. Emma she was called. She got herself into trouble, and she didn't want to bring him up on her own. Emma's mother was an old school friend, and she arranged it.'

So there it was, Laura thought, confirmation of what Jack had told her.

'How?'

Ida sighed and wiped her nose. 'We agreed that when the baby was born, I would take him in and treat him as my own. We had Amanda, but she took a long time to come, and we didn't want to wait that long again, because we would be too old to adopt if we did, and so this seemed like the best way. It suited both of us.'

'It didn't suit the baby's mother,' Laura said.

Ida shook her head and sniffled. 'Even the

340

money we handed over was just frittered away.'

'What, you bought Shane?' Amanda said, incredulous.

Ida looked up, and Laura saw shame on her face.

'It was supposed to give Emma a fresh start,' Ida said. 'She signed the papers, but it seemed like it made it worse.'

'What do you mean?'

'We kept in touch with Emma's mother at first, but she stopped calling us, because Emma just spent the money on drink, and then it was drugs. It was supposed to help her, but I don't think it did. And when Shane found out, like I told you before, it seemed to make him more cruel, more angry, except that Shane being angry was different to most people, because he didn't shout or anything. He simmered. Yes, that's what it was. He would get angry in a quiet way, and then take it out on me in a cruel way. Pieces of jewellery I liked would go missing, and then I would find them mashed up, broken. That was Shane all over.'

Laura reached across and held Ida's hand, felt the tremble between her own fingers. 'You did what you thought was right, I know that.'

Ida looked into Laura's eyes, and Laura could see the turmoil, the regret, and the guilt for that decision made all those years ago.

'Do you think it is Shane?' Ida said.

Laura gripped Ida's hands tighter and nodded. 'Like you said, Doctor Barker thought it was Shane, and he died the same day. So if you see him, remember that Shane is dangerous. Don't try and speak to him. Call us.' Ida didn't respond at first, and so Laura gave her hand a shake. 'Promise me, Ida.'

Ida nodded eventually and looked down, although Laura wasn't convinced by the response, because Ida let go of her hand and wrapped it around her own cup again, defensive once more.

'Do you have any photographs of Shane we can use?' Laura asked.

Ida nodded and then reached into her bag. She pulled out a small colour photograph, the corners creased, as if she had spent the afternoon with it clutched in her hand, comparing the young boy to the men in their thirties walking past. Which, of course, Laura guessed that she had.

Laura looked down at the image. The tilt of the head, the straggly blond hair, the half-smile, as if he knew something no one else did.

'Is there anywhere I can take you both?' Laura said.

'Could you please take us to Emma's mother? She lives in a home now. I've got the address,' Ida replied, producing a scrap of paper from her bag.

Laura smiled and patted her hand. 'Of course, I can do that.'

Chapter Fifty-Seven

Jack ran into the *Blackley Telegraph* office, setting off the door buzzer and flashing a smile at the woman behind the counter, who was reaching for her bag.

'We're closing, Jack,' she said.

'I know, I'm sorry,' Jack said, out of breath. 'Is Dolby in?'

She smiled and nodded that he was, and so Jack ran through.

Dolby was near the window, talking to one of the sales assistants as she put on her coat. He looked over towards Jack and was about to say something, but Jack pointed to his office. 'Me first,' he said.

Jack pushed open the door and paced up and down as Dolby sauntered over.

'Jack, what's the rush?' he said casually, although he didn't sound pleased. 'I'm just applying the same amount of effort as you are to my fucking Whitcroft article,' and then he sat down heavily, making his chair creak as he leaned back and propped his feet on the desk.

'I've got something better than that, and it ties in with the murders,' Jack said.

'But that's not the article I commissioned,' Dolby said, raising his voice.

'Forget about that. This story is much better,' and Jack told him all about Manero's and the link between Don Roberts and Mike Corley.

343

Dolby pulled a face and then began to applaud, mockingly. 'Well done. Prize-winning, but not good enough for this paper. It all rests on some middle-aged drinker with a grudge, and we can't prove it's true. We can't run stuff like this unless it's cast-iron screwed tight, because a libel action would bring us down.'

'So that's it, we just ignore it?'

'Jack, we're a newspaper, not some local victim group. We need to stay afloat. Newspapers are dying, you know that. It would only take one good kick from a High Court judge to finish us.'

'What if I can get you proof?'

Dolby sighed and sat up straight, his hands palm-down on the desk now. 'If you can, I'll look at it again, but until then it's just pub gossip.'

He sat back in the seat of his van, the engine off, just waiting. She wouldn't be long.

The day had been spent idling, trying to quell the clamour in his head. He could push the noises back sometimes, but it took concentration and he didn't want to make the effort. They had been like a rolling chant, urging him on, to kill her, that just one more would give him the high he needed. He didn't believe it, he had been let down too often, but the need had been inside him all day, unfulfilled from the night before.

It was too quiet, as if the world was waiting for him to act. A fly danced in front of the windscreen and then settled on the glass. He went to switch on the wipers to get rid of it, but he stopped. Leave it, he thought. He watched it as it tapped on the windscreen, and he thought he could hear it, just squeaks on the glass.

He closed his eyes. It must be the lack of sleep. He couldn't hold it together for much longer. And how was he supposed to sleep, with all of that fucking noise? The whispers and then the shouts.

He snapped his eyes open quickly. He couldn't fall asleep. Not now. There wasn't much longer to wait, he knew that.

And as he thought of her again, he felt his arousal grow. It had been there all day, like an ache, but it was stronger now.

He glanced towards his passenger seat. The handcuffs were there, and the gloves. Was this to be the last time, a climax to match the first time?

He smiled. Not much longer.

Chapter Fifty-Eight

Laura dropped Ida and her daughter at the rest home where Emma's mother lived, and decided to leave them to it. It was early evening now, and she was anxious to get back to the station.

The rest home was near the canal, just further along from the police station, and she only had to drive through an industrial estate for the quickest route back. She wanted to be there in case the PC Abbott lead turned out to be useful. Her route took her towards the dark band of the canal, the towpath running alongside, long grasses trailing on the water and flies buzzing around something on the surface. She stopped at a junction, and as she looked along she saw a familiar figure jogging along the canal towpath, her head bobbing up and down in time with her steps. Rachel Mason.

Laura watched her as she ran past, transfixed for a moment by Rachel's ponytail as it swished along the back of her Lycra vest, her shoulders muscular, a bottle of water in one hand, the small white wires of her headphones connected to a music player that was clipped on to a band around her arm.

Laura looked away. She didn't need to see Rachel's pert little arse to remind her that she wasn't in the shape she ought to be. Laura glanced at herself in the rear view mirror. Those laughter lines didn't disappear anymore. The memory of her last run came back to her and she shuddered.

Rachel appeared in the rear view mirror. The sun was getting low and so she had to squint as the evening rays put everything into silhouette.

She put her car into gear and set off. She glanced down the side streets as she drove, those that headed towards the canal, and then came to a stop at the next junction. She was looking along the road, waiting for a gap, when something troubled her, just a sense that she shouldn't go on. Had she seen something in one of the empty side streets? She rewound her journey in her mind and tried to sift through the images. All she'd passed were long strips of industrial units, some large warehouses with lorries parked behind high fences, some small square brick blocks. But she had seen something, she knew it.

She checked her watch. She needed to get back to the police station, and she was about to shake off her doubts and start driving again, but she stopped herself. Being a cop was about instinct, about running with the gut feeling, and her gut feeling was telling her that something wasn't right.

Laura sensed movement behind her, and so her eyes shot to her mirror. There was a van, small and brown, just nudging out from one of the side streets, just the front wing visible. As soon as she saw it, the bad memory rushed at her. It was the colour, drab and dull, with the pitted signs of rust near the headlight. Her mouth went dry, her palms slick on the steering wheel. It was the van that had almost knocked her over during her run.

It seemed like it was waiting, exhaust fumes drifting forward. Was it following her? Laura realised now what she had seen as she went past the side streets. It had been the van, parked further along, facing the canal. How long had it been there? If it was following her, how long had it been following her for? She looked down into the door pocket, to see whether there was any-thing she could use as a weapon. Nothing.

She clicked on her phone, her hands shaking as she selected the hands-free option.

'Joe, he's here.' Laura tried to speak calmly but her breathing was shallow, the adrenaline flood-ing into her veins.

'Who's here?'

'The man in the van. The emailer. He's behind me.'

'Where are you?'

'I'm by the canal,' she said. 'Pendle Street.'

'Keep driving normally,' he said. 'Make him follow you. Keep a commentary. We'll get someone there.'

She set off slowly, watching in her rear view mirror all the time. The van stayed in the junction, just waiting, trails of fumes drifting forward. Her hands gripped the steering wheel, waiting for it to pull out, but then it set off and turned to go in the opposite direction. Then she saw it again, the missing number plate.

The van blew smoke as it went, obscuring the rear window. She watched it crawl slowly to a bend further along that would take it away from the canal. As she saw it go out of sight, she caught a final glimpse of Rachel as she went along the towpath, just the tip of her blonde hair bobbing up and down.

'Joe, it's gone the other way.'

'We've got cars coming to you.'

'Rachel is that way.'

'What way?'

'She's jogging. He's followed her.'

'Shit! Try and get to her, warn her.'

'Okay, I'm following,' she said, and turned the car around in the road, thinking about the route, about where it would come out.

The road followed the line of the canal mostly, a remnant of the days when it passed the front of the old mills and wharfs. It was a quieter route now, because the thing that had kept the canal in business so long – the cotton industry – had died, leaving just patches of open land and the occasional derelict building. There were new houses further along that had been mocked up to look like stone cottages but that was about it, the re-generation creeping slowly along the waterfront.

Laura set off in the direction of the van, want-ing to get behind it but not wanting to spook the driver. She tried to see along the towpath, to check that Rachel was still there, but the canal curved away, so that she couldn't see much more than twenty yards ahead. She looked along the road. Laura thought that it returned to the canal-side around half a mile further along, just before the houses started.

She followed the road round, past the shells of old mills, the roofs crumbled to just trestles, the windows sealed shut with metal plates to keep people away. But people still found a way in, and so the metal shutters hung a bit loose, and Laura guessed that the inside would be littered with discarded needles and old beer cans.

As the road curved back round to the canal, Laura felt a jolt. She couldn't see the van. She should have caught it up by now. And where was Rachel? She should have appeared by now too. What if she had stopped for a rest? Or would she be further along and almost home?

As the road got closer to the canal, Laura saw that there was a place to park in front of some old wooden bollards, now almost covered by trailing blackberry bushes. Laura climbed out of the car and looked around. The streets were deserted, the evening rush hour gone, and so all she had were shadows as she tried to get her bearings. She was nervous, aware of how deserted it was.

349

She stopped by the bank and looked along both ways, her feet making soft crunches in the gravel as she turned, but it seemed loud as the sound bounced off the water and the high wall on the other side. What would she say if Rachel appeared around the bend? Except that Rachel didn't appear. There was no other sound, apart from the soft brush of trailing branches along the canal surface, the only ripple in the dark ribbon of water that curved round to the heavy black lock-gates Laura could see in the distance. Rachel could not have got that far ahead, not in the time she had.

Laura turned around, unsure what to do, waiting for the wail of sirens.

Then she heard a noise, like a scream and a bang.

Laura tracked the noise, her senses heightened. It had come from further back, from the direction she had come from. Laura moved slowly along the towpath, looking for shadows moving in the bushes that grew over it, waiting for an attack. She wished that she had brought a pepper spray with her. The towpath ran alongside a patch of open ground and an old factory further along, with holes in the roof and the windows like all the rest, made tight by metal plates.

Her ears were keen as she went, listening out. There were some bushes ahead, and long branches that trailed forward, but she knew that the noise had come from further away. She kept on walking, swatting away the midges that were enjoying the final strains of daylight. The old factory was a hundred yards further along, but all she could hear was the slow crunch of her feet and the nervous rasps of her breaths. She could feel her heartbeat, like someone tapping on her chest.

Then she saw it, the van, the back corner just visible behind the factory.

Laura ran, every cell in her body telling her that something wasn't right. Her breaths came faster, adrenaline coursing through her, as she strained to get to the factory.

She threw herself against the factory wall, all in shadow, and looked along the brickwork. She was closer to the van now and so she knew that it was the same one. She wiped her forehead with her hand, slick with sweat from the exertion. Laura crept along, her back pressed against the wall, trying to keep her breaths quiet, her phone in her hand, ready to dial as soon as she saw something to report. The bricks were cold through her shirt, her back clammy, and the ground was uneven and littered with old cigarette ends and beer cans. There was a bag on the ground nearby that looked like it might have once had glue inside. She tried to be as quiet as possible, her footsteps just light squeaks on damp grass, and when she got to the end of the wall, she put her head round slowly. The van was there, the engine off, the doors closed.

Laura looked at the floor for a second, deciding what to do. She was on her own, but she knew that time was important. Then she looked along the wall again and saw something. It was an old door, propped against a window opening, just along from the van, but the window didn't have the usual metal plate over it. It looked like there might be a way into the building.

Laura walked slowly towards it, checking behind her as she went, her back still against the wall.

The door was old and splintered. When Laura moved it back, she was able to look behind it and into the gloom of the factory. She had to let her eyes adjust, some light crept in from behind her, but it was still mostly dark, starting to match the evening outside, but she could tell that the building was huge and empty. Her efforts with the door seemed to echo inside. There were rectangular outlines of light along the walls, the remnants of the day trying to creep in around the metal plates opposite, and the holes in the roof let in straight beams of light that caught the dust thrown up by the movement of the door.

Then she heard something again. It was the sound of movement, scuffling on the floor, then a muffled shout. No, not a shout. A muffled scream.

Laura scrambled over the wide stone sill to get inside and looked along the walls to make sure that no one was waiting for her.

'Hey, who's there?' she shouted. It echoed back. She took her phone out of her pocket.

The muffled screams started up again, the sounds of a struggle, feet kicking on the floor. Then there was movement further into the building, towards the wall at the other end. Someone was crouching down, and there was motion, a flurry.

'Stop it!' Laura shouted, and began to run in the direction of the movement. The floor was covered in debris and loose cables, with metal brackets sticking up, but Laura knew that she couldn't afford to tiptoe her way through. She jabbed 999 on her phone and shouted out where she was when the phone was answered.

It got darker as she got further in, but when she got within twenty yards of the shape, she saw that whoever was on the floor was struggling, the legs kicking up.

Laura shouted again, and then she saw a shadow get bigger and turn towards her.

It was a man, she could tell that from the height, and as Laura's eyes shot back to the floor, she saw that there was still someone there. The remnants of light that streamed in through a hole in the roof shone back off bare skin. There were more muffled shouts, and as Laura processed what she could see, she knew that it was Rachel on the floor.

'It's over!' Laura shouted, stepping closer. 'Move away from her.'

The shadow didn't move. It looked like he was all in black, not much visible in the poor light, although Laura could tell that he was coming towards her.

'Stop now!' Laura shouted, her arms out, making herself look big. 'You're under arrest. You're done.'

Laura shivered and felt the hairs on her neck stand up as she heard a chuckle, deep and mean. Her ears went keen, and she heard the noise of sirens. There was no flicker of blue lights though, and so it was still just her and the shadow, now around fifteen feet from her.

Laura stepped forward. 'They're on their way

now,' she said, a tremble in her voice. 'It's over.'

The shadow moved towards her. It was fight or flight, Laura knew that now, and she was choosing fight. All the self-defence moves she knew raced through her head, but they scrambled for attention, and all she could do was follow her instincts. She took one more step forward. Then she saw it. The raised arm. He was holding something. No, not holding. Aiming. She stopped, her breathing halted. Then there was that chuckle again.

There was a noise, like a whistle in the air, and then it seemed like everything stopped working. Her arms went down, her legs straight, there was a sharp pain in her chest, and then she was falling backwards, the holes in the roof swirling, her muscles not working. Nothing was working. She hit the floor hard and went into spasms, her feet thrashing on the floor, her teeth clenched. She couldn't do anything as he came towards her, his steps heavy. Her brain registered that he was standing over her, looking down, his head cocked to one side.

Chapter Fifty-Nine

Laura lifted her head off the floor and tried to roll onto her front. The spasms had ended now, but she felt drained and sweaty, her shirt sticking to her chest. Her head had hit the floor, so she reached behind gingerly, and then winced when her hand came into contact with damp hair. She knew that the stickiness on her fingers was blood.

The attacker had gone now, or at least it seemed that way. The sirens were getting louder. He must have made his escape before the cars arrived.

She rubbed her chest. She knew what she had been hit with. It hadn't been a gun, or at least not one with bullets. It had been a Taser, a stun gun, two electrically charged wires with a fine needle on the end of each one. It had dug into her chest and paralysed her muscles, sent her into spasms on the floor. He had stood over her to take the needles out and then he had gone.

She creaked to her knees, panting hard, her hair hanging down in sweaty trails, sticking to her forehead. Then she crawled over to the form on the floor. Rachel was lying in a foetal position, choking noises coming from her.

'I'm sorry, I'm sorry,' Laura said, tears streaming down her face now. She reached into Rachel's mouth and started to scoop out the grit and small stones, throwing them onto the floor, Laura's fingers caked in saliva and vomit. She got enough out so that Rachel could start to spit out the rest, and Laura put her arms round Rachel's shoulder as she gagged and spat onto the floor.

Once her mouth was empty, Rachel began to wail, but it came in short bursts as the air tried to force its way back into her lungs. Laura held her close, tried to be a comfort, but tears were running down her own face. Rachel's hands were still cuffed, and so all she could do was submit to Laura's hold. The horror of what had happened struck Laura hard. 'I should have got here sooner, I'm sorry. It's all over now.'

Rachel's head dipped onto Laura's shoulder, and she felt her neck go damp.

Where were the police vans? She pulled out her phone and dialled Joe's number, but when it started to ring, she felt sick, knew that she didn't want to pass on the news. She couldn't call him with Rachel crying and retching next to her, and she couldn't let Rachel go, not here, alone, in a dark and derelict factory. She clicked off the phone.

Laura thought of the police cars that should be on their way, Rachel's colleagues heading for them. She used her phone to cast some light, and as she ran it up Rachel's body, she saw that she was still wearing her vest although it was torn, but there was nothing below her waist apart from her running shoes. There were red scratches on the inside of her thighs, her skin like a pale glow in the light of the screen.

'Are there stones anywhere else?' Laura asked, quietly.

Rachel looked at her, her mouth trembling, her eyes rimmed red and wide with fear. Then she nodded slowly and looked down.

Laura closed her eyes for a moment, and then nodded, trying to stay in control of the situation.

'I'm going to leave it there,' Laura said. 'Are you okay with that? Or do you want me to get it out?'

Rachel shook her head violently and began to sob again, before her head slipped forward onto Laura's chest.

Laura put her arms around her again and pulled her in close, let Rachel sob into her chest, one hand stroking Rachel's hair, trying to make it better. Except that she knew she couldn't do that. Rachel would never be better again, and it would take more than just hugs and comfort to make her a lot less broken.

As the sound of sirens drew close, Laura pulled away to take her jacket off, and then she put it around Rachel's shoulders, trailing it over her thighs to allow her a shred of dignity before their colleagues burst into the building.

Laura felt cold. It wasn't the lack of a jacket though. It was the shiver of anger that she was feeling, and as she pulled Rachel close once more, she wondered whether anything would ever be the same again, because of what had happened to Rachel. Because of what had almost happened to her.

Chapter Sixty

Jack was outside the bar that had once been called Manero's when he got the call. He had been waiting for the doormen to open the doors, to try and get some quotes on Don Roberts, in the hope that someone may have remembered stories from the old days. There was the germ of a good story there, and Jack wanted to make it stronger, for Emma's sake, to bring some justice for her.

He looked at his phone and saw that it was Laura, but when he answered, there was no one on the other end.

'Laura? Are you there?'

There were some deep breaths, and then she said, 'I need to see you, Jack.' Her voice sounded strained.

'Are you okay?'

There was a pause, and then, 'No, I'm not.'

Jack felt a stab of panic, his stomach lurching. 'Where are you?'

'The hospital.'

'I'll be right there,' he said, and ran for his car.

The journey didn't take long, because it seemed like he skidded around every corner in his rush to get there, chancing red lights and speed cameras. He dumped the car in the nearest parking space and ran towards the casualty department, passing rows of seats filled by people feeling sorry for themselves, faced by a counter and a receptionist who didn't look like she cared either way.

He found out that Laura had been taken through just after her call. He heard her voice, and as he pulled the curtain back, Jack saw her wince as the casualty doctor inserted the last of seven stitches into a small patch shaved into the back of her head.

'There you go,' the doctor said, his Indian accent strong. 'Should keep the sawdust from falling out.' His voice was too cheery, and Laura faked a smile.

'Could I have a moment?' Laura asked, and gestured towards Jack.

The doctor looked doubtful for a moment, but eventually he nodded and left them alone. Laura wrapped her arms tight around Jack and he pulled her close, whispering in her ear, 'What happened?'

Laura pulled away. 'Rachel was attacked. She was his next victim, but I got in the way.'

Jack was surprised. 'Tell me.'

She shook her head. 'I'll give you the full story later, but I'm sure you can imagine it,' she said, looking vulnerable again. 'Danger is part of the job, I know that, but this was different. It's sexual violation. It's too personal, too invasive. I've just been stitched, but what will Rachel be going through? Probed and examined, checked for injuries, for evidence, those small traces that get left behind, violated for the second time today. And why? So they can build a case and lock someone away for what, twenty years?'

Jack didn't respond, because he knew what she meant. The judge will say life, but when does it ever mean that? There will always be some rosy-eyed do-gooder ready to fight his corner, to campaign for his release, to say that it is wrong to cage someone up for ever. Even the Yorkshire Ripper found someone to speak up on his behalf, as if a portion of regret could somehow make up for thirteen dead. Jack believed that some people should never get out, because they'd foregone their right to a decent life, but sometimes it only took for the memories to fade, for the press to forget, and killers walked the streets again. What would happen in this case, if he was ever caught? What about Deborah and Jane? And now Rachel.

She would bear those scars for the rest of her life, long after the physical wounds had healed. Why didn't that ever seem to matter?

They both looked around when they heard a voice, and then the privacy curtain parted and a familiar face came into view. Joe Kinsella. He looked confused, his face filled with pain.

Laura took a deep breath and pulled away from Jack. Joe came over to her, and Jack saw tears in his eyes. Joe clenched his jaw as he tried to control his emotions.

Jack stepped out of the cubicle, not wanting to intrude on Joe's distress. The curtain didn't close though, so he watched as Joe took a deep breath and tried a smile, but it was forced. Joe wasn't ready to crumble yet, not in public.

As Joe got close, Laura put her arms around him, and as he pulled himself closer, Jack heard her whisper, 'I'm sorry, Joe. I should have got there quicker.' Joe stepped back and took hold of her hands. 'No, you saved her,' he said quietly, his voice breaking as he pumped her hands. 'I don't know what will be left of her, but whatever there is, it will be thanks to you.'

Laura gave him a watery smile. 'So what now?'

At that, Joe's gaze hardened and he dropped her hands. 'We catch him, that's what.'

'But we're too involved,' she said. 'We might make mistakes, and it will haunt us, because he's dragged us closer.'

'No, that isn't how it is,' Joe said, his voice sterner than before. 'It will haunt us if we don't go after him. You saw him, Laura. You can take us nearer. You can describe him. Have you got a voice recorder on your phone?'

Laura nodded.

'Good. Go to a dark room, or somewhere quiet where you can close your eyes. Like you said to Angel, think of him. His age. His size. His smell. How he held himself. All of those things will take us closer. Do that, and then let Carson know.'

Laura agreed, though the thought made her stomach roll. 'I will. And what about you?'

Joe stroked his stubble and then looked up at Laura. 'I'm going to wait for Rachel, to make sure she can cope.' Some more tears came into his eyes, and he looked down and chewed his lip until they'd gone. 'I'm not sure I'm the right person for her just now.'

'What do you mean?'

'We weren't serious, you know that,' Joe said. 'She would stay over, and we would be there for each other, you know, fulfilling a need, but we both knew it wasn't going to last. And now this. It makes it serious, but she needs someone she can rely on, someone who really loves her. But then it makes me feel like a coward, because I'm running at the first sign of bad times. I thought I was better than that.'

'Maybe she won't want you that close,' Laura said. 'Be there, as a friend. Forget about how you were. That's probably all she wants.'

Joe nodded. 'I've called her parents, but they're on holiday, so it's just me until they get a flight. She needs them though. It's time she stopped being a cop for a while and went back to being someone's daughter.'

Laura hugged Joe again, but he pulled away

361

sooner this time. He seemed more determined than before. 'What about you?' he said.

Laura looked through the gap in the curtain and looked at Jack. 'I want to go home,' she said.

He was in his chair in the living room, his hands gripping the arms. His clothes were covered in dust and he was sweating, the exertion of his dash from the factory. He had left the van behind and escaped on foot, running through alleys. Now he was back, the house was silent but he was wincing from the noise. Laughs. Shouts. Screams.

He closed his eyes. He thought of Doctor Barker again, but the memory he had wasn't from the day before, but more than twenty years earlier. It was the doctor's voice, friendly, caring, but it hadn't changed anything. Then there were faces through the years. First girls, then women. He hadn't hurt all of them. Some he had just followed and then fantasised about, and those were the special ones, the ones that hadn't disappointed.

He was still aroused, unfulfilled from the attack before. He'd heard the sirens and known that he had to get away. But he also knew he'd only delayed the inevitable. They would come for him.

His fingers dug into the fabric. He thought of his mother. He had heard her, had sat on the landing, listened as she argued with his adoptive parents. He'd always felt that there was something missing from his life, and as he listened, he had wanted to go down, to see her, to let her see him. But he had been scared, not wanting to meet her in case she didn't like what she saw. He had stood up, ready to go down, when he heard the final shout from her, and then the back door slammed.

That's when he'd first heard them, the noises. It was just whispers then, so quiet that he could hardly hear them, and so he had to concentrate hard to work out what they were saying.

He heard footsteps. At first he thought they were rumbles in his head, but as he looked to the window he saw that it was a real noise, not the ones he heard most of the time. They were marching up the garden path.

He stared ahead. He had been expecting them ever since he had failed. He wouldn't do anything to stop them. The door was unlocked. They could get him. He was ready.

The door banged against the wall as they burst in. He could hear mocking laughter, but as he looked up, their faces were full of menace. No one was laughing.

He didn't say anything as they grabbed his arms and pulled him towards the door. It was his time.

Chapter Sixty-One

Jack went for a drive.

Laura was at home trying to revive herself after the horrors of the day's events. Jack felt an intense need to protect her, to be with her, but he didn't want to suffocate her. She said she needed her space to process what had happened, and had told Jack to go out and keep up with the investigation. She was even more determined to catch the killer now.

He didn't know where to go at first. Joe was still at the hospital with Rachel, and so he just drove the country roads, enjoying the echo of the engine as he went along hedgerow lanes and the cool night breeze. But all the roads around Turners Fold seemed to head towards Blackley, the countryside spoiled eventually by the orange strips of street lighting that rolled down the seven hills of the town. The Whitcroft estate was on the fringes of Blackley, and Jack found himself driving towards it.

The estate seemed quiet, although the aroma of barbecues drifted in the warm night air, the laughs and chatter loud in the darkness He thought he heard a bottle smash somewhere, and then there was a shout. A balmy Saturday night would bring the drinkers onto the streets, provide Dolby with the kind of story he wanted, even if it was only a few shots of teenagers sharing alco-pops.

A couple of circuits didn't reveal much, and so he cut onto the side streets, hoping to catch people looking like they were up to no good. Even the side streets were quiet though, and it didn't look like Dolby was going to get much to write about. He was about to head away from the estate when he felt his phone buzzing in his pocket.

'Hello?'

'Jack? Is that Jack?'

He recognised the voice straight away. It was

Emma. She was slurring more than before, but there was something else there too. Her voice was higher, more frantic.

'Emma, it's me. Are you okay?'

'They've taken him,' she said, and then she started to sob.

'Who have they taken?'

'Simon. They've taken Simon.'

Jack gave a sigh of relief and then smiled to himself. They had him. It was over.

'It's okay, Emma, everything will be all right. Let the police do their job.'

'It wasn't the police,' she said. 'It was Don. I saw him.' Her words came out thick with tears.

He pulled up to the kerb. 'Calm down. Talk to me. What do you mean?'

Jack listened as Emma poured out the story between deep breaths.

'I went to Simon's house,' she said. 'I know where he lives. He doesn't know that, but I saw his van one day, just at the side of his house. I waited outside and I saw him. So after you'd gone, I thought some more about what had happened, and I just needed someone to talk to. I went to his house, and I saw them, Don and two of his men, pulling him to a car.'

She started to cry again.

'Why are they taking him, Jack? Did you tell Don what I said? Is that why?'

His mind raced with the implications. If they had taken PC Abbott, what if he wasn't the killer? 'Wait there,' he said. 'I'm on my way.'

He tried calling Laura, but there was no reply.

'Shit!' he said, his tyres screeching as he set off.

365

Laura sat on the side of the bath as the water filled the tub behind her, wincing as she took off her clothes, the stretching and moving aggravating her aches and bruises. She just needed to get herself clean, to somehow wash off the events of the day. She heard her phone ring but left it. She wanted to empty her mind so that she could recall her attacker.

She caught herself in the mirror as her clothes slipped to the floor, and she stepped forward to examine her bruises. There was a large one on her shoulder, and her elbow was grazed.

As she slid into the water, some of her tension slipped away. The bubbles gathered around her neck as she sank deeper into the water, the lavender scents relaxing her, and she closed her eyes. Suddenly the light and calmness of the bathroom was replaced by the darkness of the factory. The warmth of the water and the scent of the bubbles made her feel like she was floating, and she was able to take herself back to the deserted building, to the echoes and the dust.

Laura tried to recall her first impression of him, her glimpse through the gloom as he rose up. He was tall. That had been her first thought. And slim. No, it was more than slim. Skinny, so that he seemed to stoop, uncomfortable with his size. He wasn't a big man. Just a tall one.

She thought of him as he had stood over Rachel. That distracted her for a moment as she thought of what he had done to her. She concentrated on getting rid of those images. She had to think about him, not Rachel. She thought at the time that she hadn't been able to see his face, that he was always in shadow, but as she thought some more, there was something. It was the way he cocked his head, like a bird, curious, as he watched her come towards him. He never lost his nerve. He just waited for her to get close, so that he could get her with the Taser. Laura knew that she had to get within fifteen feet for the Taser to be effective, and so he had been patient. For Laura, that made him dangerous.

She tried to think of how he seemed when he had leaned over her. Laura's body hadn't been working, but her senses were, and she remembered there was a smell, and with her eyes closed, it came back to her. It was something damp and musty. And cigarettes. But not filtered cigarettes. No, it was the rich, cloying smell of roll-up cigarettes.

Laura thought of him as he leaned over her, her body incapable of reacting, his hands long and thin. Then she thought of the way he looked again, his head cocked. And something about that niggled her. It seemed familiar, she had definitely seen it before, but she couldn't be sure where.

He was a police officer, that's where all the clues pointed. The Taser gun. The handcuffs. Was he killing people when he was on duty, using his uniform to lull these women into a false sense of security? They hadn't found Simon Abbott as he wasn't on duty and wasn't at home, but it wouldn't take long, she was sure of that. But Shane was dead, so they thought, and so was

Simon Abbott just exacting some revenge for a friend?

But it might not be Abbott. She tried to think of all the officers who passed through the station. Was there anyone that tall who struck her as being too quiet, maybe too attentive towards her? But she knew that that line of thinking wouldn't lead her anywhere, because murderers often appeared to be the most ordinary people in the world. The nice man from down the street, or the one who helped out with church on Sunday.

Then she thought of something. She remembered the van. It had been behind her when she was jogging home, which meant that the killer knew where she lived. She sat up straight in the bath, goosebumps on her arms. He could come to her home. She was naked, vulnerable. Why had she told Jack to go out!

Laura stepped quickly out of the bath, wrapping a towel around her body. She needed to get away from the house.

Chapter Sixty-Two

Emma was sitting on her doorstep when Jack got there, her head against the door frame, her eyes almost closed. There was a glass in front of her, half-filled with cider. Her eyes opened slowly when Jack got closer.

'You're back,' she said, and her hand moved

unsteadily towards the glass.

He kneeled down in front of her and moved her drink away.

'What did you see?' he said urgently.

She went as if to grab the glass, but Jack held it further away, so that she slumped backwards against the door frame. She took a few deep breaths, and Jack thought she was going to be sick, but eventually she said, 'I told you, Don took him.'

'When was this?'

She shrugged, her movements uncoordinated. 'I came home, and then I rang you. Thirty minutes before. Maybe.'

'Are you sure it was Don?'

Her look darkened at that, her face seemed to gain a bit more focus. 'Do you think I don't know Don Roberts when I see him? He was dragging Simon to the car. Two men were holding his arms.'

'Do you know where they were taking him?'

'I didn't ask. I just watched.'

Jack stood up, frustrated. He was about to leave Emma when she added, 'Don's got something in town.'

'What do you mean, something?'

'Like a workshop.'

'How do you know that?'

Emma wiped her nose with her hand and beckoned for him to hand the glass over. She drank some greedily when he gave it to her, and then said, 'I make it my business to know about him. I wanted to burn the fucking place down. But what's the point?'

'Where is it?'

Emma gave him vague details, her memory blurred by drink, and then he ran back to his car, leaving Emma on her doorstep, with an almost empty glass of cider for company.

Laura ran into the police station, banging the door against the wall. She was wincing from her bruises, the cuts on her knee bleeding again, making small stains on her trousers, but she tried to rush through, to get to the top floor. She avoided the lift, despite her sense of urgency, and climbed the three flights of stairs instead. When she reached the top, she grimaced and took a moment to catch her breath, before hobbling along to the CCTV room.

The operator barely moved a muscle as she walked in. He was drinking coffee and eating a sandwich from a small plastic box he had brought in from home.

'Do you remember the footage I asked you to look at yesterday, of the man who came to the police station?' she said, still panting a little.

He shrugged. 'Yeah, why?' he said, his mouth full of bread.

'Have you still got it?'

He nodded. 'You asked me to save it for you, so I did,' he said, putting his food down. He sighed as he rummaged under some papers on one side of his desk and found a disc. 'Here it is.'

Laura went to a computer terminal at the end of the screens and inserted it. The software seemed to take an age to load, and she was about to turn around to get some help when familiar images jumped onto the screen, the view from the camera that overlooked the reception area.

She was impatient as she scrolled quickly through the footage, the washed-out outlines like flashes as she went through it, and then she stopped when she saw him, the slow nervous shuffle of Rupert Barker fast-forwarded into a rush. She took the footage back and pressed play, and then watched carefully, looking for something she had missed from her last viewing.

The camera looked towards the large exit doors and the row of seats opposite the glass kiosks. The chairs were in front of a window, but it was hard to see what was in the car park because there was a van parked there, a white Transit with the police crest on the side.

Rupert looked hesitant and nervous, she thought, his hand stroking his cheek, and at one point it seemed like he was about to turn around and leave. But she told herself to ignore Rupert Barker. She knew already what he was thinking about when he came to the station. Shane Grix, the file he had uncovered. It was the people at the station she was interested in now.

Laura watched as Rupert looked along the row of seats. There weren't many people in the station, just a bored-looking teenager in the obligatory tracksuit and a solicitor preening herself at the end of the row. Rupert sat down and fidgeted. Two police officers went through the reception area, their belts heavy with equipment, and Laura looked closely to see whether either of them glanced Rupert's way. Neither did.

Then Rupert walked off camera. That must have been when he spoke to the counter assistant.

There was a delay before Rupert appeared back on screen, when he sat down on one of the seats, his head forward, his hands clasped together, looking towards the floor, his feet tapping on the ground.

Another police officer marched in through the doors, just moving out of the way to let two female officers out, closely followed by a police driver, who was dragging a trolley of bags to the exit.

Laura straightened, frustrated, and looked away for a moment, sure that the answer must lie somewhere else, glancing back at the CCTV operator, ready to ask him to tee up the external footage. Then she saw something. She looked back at the screen and watched Rupert again, who was still sitting down, looking nervous. There were no more police officers, and the driver was just banging through the doors with his trolley.

She went to scratch her head, but then remembered the stitches and pulled her hand away. She had seen something, she knew it.

She leaned forward to take the footage back again, but then she stopped. It was the driver who drew her attention. He was tall and skinny, the sharpness of his shoulder blades visible through his thin blue jacket. He was standing by his van, visible through the window behind Rupert, not moving. But it was the way he held his head, cocked to one side, like a bird listening out, that made her heart beat faster.

Laura felt a shiver of recognition and cold goosebumps prickled the back of her neck. Her mouth went dry and she felt light-headed as she thought back to the person who had stood over Rachel. She swallowed hard and tried to focus on the screen, ignoring what had happened earlier. Her hand went to the mouse and it felt slick under her hand as she dragged the footage back to where the driver first came into view.

Laura watched as he seemed to slink in, just the top of his head visible at first, a bald patch spreading on the crown of his head, hair light, and his head forward, so that his shoulders were hunched, one arm down to pull the trolley loaded with blue bags, ready for delivery to the prosecution in their office on the other side of Blackley. Then it was there. The glance over to Rupert and a stutter in his walk, just for a moment, barely noticeable, but that falter was what she had seen before. He kept on going though, but he seemed quicker as he went, banging through the doors with his trolley.

Then Laura watched him as he paused by the van, his head cocked, making no effort to load it.

Her eyes went back to Rupert, who was now looking up, towards the doors that Laura had headed for when she had got the message about him. Rupert hadn't noticed the driver, and Laura saw the final nervous look on Rupert's face as he turned and walked quickly out of the station, rushing past the van, the driver looking down, his arms by his side. As Rupert went out of shot, the driver looked up, and he seemed to be watching in the direction Rupert had just gone.

Laura jabbed the eject button and almost shouted at the computer as it took an age for the drawer to open. Then she grabbed it and hobbled towards the door, going to the balcony to look out into the atrium. She was seeing if there was someone there she knew, or even the driver himself, but as she looked down, she saw only empty tables, the metal shutter on the canteen fastened down.

She headed for the stairs, taking two at a time, despite the complaints from her knee, and went towards the Incident Room, bursting through the door.

Carson was there, in conversation with the other detectives, their expressions pained, and Laura knew that they were talking about Rachel, how the case had come too close to the team.

'I've got something,' she said, and held up the disc. 'It's not Simon Abbott we're looking for.'

'What is it?' Carson said, moving towards her.

'Joe talked about the killer being Mr Invisible, about his frustration at being just an anonymous little man,' she said. When Carson folded his arms, she continued, 'What if he isn't a police officer after all? What if he is just someone who works here, who floats around the station, ignored by all of us?'

Carson's lips pursed as he thought about that. 'What's on there?' and he pointed towards the disc.

'I'll show you,' she said, and went to one of the computers and opened the disc drive. As the software loaded, she said, 'It's one of the drivers. Is there anyone more invisible? They get full access to everything, to deliver files and exhibits, but do we ever really notice them?'

Carson started to nod. 'It would fit,' he said.

'So watch this,' Laura said, and leaned forward to take control of the computer. She took the footage forward to where Rupert came into the police station.

As Carson watched Rupert, Laura said, 'We thought yesterday that the killer knew that Rupert would recognise the methods he'd used, or else he knew that Rupert had been to the police station.' Laura watched for Carson's re-action, and when she noticed the slight widening of the eyes as the driver came into view, at the stutter in his walk, and the way he loitered by his van, Laura knew that Carson had seen what she had.

'Does it look like him?' he said, his lips tight, a flush to his cheeks.

Laura nodded. 'Very much,' and then she watched as Carson ran from the Incident Room.

The other detectives crowded round to look at the footage.

'We know who he is now,' she said, almost to herself. 'We've got him.'

Suddenly, Carson came crashing through with one of the drivers, dressed in a blue jacket and trousers, a Lancashire Constabulary crest on his chest.

'Who is that?' Carson barked, pointing at the screen.

The driver looked scared, not used to having people shouting at him, but he took a deep breath as he realised that this wasn't some minor enquiry.

'It's Peter Williams,' he said.

Carson slapped him on the back and then told him to sit down. 'Stay there,' he said. 'Don't call anyone, don't speak to anyone,' and then Carson gestured for Laura to follow him. As she ran out of the room, she felt a certainty that they were almost there.

Chapter Sixty-Three

Carson drove quickly away from the station.

'Do you think he'll be expecting us?' Laura said.

'Murderers are always expecting us, because they know we don't give up. He'll have his story worked out. I just don't want him getting rid of any evidence before we get there.'

Laura looked out of the window, her jaw set, her mind working its way through the different stages of guilt. She should have got a better view of him. And just a couple of hours earlier, could she have done more? She should have rushed him, but she hesitated and let him get away.

They had to cross town to get to where Williams lived, along terraced strips and up a long climb away from the town centre that took them towards the town's hospital, which overlooked the green roll of the moors, an antidote to the glass and steel of the hospital building.

Laura's phone rang. It was Archie, one of the detectives from the squad. 'I've just spoken to the agency that recruits the drivers for us,' he said. 'He joined us six years ago. He said that he had been working as a motor cycle courier in London, and then a delivery driver, but both companies have since gone bust. His national insurance number was checked out, and he had no convictions, and so all the tests were passed.'

'What about his personal history?' Laura said.

'That's where it gets interesting,' Archie said. 'They've pulled his application form, and he said that he went to school in Stoke, but I've just tried to find it on the internet and it doesn't seem to exist.'

'So he's got a made-up past,' Laura said, catching Carson's gaze as he drove.

'At least some of it,' Archie said. 'He does have a clean driving licence, and so he is official.'

'Except that if he is Shane Grix, he was supposed to have been murdered in a London alleyway,' Laura said, and then she paused as she thought of something. 'I'll call you back, Archie. I'll just give Sandy a ring.'

She went through her contacts list to find the number of her old London colleague. The phone rang out until she heard the London chirp. 'I need another favour,' she said.

'Make it quick, darlin',' he replied. 'I love a friendly voice, but it's Saturday night and I'm in the boozer.'

'Which one? The Green Man?'

'Yes, why?'

'Because you're only across the road from the

station. Could you go across and look in the Shane Grix murder file?'

There was a sigh. 'Laura, the night's just getting going. I've had too many drinks. Don't make me do this.'

'You'll get the credit for solving that murder if you do,' she said. 'See if there is a list of Shane's associates in the file.'

'There is,' he said. 'I was looking at the file the other day, remember. We couldn't track down most of them, because they were like him, homeless and drifting, keeping away from people like me.'

'Look for a Peter Williams,' she said.

Laura could hear his deliberations, but she knew that he would do what she asked, because for all the city boy charm he thought he had, he was a good copper at heart.

She smiled as he said, 'Give me a few minutes, the file is still out. I'll call you back.'

Carson glanced at Laura. 'Are you thinking that the young man killed in the alleyway is really Peter Williams?' he said.

'We can guess that it probably isn't Shane Grix,' she said. 'And so if it isn't him, who else can it be? He must have stolen his identity when he killed him and started again.'

Carson frowned and drummed his fingers on the steering wheel. 'Perhaps it's even simpler than that.'

'What do you mean?'

'Maybe Williams was killed because of his identity, so that Grix could come back up here and do this.'

'What, targeted murder?'

Carson nodded. 'Why not? Perhaps Williams was his route back up north, where he could return and be anonymous, because Williams looked like him and so might pass for Shane once he was set on fire.'

Laura looked down when she felt her phone buzz in her hand. It was Sandy from London. She could feel the tension in the car as she listened to what Sandy had to say. When he'd finished, Laura thanked him and then turned to Carson. 'It all fits,' she said. 'Peter Williams was one of the people on the list. They were seen together a few times before the body was found, sleeping in the same shelters. He was a couple of years older and had been in London a year longer. But he was invisible. Grew up in care, no family to speak of, and so he just headed south.'

'And no one to look for him when he didn't go home,' Carson said.

'That's right,' Laura said, nodding. 'He wasn't a suspect, just one of Shane's friends, and so the police in London weren't hunting him down. And like Sandy said, Shane was just another London homeless. They die all the time.'

'So he came back north and ended up in Blackley.'

'In the same town as Shane's real mother,' Laura said. 'Now that is too much of a coincidence. So if Peter Williams really is Shane Grix, we know why he is here, to be near his real mother.'

'Hopefully he can tell us all about it in a minute,' Carson said, as he turned onto a long straight road of terraced houses lined by old

Fords and souped-up small cars, all smoothed out rear ends and tin-can exhausts. Carson scraped his wheels along the kerb outside an end-terrace. Laura jumped out and ran for the door, dirty white PVC. She heard Carson behind her.

'Just go in,' he said, puffing as he ran. 'We're not waiting for an invite.'

Laura reached for the handle, expecting it to be locked, but instead it swung open in front of her. There was no hallway, so that the door opened straight into a small square living room. She could see the kitchen behind, a square room of the same size.

'Peter Williams?' she shouted, but there was no response. She saw that the back door was closed, and so she guessed that he hadn't run out through the yard.

The room in front of her was unremarkable. There was a flat screen television and cheap leather furniture, with a coffee table in the middle of the room, covered in old cups and flakes of rolling tobacco. There were no photographs on the wall, nothing to make it homely, just woodchip painted in cream.

The stairs ran out of the corner of the room, and she was about to head for them when she noticed a small cupboard built into the space under the stairs. She used her toe to open the door, and as it swung open she was surprised. She had expected old coats and a vacuum cleaner, but there was a computer on a small desk, along with a small blue chair, crammed into the space. There was no light.

Carson appeared on her shoulder. 'It must get cosy in there,' he said. 'It must help him with the fantasy, to shut himself away, just the colours on the screen bouncing around the walls. We'll get the computer unit to have a look, see if we can find his emails.'

'Let's try upstairs,' she said.

Carson trailed her again, and as she climbed the stairs, she thought the house smelled musty and stale. It was the smell of beds that didn't get changed too often, or carpets that had never felt the hum of a vacuum cleaner.

There were two bedrooms upstairs, one on either side of the stairs, along with a bathroom. Laura got a glimpse as she went past. It was old fashioned, with an avocado-coloured sink splashed by toothpaste and soap scum. There was only one toothbrush on the sill.

The rear bedroom was just a dumping ground, with bin liners filled with old clothes, some books piled up in one corner.

Laura backed out of the room. She wanted to see what was in the main bedroom. She stood in front of the door and gave it a push, letting the view inside slowly reveal itself. The curtains were open and the street light outside made the room bright.

The bedroom was like the rest of the house, simple and cheap, no frills, with old white bedding and chipped brown cupboards. There was an old coffee cup next to the bed.

'No woman's touch?' Laura said.

Carson brushed past her and flicked the light switch as Laura went to a wardrobe opposite the bed and opened the doors. When she saw what was inside, she whistled.

'What is it?' Carson said.

'Police uniforms,' she said. 'Yellow jackets, caps, full tunics, equipment belts.'

'It would explain how he is able to convince them to talk to him,' Carson said, coming up behind her. 'That's Abbott's number,' he pointed to the collar number on the jacket. 'Abbott will get it for losing a uniform, but where is Williams?'

Then Laura's phone rang.

Chapter Sixty-Four

'Don Roberts has got him,' Jack said, as he drove too quickly through the town centre.

'What do you mean, got him?'

'I've spoken to Emma, Shane's birth mother. She saw Don and two of his men dragging Simon Abbott away.'

'We don't think it's Simon Abbott,' she said.

'Why not?'

'Because I'm in Shane's home, looking at a wardrobe filled with Abbott's uniforms. It looked like Shane used Abbott's name as a cover when he spoke to Emma, so that he could hear her story. But Shane worked for the police as a driver.'

'So they've got Shane?'

'He's not here, and so I'd guess so.'

382

'How long have you known about Shane?' Jack said.

'What do you mean?'

He stopped speaking as he came to a junction. He wasn't really sure what he was looking for. Emma had only given him a general description, because she couldn't remember the street, just the area. So he had driven along rows of houses, the streets lined by cars, and now the bright pub lights were in front of him, glittering beneath the brooding shadow of the viaduct in the distance, the route for the trains that snaked through the hills and connected all the old cotton towns.

'How many people have seen him today?' Jack said.

'Me, and Rachel,' she said.

'And how long have you known the full story?'

'Minutes ago.'

'So Don knew before you worked it out, and I can guess that you didn't tell Don Roberts,' Jack said. 'So who else could have told him?'

Laura didn't answer for a few seconds, and then she said, 'I'll speak later,' before the phone went quiet.

Jack threw his phone onto the passenger seat and carried on with his drive through the town centre again, once more on the one-way loop, trying to spot a building that was different from the pubs, clubs and takeaways, peering through the groups of short-sleeve muscle and tight white skirts. The town centre petered out eventually into industrial units and derelict back streets, the shadows filled by women who traded themselves at night, their skirts high, small glittery bags slung over their shoulders.

He had driven two circuits already, and guessed that he'd been spotted by the police who looked out for kerb crawlers, but he kept on driving. Then he saw it: David Hoyle's car.

Jack almost missed it. It was parked in the shadows of a high brick wall, away from the streetlights, but he spotted the chrome spokes, just catching enough of a gleam. As he drove towards it, his headlights caught a sign: DR Security.

The night went quiet when he turned off the engine.

'Don's got him,' Laura said to Carson. 'Emma saw Don take him.'

'How would Don know?'

'Rachel.'

Carson looked over, scowling. 'What are you saying?'

'She got nearer than I did. Really close. How else would Don find out?'

'You need to be absolutely sure, McGanity, before you accuse her.'

'It fits,' she said. 'Shane is snatched around the same time Rachel left hospital, after all this time looking for him. Bit of a coincidence, don't you think? Once Don had a name and an occupation, it wouldn't take him long to find him.'

'Let's go ask her,' Carson said. 'It's on the way to Don's house, and I'm being sent the wrong way by some pisshead related to the killer.'

Laura followed him outside and jumped into the car, and then she gripped the door handle as

Carson accelerated away.

Laura watched the houses flash by, tall Victorian rows, with stone-framed bay windows and stained glass above the front doors, most divided up into bedsits and dole flats. Carson braked hard for a speed camera, the bright yellow box catching the glare from his headlight, making a small crowd of young men clustered by a lamppost look up startled. From the way they quietly walked separate ways, their hands back in their pockets, Laura knew that a street deal had just been thwarted, although there would be a reunion as soon as Carson was out of sight. Darkness brought out the night rats. A job for someone else on a different day.

Carson turned into a steep terraced street as a short cut, the hill so sharp that the houses looked like they were leaning against each other for support, clinging onto the slope. Laura's feet dug into the mat, phantom-braking as the car raced towards the junction at the bottom. The lights were still showing red, but they started to change just as they got closer. There was just the first flicker of a green light as Carson flew through, brightened by the orange flicker of sparks as the exhaust caught the tarmac and the hill bottomed out.

Laura knew they weren't far away, some of the landmarks were familiar now, as the terraced strips gave way to the gentle curves and leaves of suburbia, and then Carson swung into the bright new boxes of Joe's estate before coming to a halt behind Joe's car.

'You better do the talking,' Carson said. 'It's

time for a gentle touch.'

The front door opened before Laura could get there, Joe Kinsella blocking her way.

'How is she?' Laura said.

Joe shook his head. 'Not good. And I know why you're here. You want her to be examined for forensics, but she won't go, and I'm not going to make her.'

'Why won't she go?'

'Right now, she's embarrassed, violated, and doesn't want to think of her intimate examination being read by her colleagues,' Joe said. Laura was about to say something, but Joe held up his hand. 'I know what you're thinking, that she has nothing to hide, but that's how she feels right now.'

Laura nodded and sighed. 'I understand, but that isn't why we are here, and it's not just a get well visit.'

Joe looked confused. 'What do you mean?'

'We think we know who Rachel's attacker is,' she said. 'A police driver called Peter Williams, although he is really Shane.'

Joe's mouth opened in surprise, and then he looked down, and Laura could almost see the thoughts racing through his mind. Then he looked up.

'Of course, it makes sense,' he said, his eyes wide. 'Not a low-ranking police officer, but someone who floats around the police station, overhearing stuff, the person you never notice coming into the room. Mr Invisible. So have you got him?'

Laura grimaced. 'That's why we need to speak

to Rachel.'

'What do you mean?'

Laura reached out to Joe and placed her hand on his. 'Joe, I'm sorry, but I think Rachel knows who her attacker is. I think she recognised him.'

Joe shook his head. 'She would have told someone.'

'She already has,' Laura said. 'Don Roberts.'

Joe looked surprised at that. 'Why would she do that?'

'Revenge, Joe. She knows what Don Roberts will do to him, and we think Don has already got him. I identified him from the footage when Doctor Barker came to the station, and no one could have leaked it so soon. So the only way Don could have known is if Rachel told him.'

Joe's look darkened, and he glanced into the house. 'She wouldn't do that. She's a cop, she knows the rules.'

'She's also hurting,' Laura said softly. 'Let me speak to her, just to check.'

Joe looked like he was going to object, but Laura saw in his eyes an acceptance that what she had said made some sense. He gave the door a push and then stepped to one side.

The house was in darkness when Laura went in. The curtains were drawn, and whatever light there was came from the flicker of a small candle on a table in the corner of the room.

Rachel was sleeping on the sofa, or so it seemed. She was wrapped up in a blanket, her blonde hair fanning out over the edge of the cushion.

'Rachel? Hi, it's me. How are you?'

Rachel turned over so that she could see Laura,

and then began to sit up.

'No, please don't get up,' Laura said, her voice soft and low. As Rachel's face caught the glow of the candle, Laura thought her eyes looked swollen and puffy from crying.

Rachel settled back down and then turned to look at Laura.

'I'm not ill or anything,' she said. 'I've just taken a shock, that's all.'

'It's not a sign of weakness,' Laura said.

'That's how some will see it.'

'Not the ones that matter,' Laura said. 'Take some time, make yourself right.' When Rachel didn't respond, Laura said, 'We know who it is.'

Rachel stayed still for a moment, and then she looked at Laura. 'Who is it?'

'A police driver called Peter Williams,' Laura replied, watching Rachel carefully. There was no look of surprise, and Laura thought she saw something else. Relief? 'But you know that already, don't you?'

'What do you mean?'

'We think Don Roberts has taken him. We don't know where, but we need to find him before he kills him.'

Rachel took a deep breath, and then said, 'I hope you fail.'

'You told Don, didn't you?' Laura said.

Rachel stared at her, but Laura didn't blink, didn't waver, and then Rachel looked away, drawing the blanket around her shoulders.

Laura reached out and put her hand on Rachel, but it was shrugged off.

Joe appeared in the doorway, just a silhouette

against the light shining in from outside. Laura nodded at him, by way of confirmation of what she had found out, before she headed for the car. Joe didn't look at her as she went past.

Carson followed Laura outside, and when they were in the car, Laura nodded and then looked away.

Carson banged the steering wheel in anger and then simmered for a few seconds, before he snapped, 'We need to find Roberts.'

Laura thought she saw Joe looking out of the window as Carson sped off.

Chapter Sixty-Five

It was dark, almost pitch black, as Jack approached the DR Security building. The streetlights further along were broken, the glass pitted by holes, and the one right outside fizzed off and on, as if someone was trying to hotwire it. It was as if he was getting his impression of the building under a strobe light.

He could make out that it was squat and square, with a large roller shutter at the front, next to a more conventional office door and a small reinforced window. There was nothing preventing access to the front, but the flashes of light caught the gleam of barbed wire that topped high metal fencing. It ran down each side and along the back, so that access to the sides of the building was through two metal security gates.

He should call Laura to tell her, but he wanted to be sure. All he had was the word of a drunk and some guesswork.

His footsteps echoed as loud crunches as he walked slowly towards the roller shutter. He pressed his ear against the cold metal. He guessed that there was nothing behind it, just access into the building, like a garage entrance. There was no sound.

He moved slowly towards the office door, listening out for movement, expecting to be confronted. He didn't breathe as he tried the handle, but the door was locked. He went to the small window, criss-crossed by wire, reinforced glass, and peered in, but he couldn't see anything, the white office blind blocking his view. He stepped back to look for an outline of light, some sign that someone was inside, but there was nothing, just his own shadow against the glass.

He stepped back. The building looked empty. No noise. No lights. But there was another car there, not just Hoyle's. As Jack peered into the patch of darkness behind the building, he saw the outline of a black car, an urban cruiser, barely visible, except for a glint from the windscreen. Jack's mind flashed back to the cars outside Don's house. It was the same type.

The security gates at each side of the building were six feet high, heavy metal, with sturdy struts going their length. He went to the one to his left and gave it a shake. It felt solid. He looked for a foothold to clamber over, but there was only a lock chamber. It would have to do.

He lifted his foot onto the lock and then

gripped the struts, before hauling himself up. The gate clanged against its frame, the noise bouncing back from the brick wall at the end of the street. He paused to listen out for any doors opening, someone reacting to the noise. If he kept on going, he would be trapped. Still nothing. He let out a breath and his tongue flicked at his lips. His mouth was dry and his stomach was rolling with nerves. He decided to keep going. He knew he should call Laura, to tell her where he was, but he wanted to find out what was going on first.

He leaned back and threw his leg up, making more noise, the muscles in his thighs taut from the stretch. Then he forced his leg over and dropped to the ground on the other side. As he got his breath back, he became aware of the silence, and how much he had broken it.

Jack looked along the building. There was a window further along, to match the one on the other side, and his view was towards the cars parked behind. He tried to see through the darkness, to check for obstacles that might cause a noisy trip. The fence created some space for rubbish bins and so he knew he had to tread carefully. There were piles of cardboard, along with discarded pieces of metal that looked like broken car clamps.

His hands edged slowly along the wall, his feet feeling their way forward, trying to avoid a clang or a stumble. His clothes rustled against the bricks. The window crept into view, a faint glow of light getting closer. It wasn't blocked out.

He dropped to his knees and shuffled to get

under the window. He wanted to listen out for noise before he lifted himself up, to check that whoever was inside wasn't right by the glass. There were voices, just bass rumbles. It was impossible to make out what was being said. He raised himself slowly. The glass came into view, and he wondered whether there was someone on the other side watching him.

The window was dirty, covered in dust and cobwebs, and so there was no clear view. He pressed his face to the glass and rubbed away a small circle in the dirt. The interior was visible, but if he could see in, then they could see him. His breath misted up the glass, but as it melted away, Jack saw a large open space, with two vans against the back wall. And there were people stood around, focussed on something in the middle of the room, cast in the light of a simple bulb. He rubbed some more dirt away from the window, used the mist from his breath to clean a neat circle.

And then Jack saw what they were standing around. Or rather who. It was a man on a small metal chair, his head pulled back.

Jack reached for his phone, about to call Laura, but he jumped when a scream came through the glass, a shriek of pure agony.

Shit. He stepped back and dropped his phone, stumbled against an old clamp bracket. He reached out with his hand but there was nothing there to stop him. He clattered against one of the large metal rubbish bins, the noise cutting through the night.

He cursed and went to his knees, scouring the

ground for his phone, fingers scrambling around in the grit and debris. When his fingers bounced against it, he clicked it on to check that it was still working, and then eased himself back up to the window, to check whether anyone had heard him.

His heartbeat sounded loud as he peered into the glass. He dropped down again quickly, cursing, because everyone in there was looking towards the window.

Jack tried to stay still so that he could listen out, and then he heard the shouts. They were coming for him.

He ran for the locked gate, kicking rusted pieces of metal out of the way. He had to get back to his car, to phone for help. He took a jump at the gate, ready to go over the same way, his hands gripping the top, but then a large black shape appeared on the other side, his hands around the struts like a jailbird. Except that Jack was the one who was imprisoned.

'You've made a big mistake,' said a deep voice, and then there was the clink of the key as it went into the lock on the gate. As it swung slowly open with a creak, large hands went for him.

Chapter Sixty-Six

Carson banged on Don's door.

'If he's got Williams, he's not going to be here,' Laura said.

'I know that, but someone here must be able to talk,' Carson snapped back, before banging again on the door.

There was a click as the door opened. It was Helen, Don's wife.

'Where is he?' demanded Carson.

'Who?'

'Don't piss me about. Your husband. Is he in?'

She stared at Laura, and then at Carson, and then shook her head. 'He's busy,' she said and went to close the door.

Carson banged his hand on the door with such force that Helen was thrown back a few steps into the hall. He went inside, Laura right behind him.

They went into the living room. It was empty, but then Laura noticed the open bottle of vodka on the desk, next to a large bottle of cola.

'It's dangerous to drink on your own,' Laura said, turning to Helen.

Before she could answer, there was a noise from the kitchen, and Angel, David Hoyle's girlfriend, appeared.

'She isn't alone,' Angel said.

Laura was surprised to see her, and she detected

a slur to Angel's voice. 'What are you doing here?' Laura said. 'I didn't know you were friends.'

Angel didn't answer. She looked at Helen instead.

I get it,' Laura said. 'You're here so that Helen can keep an eye on you, so that you don't call me to tell me what David is doing, because you don't look like the sort of person who hangs around with crooks and their families.' When Helen folded her arms at that, Laura added, 'And don't you look so offended. We both know that more than hard work has given you all this.'

'Cut the small talk,' Carson said. 'Sit down, both of you.' Both women stayed on their feet, and so Carson pushed them, his fingers jabbing into their chests.

'That's assault,' Angel shouted.

'And I'm talking about murder, so leave your middle-class neurosis behind, and sit down,' Carson snapped back.

Angel looked at Helen, and then went to sit next to her, her face set in a scowl.

'What do you want?' Helen said.

'Your husband,' Carson said.

'I don't know where he is.'

'You're lying,' Carson said, before he looked towards Angel, stepping closer, making her cross her legs, protective, nervous. 'You'd be popular in prison.'

'Prison?'

'Is there an echo in here?' he said, tapping his knuckles on Angel's head. 'Yes, prison, and you're a sweet middle-class girl, nice skin, nice figure. A step up from the usual druggies and angry dykes they get in there, so you'll never get lonely, because it can be a killer in there, loneliness, when you've so much time to get through.'

'Why would I go to prison?'

'Assisting an offender,' Carson said. 'Maybe even conspiracy to murder, if we can sweet talk the prosecution into dragging everyone in. And you're really fucked, because you promised to help us, but when it came down to it, you didn't.'

'You promised to help?' Helen said.

'Ignore her,' Carson said. 'Where is Don Roberts?'

Angel looked at Helen, and then back at Carson. 'I can't help you.'

'Yes, you can, but this is your last chance,' Laura said. 'Call David. Tell him to call it off. Turn Williams in. David might even get a reward. But don't kill Williams, or everyone's life will be ruined. David's. Don's. Everyone.'

'We don't talk to the police,' Helen said, her voice filled with a sneer.

'You don't, we know that,' Carson replied. 'But Angel isn't like you. David dropped her here to make her stay quiet, and now David has gone with them to get revenge for Angel, but does she really want that?' He looked at Angel. 'Don't side with Don. Let this end properly, and then David can go back to his life, doing what he does to make your life better. He's crossed the line, but you don't have to go with him.'

Angel's chin was trembling, tears forming in her eyes. She looked at Helen.

'Remember what we told you,' Helen said, her

eyes filled with menace.

Angel looked down and stayed silent. Helen folded her arms. They were going to get nothing else.

Chapter Sixty-Seven

Strong hands gripped Jack's shoulders and pushed him against the wall. His head banged hard against the brickwork. He had to focus to stop his knees from buckling, the night turning into colour-filled speckles of light. The smell of stale cigarettes filled Jack's nostrils and spittle flecked his cheeks as his captor got up close, a forearm pushed against his throat.

Jack tried to see past the man, but it was too dark, the speckles fading. Shadows moved around him. There were noises, angry hisses, and a hand was in his pocket, searching. His phone was pulled out and Jack's face was lit up by the screen as it was held in front of him. Jack could see a snarl and a shaved head, and the gleam of a silver ring that pierced an eyebrow. Then it went dark again as the phone was dropped to the floor, and the crunch of glass and plastic told Jack that it had been crushed under someone's foot.

He was about to protest when he was pulled away from the wall, grabbed by his shirt, and pushed towards the open front door. His arms were pulled up behind him, and his head hit the door frame on the way in. His forehead went numb, and there was the warm trickle of blood in his eye.

Jack tried to struggle against the pain, but he was pushed faster than he could walk, his feet stumbling.

'What the fuck are you doing?' Jack shouted.

There was no response. Jack was thrown forward until he slithered on his knees, smooth across a concrete floor, his hands breaking his fall. He looked up as he landed. Wheel clamps were piled up in a corner, next to a small white van and a stack of clamping warning signs. But it was what was in the middle of the floor that made Jack gasp. It was what he had seen through the window, but it was clearer now, closer.

There was a man tied to a chair, his ankles bound around the chair legs, his hands behind his back. He was skinny, his shirt ripped open, and Jack could see the outline of his ribs. His legs were exposed, and they were red and blistered. It was his face that attracted Jack's attention though. It was swollen and bloodied. His mouth was just a red shadow, and through his grimace Jack saw gaps where there had been teeth not long before. The man's eyes were virtually closed by vivid purple swelling around them. Blood ran down both cheeks and pooled around the base of his neck, soaking his shirt.

Don Roberts was in front of him, sitting in a chair, leaning forward, his feet tapping on the floor, making soft clicks as the prisoner moaned.

Jack's gut churned, fear making sweat prickle onto his face.

Then Jack saw something else that made him close his eyes and wish that he had called the police before poking around.

There was a clothes iron plugged into an extension cord, steam belching out as it reached the top temperature, the orange light still showing. Jack looked again at the figure strapped to the chair, and this time he spotted a triangular blister on his chest, red and inflamed. Next to the iron was a kettle, wisps of steam just visible from the spout. Jack knew now why his legs were blistered.

Jack looked at Don. 'You've gone far enough,' he shouted. 'Call the police. You've had some revenge.'

Don's feet stopped tapping, and someone cleared their throat behind him. Don Roberts got to his feet and walked right up to Jack. His arms were by his side as he looked down. There was blood on his knuckles and some smears across his shirt.

'There is no such thing as far enough,' Don answered, his voice deep and angry.

'Let the police handle it,' Jack said.

Don shook his head. 'Would they do this?' he said, and went back to the steaming iron. He picked it up and held it close to the man's face, who tried to squirm away. He couldn't, he was bound too tightly.

'No!' Jack shouted, which mixed in with the man's scream, but the sounds faded as Jack's head was banged against the concrete. Everything faded. Sounds. Vision. Don's movements seemed slower, as if there was a time-lag, but then Jack's vision cleared just in time to see Don

399

press the iron against the man's chest.

He bucked and screeched with pain. Jack tried to bury his face in the floor, unable to watch.

The screams quietened down into a gasping sob, and Jack looked up to see Don putting the iron down. Hands gripped Jack and pulled him up, and then he was dragged back towards the end of the room. He was thrown onto a chair, and a voice said, 'If you move, you take his place.'

Jack looked around at his captors. There was Don, with a few of his goons, and then he saw Mike Corley against the wall. He was wearing the same expression as Don: anger mixed with hatred and revenge.

'Why are you here?' Jack said to Mike Corley. 'You're a policeman for Christ's sake.'

Mike glared at him and said, 'If you ever lose a daughter, tell me what you would do. And if it's something different, you're no man.'

Jack looked along the wall and saw David Hoyle. He didn't look so brash and confident anymore.

'What's wrong, David?' Jack said, breathing hard. 'Revenge for Angel too sweet for you?'

David Hoyle looked down.

'You don't want to be here, I can tell, David,' Jack shouted. 'You can end this.'

A hand gripped Jack's hair and pulled it back. He grimaced with pain and heard the click of footsteps again. As his head was thrown forward, he saw Don Roberts standing in front of him.

'Why did you come here?' Don said.

'To stop this,' Jack said, between sharp breaths.

'You should have stayed away. You've put me at

risk,' Don said. 'I can't allow that to happen.'

Jack looked around the group, looking for a sign that he wasn't in danger, but everyone looked angry.

'What, you're going to kill me?' Jack said.

Don didn't answer. Instead, he turned and walked towards the man in the chair. When he got close, he pulled his fist back and punched him hard on the jaw. The man's chin hung slack as blood spewed out of his mouth.

Jack looked towards David Hoye. 'How are you going to defend this?' Jack shouted, before he felt the sharp sting of a slap across his face.

Hoyle just cast his eyes to the ground. He wasn't enjoying this.

Jack looked back at Don. 'How do you know it was him?' Jack said. 'What if you're torturing an innocent man?'

Don shook his head. 'But I'm not.'

'The police don't know who he is. What makes you so sure you've got it right?'

Don crouched down in front of Jack. 'Let's just say that at least one police officer knows who he is.'

'What do you mean?'

Don grinned, although the brightness never got to his eyes. 'A little birdie made a call,' he said, and creaked back to his feet.

Jack closed his eyes. Rachel Mason. He had guessed right. She had been closest, pinned underneath him in that derelict factory. It all clicked into place. So she had recognised him but not told her colleagues. Rachel had chosen vengeance, not justice.

'My girlfriend knows where I am,' Jack blurted out.

Don turned round. 'Why should I care?'

'I told her that I was just checking it out,' he lied. 'And you know that she's a detective on the case.' Don's eyes just widened for a moment, a hint of panic. 'Had you forgotten?' Jack nodded his head towards the front door. 'You could check on my phone, except that you've smashed it.'

Don looked around at his men, as if he was suddenly unsure what to do.

Then he turned back and pointed to the prisoner. 'We haven't got much time,' Don said. 'Let's finish it.'

Jack closed his eyes.

Chapter Sixty-Eight

Carson waited outside Don's house, looking down the road. Laura watched from inside the hallway, keeping Helen Roberts and Angel in sight.

'Where the fuck are they?' Carson hissed, pacing up and down.

'We can't stay much longer,' Laura said.

Carson turned back to flash Laura a look that told her he knew exactly how urgent it was, but he was distracted by the flicker of blue lights on the houses opposite. He ran onto the road and waved his arms, and as the squad car pulled over at the side of the road, Carson pointed into the

402

house. 'Get them.'

Laura knew what he meant.

She went back into the living room and grabbed Helen Roberts by her arm. 'You're under arrest,' she said, and yanked her towards the door. Her dog started to growl and then bark, but Laura ignored it, twisting Helen's arm up her back.

'What for?' Helen shouted.

'All the things that the inspector mentioned, so shut your mouth and get outside,' Laura snapped in her ear. 'You're going to the station.'

Helen looked back at Angel, whose hand was over her mouth, and Helen started to say something, but Laura pushed her hard through the doorway, her shoulders banging against the door frame.

'You're hurting me,' Helen said, her voice angry.

'Tell your lawyer that,' Laura said. 'He might be in the next cell before morning.'

The uniformed officer walked towards the front door, a young male officer, uncertainty in his eyes, unclear as to why he was there.

'We needed cuffs and a car with proper locks,' Laura said, and pushed Helen towards him. 'Take her with you.'

Carson walked past Laura and went into the house as the handcuffs snapped around Helen's wrists. Laura followed him.

'She's gone now,' Carson said to Angel. 'I think we need to talk, don't you?'

Angel began to nod, tears streaming down her face. She slumped backwards onto the sofa. 'I'm scared,' she said.

Laura pushed past Carson and kneeled down in front of Angel. 'We need to stop David from helping them kill someone.'

Angel nodded again.

'Where are they?' Laura said.

Angel looked towards the window as shouting came from outside. It sounded like the uniform was struggling with Helen. Then she wiped away the tears.

'I heard them talking. Don's got premises, where he keeps his vans. They were taking him there.'

'Did they say where?'

Angel shook her head. 'Sorry,' and then the tears started to flow again.

Laura got up and looked around the room. She was looking for something with Don's business details on it. The room was just filled with gadgets and videos, with computer games stacked by the television. Then she saw them, a pile of papers on a shelf in the corner.

Laura went to them, and saw they were carbonated sheets filled out with vehicle details. Clamping tickets. There was a number and the name of the company, DR Security, emblazoned across the top. Underneath that there was an address. 'We've got it,' she said.

'And what about me?' Angel said.

'You're coming with us,' Laura replied, and they all headed for Carson's car outside.

Don Roberts went to the back of one of the vans and re-appeared holding a long tow-rope. He fashioned a noose at one end, his eyes on Jack, and then turned away to throw the rope over a roof beam. The noose dangled a few feet above the head of his prisoner.

'Help me,' Don barked at David Hoyle, who stayed silent and just shook his head. Don glared a look of disapproval. He had spotted Hoyle for what most lawyers were, tough with a pen, cruel with their actions, but they couldn't cope when it didn't stay clean.

One of Don's muscle men stepped forward instead and kneeled down to untie the rope that bound the prisoner's feet to the chair. When they came loose, he flopped forward, his hands behind his back, the only thing keeping him up.

'Get him on the chair,' Don said, his voice a growl now.

The goon hooked his arms under his prisoner's and then hoisted him to his feet.

'If you do it, you'll die,' Jack shouted.

The man looked up slowly, his mouth hanging slack, bloodied drool forming a tentacle on its way to the floor. He peered at Jack through his swollen lids and then put his head down.

Don stared at Jack, his expression a mix of rage and confusion, wondering why he cared.

'He did it for Emma,' Jack blurted out. When Don didn't answer, he continued, 'You remember her, don't you, Don? Corley knows. Ask him.' A look flashed between them. 'The teenage girl you both abused all those years ago. No, not abused. Raped. Under age. Ringing any bells, Don? I never took you for a kiddy-fiddler.'

Don clenched his jaw and then said, 'You don't know what you're talking about.'

'Don't I? Or maybe there were a few more?

How many, Don? The one I spoke to seemed pretty certain. Emma she was called. And there's something else you don't know: she had the baby. Didn't Mike tell you all this?'

Don whirled around to Mike Corley. 'Did you know about this?'

'He told me before,' Mike said.

'Why didn't you mention it?'

'This isn't some fucking cosy reunion,' Mike snapped. 'Once we've finished here, we go back to being cop and criminal. He's got it all down on tape anyway. I just want him dead,' and he pointed to the figure on the chair. 'I don't care what happens after that.'

Don clicked his fingers at one of his goons and pointed towards the door. 'Check out his car for a tape machine.' Then he walked over towards Jack, the click of his shoes louder now as everyone descended into silence. He stood over Jack, his fists clenched. 'You need to learn to keep your mouth shut,' he said, his voice trembling with anger.

Jack looked up, tried to gauge what Don would do. The iron was still plugged in, the orange light clicking on and off as it maintained its heat. Jack could feel the tension in the room. He had changed the dynamic, from the simple murder of someone who perhaps deserved it, to a scenario where someone could expose them and send them to prison. There were more people there than just Don and Mike though. If he could turn the others against them, maybe he could find a way out of this.

'If you like fucking children, that's your business,' Jack said. 'Does it make him much worse than you?'

Jack felt a burst of pain as Don punched him. His jaw went slack and blood spewed onto the floor, and he coughed a tooth onto the concrete. He took some deep breaths through his nose and looked at Don again. 'She had a bouncing baby boy, but she had to give him away. She couldn't give him a proper life, because she was just a child herself, but babies get bigger, and eventually they grow up.'

Jack nodded towards Don's prisoner. 'Say hello to your son.'

Don swallowed.

'Although you've already acquainted yourself,' Jack continued, 'because you've just had your son tied to a chair.'

Don looked back to the bloodied figure by the chair, his face filled with confusion now, and then at Mike Corley, who was ashen.

'He was adopted,' Jack said. 'Emma doesn't know whose child it is. Maybe it's your son, Mike. Are you going to save him? His real name is Shane. Say hello.'

'This is bullshit,' Don said, but his tone was unconvincing.

Jack shook his head slowly and then pointed towards the prisoner. 'Ask him.'

Don followed his gaze, and the prisoner looked around the room, his face screwed up with pain, and then he started to nod. He tried to say something, but blood speckled his chin. Then he lifted his head and tried again.

'I fucked up your daughters like you both fucked

407

up my mother,' he said, and then he started to cackle.

Don marched over and gripped him by the shirt. He hoisted him onto the chair, his rage giving him extra strength, so that his head was level with the noose. Don hesitated, just for a moment, but when Shane started to grin, Don reached for the noose and wrapped it around Shane's neck. Don stepped back.

Shane was standing on the chair, his hands still tied behind his back. Don reached forward with his foot until it rested on the edge of the chair, ready to kick it over. He looked back at Jack, and then back at Shane. He seemed to be having second thoughts, as if he had seen something in Shane, a recognition of his own flesh.

But Jack was wrong.

Don moved away and walked quickly to his office. When he returned, he was holding a baseball bat. He tossed it to Mike Corley, who weighed it in his hand for a moment, and then Mike strode towards Shane, who was twisting his body, waiting for the blow. Mike pulled the bat back, ready for a swing. When he got within striking distance, he swung hard, the bat aiming right between Shane's legs.

Shane groaned in pain and then vomited onto the floor, the splash onto the concrete making someone retch behind Jack. Shane slumped forward, his neck straining in the noose, his feet just staying on the chair, taking his weight, so that he was being twirled in an arc before he was able to straighten himself.

Jack got up, ready to rush forward, not prepared to watch any more, but Mike turned back to him and swung the bat at his thigh.

Jack screamed in agony. He went to the floor and almost passed out with the pain.

'Get another chair, and some more rope,' Don shouted. There were the sounds of movement. Hands lifted Jack under his arms and hoisted him to his feet.

Jack shouted out when his foot hit the floor, but still he was dragged forward. As he opened his eyes, Jack saw another chair, just a foot away from Shane's. Jack looked up and saw that another rope had been hooked over a beam, so that a noose hung down. He tried to struggle, but the pain was excruciating every time he moved his leg and so he couldn't resist when he was lifted onto the chair.

Jack tried to move his head so that they couldn't put the noose over it, but someone gave his hair a yank. His yelp was quietened by the coarseness of the rope as it went tight around his neck, a slip knot at the back jamming tight.

Sweat gathered around the rope, and Jack struggled to swallow. His arms were still pulled back, but he felt something go around them. More rope. His hands were bound now. He couldn't pull off the noose. Images rushed through his brain. Laura. Bobby. His parents. Dolby. He saw a front page headline: *Local Reporter Dead.*

Jack's leg was sending sharp jabs of pain through his body, making him sag, but every time he dipped, just looking for a way of taking the weight off it, the rope carved into his neck a little more, so that he had to force himself to stand.

'So this is it?' Jack said, grimacing, gasping. 'You're going to kill us both? For what? Finding out? Is that all it takes?'

Don grabbed the bat back from Mike Corley and stepped towards Jack. He swung the bat in a lazy arc. Jack braced himself for another blow, unable to defend himself this time. But there was no pain, no hard strike with the bat. When Jack opened his eyes, Don was smirking.

'No,' Don said, his voice low. 'I'm not going to kill you both. You're going to do it.'

'I don't understand,' Jack said, confused.

Don pointed towards Shane. 'If I kick his chair away, I'll kick your chair too. He is revenge. You're just expedient, because I'm not having a witness.' Then he raised his eyebrows. 'But there is another way.'

Jack swallowed, it was more difficult than before. He tried bravado. 'Enlighten me,' he said.

Don prodded Shane, who looked like he was fighting to stay conscious, with the tip of the baseball bat. 'You kick his chair away and you survive.'

'Explain. I don't understand.'

'It's quite simple. The easiest way to protect yourself is to make your enemy your ally. Take this monster on the chair next to you.'

'Don't you feel anything, that he might be your son?' Jack said.

Don jabbed Shane again, this time in the groin. 'He's not my son. He's nothing, and within five minutes, he'll be dead. And so will you be if you don't kick his chair away.'

'I'm not like you. Why should I do it?'

'Because it will make you his killer,' Don said,

with relish. 'With my career choices, you get to know a bit about the law, and I know one thing: you have no defence to murder if you kick that chair. The law doesn't allow you to be a coward. Isn't that right, David?' And he looked towards David Hoyle.

David Hoyle didn't say anything.

'Hoyle!' Don shouted. 'Give this fucker some legal advice.'

Hoyle nodded slowly. When he spoke, it came out with a stammer.

'H-h-he's right. You would call it duress, where you did what you did because you were under threat, but it doesn't count if you kill someone.'

Don grinned malevolently. 'You see, it's fucking genius. The law won't let you kill someone else to save yourself, because that would be a coward's charter, but it's the only choice you've got. If you kick his chair away, you live. You won't tell anyone, because if you do you'll spend your life in prison, and I don't think you like that idea. But if you don't, and there's a fucking time limit on this, then I kick both, and you'll be buried on the moors with him.'

Jack looked upwards. He noticed the cobwebs on the steel roof beams, and the pinpricks of stars through a skylight. Was that to be his last view? He listened out for the sound of sirens, hoping that Laura had followed the same thought process that he had, but all he could hear was the tap-tap of Don's shoes. His mind flashed through his life, with images of his father, strong and silent, and the warmth of his mother. Friends. Past girlfriends. All rushing through his head like

411

a flickbook, and as he recognised them, all those people who would judge him, he knew that there was only one thing he would do.

He knew what he was going to do, and his lip trembled as he realised that it might be the last thing he would ever say. He closed his eyes and tried to imagine how it would feel when the chair shifted underneath him, as the tow-rope gripped tightly around his neck and he felt the swing of his body.

It didn't make him change his mind.

He opened his eyes and glared at Don Roberts. 'You might be a murderer, Don, but I'm not. Go fuck yourself.'

Chapter Sixty-Nine

Carson had called up more marked cars and they were clearing the way with sirens and lights. The blue flashes were bright between the buildings as they raced through the suburban streets.

'You need to stay in the car when we get there,' Carson shouted to Angel.

She nodded but didn't say anything. Her fear seemed to have sobered her up, and now she was grim-faced in the back of the car.

'How certain are you about this?'

'I heard them talking outside,' Angel said. 'They had that pervert tied up in the back of the car, and they were discussing where to take him.'

Laura turned around. 'Why did David get involved? It's a step too far for him.'

'Because Don wanted him there,' Angel said. 'I told David not to go, and he didn't want to, but he does everything Don asks, because he's too frightened to say no. You were right, I was at Don's house so that hard-faced bitch could keep an eye on me.'

'It was to give you both too much to lose,' Carson said. 'By taking David along, Don's got him forever, and nothing will be too illegal, because Don will always have something over him. And once he has that hold, you'll stay quiet too. Being a career criminal is just about stopping the whispers, nothing more.'

'I'm not like them,' Angel said softly.

'Yes, I know, and that's why you wouldn't have held out. It would have split you and David up.'

Carson made a sharp turn, and Laura had to grip the door handle herself, thinking that only good luck was keeping them from a crash.

They were racing round the edge of the town centre, on whatever counted as the inner ring road in Blackley – really just a succession of traffic lights – and so Carson was stop-start all the way down, edging his way through the red lights. They had an address.

'How far now?' he shouted.

'Turn left here,' Laura said. 'It's somewhere around here.'

Carson screeched his tyres as he turned into a road that took them towards the viaduct, a large shadow at the end of the street. Laura was trying to see along the side streets, looking for signs of Don's business, the signs and hoardings lit up by

413

blue flashes. Then the headlights caught something else. A Triumph Stag.

'Pull over!' Laura screamed.

The car hadn't fully stopped before Laura opened the door and started to run.

Chapter Seventy

Jack waited for the swing, for the drop, his nails digging into his clenched fists, his chest rising and falling fast, his heart like a drum roll, but nothing came. He opened his eyes. Don was staring at Shane, his jaw set, Mike just behind him. Shane laughed, but it came out with a wince as the beating took effect again.

'What are you laughing at?' Don said.

'You,' Shane said, his voice muffled through the swelling. He spat blood onto the floor. 'What do you want, for me to feel fear? Or is it that you're too scared to do it?'

'Don't, Shane,' Jack shouted.

'Oh, fuck off,' Shane snarled at Jack. 'Stop playing the hero. I'd have had your girl too if that other car hadn't come along. So go on, kick away my chair, like the big man wants you to.'

Don stepped forward and raised his foot. It rested on the edge of Shane's chair. 'I want you to feel the terror that my daughter felt, in the last moments before she died.'

'Those weren't moments,' Shane said. 'They were minutes.'

414

Don went pale.

'It's not like the movies,' Shane continued, his voice gloating. 'There's no quick squeeze and then it's over. No, they can hold on for fucking ages. Can you imagine how long someone can hold their breath for? It's like that, big man.' He laughed again, and then he was wracked by coughs. 'I had to take a break, my hands were cramping up.'

An unhealthy flush was colouring Don's cheeks.

'He's trying to make you angry,' David Hoyle said to Don. 'Don't do it. Stick to what you said.'

Shane nodded, and tried to peer at David Hoyle through swollen eyes. 'He's fucking sharp, that one. I remember when I was creeping around his house, but I fucked that one up, because it was all a bit off the cuff.'

'Why me?' Hoyle said, his voice hardening.

Shane spat out some more blood, and Don and Mike had to move quickly to avoid being hit. 'Because you're as guilty as everyone else for making her life miserable. I saw you, at the police station, on the day you released Don's pets into the wild. Those little shits have made Emma's life a misery, and all you could do was grin as they laughed at how they'd got off again.'

'That was the lack of evidence, not me,' Hoyle said.

'Oh spare me your fucking morality,' Shane snapped, drawing deep breaths as he battled his injuries. 'It's just a big game to you. I was there, I saw you. I was wheeling some files through, and you looked so fucking pleased with yourself. So I improvised, and it didn't pay off.' He tried to hold his head up so he could stare at Hoyle, but he just grimaced with pain. 'Now you want to do it, Hoyle, I can tell. Go on then, you do it, although you're already as guilty as everyone else, because you're all wanting the same thing to happen. Tell them, Hoyle, that it won't get you off, it doesn't matter who kicks away my chair.'

Don jabbed Shane in the groin again. Shane went to double up, but the noose stopped him.

'It's not about us,' Don said. 'It's about stopping him talking,' and he gave Jack a jab on his leg.

'But you want to make me scared,' Shane said. 'But I don't get scared, and that's what makes me different to you.'

Hoyle stepped forward. 'He's trying to make you do it, Don, that's all. He wants you to end it.'

Shane cackled. 'Frightened, are we, Mr Hoyle?'

Don stared at Jack, and then back at Shane. He raised his foot onto Jack's chair and tensed.

'You've got ten seconds to push that bastard's chair over, and if you don't, your chair goes first.'

Jack tried to delay it. He turned to Shane. 'Why Rachel Mason? What was she to you?'

Shane coughed out some more blood. 'Just for fun,' he said. 'Snooty little cow had it coming.'

'So that was it? You just didn't like her?'

Shane paused, and then he grinned, blood gathering where his teeth used to be. 'Oh, I liked her all right. I had been looking forward to her most of all.'

'You're wasting your own time, not mine,' Don said. 'Do it.'

Jack looked down and saw Don's foot tense against his chair. He expected Don to count the seconds out, but instead he let the time hover, the room silent. Jack looked up again, closed his eyes, refused to take part, made a silent prayer that it was an empty threat. But he knew it made sense, that he was a witness, and people like Don Roberts don't like witnesses. He could feel Don's foot push against the chair, making it rock onto the back legs, and Jack's leg was struggling to support him now. He was shaking. He said goodbye to Laura, to Bobby. He was angry that he was acting like a coward, except that it didn't feel like cowardice, because he was doing what was right: he was refusing to kill a man. But even if it felt like the right thing to do, whatever Shane had done, it would be a short-lived victory, because his conscience would die with him.

Jack knew the ten seconds had passed, and he opened his eyes to the view of the skylight. Then he saw them.

Jack had been looking at the stars, silver dots in the dark blue, but then the light seemed to change. It acquired a flicker, like a strobe effect, and as he watched, the flickers got brighter. Blue flickers.

Jack looked down. Don was tense and still. Hoyle was turning towards the front of the office. So was Mike Corley.

Then Jack heard them. A distant wail. The soundtrack for the flickers. Sirens, far off, but getting closer.

'Cut us down,' Jack shouted, his pulse racing now, adrenaline making his cheeks flush, his

417

fingers trembling. 'All you will have is some beatings. Go on, do it, Don, while you still have the chance.' His tongue flicked across his lips as his mouth went dry.

The sirens sounded like they were close now. Don looked at Jack, then at Hoyle, and then at Shane. He looked angry, and he looked scared, like an animal caught in the headlights, not sure which way to turn.

'We need to go, Don,' Hoyle said, panic in his voice.

Corley headed for the front door, but Don shouted, 'No, out the back.'

Mike turned, but then his attention was dragged back to the front by the sound of sirens in the street outside. 'We need to go, Don, now.'

Don looked towards the rear of the building, and then at Jack again, before he started to move. 'Let's go,' Don said. He pulled out a knife from his pocket and started to look around for a way to get level with the rope, but then there was a screech of tyres outside and the sound of shouting.

They ran towards the back of the room, all in a rush to get away. There was a hammering at the front door, and then the sound of someone trying to kick their way in. Jack felt relief course through him, sweat breaking across his forehead, the pain in his knee coming into focus.

Jack looked at Shane, and realised that he knew what was going on.

'It's over,' Jack said to him.

Shane looked at the door as it sounded like the wood was splintering, the banging incessant.

Then he turned to Jack and shook his head.

Shane kicked at Jack's chair and it wobbled. Jack shouted for him to stop, pressed his feet down to try and apply some weight. He felt the rope go tight against his neck as he tottered on the chair, the knot digging into his skin. Shane took another go at kicking the chair, and this time he caught it with more force.

The chair started to lean to one side. Jack tried to balance on it, to bring it back. He heard Shane cackle behind him, and the sound of shouting from outside. Jack lashed out with his foot but his leg gave way, just for a second, and as he struggled to control it, he felt himself lose balance.

Jack's chair hit the floor with a clatter and he felt his legs swing into the air. He tried to shout out but the rope clamped tightly around his neck, and all he could hear for a couple of seconds was the creak of the rope. Then there was another noise, another clatter of a chair going over, followed by a short scream and then the sound of a crack.

Shane was swinging too.

The knot dug hard into Jack's neck. He tried to take a breath but couldn't. Panic surged through him and he felt his chest strain when he couldn't fill his lungs with air. He struggled and thrashed, but it was a reflex, and the rope just seemed to get tighter. The view of the room moved around as he swayed. He caught a glance downwards, saw his feet floating in the air, a couple of feet above the concrete floor. They banged against Shane's feet, who was swinging next to him. His vision started to blur, the room began to vanish into white, the sounds outside fading, until the only sound he could hear was the creaking of the rope.

As the room went faint, he realised that he hadn't had the chance to say goodbye to the people he loved.

Chapter Seventy-One

Laura ran for the front door. Carson and a uniformed officer were right behind her.

'Jack!' she shouted, and pushed on the door handle, her shoulder slamming into it at the same time. It was locked, wouldn't budge. She kicked at the door. It was solid. There was shouting coming from inside. She turned around to the uniforms spilling out of the cars. There was another car coming along the road. 'Two of you go round the back!'

She tried to give the door another kick, but it wouldn't move.

Carson appeared on her shoulder and pushed her out of the way. He kicked at the lock. Still nothing.

Then there was a scream from inside.

'Give me your baton!' Laura shouted to the uniform stood next to her. He reached to his belt quickly and handed it over. She hit the window hard, not caring about flying glass, but the baton just bounced back. It was toughened glass, reinforced by a metal mesh. She hit it again. Still nothing. She looked around for something to throw through the window. There was some rubble by the wall, she could make it out in the glare from the headlights. She ran over and found a half-brick, some mortar still attached to it. As she ran back, she raised her arm and then launched it at the window when she got close.

It bounced off and back onto the floor, but this time Laura saw that there was a crack. She picked up the brick and threw it again. It bounced off the window once more, except this time the glass didn't look as clear. The skin had been broken, and so she grabbed the baton once more and began to hit the window.

A hole appeared on the third strike. She was breathless but didn't stop. A few more baton strikes and there was a hole big enough for her to get her shoulders through.

Laura threw the baton onto the floor and started to haul herself through the window. Shards of glass dug into her stomach, and she winced as her hands took her weight. She could see the shimmer of sharp fragments of glass scattered on a desk in front of the window. With a final effort she got herself through, sliding across the desk and onto the floor. She could feel something damp on her stomach, and she knew it was blood from the way her shirt stuck to it, but she didn't have time to check herself. She rushed out of the small office and to the front door, expecting someone to shout from inside, but no one bothered her as she unlocked the bolts, top and bottom, the rest of the door just held with a Yale lock.

The uniforms ran through, shouting that they were the police, and Laura followed them, panting with exertion, scared of what she would find.

The building opened up into a large open space, and she saw that it was filled by two white vans. But it was what was in front of the vehicles that made her gasp and shout.

There were two people, their heads in nooses, swinging. One face was covered in blood and bunched against his noose, his hands behind his back, a chair behind him, toppled over.

But it was the other person that made her heart stop.

'Jack!'

She ran forward, covering the ground fast even though every step seemed to be in slow motion. She grabbed him by the legs to take his weight, but she saw that the rope was tight against his neck.

'Get a knife someone!' she shouted.

There was banging from a nearby storeroom, someone looking for tools, and then she heard footsteps, someone moving towards her. Jack's body bucked as the other person hacked at the rope with something. A hacksaw or a blade, she couldn't tell, but too many seconds passed before the rope went slack and she went to the floor, Jack on top of her.

Her hands went straight to the knot at the back of his neck but it was too tight, too embedded into the skin. She heard someone next to her. She looked. It was Carson. There was the glint of a silver blade in his hand, the edge jagged. He was cutting into the rope around the neck, sawing madly, the blade turning red, but Laura didn't care about that. And then Carson gave a shout as he was able to throw the rope to one side.

Jack flopped forward, and there were tears running down her face as she put her hands on his cheeks, willing some life into him.

And then he seemed to take a deep breath and cough, blood and spittle flicking on to her cheek. But that didn't matter, and she held onto him, still underneath, as his chest began to rise and fall and his eyelids started to flicker.

She could hear the exertions of someone cutting at the rope that held Shane Grix, and then there was the sound of a body falling to the floor, the smack of dead flesh on concrete, like a pig carcass thrown onto a cold butcher's slab.

Laura didn't look over. Instead, she stroked Jack's hair, held his head in her arms, tears rolling down her face. It was over, she kept on saying. It was over.

Chapter Seventy-Two

The next few days seemed to pass in a blur – from Jack's time in hospital to the police statements and constant press attention.

Jack had been saved by Don's impatience. Don had fashioned a proper fixed knot for Shane, spent time making sure that the knot was strong and wouldn't come loose when he started to swing. Once Shane kicked his chair away, the rope had jammed under his jaw, the sudden jolt breaking his neck. He was dead before the police broke in. When it came to Jack, Don was getting angry, was working off-plan, and so he just threaded a slipknot, so that when Shane kicked away Jack's chair, it throttled him, tight and hard.

Laura had just about got there in time and the knot slackened a touch when he was cut down, but they had to cut away the whole thing to get Jack breathing again.

Jack looked down at his hands. They were shaking, his palms slick with sweat. He tried not to think back to that time. He had recovered from the physical threat. It had been other things that came back to him more often, like the thoughts he'd had when on the chair. It had been the jolt he'd needed, as frightening as it was, the realisation that if he'd died, there wouldn't have been too many people to scatter petals on his grave. He had friends, but they were casual, just good for a drink or a phone call. The circle of people who loved Jack was too small. The only people he'd had to say goodbye to were Laura and Bobby. He vowed to change that, to meet more people, to make his life a little less about writing articles not many people read.

His finger ran around his neck, and he felt the rough skin that still marked out the loop of the rope. He pulled his shirt collar away. It felt too tight.

Shane's funeral had attracted more photographers than mourners. There were just two people who shed tears, Ida and Emma, on opposite sides of the grave, each in black, one crying because she blamed herself for what he had done, the other because she hadn't been there to stop him. They left separately, each partly blaming the other. Bad upbringing. Bad genes. Maybe just a combination of the two.

Rachel had no choice but to resign. The force had allowed her to do that – fall or be pushed. It was the only way to keep the small pension she had built up. Jack had seen her once, coming out of the college, dressed in old jeans and a T-shirt, holding papers in her hand. It looked like she was trying to get on a course, approaching the resignation as an opportunity, not a punishment. Jack smiled when he saw her, pleased that she was doing something with her life.

The future of Don and his men, and Mike Corley and David Hoyle, was not quite so bright. They had been charged with conspiring to murder Shane, all of them in custody awaiting their trial. Jack was the star witness, the only person who was in that room who wasn't in a cell, and he felt no nerves at the thought of sending men to prison for many years.

Jack knew that David Hoyle would suffer the most in prison. Mike Corley would get some protection because he was an ex-copper. His own cell, with a television, provided that he didn't mind sharing a wing with rapists and child molesters. David Hoyle would have to mix with the general population, and he wasn't tough enough for that.

Jack had no sympathy. David Hoyle was a lawyer, he knew where the line was, and he shouldn't have crossed it.

Jack took some deep breaths and looked at the floor. He shouldn't feel like this. He could hear the soft murmurs of people around him, but they seemed distant, as if he was sitting in a bubble. He looked up instead, tried to focus on the view through the large window, past clusters of trees and towards a line of cottages on a distant brow. It was going to be all right, he told himself.

Then his thoughts were broken by the sound of music from the back of the room and the rumble of people rising to their feet. He recognised the tune. It was the one Laura had wanted for her entrance.

Jack felt a tap on his arm. It was Joe Kinsella, who smiled and said, 'It's time.'

Jack rose slowly to his feet, winced as his leg ached, and then as he looked round, his nerves melted away.

Laura was in an ivory-coloured dress, neat and simple, her shoulders bare, the train short, clutching a hand-tied bouquet of white calla lilies and roses, the colour provided by her stream of dark hair. Her dimples flickered in her cheeks. As beautiful as she looked the first time he'd met her.

As she reached him, he held out his hand and squeezed hers.

'I love you,' he whispered.

Tears sprang to her eyes before she gave his fingers a small squeeze and then they turned to the Registrar.

Jack knew then that everything was going to be all right.

The publishers hope that this book has given you enjoyable reading. Large Print Books are especially designed to be as easy to see and hold as possible. If you wish a complete list of our books please ask at your local library or write directly to:

Magna Large Print Books
Magna House, Long Preston,
Skipton, North Yorkshire.
BD23 4ND

This Large Print Book for the partially sighted, who cannot read normal print, is published under the auspices of

THE ULVERSCROFT FOUNDATION